THE NIGHT HUNT

ALSO BY ALEXANDRA CHRISTO

THE HUNDRED KINGDOMS NOVELS

To Kill a Kingdom

Princess of Souls

THE CROOKED DUOLOGY

Into the Crooked Place

City of Spells

THE
NIGHT
HUNT

ALEXANDRA CHRISTO

HOT
KEY
BOOKS

First published in Great Britain in 2023 by
HOT KEY BOOKS
4th Floor, Victoria House, Bloomsbury Square
London WC1B 4DA
Owned by Bonnier Books
Sveavägen 56, Stockholm, Sweden
bonnierbooks.co.uk/HotKeyBooks

A CIP catalogue record for this book is available from the British Library.

ISBN: 978-1-4714-1399-5
Also available as an ebook and in audio

1

Design by Meg Sayre
Printed and bound in Great Britain by Clays Ltd, Elcograf S.p.A.

Hot Key Books is an imprint of Bonnier Books UK
bonnierbooks.co.uk

FOR DANIEL,
FOR ALWAYS TAKING ON THE WORLD'S
GODS AND MONSTERS
BY MY SIDE

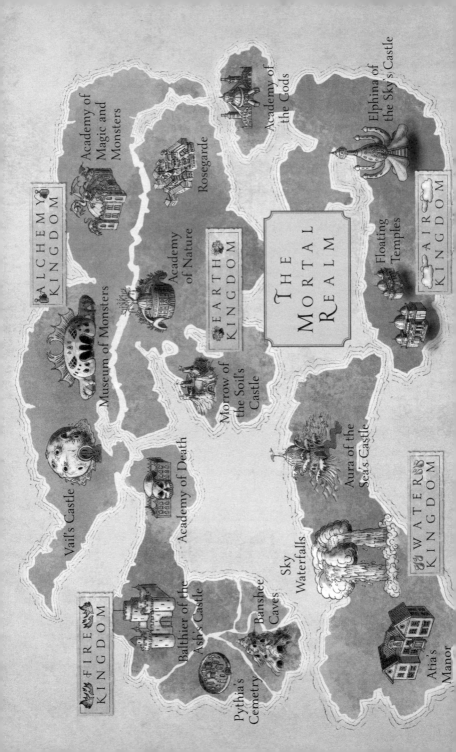

ENTRANCE TO OKSENYA

River of Fire

River of Oblivion

River of Sorrow

LIBRARY BETWEEN WORLDS

River of Death

TO THE SORTING ZONE

River of Eternity

PROLOGUE

Once upon a time, a man died.

Many men, actually. They're prone to it, after all, because humans are fragile things and tend to fade with the stars.

The important thing isn't really the man, but what killed him and what happened after.

That thing was a monster—which shouldn't surprise you—and her name was Atia. Which should surprise you, because not many monsters liked to have their names known to outsiders.

They preferred sounds instead. A certain creak to the floorboard, a familiar sob, or the song that carried in a scream. That was their desired infamy. And it wasn't just the monsters. Even creatures who would've considered themselves Godly had sacrificed their names for a sound.

Death, for instance, liked wind chimes. That was the noise his Heralds made. The delicate tickle of music they brought into the world before they sprang from the shadows and ferried their souls.

But Atia liked having her name known.

With names came purpose and power. People gave them like gifts: so you could be recognized and remembered.

Atia liked gifts too. Fear was one she collected often.

Her reputation drifted through the world in whispers, so she was never just a howl in the night, or the slam of a door, or the slow swallow of a dry throat.

She was Atia. The Last of the Nefas.

And the Gods did not like it.

ATIA

Fear tastes like spiced honey.

It's thick and sweet as it moves across my tongue, and carries a distinctly familiar warmth once it slides down my throat and fills my empty belly.

"Atia," Sapphir says in a frantic whisper. "Are you done yet?"

I shake my head and start to hum a little sea ditty I once overheard by the docks.

Sailors like singing, even if they should know better what kinds of creatures it attracts.

"That melody is awfully sinister," Sapphir says.

"I hope so," I tell her.

She laughs and her fangs shine under the light of the moon. "No wonder you don't have any other friends."

"I have plenty of friends," I say. "They're just all dead."

Like my parents and the rest of my kind.

Sapphir's laughter trickles over to me. "That doesn't bode well for me."

I reach out a hand to the lake below, my fingers circling ripples across the muddied water. "You're already dead, Sapphir," I remind her.

Though not in any permanent way.

Vampires have that luxury.

I sigh as the moon cascades over us, casting a cool glow on the small fishing plank that overlooks the waters of this village. Its splinters are damp enough to smell like rot. Behind us a forest of purple thorn trees lingers like a watchful audience, the branches kissing a clouded winter sky that promises snowfall come morning.

It is quiet and deserted, save for us.

"Well?" Sapphir presses. "Your kill or mine?"

I look down at the human, trembling between us.

The only fun I ever get these days is from tormenting them.

Humans who stumble from the one tavern this village of Rosegarde has to offer, or those who sail across oceans and worlds, seeking adventure.

It's the adventure that I take. The hopes and the comforts—things I can never truly have for myself—until fear is all that remains.

And I like fear.

"I'm still feeding," I say, as the man's dread clings to the air.

Even seeing me in my human form, he's scared.

The Nefas can change shapes with our whim, and while we can appear human—perfect for inconspicuous hunting—in our true form our hair is cast from moonlight, skin blue from the tears we drink, and ears receding back in golden spirals. Our great wings are made from thorn and bramble, tree-branch veined and dressed with forest leaves.

When we fly, it sounds like screaming.

Like the nightmares we steal while the sun sleeps.

Now, though, I look like any human. The only exception being my eyes, which turn white with magic when I feed.

The man sobs beneath me, and I smile.

The Nefas thrive on chaos and illusion, but for most centuries we've stuck to nightmares. It's safer to feed in the shadows.

That's what my parents always taught me.

Fear is an easy meal to take while our prey sleeps, my father always said. *Do nothing to draw attention and risk the wrath of the Gods.*

But I've never wanted to live my life rationed to the darkness like they did. I want to bring my illusions out into the open. Creating worlds from other people's horrors is the only way I know I'm real.

Besides, a girl needs a little fun.

"Please," the human man begs, as he is surrounded by visions of his greatest fears.

Spiders, crawling up his pant legs and down the crease of his neck.

Earth, splattered on top of him, choking into his throat as he is buried alive.

Conjuring them is like plucking flower petals. My mind reaches into his, moving about memories and sifting through dreams until I get to the root of what makes him shudder.

Then I pluck them out one by one and scatter them into the world.

To him, it's as real as anything.

His hair stripes white with fear.

"You must hurry and drain him already," Sapphir says impatiently. "I want my share, Atia."

She's always a little greedy when we hunt together.

It's been three years, ever since I was fourteen and the man who smelled like ash told me to *run, run as fast as I could* from the screams of my parents.

Those years have spanned many villages and forests, but the human realm is small and closed in, just five elemental kingdoms making up the land. So my path has crossed with Sapphir's more than once.

The first time was far on the other side of the Earth Kingdom, high in the reaches of the tree mountains. What I thought was an excellent place to hide turned out to be Sapphir's preferred hunting grounds for unsuspecting campers.

She pounced down from high up in the branches with her teeth bared, leaping onto my shoulders and sending me rolling down a large hill.

I smacked my nose against a rock and the blood gushed onto my shirt like a waterfall.

Sapphir sneered and licked her lips.

Then my scent caught the air and she wrinkled her nose.

"You're not human," she said, as if I needed reminding.

"And you're not going to live past today if you do that again," I shot back.

I may have been young, but I didn't have any fear left in me after what I saw happen to my family.

Sapphir smiled, fangs like pure white daggers that grated along her lips. She said: "Little monster, do you want to share a meal?"

So we did.

We found a group of campers who'd come to forage, and we delighted.

After we parted ways, we'd always find each other again, in new towns and new forests. It's almost like having a friend, except the only reason Sapphir hasn't tried to kill me is because it would do nothing to satiate her hunger, and the only reason I haven't fed off her fear is because a monster's fear doesn't taste the same as a human's.

It's more like a truce than a friendship, but I treasure it all the same. Sometimes it's nice to have company in the shadows, to duet in torment.

To know that I don't always have to be alone.

"I'm hungry," Sapphir says.

Other times, like tonight, it's nothing but an irritation.

"*I know*," I tell her tightly.

She always is.

Sapphir likes to eat humans, like all vampires. And she won't simply drain their blood, as the old stories say. She eats everything but the bones.

Even their *toes*.

I shudder a little at the thought.

I don't think humans would taste very nice, all sweaty from the day with dirt under their fingernails. Especially ones like this, stinking of stale ale and someone else's perfume.

Besides, killing is a surefire way to get cursed.

There are rules for the night and the things that crawl in the shadows. There are even rules for the shadows. Monsters can wreak havoc among humans and each other, feeding on fear or sadness or blood.

But killing is forbidden.

The Gods and their Heralds put that rule into place centuries ago, after the great war, when the God of Eternity was killed and my kind were banished to this world. That's why most vampires just drain a little blood here and there. It keeps them under the Gods' radar.

Not Sapphir.

She knows that breaking the rules comes at a price, the magic that binds us shattering like glass, and she doesn't care. It works in different ways for different monsters, but for Sapphir it means the youthful glow her vampirism should give her fades away. She ages rapidly, looking like a teenager one day, then a woman headed for the grave the next.

So Sapphir eats more often to quell it, the blood and hearts giving her back her youth, but after a time, the act of killing makes her age again, even quicker.

So she feeds again.

Really, I've always thought Sapphir was quite the addict.

And one day she'll wither beyond repair, her appetite not quick enough to placate the Gods' curse.

In the end, they always win.

"Are you finished now?" she presses.

The man's body is racked with silent sobs.

He's too scared to even scream.

I press my hand to his heart.

His fear thickens and I gulp down the last of its honey.

"It's okay," I promise him, twisting my voice to a lie. "It's all over now."

I turn to Sapphir.

She's crouched on the plank beside me, her stance like a wild animal ready to attack. Her long fingernails curl into the rotting wood, holding herself back the best she can.

I don't know how old she truly is, but right now Sapphir looks my age. Seventeen, with long black hair floating down her shoulders in large curls. Even so, I see the streaks of gray beginning to appear, and on her beautiful brown skin a wrinkle creases the sides of her eyes. Another dimples her chin and cuts across her cheeks.

She's aging before me.

My chest tugs.

If Sapphir were to die, I would truly be alone again.

"Have your fun," I say to her.

Sapphir's fangs grow large with her smile.

"Wait, wait." I hold up a hand and get to my feet, dusting the lake dirt from my legs. "Let me leave first. I really don't want to watch."

"It won't last long," Sapphir says.

Her eyes turn red with hunger and I quickly walk away, not waiting for what comes next.

I've never had much taste for blood. Most monsters delight in it, but I've always thought tearing people limb from limb is a little overboard.

Chaos is so much more appealing than carnage.

Bones crack behind me and the man barely has the chance to cry out before Sapphir screeches. The next sound I hear is the gurgle of his blood in her mouth.

I shake my head and resist the urge to look back.

If she doesn't hurry, the Heralds are going to catch her, and they'd love nothing more than to curse her twice over.

I wave my arm and a gateway appears in front of me.

"Better her than me," I mumble under my breath.

My gateway splinters through the forest trees, like a tear in the papers of a book making way for the lines on the next page. It glistens in bright blue light, brushing the nearest leaves from the dirt floor and clearing a path for me to approach.

Opening a gateway is as easy as breathing. A quick inhale as I picture where I want to go, and then a sigh parting my lips as I blow new worlds into view.

My father said the Nefas used to be able to hop in and out of dimensions—from the land of the Gods to the land of the humans—until they were kicked out of Oksenya. When the Gods threw them to the mortals, they stifled their powers.

I think that's what destroyed the others over the centuries. Destroyed their spirits, long before the Gods hunted them to their deaths.

But I never lived in Oksenya to know any different. As the only Nefas to be born here, my gateways have only ever led to places within the human realm.

I step toward my gate, ready to make my way home, when the sound of wind chimes fills the air.

I hear Sapphir growl and curse loudly at the interruption of her meal, but by the time I turn around, she's already scurried into a nearby brush of trees, leaving the broken body behind.

She's quick, I'll give her that.

The world creaks and I narrow my eyes.

I watch the shadows beside the dead man's feet wither. They shrink into themselves and then grow taller, coming out from the ground and up into the world.

They mold themselves into a human form.

At first it's just smoke in the shape of wings, with thin legs and long arms jutting out from black feathers. Then a body takes shape.

A face.

A boy.

A Herald of the Gods.

He hovers over the dead man and sighs.

He looks young, I think. Though I know he isn't.

His face is sharp and soft at once, high round cheekbones set against an angular jaw. He shrugs his shoulders and the feathered wings that engulfed his body shrivel into a small gold tie pin on his chest.

He's dressed all in black, with a waistcoat tight against his slim frame and an overcoat hanging from his shoulders. His hair is just as dark against his narrow, hooded eyes, which echo a muted gray. Though his skin is bright and *alive*, pale as starlight.

The only hint of color on him is from the pocket watch that hooks over the buttons of his waistcoat and hangs delicately at his side.

The Herald peers over the body, taking a moment to assess.

Then he turns to me.

"Monster of mischief," he says.

Like I've just made his day longer.

I should leave.

Turn back to my gate and disappear to the small room atop the tavern that I've called home these past weeks. The last thing I need is to give the Gods an excuse to turn on me.

Yet I stay, watching the Herald as intently as he watches me.

"Vampire?" he asks, his voice cutting through the air like a blade. "It doesn't look like your handiwork."

I don't reply.

Heralds are meddlers by trade. Not just in human affairs, but the affairs of monsters. Stupid little messengers delivering decrees and punishments, or guiding the souls of the dead into the After, thinking it makes them all-powerful because they work directly for the Gods.

There is nothing I have to say to him.

"It's against the rules to kill humans, you know," the Herald says, more to himself than to me. "But I guess you've never had a taste for rules."

He kneels down beside what's left of the man's body, paying no more attention to me.

"Out you come," he says, voice husky and almost bored. "It's over now."

I frown, as his words echo mine so closely.

I'd told the dead man that same thing, before he became a dead man.

The light across his body shimmers in response to the Herald, gathering in an orb at his heart. A glow of hope and a bright, bright future lost.

It expels in a firework of light, exploding into form.

The man, ghostly and translucent, looks down at what he once was.

The Herald pushes himself to his feet. He turns to me with those curious dead eyes.

"Nefas," he says. "You should be careful of the company you keep. Another Herald might try to blame you for this. Then you'd face the Gods' wrath as those before you have."

At this, I laugh.

The idea of him threatening me is the funniest thing I've heard in years.

I tilt my chin high; his threat rolls off me like rainwater.

I won't cower as my parents did.

"Another Nefas might kill you for suggesting that."

The Herald's smile is slow and cutting. "There are no other Nefas," he says.

Like I wasn't aware.

Like I haven't spent the last three years alone, and the years before that forced to hide and bend to the shadows.

"The Gods wouldn't kill me," I challenge. "The last of a race is a precious thing."

The Herald's eyebrows lift, like he finds this amusing. If I didn't know what stiffs his kind were, I'd swear he wanted to laugh.

"Is that what you think?" he asks. The dead man's soul flickers beside him. "That you're precious? That the Gods would ever covet a monster?"

I'm precious enough not to be killed, I think.

After all, they let me go once before.

"Enjoy guiding your soul, cursed little messenger." I turn from him and back to my gate. "I imagine it won't be the last errand you'll have to run today."

"Enjoy your time, monster of mischief," he calls back to me. "I imagine it'll soon run out."

I ignore him. The words of a Herald have no power over me.

Whatever this shadow boy thinks, he's wrong. The Gods wouldn't turn on me when I haven't broken any rules.

My gateway flares before me, pulling me inward, and I step into it without hesitation. Without looking back at the two dead things behind me.

I let it swallow me whole and whisk me away from the night.

2

SILAS

I've been dead—then a guide for the dead—for an eternity.
Or at least it feels that way.

I wait with the dead man and regard his body.

It's not the worst I've seen.

He lies flat on the fishing plank, eyes wide and still in terror. His neck is red, a chunk of flesh hanging loosely from his jugular.

The vampire didn't have time to do much past killing him.

If I was any later, he would've been strewn across the ground in pieces.

Now that would have rocked this tiny village of Rosegarde and made certain the residents locked themselves in their homes for months, barricading their doors and stapling garlic over their window ledges.

They'd start selling stakes at the local store and preparing their pitchforks.

It's the same routine whenever a monster breaks the rules.

Humans gather; they riot. They tread carefully for as long as it takes them to convince themselves they've scared away whatever monster dared cross into their village. And then they forget.

I've seen it hundreds of times.

Not just in Rosegarde, but in many places within my territory.

Each Herald has a territory. We work as messengers for the

Gods, conveying their decrees and curses to the monsters of the land. And on behalf of Thentos—the God of Death—we also guide souls to the After or the Never.

You'd think with all that interaction we'd be quite personable, but none of us work well in teams. So we broke off pieces of the world and divided them among ourselves. The mountains, the seas, the scraps of land that hover between.

All of it sectioned into tidy little territories so we can be responsible for our own monsters and messes.

What I wouldn't give to travel this world, to not be confined to one piece of land. To one kingdom. To Rosegarde and all the other tiny villages just like it that I patrol in and out of.

Existing, but never doing anything so bold as living.

I wonder if I traveled back when I was a human. I could've been an adventurer or a pirate for all I know, sailing the seas from the Fire Kingdom to the Alchemy Kingdom, pilfering from wealthy landowners who hoarded their gold and magic.

Then again, I could have also been a librarian.

I check my pocket watch and then ensure I have the obol coin, marked with the face of one of the three High Gods. The Charon's boat will be here soon, to ferry this man across the death shores and toward his afterlife, and he will require payment.

The same routine, every time.

"Must we go?" the man asks.

I've already done the hard job of explaining that he's dead, but next is trying to convince him not to be so angry about it.

Sometimes, that's easier said than done. Not all souls go peacefully. Most want to cling to their humanity. I understand the urge.

If I could remember anything about my past, I'd cling to it too.

"We must," I tell him, as firmly as I can.

I'm in no mood to bargain.

"The one with the white hair," the man says. "Every fear that sprang to my mind invaded the world when she touched me. How is that possible?"

The Nefas.

Monsters of mischief and illusion, devourers of fear and nightmare, so troublesome that the Gods threw them to the mortal realm over two hundred years ago and wiped their trace from every page of every story they could find.

Most of them were cursed and killed in the first decade of being sent here. I'd heard of a couple surviving, but as far as I knew, they were taken care of years ago.

I guess one slipped through the cracks.

And now she's here, in the Earth Kingdom.

In *my* territory.

It's just my luck.

"I thought her hair looked more silver" is all I say to the dead man. "And believe me, I'm not happy about her being here either."

I flip my pocket watch closed and tuck it back into my waistcoat.

All the territories in all the world and I have to get the one filled with monsters who don't follow the rules.

The water beyond us ripples, and I see the carcass of a boat come into view. It's small and unassuming, the wood rusted and burned with age. Its smoky oars slip in and out of the water on their own.

Each billow from them darkens the river, transforming it into the death currents that'll take this man's soul to where it deserves.

If a person is good, they go to the After.

If they're bad, their soul is banished to the Never.

And if they fall too close to the middle, they might just end up like me. A Herald, forced to serve the Gods.

I don't remember anything about my past, but I know this: All Heralds are humans who weren't good enough for the After or bad enough for the Never. My fate was balanced and so I am sentenced to serve until it can be swung one way or the other.

My past was taken from me. Every memory. Every ounce of pain or joy. They even took my true name.

One hundred years of service. That's how long I have to wait until I can earn the chance to move on to the After and regain my memories.

I'm only halfway through, but it feels like it's been an age. Sometimes I get a low, twisted pull in my heart that makes me think I'll be stuck this way forever.

"The girl with the white hair," the man says, as the boat docks beside us. "What is she really?"

What is she? I think.

She's a creature of night and shadow. A thing that wears humanity like a mask to lull her prey in close. And she does it well. I could barely see her true self flicker beyond it. Her wings, unused, shedding feathers like black snowfall as she stepped through her gateway.

The Last of the Nefas.

"She's a monster, just like all the others," I tell him. "She's not special."

I nod to the boat as it rocks gently against the riverbed, beckoning the man forward.

"It's time," I say.

I lead him onto the boat, and it steadies as soon as his feet touch the wood, settled as it hooks onto his soul. Then I do what I always do. What I've done for so many years and what I'll have to do for so many more: I help ferry his soul across the shores and to the River of Death.

I take him to the one place I wish I could go.

Giving him the destiny I want so badly for myself.

I flick through the dead man's file from earlier, ready to add it to the Library of Souls. Which is just a fancy term for a filing cabinet in a room of blue-gray that stretches eons long.

It lies deep within the sorting zone, which is about as exciting as it sounds. At the mouth of the River of Death, it's a realm masquerading as a building. A half space caught between the dead and the living that only we can access.

And every time I come here, it looks new.

Sometimes I can't put my finger on what it is, but there's always a vague sense of change. A lantern might flicker differently, or a corridor might shape itself to the latest dead human's whim. Sometimes the floors will turn from marble to river water, slicking across my shoes.

It all sounds magical and exciting until you have to navigate the same damn corridor one hundred different ways just to put someone's file to rest.

Besides, however much this place shifts, there's no denying the gray tint it always has. Or that morbid musk I can never quite get out of my suits.

"One more down," I say.

I stamp the man's file with the word *delivered* and then light a match to char the edges closed.

It's the same routine, all day every day.

If it wasn't for my immortality, I'd probably die of boredom.

I think about filing it under *D* for *damn, I'm sick of this*, but I remember the dead man saying his name was Jared Mores, and since he was also torn apart by a vampire, I start to feel bad.

Knowing someone's name always makes it hard to have any fun in this place.

I slip the file under *M* for *Mores* and pat myself on the back for being a good little Herald who always does as he should.

Well done, Silas. Gold star for you.

Only when I push his drawer closed, my hand lingers. My own file is down here somewhere, lost to the endless rows.

I pull open a drawer at random and pick out a file I don't recognize, tearing the char to flick through its pages.

Would I know my true name if I came across it?

I steel myself and close my eyes, moving my hand from side to side and across the drawers until one brings an uneasy feeling in my stomach.

I open my eyes and curve my fingers around the handle, wondering if maybe—

"It's not in there," a voice says.

A figure pokes out from a nearby drawer.

The Keeper of Files.

He crawls from the cabinet, gray limbs fluid as his hands slick around the drawer to lever himself back to the floor. His suit is tinted green and bunches up over his head, where no clear line draws between his neck and his chin.

He is a solid blob of a creature, no more than half my size.

A creature of riddles.

"You won't find it," he says, as I begin to walk away. His voice drifts through the room like a taunt. "At least, not in the places you'd think to look."

I turn back to him. "How do you know where I'd look?"

"Your name would be a good start," he says. "But since you can't remember it, you wouldn't think to look there."

I hold back my glare. "I guess you'd know what my real name was?"

"I'm the Keeper of Files. You're a file. Yes, yes, *I* remember."

"Don't suppose you'd tell me?" I ask, trying my luck.

The Keeper of Files tugs his lips upward in a cracked smile. "Heralds are not meant to consider their service so woefully, young boy of old worlds. That's why their memories are wiped. You are in this play now, so you must perform your lines with gusto. Yes, yes, play the part!"

I arch an eyebrow. "So that's a *no* to telling me about my past then?"

When the Keeper doesn't blink for a good minute, I realize I'd be better off talking to a brick wall.

You're supposed to be atoning for your sins, Silas, not trying to remember them, I remind myself.

I should be focused only on my service. Being a Herald is not about me. It's about the word and will of the Gods that must be conveyed.

Blah, blah, blah.

That spiel is the first memory I have: waking up in the sorting zone surrounded by thick curtains and a man in a purple suit telling me I had a sin to make amends for and that I must serve the Gods until my fate is decided. Then he pressed a dagger into my hand and told me it would help to keep the villains at bay.

I later found out it was Thentos himself, God of Death.

On the few occasions I've spoken to other Heralds, they recall their first day as hazy. A blur of etiquette and edicts they scarcely remember the specifics of, but I remember every detail.

Most of all, how every strange thing Thentos said didn't feel so strange at all. His words and instructions—even the damn suit he was wearing—felt like a dream I'd already had, a dozen times over.

Only of course it wasn't.

Dreams imply the possibility of waking up and I've never woken up from this.

"Since you're here, I need you to do me a favor," I say to the Keeper now, straightening my tie as if it'll straighten out my priorities. "Convey a message to the Gods. Let them know that I encountered a Nefas in the Earth Kingdom, in the village of Rosegarde. They may want to keep an eye on her. She seemed the type to cause trouble."

I almost feel jealous of that.

How fun it would be to cause a little trouble every now and again.

"You saw a Nefas?" the Keeper of Files asks.

The curiosity in his tone doesn't go amiss, but there was nothing peculiar about the monster to report beyond her existence.

Not including her arrogance, of course.

But then all monsters are arrogant. They all think they're something special when really they're just nameless creatures, whose mess I have to tidy up and whose curses I have to relay when they inevitably break the rules.

Nameless.

That thought makes me wonder.

Most monsters prefer distinct scratching on the forest floors or some other calling card to set them apart, but that Nefas…the way she regarded herself.

I bet she has a name.

I wonder what it tastes like.

"How impressive to escape a Nefas unharmed!" the Keeper of Files says.

I shrug. "That isn't saying much, since I can't die."

He grins. His teeth are filed to points. "Lived to tell the tale but you want me to tell it instead," he says. "I imagine the higher-ups are interested in what you have to say."

Higher-ups?

I almost laugh at the idea.

The High Gods who rule the blessed realm of Oksenya never leave it, and the River Gods who protect them rarely abandon their positions.

Instead, we get our messages right here in the sorting zone. Whenever the Gods have something for us to pass on, it appears in our respective pigeonholes as a small quill, with purple flower petals for feathers. Only when we put the pen to sacred parchment does the message write itself, ready for us to relay.

That's not going to change because of one little Nefas.

"If the Gods want any further information, they know where to find me," I say. "Here. As always."

The Keeper of Files clucks at my wry tone. "You'll do well to remember who you are," he says. "Yes, yes, try your best."

The seriousness in his voice almost makes me chuckle.

Remembering who I am is the one thing I can't do and this creature knows it. I'd kill to even remember my real name.

Silas is a name I saw carved on a headstone during my very first visit to a cemetery. I took it for myself to make sure I don't forget that I'm somebody to be remembered too, even if I don't know who that somebody is.

You can't forget yourself if you have a name.

A place like this swallows people up, turning them into mindless servants until their one hundred years are up.

It won't happen to me if I keep ahold of that.

Silas. Silas. Silas.

"Did the Nefas say anything to you?" the Keeper of Files asks.

I raise an eyebrow. "Anything like what?"

"Monsters whisper many things." The Keeper taps a nearby file drawer with a spindled finger, the sound like a ticking clock. "Betrayal and woe and curses."

Each word is punctuated by the drum of his long fingers.

"Curses," I repeat, thinking back to the encounter.

Cursed little messenger.

That's what the Nefas had called me. And she wasn't exactly wrong.

"Not that such things are of interest to me," the Keeper says quickly. "Not in my play. Not in my lines. My only interest is the files and nothing more."

He stretches his arms across the various drawers in a hug.

As though he didn't start this conversation in the first place.

Still, it makes me think.

Every monster who breaks the rules and takes the life of a human is cursed by the Gods. Only, the great secret that the monsters of the world don't know—and that only we as Heralds are privy to—is that the rules can be broken.

The Gods' curse isn't without flaws. It has rules, as all magic must.

A counter-magic, to ensure there is always balance.

If a monster wants to break their curse, they must absorb the blood and power of three formidable beings: a vampire—to attain their chance at new life; a banshee—to claim their daunting; and a God—to regain their magic. And of course, drink from the River of Eternity, to reclaim their immortality.

Lucky for them.

I wish there was a hidden solution to unbind me from my fate, but for Heralds there's no such loophole.

Besides we *can't* kill.

Not even vampires or banshees. If any Herald were to try, we would be struck down in flames and erased from the world.

The Keeper of Files opens a drawer and then crawls inside.

"Why do you think you can't accept your duties like the other Heralds?" he asks, his voice muffled by the files he roots around in. "Why do you think you are strange?"

I pause at the question.

Truthfully, I'm not sure. It would be easier if I could accept my duty, but the gnawing in my heart is inescapable.

If I ever slept, it would keep me awake.

"I don't think I'm meant to be like this," I say.

"You believe the Gods made a mistake when they turned you into a Herald."

It is not a question.

"I just know that I don't belong here."

The Keeper of Files pops his head out of the drawer and

blinks for the first time. "A Herald can only be unmade by the God of Death, and memories can only be unmade by the God of Forgetting," he says.

I smirk. "Thanks, but I don't think pleading with a God for my life back will work."

"Not plead with," he answers, gaze sharpening. "Why, you could simply absorb their power to use for your own, then make or unmake yourself! What fun!"

I grimace at his cavalier suggestion of treachery.

The Keeper of Files has always had an odd sense of humor.

"Gods don't die by mortal blades," I remind him, brushing the suggestion off. "I guess I'll have to pass on trying to murder one. But thanks for the tip."

The Keeper of Files merely gestures to my belt, where my dagger is fixed. Two snakes loop around the blade, their tongues hissing at a handle shaped like wings.

My gift from Thentos when I first became a Herald.

To keep the villains at bay.

"Is that a mortal blade?" he asks.

His eyes do not leave mine.

I grit my teeth in place of gripping the dagger.

"I'm no killer."

He cocks his head to one side. "How would you know?"

I glower.

I don't need the reminder that my past is a mystery, or that I could have done something truly awful to deserve the hand of fate I've been dealt, but I'm a Herald now.

And Heralds can't kill, even if we wanted to.

That blade is for defense only.

So get someone to use it for you, a voice in my head says.

I nearly snort at the thought.

What being, monster or otherwise, would be desperate enough to help me kill a God and steal back my life?

"If treachery is rejected, then I think I'm bored," the Keeper of Files tells me, snapping me back to reality. "Don't hurt yourself overthinking. And remember, your service is appreciated. It will be for an eternity."

He leans down to whisper.

"But shhh, don't tell anyone I told you that."

I adjust my tie, making sure the winged pin that allows me to travel through the world is perfectly straight.

"There is no eternity in my contract," I correct him. "I've served fifty years and I only have another fifty until I'm free."

The Keeper of Files tilts his head, studying my neatly pressed suit. "Eternities are ever changing."

Not mine, I think sharply.

I won't allow it.

I could not handle another clump of seemingly indefinite years, relaying the Gods' every whim alongside so many Heralds waiting for their chance at redemption.

Unquestioning. Unliving.

So do something about it, that voice in my head says. *Find your loophole.*

3

ATIA

Deep in the vein of Rosegarde, there's only ever one place that people gather come sundown.

The Covet sits on the very edge of the canals, with tree veins encasing its windows in a forest of rich orange ivy, no matter the season. The swells of music—soft violin strings bolstered by drums and brassy horns—cascade from every open crevice and cracked door. When you look straight at it on a bright day, the building could masquerade as normal, but if you catch it out of the corner of your eye, in the sketch of night, you might very well see it sway and curve.

Of course, that could be the ale talking. Or the magic.

There's rarely a difference between the two.

And for the past two months, it's become all too familiar. I've been in one place for too long and my parents taught me better.

Keep moving, they always said. *Never let them track you.*

Never let them see you, they meant.

And definitely don't talk to a Herald.

If my parents could've seen me the other night, they'd be furious.

No, I correct myself. *They'd be worried.*

Being worried was their favorite pastime.

"You're in late today," a chirpy voice says.

I look across the bar to see a young boy with deep brown skin and light blond hair dressed, as always, in the navy robes of the Academics.

Tristan.

He wipes his robes, scowling at the ale stain on his front pocket.

"I've spent hours writing about banshees," he tells me.

He picks up a notebook that's resting on the bar and holds it up like a prize.

"I can't wait for you to hear about what I found at the library."

Tristan is always far too eager to talk, *especially* when it's about the library. He spends half his time there, when he's not spending the other half in the corner of the Covet scribbling furiously in his notebook.

I take said notebook out of Tristan's hands and try to focus.

Around us, the Covet is alive with night.

People gather everywhere: on tables and the rickety stairs that lead up to the guest rooms. Above us, the candle lanterns sway as the dancing shakes the very walls.

"How long were you waiting for me?" I ask Tristan over the noise.

"Technically I wasn't waiting, I was working," he says. "But also, two hours."

I snort a laugh and crack open the notebook's ink-soaked pages.

"You should spend less time studying monsters and more time making actual friends."

"I don't need friends when I have my books," Tristan proclaims. "And you."

I'm a little outraged. "We're not friends, Tristan."

I've been reminding him of that every day since I got here.

Then again, on the list of humans I can stand, his name is at the top. He's also the only one whose nightmares I haven't touched.

Tristan's far too amiable to be riddled with fear. I think I might actually feel guilty if I plagued him with his worst terrors.

I'm also not sure what his fears would be if I tried to find them. Buried under a mountain of books? Something tells me he'd quite enjoy that.

"So, banshees," I say, flicking through the notebook. "What did you find?"

Tristan's face lights up.

Before his parents moved to Queen Morrow of the Soil's Earth Kingdom, where scholars study nature, he lived in the Alchemy Kingdom. Their specialty is magic and monsters, and despite the move, Tristan hasn't switched studies.

"Right here," he says, pointing excitedly to a page.

"Thanks to this text, I'm working on a theory that banshees don't just predict death, but cause it too. I think they're hunters, not omens."

I mumble a *huh* as though the idea is revolutionary. Really, banshees are a mix of both legends.

"Interesting theory" is all I say.

I push the notebook back over and Tristan pockets it with a grin.

"It won't be a theory for long. I'll prove it once I find one."

I pause to eye him curiously. "You're going banshee hunting?"

"If I'm going to write about monsters, I probably need to meet one," Tristan says.

The irony of it makes me stifle a laugh. "Good luck with that."

"I won't need luck," he tells me, ever confident. "There are monsters lurking among us, Atia. They could even be here, in this very tavern."

"Wow. How frightening."

Tristan leans in close across the bar, his eyes darting around us to make sure nobody is listening in. I can smell the garlic wards on him that all the villagers have been wearing since Sapphir's attack two nights ago.

"Did you see the traveler?" he asks in a whisper. "The man who came through here selling elixirs from the Water Kingdom?"

I stiffen.

The man at the fishing plank did mention being a trader, but I stopped listening after he started talking about phial sizes.

"Why do you ask?"

"He was killed two nights ago," Tristan says. "Throat ripped out. People are saying that it's a vampire."

"But not a banshee."

Tristan shakes his head. "Where one monster goes, another follows."

I nod. "I'm sure banshees and vampires are the best of friends."

Tristan is undeterred by my sarcasm. "How can a seer be so close-minded?"

A *seer*.

Now that's an identity that has come to bite me in the backside.

I may be able to travel from kingdom to kingdom at the wave of a gateway, but even I need a place to rest. Coin to rent a room. Some monsters might want to sleep on forest floors in the freezing rain, but I'd rather have my comforts. And in the human world, gold is given in exchange for goods.

The best goods I could think to trade for were fake futures.

In other kingdoms I've been a painter or a storyteller. Once I was even a jailer. But a traveling seer draws the least attention and the most gold, and the white of my hair lends perfectly to the lie.

People are superstitious and love nothing more than to be told they're *on the right path*.

"You're barking up the wrong tree if you want someone open," I tell Tristan. "Come to me when you want sarcasm and pessimism, or anything else that means I don't have to smile."

"But you've got a beautiful smile," Tristan says.

A sheepish blush creeps onto his cheeks and he looks down to the floor, as though he hadn't expected himself to say that.

He clears his throat and I know what he's going to ask me next. It wouldn't be the first time.

"Did you want to go for a walk later?" He bites his lip. "We could head to the lake and watch the stars."

His fingers tap against the bar, as they always do when he's nervous.

I swallow down my sigh, feeling a pang of guilt I'm not used to.

We could head to the lake and watch the stars if Tristan wasn't human and I wasn't the kind of thing that hunted them.

If he wasn't nice and I wasn't the opposite of all things nice.

We could play out the romantic scene, skipping stones in the water.

If it were any other man or woman, Tristan's words would make their heart pound. A pretty boy asking pretty things.

But I can't see him that way.

He's too delicate—*breakable*—and there isn't a spark or hunger there. Though even if there was someone I felt that with, I would never allow myself to give in to it.

Don't ever let them see you.

And I never have.

Tristan told me I was pretty once, but it was only because he hasn't seen my true face.

"You don't want to go to the lake with me, Tristan."

The last man who did didn't survive.

Tristan doesn't press further.

He takes care not to look too disappointed.

"I'll have to stick to talking your ear off," he says, a large smile covering up any awkwardness that was there before. "Do you know how rare it is to find another scholar from the Alchemy Kingdom?"

I shrug. "I'm guessing rare."

"*Very*," he says. "As in two. You and me."

Or just him, since I've never actually been to the Alchemy Kingdom. Still, it made a convenient cover story for every time I let slip more knowledge on monsters than I should have.

I left Alchemy once my parents died, I told him.

A lie that stopped Tristan inquiring any more. I didn't need to tell him how they were ripped apart by Gods and how it was partly my fault.

How I'd never imagined that after every lesson they taught me about being gentle when invading nightmares, they could ever break the Gods' rules and kill a human.

Or how when I tried to escape that night, a strange man caught me by the wrist and I still feel his grip and smell the ash of his skin.

All Tristan needed to know was that I once had parents and now I don't.

"Are you Tristan Berrow?" someone asks.

Tristan's eyes quickly darken as they're drawn to the voice.

I turn and see a man with a collar that funnels up to his chin, a cigarette pinched between his lips.

He moves like water reeds, swaying slightly on his feet, jittering up and down as if there are things inside he can't contain. His skin is pale, and though he's short, something about him towers over Tristan.

"Where are your parents?" the stranger asks, voice scratchy.

Tristan puffs his chest out in an effort to appear bigger. "I'm managing things tonight."

The stranger blows a thick cloud of smoke into the air and Tristan immediately wafts it away.

"So grown-up."

I watch with interest.

Such a tiny speck of a man and yet his every word seems to ruffle Tristan. I can taste the sweetness of his fear. My stomach growls.

"It's time to give what you owe, thief," the man says.

Tristan's eyes grow wide with the accusation. "We've settled our debts."

"And what about your promises?"

The man steps closer and stamps his cigarette out on the bar, crushing it into the woodgrain.

"Give what you owe, or I'll make you watch while I gut your parents."

His words are intended for Tristan, but they hit me instead.

Not while she's here, my father's memory yells.

My mother screams, as his head bounces onto the floor beside her.

The blade cuts into her heart next.

Atia, run!

And I did.

I ran because my wings were too small to fly, and I was sure it was fast enough until—

Your parents' disobedience could never be forgiven, the ashen man had said, hand tight around my wrist. His violet suit glimmered in the darkness. *Now take this mercy and run. Run far and as fast as you can.*

Something sharp and jagged splinters inside me at the memory and suddenly I am so angry it cannot be controlled.

I stand, my chair clattering violently to the floor.

Tristan and the stranger turn to me in surprise.

My heart pounds relentlessly inside my chest. When I look down at my hands, I realize they're shaking.

"Don't threaten him like that."

My voice is guttural, more a growl than anything else. I haven't thought about that day—haven't heard my mother's screams fill my memories and let the smell of the ashen man invade my nostrils—in years.

I haven't let myself.

"Mind your business, girl," the man says.

I should.

Monsters should never get involved in the business of humans, but I can't help it.

"That's enough," I say, controlling my temper the best I can.

The stranger looks amused. There is no sign of fear in his eyes as he regards my human form. "Listen here, little girl—"

I thrust my palm up and straight into his face.

The stranger's fragile nose shatters easily in my hand.

He slumps backward onto the floor, eyes bulging at the outburst. The blood leaks from him like an old pipe.

"You—you—"

"I said, *that's enough*," I repeat, the finality in my words unwavering.

I take another step toward him.

The stranger skitters backward.

Now there is fear in his eyes.

I could make your worst nightmares come true, I think.

I could crawl into your mind and skitter through your every fear until you beg me for mercy.

I could drink the air as it turned black with your fear, letting it slip down my throat and across my skin like a warm blanket.

I could coat this building in your blood and let the Gods and their rules be damned.

I swallow, knowing I can't do any of that.

Not here.

Not with Tristan and the Covet's patrons now turning to stare.

I may want to show this man my true face and watch the color drain from his cheeks, but revealing myself to an entire village of humans is just asking to be hunted.

By them and the Gods.

Better to leave Rosegarde of my own choice than be chased out.

I take in a steadying breath.

"I'm the village's new seer," I say, swallowing my fury. "I could look into your mind and find every dirty secret you've ever hidden. Every body."

The stranger's eyes narrow.

"I could reveal it all to the village guards. Or to your other clients. I'm sure they'd appreciate the leverage to wipe off their debts."

The stranger's lips curl in hatred.

Perhaps he knows it's a lie and that every word I've spoken is a farce, but I can sense his worry as he mulls over what it would mean if it were true.

How I could ruin him.

"Hide behind your seer." He sneers at Tristan, dragging his sleeve across his nose to wipe the blood. "This won't end here. You know she always gets what she's owed."

She? I watch the stranger's retreating figure, until he rips open the street door and it slams back behind him, nearly ripping the bell from its hinges.

Who is this mysterious she?

"I can't believe you just did that," Tristan says.

"Would you rather I didn't?"

He gapes at me like he's not sure either way.

I shrug and pick up the chair I'd thrown to the floor. I settle back down into the rickety thing, still feeling the fire of the confrontation unsettled in my bones.

"We're good people, by the way," Tristan says suddenly. "My parents and I. We're *not* thieves."

"I didn't say you were."

"You must have wondered what he meant."

"I make it a habit never to wonder about other people," I say. "They always turn out to be far less interesting than I imagine."

Tristan snorts. "You're strange, Atia. Maybe even stranger than I thought."

I quirk a brow.

"In a nice way," he says hurriedly. "Strange is better than boring."

I muse over this. "I could be boring."

"I wish you wouldn't," he says. "I'd have nobody to talk to."

"I suppose talking about monsters doesn't get you far in social circles."

"I'm not sure why," Tristan says. "We all have a bit of monster in us. But we all have a bit of something else too."

Not me, I think.

"What else?"

"Hope," he says confidently. The voice of someone who's never had it stolen from them. "Family. Friends. People who make us want to do better."

I swallow, a pit growing large in my stomach.

Tristan might have all that, but I don't.

The Gods took it from me long ago and it's time I left Rosegarde before I trick myself into thinking I could ever have it again.

I must disappear.

Let the people I've crossed paths with forget I ever existed.

Become a story and nothing more.

4

ATIA

Despite what you might have heard, the night was not actually made for monsters.

It was made for the humans to find freedom from the harsh light of being seen. To let them loose from the restraints they'd chosen for themselves or the ones that had been put onto them.

It was made to let them be vulnerable, exposed.

That's when the monsters came.

When we claimed the night for ourselves.

We have no choice, my father once said as I, eight years old, stared up at him. *After Oksenya, this is all the Gods left for us. Just the night. Just the shadows. And we must treat those shadows well, for they keep us hidden.*

Despite its apparent beauty, when my father spoke of Oksenya, his voice was always carved from the narrows of the world, quiet and foreboding. Only when he spoke of the human realm and the memories we'd make was it filled with warmth and comfort.

That's the thing I remember most about him.

Not the large spiraled horns that were so grand and intricate they looked like mazes on his head. Riddles that had sprung from his mind to take shape for all to see.

I remember his voice and how safe it made me feel. How it made me wonder about others of our kind and if they were all so reverent.

As for my mother, I remember the way she sang in clucks and hums, a mix of sweet murmurs and clicking tongues. The melody of her, even in the way she walked around the small barn that we called home.

She fed the crowing roosters with a spring in her step that felt like a dance, and gave the horses bushels of apples that made them nuzzle into her neck like they were telling her secrets.

The farm had all manner of arias and so did my mother.

She was a song. She made me smile the way music makes the humans smile. Made me dance and laugh, the way their favorite ditties do.

Whenever she held my hand, I couldn't imagine why the Gods hated us enough to start a war. Why they blamed us when one of their own died for it. Or why others of our kind would have killed humans when they were thrown to this realm.

Yes, we fed on nightmares. We left the farm to steal fear, but that was chaos, not carnage. Dream, not reality.

How could it have all been a lie?

I grit my teeth now as the moon hides behind a growing cloud, darkening the streets.

I linger in wait at the top of one of the stone staircases that connect the streets of Rosegarde. It is a village of hills and steps, with houses that connect up a mossy backdrop and canals that slip between them like delicate veins, leading to the forested lake below.

I watch the drunks stumble through the streets.

There's a knack to hunting.

For the first year I was alone after my parents were killed, I'd hunt anyone and anything, crawling through windows to steal whatever nightmares I could. Now I prefer to be more meticulous in the hunt. Savor it. Take the time to find the perfect prey.

I lick my hungry lips.

The confrontation with Tristan's stranger has left me famished and the beast inside me must be fed. It must be settled.

So I watch.

It doesn't take long before I see Tristan meandering into a nearby alley.

The moon is dark and the air bites hard enough for him to pull the collar of his thin coat up high to his chin. He exhales a cold breath and holds his books close to his chest, as if protecting them from the harsh wind.

A scholar, through and through.

I smile a little.

Tristan is a strange kind of human, untouched by any horrors the world has to hold. He studies monsters, but he knows nothing real of them.

I hope it stays that way. Let him be wide-eyed forever, speaking of myths like they are magic. Leave the shadows and their world for creatures like me to deal with.

Tristan looks up to the moon and holds his thumb out to it. Then, with a large grin, he turns on his heel and heads down the alley that leads toward the first of many canals.

It's only a moment later that I see a figure slip after him.

I pause and step forward, peering closer through the brush that hides me.

The stranger from earlier throws his cigar to the ground, the end blazing against the cobbles.

He was waiting for Tristan.

How could he even be so sure Tristan would take this route?

The slopes of the alleys are certainly not the quickest way to his home. They're a far more winding and scenic path.

The man stares after him.

I recognize that stare. It's the same look I've had for the past few hours—of wanting to make prey from someone.

Never get involved in the business of humans, Atia.

That is how they trap you.

I hear my father's scolding voice, warning me to keep my mind on my own problems and not those of mortals.

Yet as this man follows Tristan through the narrow alleyways, I follow too.

5

SILAS

I approach my designated pigeonhole. I can see the quill already, feathered with purple flower petals, practically glowing in the small space.

A message from the Gods.

Yet another decree to be ferried.

Yet another day of the same.

I close my eyes and blow out a breath as I step forward.

"That looks important."

The Keeper of Files is sprawled across the floor at my feet, eyebrows wiggling by my toes.

I jump back. "What are you doing?"

"Napping," he says. "You nearly stepped on me."

"Why were you napping on the floor?"

"I was tired. Why were you walking around with your eyes closed?" He pulls himself to standing.

I exhale, knowing there's no use in trying to reason with a creature who spends his days doing nothing but watching souls be alphabetized.

"Shouldn't you be guarding the files or something?" I ask. "Why are you by the quills?"

"I delivered your message about the Nefas to the Gods. Yes, yes, just like you asked." He says it with a grumble that tells me he was not happy about it. "It seems they replied. Very quick indeed. I bet the play will be starting again! Do you have your lines ready?"

"Sometimes I think that you must be very drunk," I say.

The Keeper looks indignant. "That's beside the point."

Does any of this have a point? I think. *The messages, the Gods, the repetition of my entire life.*

As I think it, the door to the file room swings open and three Heralds appear in a perfect row. Their suits are crisp black, each with the same tie pin I have that holds our wings and allows us to fly through the shadows.

Their short hair is cut to the perfect centimeter above their ears. They are copies of each other, their differences smudging away so that none of the humanity remains in their blond hair or green eyes.

They are nothing but what the Gods have made them, only the smallest shards of who they once were seem to remain.

Is that what I look like? Is it what they think of me too?

Maybe we're all just masquerading.

"Earth Kingdom Herald," one greets me.

Silas, I want to scream.

My damn name is Silas.

"Hello, Fire Kingdom Herald," I say back. "I see you're wearing the black suit today. Very fetching."

The Herald doesn't smile.

She looks down to regard her unchanging attire, the same as all the others. I don't know why they won't wear anything else, shifting our attire at will as I do.

Apparently, I'm the only one who wants some kind of variety in this day-to-day monotony.

"May we check our messages too?" she asks. She looks down at the Keeper. "Then I'll need to file. I had a decapitation and I would like it off my hands."

"Literally?" I ask.

"It nearly was," she says. "There was a splatter as I arrived. It could've stained my tie."

I blink. "That would've been unfortunate."

"I have spares," she says. "It wouldn't have mattered."

"Except to the human."

The Herald rolls her eyes. "Everything matters to them."

As though we were not once *them*.

"And to the monsters," one of the others says.

An Alchemy Kingdom Herald, whose voice is as deep as a cavern. He polishes his tie pin with his sleeve.

"They are all sentimental. I've heard the rumblings," he says. "Up in arms about missing monsters. I ferried a soul today and a lykai was there waiting. It begged me to look into its lost mate and *ask the Gods* if they knew anything. As though we relay messages for just anyone."

"Let us pretend we care about their petty messages," the Fire Kingdom Herald says. "Let us pretend less monsters is a bad thing."

"Let us congratulate whoever is stealing them away," the Alchemy Kingdom Herald agrees with a hint of a laugh.

It doesn't quite reach his lips. A Herald could never do something as human as smile.

My brows knit together.

I hadn't heard any whispers about missing monsters, but I suppose you have to actually talk to other Heralds to be in the know.

I'd really rather not.

"I should return to the files then," the Keeper says to me.

He grumbles at the end of our conversation and slinks toward the door to retreat back to the library.

"Do not ask me for help with your lost head," he intones over his shoulder. "I am a busy thing, yes, yes. And I have helped you enough."

"I'm actually quite busy too," I say, trying to dismiss myself from the other Heralds.

But they have already brushed past me and begun heading toward their pigeonholes.

I wasn't joking when I said we weren't team players. Most prefer to be alone. Maybe that's how they were in life too. Silent and unblinking in the face of decapitation, unless it were to stain their suits.

Maybe that's what I was like.

I take the quill from the pigeonhole.

Who were you, Silas? I ask myself. *A coward or a killer? An adventurer or a giant drip?*

I grab a nearby piece of parchment and put the quill to it, letting the pen come alive in my hand. The ink scribbles quickly, scratching its message in cursive across the page.

I lean in closer, reading it twice over to ensure I'm not mistaken, but there it is, clear as day.

The Gods' latest command.

I don't expect to smile, but I do.

It's late when I find myself at the Rosegarde lake, on the small fishing plank where the scent of the Nefas still lingers.

I reach out a hand to touch the air where she opened her

gateway. It still feels warm with her magic and the promise of death that follows her.

It's a scent I know well.

I can smell it, smell *her*, still hiding in this village somewhere. The remnants of her power are like the last waves of a storm, and there's enough of it left to linger that I could find her easily if I wanted.

I could track her through this village in a heartbeat.

Are you sure this is a good idea, Silas? I ask myself. *Are you sure this is right?*

"No," I say out loud.

But I do it anyway.

I close my fist around the warm air, trapping a shard of her magic in my palm.

I'm coming, little monster.

ATIA

My footsteps are light against the broken cobbles, hidden under the light smear of snowfall.

The stranger makes smart work of following Tristan. I can tell it isn't the first time he has done something like this.

Luckily for Tristan, it's not the first time I have either.

I keep to the creases of the pathways, careful not to be seen as I trace them through the alleys of Rosegarde.

The stranger is well-practiced. He waits until Tristan reaches the nook of his journey where the torchlights are lowest and the pathways are barren.

"Boy," he says.

One word pierces through the quiet of the night.

Tristan turns around and sees the man. Then he sees the knife.

The panic edges into his face until his eyes drift behind the man and find me.

Tristan gapes.

"*Atia?*" he asks. "What are you doing here?"

"Following you," I say simply, stepping fully into view. "Actually, I was following the man who was following you."

I nod over to the stranger.

"Semantics."

"Stay out of this," the man sneers. "It's between me and the boy."

"It's between you and his parents," I correct. "Tristan shouldn't suffer for their misdoings. Whatever debt you're after is surely theirs to provide."

No child should pay for their parents' sins. That's a lesson I've already learned well enough.

"You don't know what you're talking about," the man says. "Or who you're dealing with."

I walk toward him, my eyes darkening with the growing night. I can feel the wind whipping the ends of my hair.

"Do you?" I ask.

This stranger is tarnished. I can smell not just his own fear but the last traces of fear from the lives he has taken. They cling to him like weeds.

He is a killer and he would kill Tristan given half the chance.

"People like you are why monsters like me exist," I say.

The man's brows pinch together. "Who are you?"

"Not *who*."

I waste no time in reaching out to him.

With just one touch the man seizes and I'm able to climb into the field of his mind, plucking which fears look the most appetizing.

He shakes, the terror settling into his bones.

My final meal in Rosegarde will be a grand one indeed.

"Atia, what are you doing?" Tristan asks, panicked.

I grin and I can tell the moment my blue eyes turn white, because Tristan stumbles back, horror in his stare.

"Feeding," I say.

I shake loose my humanity, letting my skin take on its teardrop hue. My golden horns curl out from the curtain of my hair, weaving upward in great spirals, and my wings spring out in celebration, a forest in their feathers as they stretch to the size of trees.

This man is a feast.

The further I delve into his mind, the more wicked, awful things I taste. Memories of murder and blood soaking into his nail beds.

He is as much a monster as me and that means he isn't protected by his so-called humanity.

"You're—" Tristan says, voice breathy. "Atia, you're a—"

He breaks off.

I inhale the scent of the man's fear.

He's scared of needles, so I create an illusion of a thousand of them pricking into his skin.

He's afraid of thunder, so I let the noise of it batter into his eardrums, loud enough to draw blood.

But most of all, he's scared of ghosts.

That one I enjoy most. I see the faces of each victim he's had. They sit on the surface of his mind, easily captured. I conjure images of them that scream in his face and claw at his ankles.

Then a new image appears among his cries, so much clearer than all the others before. A woman with golden hair slipping across her collarbone, green eyes, and red lips that draw to a slow smile as she wags her finger from side to side, scolding.

The crown she wears is black as raven feathers.

Vail of the Arcane. The queen of the Alchemy Kingdom is engraved into this man's mind. And he is so afraid of her.

She always gets what she's owed.

That's what the man told Tristan back at the Covet.

Was he talking about Vail?

I know little of the Alchemy Queen, aside from her love of magic and monsters, and her affinity for collecting both. It's why the smarter creatures steer clear from that side of the world. That, and the rumor that she killed her father and four siblings so she could ascend to the throne faster.

Vail of the Arcane is not the kind of queen to entangle yourself with.

How did Tristan and his family become indebted to her?

I delve deeper into this man's mind to try and find my answers, but there is only her face, clawing into him like nails.

He screams until his throat is hoarse.

I could paralyze him with just one of these awful thoughts— one searing image of Vail would surely do it—but it isn't enough. I don't want his hair to simply streak white and his eyes to glaze over as he tries to escape from this nightmare.

I want him to think there is no escape.

It's what he deserves for going after Tristan and his parents.

Let Vail collect her own gold if that's what's owed, rather than sending her lackeys to destroy a family in her name.

"Wh-what's happening to him?" Tristan asks.

His hands tremble by his sides as he watches the man convulse.

"Nothing he doesn't deserve," I answer darkly.

The man's fear fills me like a black hole. There is no end to it.

Even as his fingernails dig into the cobblestones, breaking off at the ends.

Tristan falls back to the ground, but I pay no mind to him.

What matters is the man, frozen in front of me, choking on his breath as it traps in his throat. Listening to him scream is like music, filling the night and bouncing off the moon to make the shadows dance.

"Atia," Tristan says. His face is ashen as he pleads with me. "Stop it."

I don't.

I realize that I *can't*.

The monster inside me is roaring. This man's soul is tainted. He refuses to follow the rules that even us creatures are bound by.

He kills and tears families apart.

He is no better than the Gods who murdered my parents right in front of me.

Creator of his own wicked law.

And how are the humans punished for such crimes? They aren't. It is only *us* who suffer.

Once again that day fills my mind.

My mother pleaded to be spared. The memory of her cries outweigh this man's.

The Gods wouldn't have found us if it wasn't for my mistake.

I hear her begging for me to *run, run, RUN!*

As though I could outrun such horrors.

And then the hand of the man in the violet suit snaked around me.

Suddenly, I'm not just pulling this man's fears into the world, but pouring my own into him. The fear I felt that day as I watched my parents be cut down and the fear I've felt every day since, knowing I live at the whims of Gods.

I am a *Nefas*. I feed on fear and yet that very thing plagues me too.

I am so afraid and I can't stand it.

"You deserve to be punished," I spit at the man.

Sweat beads down my temple as I watch him suffer.

It's enough, I think to myself. *You should stop now.*

Only I don't, even as his breathing grows stagnant.

"Mercy," he whispers. "For the love of Gods, mercy."

"The Gods do not know love," I say. "And they do not know mercy."

Atia, I hear my mother cry my name. Then scream it. *ATIA!*

Again and again.

Then I realize it is Tristan who is screaming and not her.

I blink and step back, thrown from my haze.

The man is still on the floor.

His hair is as white as his face, not a speck of color left anywhere on him. His eyes are blanched and his mouth is ripped open, stuck rigid in a scream.

Tristan rushes to his side and places a finger to his neck, then his wrist. He lowers his ear to his mouth and his chest, to check for breath. A heartbeat.

When Tristan looks back to me, I crumple.

I know before he says it.

"He's dead," Tristan tells me.

And so am I.

Monsters have one rule bestowed on us by the Gods and I've broken it.

I've killed someone. Literally *scared* him to death. I didn't even know such a thing was possible.

"I didn't mean to," I whisper.

How did I lose control like that? Why couldn't I stop?

I've never felt so disconnected from myself, or so angry at anyone I've fed on. I've winced when seeing Sapphir mangle humans and steal their lives away, turning my back so I didn't have to look.

But now I am the same as her.

The world bends as I think it, shifting beneath my feet. The wind turns to smoke and then becomes solid before my eyes, morphing from wings into a familiar face.

"Well, well," the Herald says with a smile. "There you are."

SILAS

The Nefas is a sight to behold.

I have seen many monsters in my time, but never miracles. And the sight of her feels oddly miraculous.

Her skin has taken on the hue of the ocean, blanketing her in ripples a deep, drowning blue. Her hair, silver as a new coin, looks like the crest of a wave washing over her shoulders. She has horns, but they are not jagged and pointed, or red as blood like some of the creatures who darken the night. They are the rays of the sun made solid, too intricately woven for me to find their end.

She truly looks like she was born from Gods.

And she isn't happy to see me.

Quickly, she shakes the monster from her form and brings the illusion of humanity to her surface.

I feel a pang of disappointment.

"*You*," the Nefas says, outraged. "Are there no other Heralds this side of Rosegarde?"

She eyes the linen of my suit and scoffs.

I think about explaining our system and how the Heralds have divided up the territories within the five elemental kingdoms, but I don't think she'd care.

I survey the dead man at her feet.

It's as though all the blood in his body has dried up, leaving his face hollow and pale. His hair is the color of cobwebs and his fingernails are torn right to the beds.

I've never seen a body quite like it.

Or noticed this odd sensation in the pit of my stomach before.

Usually when someone dies in my territory, I feel the tingle of their souls like butterflies in my stomach. Then comes the ringing in my ears as they sing to me. As with everything in my life, it's always unchanged.

This time was different.

Instead of a tingle, a cold chill skittered up my spine, and in place of the ringing, there was a guttural scream beckoning me forward, louder even than the melody of Atia's magic.

For the first time in what feels like lifetimes, something new happened.

And despite there being a dead body involved, I get a thrill from it.

You'd think being a Herald would be exciting, caught between the mystical world and the human world, but it feels less like a sacred duty and more like a cage. I'm a prisoner in the mystical world, and in the human world I'm just a shadow.

I don't belong anywhere, and no matter how much I try to obey and enforce the rules, relay the Gods' curses and do their bidding, I feel like I must have been terrible in my past life to deserve being stuck this way.

So do something about it, Silas.

"Wh-what is going on? Who is that?"

For the first time I notice the human boy beside the Nefas, wide-eyed and pointing at me like he's seen a ghost.

"That's a Herald," the Nefas says.

"A *Herald*," the boy repeats. "They're real?"

"Unfortunately." She rolls her eyes.

I smirk.

The boy looks young, around the same age as I must've been when I first died, only I'm pretty sure I didn't have the same baffled look on my face.

I'm not sure what I expected when I got here, but it definitely wasn't to see him standing by my new monster's side. Nor to see the girl in question looking so conflicted.

I thought she would be pleased with the chaos she's caused, but there is a strange look in her, hidden behind the glare she shoots my way.

Her eyes are white from the kill, a hint of the creature that lies beneath her human facade. I can see the points of her teeth, sharpening as she lets the illusion slip, just a little.

She should look monstrous, but she doesn't.

She looks awful and beautiful.

She looks sad.

"This is not what it seems," she says.

I can't help but scoff.

"It's been a busy week for you."

She sighs before me, irritated. "I didn't kill that first man."

"Oh?" I say, raising a brow. "I suppose you didn't kill this one either?"

"This one was an accident."

"Bit late to tell him that you're sorry."

Not that it would matter.

"I didn't know humans could actually be scared to death," the Nefas says.

"I'm glad that this was a learning experience for you."

She glares and I can't help but smile.

It's said that her kind were the bane of the Gods before the war got them kicked out of Oksenya. I don't know the exact details, but I know the Nefas killed the God of Eternity and the High Gods banished them from Oksenya because of it. They're meant to be bloodthirsty creatures who delighted in torture.

Yet this girl won't even look at her kill, her eyes flitting to the ground by his feet and then back to me again.

She chews on the corner of her lip.

"She was just trying to protect me," the human boy says.

I turn and the Nefas steps quickly in front of him like a shield.

"Shut up, Tristan," she hisses.

I eye the two of them.

What a strange pair they make.

"Look, I don't know who you are or what's going on here," the boy—Tristan—says. "But whatever Atia did, she didn't mean it."

Atia.

So the monster does have a name.

I smile, tasting the word inside my mind, toying with saying it out loud.

"She's a good person," Tristan says.

"She's not a person at all."

And I must be the one to remind her of that.

"You have broken the most sacred of rules, the condition of a monster's peaceful presence in the mortal realm," I declare, ever the messenger. "For your sins, by the power of the High Gods and with their eternal blessing, I decree you doomed. I invoke their curse upon you."

The words themselves are chiseled by magic, a drop of the

Gods' powers coating every syllable. Once I speak them, that power erupts from me in a fragment of light.

It shoots for Atia, puncturing clear through her heart.

She stumbles backward, a hand to her chest where it struck.

Her face contorts and she bends over, heaving like she could spew it back out.

The human rushes to her side.

Does it hurt? The look of anguish on her face takes me aback in a way it never has with other monsters.

Would I have felt something similar to her, when I was cursed to become a Herald?

Who would have decreed my punishment?

"What's to come isn't to be taken lightly," I say. "The curse will soon cause you to wither."

Atia's teeth clench tightly together as she looks at me in loathing.

I wonder how it will work on her.

If the curse will start small, siphoning off a piece of her she might not even notice, before it starts slowly eating away at all that she is, causing the magic that lives inside her to turn against her.

"I warned you that your time would run out, Atia of the Nefas."

She frowns at the use of her name, a quick pinch of the brow to show her surprise that I'd dare speak it.

"I can't be cursed," she says. She lifts her chin up high.

But for all her bravado, I see the sorrow in her eyes, and the new fear creeping alongside it. Is this the first time she has felt such a thing, after a lifetime of bringing it forth in others?

"I can't be cursed," Atia repeats. I'm not sure which of us

she's trying to convince. "This was an accident. It wasn't . . . I didn't—"

She cuts herself off before she can reason an excuse.

I almost feel sorry for her, before I remind myself that she's a monster.

A killer, just like all the others.

I touch a hand to my blade, thinking back to the Keeper's words. How only killing a God could unmake a Herald, if we were ever able to do such a thing without perishing ourselves.

A killer to do my killing for me.

Someone to wield my blade in a way I could never.

"Come on, Tristan," Atia says. "We're leaving. It isn't safe with him here."

I arch a brow. "Which one of us is a monster?"

Atia sneers.

She grabs the human boy by the arm and then waves her hand in the air, pulling the threads of reality open at the seams. The gateway she creates ripples like a blanket of water over the streets, alight in the same shade of blue that threatens to spill from her skin. The world molds and reshapes against it.

Atia steps forward, ready to make her escape. But running from the body won't let her outrun the curse. She should know that. It is inside her now, and sooner or later it will overtake her. Then I'll be the one collecting her body and throwing it into the rivers with all the other once-monsters who couldn't control themselves.

There her soul will remain, drowning in eternity.

Unless . . .

"I'll see you soon," I promise.

And when I do, you'll realize there's only one way out of this, little monster. Only one bargain you can strike to undo your fate.

Atia casts one last look my way, alight in daring.

"You'll have to catch me first."

She jumps into her gateway, pulling the human through with her.

ATIA

Tristan collapses as soon as his feet hit the ground on the other side.

I've not taken him far, just to the edge of the Rosegarde forest, close to the small lake where Sapphir and I fed on our last victim.

I don't know why I chose to come here.

Because you're a killer now too, I remind myself.

"I can't believe it," Tristan says.

He sits in a heap on the forest floor. His clothes are stuck with leaves and charred slightly at the sleeves from my gateway. He looks disheveled, nothing of the scholar left in him.

"Sorry," I say. "I've never taken a human through before. But at least your head didn't explode."

"My head?" Tristan repeats, disbelieving. "That was a possibility?"

I shrug. "Apparently not."

Tristan sighs. "So if I'm a human," he says. "That makes you . . . ?"

He lets the question linger in the air. There's no judgment in it, only intrigue. I thought maybe he'd panic and try to run, but all Tristan does is stare at me.

I should have known the scholar of monsters wouldn't be scared of our world. He's curious, excited even.

He doesn't fear me, even though he should.

"What happened back there?" Tristan asks, when I don't respond to his first question.

I pace around the forest, trying to figure that out for myself.

I killed someone by bringing their fears to life. Every lesson my parents ever taught me and not once did they mention the possibility of that happening.

They warned me of so many dangers, but never the danger that simply being myself could wield.

I walk in circles around Tristan, my feet crunching against the dry brown leaves. The blue night magpies coo around me and I can hear the scurry of insects between the bramble and forest dirt, trying to escape my quickening footsteps.

The night watches me, waiting for what I'll do next.

I wish I knew.

"This is bad, isn't it?" Tristan says. "Really bad."

I stop my pacing and turn, watching as he pulls himself up from the ground to face me.

"I thought you'd be glad," I say. And then, half-hearted at best, "You always said you wanted to meet a monster."

"That man was..." Tristan trails off and shakes his head. "What are you, Atia? What kind of monster? I always thought they stayed hidden in their own societies, far away from us, and only ventured into our towns to hunt. Aren't you afraid of being caught? Can all monsters look so human?"

"Which question should I answer first?"

Tristan bites his lip, a sign I've come to recognize as nervousness.

"What are you?" he asks.

I can tell by the tentative way he says it, the hesitation and slight pauses between the words, that he's trying hard not to offend me.

"They call us the Nefas," I tell him. "We're—"

"Monsters of illusion," Tristan interrupts. Of course he'd know.

I bet he's found the rarest of volumes within the libraries he habituates. "You feed off fear, as a kind of sustenance. And you're very, very rare. Extinct, even."

"You read too much," I say.

"You were created by the Gods," he continues. "But then sent to the human realm as a punishment for something."

"Not something I did."

"But what did *you* do?" Tristan asks. "To that man? Did you feed on his fear?"

I run a hand through my hair, brushing it from my face.

I did more than just feed on that man's fear. I broke the rules.

This is what comes from getting involved with humans. I've spent years under the radar of the Gods, keeping away from the humans and their messy lives. I heeded the warning of the ashen man who killed my parents. My entire existence has been wrapped around remembering to never break the rules like my parents had, so I wouldn't suffer the same fate they did.

A lifetime of being careful, lost to one single night.

"Are you okay?" Tristan asks.

"Just be quiet," I snap. "I need to think."

He bites his lip, though I know he's desperate to ask so many questions about this world I was born to and that he has longed to discover.

I place a hand to my temple, feeling a new headache settling in. I'm dizzy, my mind swirling with all the ways the Gods' curse could punish me now the Herald has decreed it.

That damn tie pin–wielding meddler.

Sapphir's curse has been to age and lose the youth and beauty her kind rely on to lull their victims, but when my parents broke the rules, they were simply cut down where they stood.

"Atia, you don't look so well," Tristan says, concern coating his soft voice. "You need to eat something."

I just did, I think.

But he's right. I don't feel well. When I look down at my hands, I see the veins beneath my skin are plump and blue, rising to the surface.

The thrum of magic in me feels lighter somehow. Normally I sense the weight of it embedded into me, like a strong core keeping me tethered to this world. Now, it's teetering just below the surface and threatening at any moment to fade away.

Wash into the air with the next strong breeze.

My head spins.

Is this just the beginning?

When the Gods take their punishment out of me, carving up the parts of me that they deem the most just, will it hurt?

I never thought to ask Sapphir what it's like when she's forced to feed not just for pleasure or basic survival, but to make herself whole again. A rare loophole in the Gods' curse that makes vampires so unique.

"Atia," Tristan says.

He places a hand on my shoulder and the weight of it nearly pushes me to the ground.

I look down into the mud-ridden puddle at my feet and see the echo of my true face blur and then sink back. I try to push it outward, shaking my curled horns from my hair and letting my skin vein back to blue. It is only a brief glimpse of myself that flickers in and out of existence.

My wings recoil and shrivel at my back, unable to spring outward.

I should have asked, I think to myself. *How does it feel for the pieces of yourself to be undone by someone else?*

9

ATIA

I can't feed.

A man sits opposite me, his palm upward to the sky as I cradle it in my own, pretending to search the lines of his hand for a clue as to what kind of sad little future he might have.

A single magpie lurches on the open window, like a taunt for my sorrow.

"I've been feeling strange lately," the man says.

I'm barely listening, focusing instead on the feel of his skin under my fingertips. I try to fold myself into him, searching aimlessly for any fears that might be cascading over the surface of his mind.

There is only the faintest whimper, too quiet to make out amid the tavern noise.

Stakes?

No, not stakes.

I strain to hear the call of his fears.

"I don't wish to say I'm unfulfilled," he continues, unaware. "But lately I get the sense that there's something more I could be doing than being the village mason. I'm on the cusp of something great, I know it, but I just don't know what it is."

"Yes," I say, placing my hand on his wrist instead.

His pulse thrums under my touch.

Whispers as quiet as butterfly wings fill my mind, in place of the legion of fears that would normally filter into me.

Snakes?

"Are you listening to me?" he asks.

"No," I say, and get up promptly from my seat in the corner of the Covet.

Ten clients today, visiting Rosegarde's new and prolific seer, and I haven't been able to feed on a single one of them.

I've barely extracted a drop of fear to wet my lips or an ounce of terror to quiet the rumble in my stomach. The curse is stealing away the pieces of me that are the most bright.

The most monstrous.

"You're supposed to give me a reading," the man says.

He stands, more abruptly than I did, and the snow still left on his boots falls begrudgingly to the floor.

He grabs me by the arm. His bony human fingers dig into the skin below my shoulder and I'm surprised to find that it actually *hurts*.

Pain, from some pathetic mortal.

My nostrils flare in disgust.

I have never been threatened or made to feel like anything less than a being worthy of legend. Three years since my parents were killed spent traveling the five elemental kingdoms, dipping in and out of their realities, and not a single human has dared to confront me.

It's not that I've needed to threaten them or earn a reputation for violence in every new territory I explore. None of it has been necessary—because the humans know. Not what I am, but they know *something*. Call it a sense or an instinct, but one look in my eyes is all it has ever taken.

Now here this man stands, his fingers clenching into me as if I am something for him to pull and command.

"I want my reading," he says, tightening his hand around my arm in threat.

My skin pinches beneath his grip.

"The universe wants you to fully embrace new endeavors and be open to change in your life," I say to him, jaw tight. "However, an unforeseen misfortune will prevent you from ever being able to do so."

The man's eyes grow wide and his grip on me loosens, just a little. "What misfortune?"

"Me killing you if you don't let go of my arm."

The man freezes, shocked by the poison in my words. The truth I know he can sense in them.

I will tear him apart before I ever let him think he holds power over me.

Nobody holds power over me. Not him and not the wretched Gods either.

I squeeze my hands to fists and ready to push my veined wings out into view. Discretion be damned. When this man sees the true whites of my eyes and kneels before me, then he'll understand what a monster really is.

Only, however hard my fists squeeze by my sides and my true form tries to push itself free, I am stagnant.

I don't transform.

I flicker.

A blink of what I am that only makes the man frown as if his eyes are playing tricks.

The illusion of my face stays the same.

It's then I realize a horrible truth. The Gods aren't just taking my abilities from me. They're taking my form.

My horns.

My *wings*.

"Unbelievable." The man sputters before me. I'd forgotten he was still here. "Did you just threaten me?"

"I'm sure it was all just a misunderstanding."

I don't meet Tristan's eyes as he comes to my side.

"Allow me to refill your glass at no charge, mason. And I shall get you another order of fire-roasted pigeon breast," Tristan says, placating the brute.

The man doesn't argue, the promise of free ale far outweighing the need to scold some silly little seer.

I don't wait to hear the resolution of the conversation. I turn and run from the tavern and into the new snow outside, fleeing the scene in shame.

The bell clangs, announcing my escape to everyone before the door slams behind me.

"Atia, wait!"

Tristan follows me out.

He has been shadowing me for the past three days, ever since the incident. He hasn't dared to ask questions, waiting instead for me to relinquish answers.

I don't know if he's afraid of scaring me away, or if he just enjoys seeing a monster in the flesh after years of study, but he has stayed close. Sitting at the table beside me while I try to take readings, appearing first thing in the morning when I descend from the room I rent above the Covet.

The human has become a shadow.

I stumble away from him in such a hurry that I slip on a patch of ice and fall with a hard thump into the snow.

When I look down, my knee is bleeding.

I wait a few seconds.

It does not heal.

I pull myself back to my feet, cold and damp, a snarl teetering on my lips.

"Are you okay?" Tristan asks.

I whirl around on him, outraged, and point to the blood on my knee. "Can you not see this?"

"It's just a scrape, Atia."

"It isn't healing," I seethe. "I'm supposed to be immortal, Tristan. I am supposed to *heal*."

A crease forms in Tristan's brow. "Atia, I don't know what's happening, but I'd very much like to help. Especially since you helping me is what got you into this mess."

"Go away," I snap.

"Go where?" he asks. "Back to a life of mundanity and books where everything is theory and all the miracles of the world are dismissed as evil?"

"I don't care where you go," I tell him. "Just *go*."

I can't stand to be around anyone, knowing what is happening to me.

The curse is chipping away at all the pieces of me, and when it's done, what will be left? I can barely sense people's fears and I don't seem to be able to transform without possibly bursting a vein.

I'm stuck in a watercolor version of myself.

I wave my hand in front of me to create a gateway to escape Tristan's pestering. The air wavers, as if undecided on whether or not it wishes to pull apart.

Don't you dare disobey me, I growl inside my mind.

Reluctantly, the gateway appears and I'm given a brief glimpse of waterfall skies before, like an elastic, the gateway snaps shut again.

Son of a—

The Gods wish for me to be trapped.

I grit my teeth together and focus again, pulling at the pieces of the world as if with my bare hands. I am shaking with the force of it, my nails digging into my palms.

It's exhausting, but it works.

The gateway opens and this time it stays open.

I want to turn my nose to the sky and smirk at the Gods. *Hah!* Or perhaps scream at them to stop with their games and *just try to kill me already, you cowards!*

The mere thought seems to be enough.

From the nearby brush that edges the canals where I've so often lain in wait for a victim, a creature crawls out.

Her hair is a mane and her naked body is coated in a layer of thick fur. Though she's standing as a human would, her nails and teeth are like daggers as she bares them at me.

A lykai.

It's the first time I've seen one outside the pictures in Tristan's books, or heard of one outside the stories my father would tell of the wolf-like creatures who fed on human hearts. They're not the kind of monster that would ever be welcomed into Oksenya.

As my focus turns to her, my gateway pulls violently closed.

Damn it.

"What do you want?" I ask, bypassing over pleasantries.

"Your head," she says.

Her voice is that of a howl.

I swallow as the weight of her words sink into me just as her fangs might.

Monsters exist in a quiet peace, and unless somebody invades another's territory, we usually pass each other by without much fuss. Of course some like to group for hunting purposes, like the gorgons and the banshees, and others have their feuds, passed down through bloodlines too ancient for me to care about.

But the Nefas have never been a part of any quarrel that I know of.

"My head," I repeat.

"There's a bounty on it," the lykai continues. "The Gods have promised a place in Oksenya to whatever creature can deliver your head."

"That's a lie."

"I'll find out when I present it to them," the lykai says.

I glare.

"A-Atia?" Tristan stammers beside me. "Should we run?"

"Oh, yes please," the lykai says, thrilled by the thought of a hunt.

"No," I say quickly. "We can't outrun her."

She may look mostly human now, but Tristan should have read enough books to know of how a lykai's legs can snap backward, propelling them to all fours so they can gather speed faster than any mortal animal.

At full power, I could create a whirl of illusions to confuse such a creature, giving us time to retreat into the shadows. Or create a gateway to easily slip into, leaving the lykai hungry and disappointed.

But I'm already exhausted from trying the first few times. My arms ache as if I've carried a heavy load.

"Why would the Gods want me dead instead of cursed?" I ask.

Why wouldn't they? I think to myself. *They killed your parents when they broke the rules. Perhaps the Nefas are too dangerous to let wither.*

The ashen man warned me of what would come from displeasing the High Gods. The Herald did too.

He said I couldn't escape their wrath and he was right.

"I didn't ask for details," the lykai says. "In these dangerous times, I would rather do the Gods' bidding than be hunted on the streets."

Her teeth scrape against her lips as she lowers her body down to the ground in a crouch, preparing to pounce.

"I didn't murder anyone," I say out loud, so the Gods can hear. "It was an accident!"

"Shame about that," the lykai says. "You should have at least enjoyed the kill, if you're going to die for it."

I shake my head, defiant. "I'm warning you, if you lay a hand on me, then you'll suffer."

The lykai does not hesitate.

She pounces, slashing her claws through the air as she goes. Though I jump out of the way, they scratch across my shoulder and I'm thrown to the ground.

Then she's on top of me, howling, the saliva catching beneath her fangs.

I hope Tristan has run.

I hope he gets a good head start before this creature turns her attention to him.

"Goodbye, Nefas," she says, teeth bared.

She curls opens her jaw, wide enough for me to hear the bones pop as the cavern of her mouth stretches down her neck.

I dig my nails into the ground, staring her straight in the eye.

And then I smash my head into hers.

Her teeth nick my brow as she cries out in pain. I try to wiggle out from under her, but it's no use.

"Get *off* me!" I yell.

Out of the corner of my eye, the shadows shift.

They rise from the cobbles and swiftly dart out to wrap around the lykai's body.

The creature stills, her mouth just inches from me, when suddenly she is wrenched back.

The shadows surround her, closing in. They squeeze against her ribs, and the lykai howls out in pain as her bones threaten to break.

The shadows still at her cries and then throw her to the ground.

The lykai whimpers and tries to run, but after just a few paces she collapses, her breaths labored. Alive, but wounded.

It'll take her a while to recover.

I clamber to my feet, wondering if I should just finish the job while she's injured. It would serve her right for coming after me when I was not at full strength.

As I consider it, the shadows that pulled her from me begin to curve and bend, taking on a familiar form.

"You did warn her not to lay a hand on you," he says.

I look up at the face of the Herald, suit undisturbed as he stands over the weeping body of my attacker.

10

SILAS

This is the part where you say thank you."

Atia looks offended at the thought.

I guess she's not used to being saved. I enjoy knowing that I'm probably the only thing in existence to ever get that honor.

"Thank you," the human boy—Tristan, I remember—says.

He is still blanched as he stares at the unconscious lykai by my feet.

"Be quiet, Tristan," Atia scolds her human friend. "The Herald did nothing to be thanked for."

I raise an eyebrow. "Except save your life."

"Not without a motive," she says, eyeing me suspiciously.

I smile at that. The Nefas is smart. Either that, or she's so paranoid that she can't believe anyone would try to help her without wanting something first.

Not that she's wrong in this case.

"Atia doesn't like people saving her," Tristan says.

"I can see that."

"I don't *need* saving. Now let me ask you, Herald, what is it you want?" Atia tightens her hand at her side, angling her body slightly.

A defensive stance, if ever there was one.

I wonder how she plans to attack me with her powers fading.

Perhaps a week ago or even a day ago she could have done me

some serious harm, piercing my immortality however briefly to cause injury.

But not anymore.

Now she's dwindling.

Desperate.

"How would you like the chance to go to Oksenya?" I ask.

I know it's the right way to lead when Atia blinks, rapidly, like I've just shined a star directly in her face.

"What did you say?" she asks.

I hold back my smile.

The Last of the Nefas is about to fall to the Gods and that means she'll be willing to make alliances she wasn't before.

The enemy of my enemy.

If Atia wants to escape their wrath, then I have the means to help her. The secret to undoing her curse. And in doing so, I have the means to escape my own.

Someone capable of killing to do my killing for me.

My loophole to escape this servitude.

"Wait, Oksenya is real?" Tristan asks, eyes wide and eager. "The blessed realm?"

"It's real," Atia confirms, eyeing me all the while, her suspicion thickening the air. "It's a place for Gods and monsters, or the most heroic of humans, ruled by the Three High Gods: Imera, God of the Day. Skotadi, God of the Dark. And Isorropía, God of the Balance."

"Yes, I know all about it!" Tristan exclaims. "It's protected by five rivers and their Gods, right? Thentos guards the River of Death and is the protector of lost souls and creator of Heralds. Or there's Aion, guardian for the River of Eternity, where it's said all the Gods' monsters once drank from to become immortal."

I tilt my head to the side. "Aion isn't guarding anything anymore. He's dead. But you sure do know a lot about our world."

"He reads," Atia says dismissively. "And anyway, as I'm sure you know, *Herald*, after the God of Eternity was killed, my kind were kicked out. There's no way they'd let me back in. Especially now."

I can't help but find the way she glares at me amusing. It's so *human*. I wonder if that's because of the curse slowly taking her abilities, or the fact that she was born and raised in the mortal realm.

"I didn't say anything about them letting you," I clarify. "I wasn't under the impression you ever asked for anything. You take, do you not?"

"And what is it I'm supposed to be taking?" Atia asks. "A password? A hidden key to bypass their locks?"

"A life," I say, enjoying the way it makes her pause. "Or three lives, to be exact."

Atia stares.

It wouldn't be the first life she's taken, but she hesitates nonetheless, assessing the situation. Assessing me.

Heralds don't usually make a habit of helping monsters break the rules, especially when those monsters have been damned by the Gods. But damnation is what Atia and I have in common.

She has been stripped of her monstrousness and I have been stripped of my humanity. I know that we'd both like back all the things the Gods have taken from us.

This is our chance.

A truce, so we can both get what we want.

"Which three lives am I to take?" Atia asks. "I remember it didn't work out so well the first time I killed."

"This is different."

"How?"

"Because I'm going to help you."

Atia wrinkles her nose. "What makes you think I need your help to kill anyone?"

"I'm a Herald of the Gods and you barely have any power left," I say. "I suspect the answer should be obvious. Three monsters will need to be destroyed for this to work. A vampire, a banshee, and a God. You must absorb their power through blood to earn back yours. Then you must drink water from the River of Eternity and your curse shall be broken."

Atia's eyebrows rise, and slowly, she pushes her hands into her pockets, the indignation clear on her face.

"You want me to kill a God."

"To break your curse."

"And you talk about drinking from the River of Eternity like it's easy," Atia says. "It's one of the entrances to Oksenya. And in case you didn't know, Oksenya is pretty hard to get into without an invitation from the Gods."

"Except those Gods once gifted a phial containing water from the River of Eternity to the humans," I tell her. "In the time before time, as a gift for their worship. All we need to do is find it. Then you have everything you need."

"Assuming nobody has drunk it already," Atia says, shaking her head like the mere thought is impossible. "Besides, what's in it for you? I kill three creatures and gain my powers back, but what do you get?"

I consider lying at first, but what's the point?

There have been plenty of lies up until now; it wouldn't hurt to sprinkle a little truth to balance it out.

"My humanity," I say. "If I help you defeat the first two

monsters, using my powers where you have none, then when we find the Gods, you will help me kill one so I can undo *my* curse. I wish to find my humanity and be freed from being a Herald."

Surely Lahi, God of Forgetting and guardian for the River of Oblivion, should do. She allows those who pass on to the After to shed their past lives and is no doubt responsible for stealing my memories. Her powers should be able to grant me the one thing I long for: the chance for my life back.

"You're perfectly capable of killing without me," Atia says.

"Actually, I'm not."

I hadn't exactly planned on revealing that, but I know the Nefas won't trust me without an explanation.

"Heralds can't cause death; we simply manage it. Our powers aren't capable of taking life."

I'll spare her the details of what would happen if I were to try.

"Wow." Atia blinks. "So do you want to become human because Heralds are so lame? How meek and lonely your life must be to desire such things."

I glower, but this only amuses her further.

"You'd know all about being lonely, wouldn't you?" I say sharply. "Atia of the Nefas, last of your kind."

She twitches, as though I've hit the same nerve in her that she hit in me.

"If we're to do this, it must be now," I say to her. "There's a bounty on you. Others will be coming soon. Do we have a deal or not?"

"Team up to kill Gods?" she says.

She sighs as she looks down at my outstretched hand. Then without another word, she turns on her heel, stopping only briefly to stare at the lykai.

Atia shakes her head at its still-simpering form.

"Serves you right," she says to the creature, before stepping over it and continuing on her path. "Damn traitor."

Tristan scurries after her and I fall quiet, barely blinking as I watch her figure slowly retreat into the night.

When that girl disappears, so does my hope of ending my own curse.

"Are you coming?" Atia calls back to me.

She glances over her shoulder, eyebrow raised as if she expected me to be following her already.

"We have Gods to kill, don't we?" she says.

I lock my eyes with hers, the glow of them like a torch in this darkness.

I nod, letting a hint of hope unfurl into my stomach.

And then I follow.

11

ATIA

I can't have taken more than ten steps forward before Tristan huffs beside me, as if I've just made him run up a dozen flights of stairs.

"Slow down, would you?" he says, practically jogging to keep pace.

"Go home, Tristan," I tell him. "This is between monsters and Gods. It doesn't concern you."

He's already been nearly murdered twice in these recent days. I've done a lot of bad things in my life, but the worst would be allowing him to become even more wrapped up in all of this than he is already.

"But, Atia—"

"Tristan," I say, firmly as I can. "I have a bounty on my head. The Gods want me dead and they're sending any creature they can to do the job. A minion of theirs has even come to warn me"—I shoot a pointed look toward the Herald, who stops adjusting his tie to briefly frown at the use of the word *minion*—"so I hardly think this is the time for you to be following me."

Tristan pouts, chewing on the corner of his lip as he considers his imminent doom. "Where else would I go?"

"Home."

Tristan wrinkles his nose. "Ugh, boring," he says. "Let's go kill monsters instead."

I throw my hands up into the air with a huff, but truthfully there's a part of me that does want to smile.

Tristan, the scholar, wanting to go monster hunting is quite the picture.

"You'll need my help anyway," Tristan says. "You're meant to hunt a banshee, aren't you? You know how closely I've been studying them. I know their hunting patterns and where they tend to dwell. I know more about monsters than anyone else in this kingdom, Atia. Perhaps even you."

He isn't wrong.

While I've spent my time keeping to myself, Tristan has spent his learning all he could about every monster the world knows of. I'd bet he's one of the few people in the five elemental kingdoms who has even heard of a Nefas. But I have spent so long alone, become accustomed to relying on myself, that it feels odd for someone to offer me a helping hand.

Dangerous, even.

"It's not a good idea," I say.

Tristan folds his arms across his Academic robes.

"Atia," he presses, not letting it drop. "You're not the only one being hunted. That man won't be the last who comes looking for me. It's safer if I leave the Earth Kingdom for a while anyway."

I narrow my eyes to study the discomfort in his.

Why is the queen of the Alchemy Kingdom so set on collecting a debt from the son of a tavern owner in a kingdom that isn't even hers?

"You're going to get yourself killed," I warn him.

The Herald clears his throat, stepping alongside us.

"Doubtful," he says. "At least not by any monsters."

I get hit by his scent when he comes close, like spring blossoms and cut grass. He smells of comfort and warm days when the sun begins to first peer from the depths of winter.

A key part of his design. A trick to help comfort lost souls as they cross into the After.

He is *meant* to make me feel at ease.

I shift away from him.

"The monsters hunting you would hardly waste their time with a human and risk being cursed themselves," he explains. "If he's going to die, it's unlikely to be our fault. No need to be dramatic."

I blink.

In all my years of torturing humans with their greatest fears, parading the streets with stark white hair and pretending to be a host of fanciful things—from seers to rare shell collectors—I don't think I've ever been called dramatic.

Even murdering someone didn't earn me that title.

"I don't think you can talk to anyone about drama," I say to the Herald.

I stride ahead.

To the Herald's credit, while Tristan lags behind, taking three steps for every one of mine, the Herald glides seamlessly at my side, barely a noise when he moves.

If I couldn't look down and see his polished shoes pressing against the cobbles, I would almost think he was floating a hair above the ground.

"If anyone is dramatic, it's you," I say. "Arriving in a beam of winged shadows and summoning magic boats."

"A boat is needed to cross water," the Herald says simply.

The moon cascades down on his pale cheeks, sharpening them to a high point. His hair, though once slicked back, now falls messily into his face as it did that night we first met.

"You're wearing glasses right now," I say, staring pointedly at the thin circular frames perched on the edge of his nose. "A Herald has no need for such things."

"They match my suit," he says.

"You wear *suits*."

He looks indignant. "You wear humanity."

"Only some of the time," I say with a shrug, liking the offended tone he's trying so hard to mask. "It's my least favorite form and I'd cast it aside if I could. I prefer the wolf."

"As bloodthirsty as you," he says with an edge.

I smirk. I'm not sure why he thinks of that as an insult.

I take it as the highest compliment.

"Calm yourself, Herald. I didn't mean to insult your fashion sense."

He crosses his arms over his chest, stepping in front of me so I come to an abrupt stop before my nose collides into the apple of his throat.

"I have a name, you know."

I look up at him, surprised.

I thought Heralds didn't remember their pasts. Another one of the Gods' ever-so-almighty ideas. What better way to create a servant than to erase all they were before?

"I chose my own name," he says, as though he knows just what I was thinking. "A new one. Silas."

I can't conceal the wrinkle of my nose in time. "You chose that yourself?"

"It reminds me I'm more than what they made me to be, and to never accept a fate I've been given by someone else," *Silas* says.

My throat goes dry.

It seems my whole life I've been trying and failing to do just that.

I live by the rules my parents set, and no matter how many times I try to convince myself I'm carving out my own fate by not sticking to shadow and bringing my illusions to life, the truth is that I'm always thinking about their warnings and what they would've wanted for me.

I'm always thinking about how I may have led the Gods straight to their door that night.

About the man covered in their blood, who told me to run as far away as I could.

Maybe that's why I've never stayed in one kingdom for too long. What if I did and he found me again?

What if he's the one the High Gods send this time? To finish the job like he should've done all those years ago.

My nails dig into my palms.

"I'm not sure I like Silas," I say, painting a mocking smile onto my face. "How about I just call you the Herald of Doom? It'll strike more fear in the hearts of our new enemies."

Silas narrows his eyes. "Weren't the Nefas created to be amusing?"

"I'm very amused by myself," I say, sidestepping him to continue on my path.

The night grows darker as we walk and I find myself quickening my pace, even with a Herald by my side as an odd new protector. It's strange, but with every crackle of birds in the snow-coated bushes, or whistle of the wind, I get more on edge.

I've never had to walk the streets in fear. No matter the hour of day or night, or how secluded a place was, it hadn't crossed my mind to be scared of what might hide in the dark because I was always that thing.

How privileged I was to never have to worry about my own mortality, or let it pass my mind that just walking was something to be afraid of.

Is this what it feels like to be a human?

If so, I'm more desperate than ever to regain my immortality.

"Do you have a direction?" Silas asks with a sigh as we turn onto a new street at the very edge of Rosegarde's border.

The promise of the next village lingers.

The snow has coated most of the path, a thin sheet of ice trying to crack over the canals. If we walk past this street and over the edge of the next hill, we'll have officially left Rosegarde.

"We've been walking for a while," Silas says. "Forgive me, but I thought you wanted to kill Gods and their monsters? We have far to travel if we're going to do that and walking aimlessly through the night won't help."

"I'm not aimless," I tell him, at the same time Tristan asks: "How far exactly?"

"Across kingdoms," Silas answers him. "Different monsters prefer different territories, as you must know, so we should be vigilant in our search."

I sigh at the thought.

With it being so hard for me to conjure gateways, I don't wish to waste the little magic I have left in me on that, so I'm going to have to rely on Silas to get us across the five elemental kingdoms. Assuming he can transport others in his shadowed wings. If not, it would mean venturing through the territories via ferry, or on horseback, neither of which are appealing and take far too long.

Just a few days ago I could be anywhere I wanted in the blink of an eye. Humans do everything far too slowly, which is strange given how fleeting their lives are.

"Where would we go first?" Tristan asks, far more excited than I am at the thought of all this travel.

He sees it as adventure, whereas I see it as weeks, possibly months, lost in a life that has suddenly become all too short.

"I've always wanted to go to the Water Kingdom," Tristan says. "Though I don't think banshees tend to like it there. We'd probably be better off searching King Balthier's Fire Kingdom for those."

Each of the human kingdoms is ruled by one of the five Cousins, said to be descended from the elements. The story goes that when the Gods created the realm it was so heavy with wonder that it cracked. The miracles of the world split into five and from them each of the elements were birthed as holy people to rule over their share of the land.

Water, Fire, Air, Earth, and Alchemy.

Alchemy being one I'd like to avoid traveling to, lest we wind up in a glass cabinet while people debate how real we are.

"Before we roam the world looking blindly for things to kill, we could also just look right here in Rosegarde."

I point to the small house on the far end of the street we've turned into.

It's unassuming in all the ways a house would be if it didn't want to be found. Like the others, it's striped with black wood, its door rickety and splintered, but there is something about it not like the others.

Something darker and hidden.

The paintwork is a shade more aged, the view inside the

windows obscured by thick black curtains, and the heavy iron knocker that once stood proudly is now ripped out, leaving the nails clawing jaggedly from the door.

Monsters come and go in Rosegarde, and that house, unbeknownst to most, is where they tend to gather when they stay.

"Sapphir lives there for now," I tell the Herald, when he raises his eyebrows in question. "She's a friend of mine. I believe you've cleaned up one or two of her messes."

"Messes?" Tristan asks.

"Bodies," Silas clarifies. He looks at me strangely. "Are you suggesting we kill your friend?"

"Tempting, but no." I'm surprised by the brutality of the suggestion. "Sapphir is a vampire, which means she'd have a pretty good idea where we could find other vampires to kill. Knowing Sapphir, she probably has a few she'd like to see dead."

Silas's face dawns in understanding. "She makes a lot of enemies."

"Exactly."

"Something the two of you have in common."

I roll my eyes, brushing off the slight.

His insults hold no weight with me.

"She can help us," I say, though I suspect with Sapphir there will be a price for that. Something given for something gained.

Nothing in this world is ever free, even friendship. But that doesn't deter me. Someone has stolen the magic from inside me and I want it back.

No matter the price, I'll be willing to pay.

12

ATIA

Sapphir answers the door wrapped in a silk nightdress, her black hair like ribbons down her arms. She smiles when she sees me, fangs sharp and pinching the corners of her lips.

"Atia, darling," she says in a drawl.

I can smell the blood on her breath. There are lines of it in the cracks of her mouth and her skin has the glow of freshly stolen youth.

She's fed recently.

Lucky her.

"Can we come in?" I ask.

You must be invited into a vampire's lair to enter. The lore around them is spotty and confused at best, but the same magic that protects their youth also seems to protect their homes, forbidding strangers.

Consequently, a vampire cannot enter someone else's home without the same respect. It's old magic, steeped in the courtesy of ancient killers.

That magic is the very reason I'll need Sapphir's help if I'm to track and kill a vampire to relieve myself of this curse.

Even if I could find a vampire's lair, I'd have no way to enter without an invitation. Sapphir, on the other hand, could walk right in.

"You'll have to introduce me to your friends first," Sapphir says.

Her eyes flicker over Tristan, but it's Silas where her attention lingers.

Her stare presses into him, roaming over his clean black suit and the broad curve of his shoulders. I see her smirk when his jaw tenses, enjoying his discomfort at being watched.

Heralds are used to being invisible, undetected.

"This is Silas," I introduce.

Her mouth curves at the mention of his name. Names have power, after all. I wonder if I should have kept his for myself.

"He's a Herald," I say.

"A Herald, here at my doorstep." Sapphir leans against the doorway, toying with the idea of inviting him inside. "How rare. Interesting new friend you have, Atia."

"He's not my friend," I say. "He's my . . ."

The more I search for the word, the more I struggle to come up with one to describe this new alliance between us.

"Her partner," Silas finishes for me.

I scoff. "Hardly."

Tristan holds out his hand to Sapphir. "I'm Tristan. A pleasure to meet you, my lady."

Sapphir raises an eyebrow. "Human?" she asks.

"Human," I confirm.

Finally, her attention draws from Silas. "Human," she repeats with new intrigue. "How delightful. Are we having a feast tonight, Atia? Is the Herald here early to collect the corpse?"

"He's not for eating," I say.

"For *eating*?" Tristan asks, eyes widening.

I hook a hand to my hip. "Can we come in or not? Really, Sapphir, you're losing your manners in your old age."

Sapphir steps to the side, arms widening to welcome us past

the entry. "I'm only ninety-three, Atia, and I remember my manners perfectly." Her voice is husky with night and death. "Come on in."

Stepping into Sapphir's home is like stepping into a shadow. Not the kind you see on the street that can disappear in a flicker of night, but the kind that lingers. The deep, unyielding shadows that remain well into day, when the sun is at its highest. The kind that dwell in the crevices of the world, that you've never looked directly at. The ones you see move out of the corner of your eye.

Not even moonlight glimpses through the thick black curtains that cascade across every window, the only glow coming from the fire of sparsely lit torches that decorate the walls.

Even the mirrors are covered, I suspect for the days when Sapphir's curse grows stronger and her true age dimples across her features between feedings.

There is the smell of dust in the air and, unmistakably, blood. There are handprints of it on the stair railings, smudges across the walls, and when my shoes squelch against the hardwood floors, I know there are puddles of it too.

This is a halfway house for monsters.

A temporary home for Sapphir while she stays in Rosegarde, but a permanent home to other creatures like her.

"There's murder on you, Atia," Sapphir says, as she leads us into the drawing room. "I don't remember smelling that before."

I take a seat on the plush velvet sofa while Sapphir stokes the large fireplace with an iron poker. Tristan sits beside me, his breath growing heavy with the realization of where we are.

He wanted monsters, but I'm sure he never imagined being prey to so many in one night.

Silas does not move to sit.

He runs his hand along the top of a painting, wiping the dust from its frame, and then glances over to Sapphir. His hands slip into his pockets in an air of casualness, but I see the way his eyes flicker whenever she moves too quickly.

He stares at her like there is a bitter taste in his mouth.

Sapphir has killed a hundred times over and not a one of those was an accident, unlike what happened to me the other night. Sapphir has never lost control. She kills with perfect precision, and because of that she has been cursed so many times that she can't even bear to look in a mirror for fear of what she'll see.

"I've been cursed," I tell her.

"Yes," Sapphir says. "I can smell that too. Did you come here for protection? Because it seems you already have that in spades."

She bestows a quick glance toward Silas.

"Atia doesn't need protection," he says, before I can argue the point.

"Oh?" Sapphir asks. "Then what does she need?"

"To kill a vampire," he says, not missing a beat.

I think he enjoys the way Sapphir's bravado slips for a moment, her eyes darkening with the possibility of a threat.

"We thought you could lead us to one," I say quickly, trying to quash any misunderstandings.

The last thing I need right now is another enemy, for the sake of Silas's amusement.

We're not true friends, I know that, despite what I may some-times allow myself to think when I grow lonely, but Sapphir has at the very least been my ally for years.

"Why a vampire?" she asks.

"It's a long story," I say. "But take my word that killing one will help me. And I need to do it quickly. I was attacked by a lykai tonight and I suspect the Gods will be sending more monsters my way. There's a bounty on my head."

Sapphir ponders this carefully, tightening her robe around her slim waist. She looks young tonight, but there are nearly one hundred years of wisdom and cunning behind her dark eyes.

"I know where there's a nest," she finally says.

Silas pushes away from the wall and I notice that he has removed his glasses. That he discarded them, probably, before we entered Sapphir's house, slipping away any signs of decorative humanity before she could notice.

I hadn't realized how severe he looks without them. The high rounds of his cheekbones seem sharper, more harrowing, and the grays of his eyes turn almost star-bright.

I'd only been teasing before, but the glasses really did make him look human. Approachable. Now he looks far more ethereal.

Somewhat intangible.

"Where is the nest?" he asks Sapphir.

Her smile slips across her face as easily as day slips to night when you forget to look.

"Isn't it obvious?" she says. Her fangs scrape against her bottom lip, and suddenly my skin grows cold. "You're in one."

13

SILAS

The vampires seep into the room like water on a wet day, slipping from every crack and crevice.

We're surrounded by six of them. Seven, including Atia's murderous friend.

Before anything, I find myself looking to Atia and taking in the hint of betrayal on her face.

She expected loyalty from this visit and now that she's been slighted, the mask of niceties she was trying so hard to keep has slipped.

A new darkness dawns on her face.

"A whole nest just for me," Atia says. "How touching."

"You shouldn't have come," Sapphir tells her.

Atia nods. "Even after all this time, I should have known you couldn't be trusted."

"I did try to kill you when we first met," Sapphir reminds her.

"Fond memories," Atia spits back.

Sapphir only smirks. "You've spoiled the hunt by just showing up here. Though I admit I'm a little happier for it," she says. "I really could not summon the energy to track you down myself with all your gateway hopping. An annoying habit, by the way. It's far better that you walk right into my house."

The vampires have circled around us now, blocking off every

curtained window and door. They form a barrier between us and any chance of escape, their hunger hissing through their teeth.

I could still slip away.

There isn't a barricade that could keep me in.

These monsters are ruled by this realm's laws, but I'm ruled only by the Gods. And that means I can be anywhere, at any time. If they think they can trap me, then they're idiots.

Very ancient idiots.

"You don't have to do this," Atia says.

Sapphir sighs, bored of small talk. "I know I don't *have* to."

"Then why?"

"You said it yourself." There is no regret in her voice. "There's a bounty on your head and it's one I'd like to collect. Besides, there are whispers on the horizon of something new. Something hunting creatures like us, beyond the Gods. And so I want to be on the good side of the deities for now."

Missing monsters.

The Heralds back in the sorting zone had been discussing that very thing. I can't think what in the world would be hunting monsters aside from the Gods and a few humans with pitchforks, but the vampire seems rattled.

"You truly are stupid if you think that the Gods are going to let you into Oksenya because you kill me," Atia says. "Age does not breed intelligence, I see."

"I don't care about traveling to your ridiculous blessed realm," Sapphir says. "That's always been the problem with the Nefas. So concerned with that place, you failed to ever move on from it. From the war and all that happened. You are so afraid to embrace your true selves that it left you *weak*."

"I am *not* weak," Atia snaps.

"But you've never even been to Oksenya and yet thoughts of it consume you." Sapphir's tone is mocking. "I don't think I'm the stupid one."

Atia blinks, sharply, as if Sapphir had reached out and struck her.

I move forward a step, feeling the strange urge to intervene.

"What have you been promised for this then?" I ask.

"The chance to wipe her curse clean, I'll bet," Atia replies in a monotone. "She wants to be young and immortal again and she thinks the Gods will give her that if she gives them me."

Her eyes lock with Sapphir's.

"She wants her damn mirrors back."

Sapphir doesn't seem surprised that Atia would have guessed this.

"I should kill every one of you," Atia says, a snarl twisting onto her beautiful face. "Rip out your hearts and staple them to the walls with silver, like the old stories say."

Sapphir's smile is rigid. "I imagine you would, if you could. But you're outnumbered, Atia."

Sapphir turns to the others.

"Lead her and her human friend downstairs," she says simply.

The six vampires nod in unison, like a well-practiced group of killers. Two secure Tristan by his elbows and two more sandwich Atia in. She's forced to relent when one pulls her hair back and the other quickly grabs her arms. She doesn't fight, though I know she could.

She might not have all the powers of a Nefas anymore, but Atia still has strength in her. I'm not sure why she's relinquishing control so easily, especially after claiming she wanted to nail their hearts to a wall.

Why is she letting them force her across the room?

We're supposed to be fighting for the end to both our curses and after one puff of bravado she's just giving in.

When the final two vampires come for me, I'm not as amicable.

I lurch out and snap the first one's neck.

The sound of his cracking bones—the implication of death—makes me wince, but I swallow it down before anyone else can see. It's not real and I must be the stuff of their nightmarish stories for this to work.

The vampire falls to the floor with a thump, his chin set against his back.

His friend growls, which I think is supposed to be threatening. Maybe they've forgotten that we're all immortal here.

"Your friend will be fine if someone snaps him back into shape," I say.

Vampires cannot be killed so easily.

Still, the violence of it isn't lost on them. Or on me.

I tighten my fists as I see the shock dawn on their eternal faces. One of them, who looks no older than thirteen, turns to Sapphir.

"A *Herald*?" she says. "You never mentioned a Herald."

"I didn't know Atia kept such an eclectic group of friends," Sapphir says tightly. Then, to me, "I don't know why you're here or what business you have with Atia, but you must leave now. We have no quarrel with you. It is your Gods who set her bounty, so whatever orders you were under from them before, be assured these override them."

"I don't need your permission to go," I say.

I could shadow out at any time, but leaving Atia to die means leaving my one opportunity to be free behind and I won't allow that. Better I incapacitate the vampires first, knocking them out one by one before I tear Atia from this place and bring her to safety.

We can look for vampires somewhere that doesn't have an ambush.

"Don't," Atia says.

For a moment I wonder whether I've spoken the thoughts out loud, but I realize I didn't need to. It's clear Atia knows exactly what I'm thinking, but she has plans of her own.

"Don't," she says again.

Suddenly, I understand that what she really means is *not yet.*

If the vampires are taking us somewhere, Atia wants to know where. That's why she isn't resisting or putting up a fight. She wants to see every inch of this place so that she can burn it all to the ground.

She's still planning on killing them.

I smirk.

I have chosen my monster well.

"I'll stay," I tell Sapphir. "If the Gods have truly ordered her death, then I must ensure you carry it out properly."

"Very well." Sapphir doesn't look pleased, but there isn't much she can do about it. "But do not get all high-and-mighty when I bleed the human too. It is the least the Gods owe me for delivering their bounty."

I cast a glance to Tristan, who, to his credit, keeps a straight face, not letting the fear take over.

"I don't think he'd taste too good, but sure." I shove my hands into my pockets. "I promise not to shed any tears."

Tristan frowns at me. "I think I'm offended by that."

When they lead us from the room, they leave their vampire

friend with his broken neck jittering on the floor, not bothering to snap him back into place yet.

That leaves five of them, I think to myself. *Six, including Sapphir.*

We're brought to a basement, carved into the stone of the earth like a cave. A sanctuary beneath the floors of their safe house, where the sun has no chance of finding them.

The walls are bare and damp, but the floors are carved in deep mahogany, and from the cavernous ceiling elaborate candles hang, decorated with pearls and gold rosettes.

The sound of humming fills the room, and when I follow it, I see a captive hanging by his wrists in the corner.

He wears a stark white shirt and his hair hangs limp at his chin, covering his hanging head in a reddish-blond so I can't make out his face. But I do see his fingers. They are long, clawlike against delicate hands.

When he hears us enter, he peers up and the humming stops. There is something not quite human about him. He isn't there for food. Vampires don't feed on other monsters. So he's there for a vendetta, maybe. Or perhaps just the delight of torment.

Vampires like to feed on pain, just as much as blood.

"What is this place?" Tristan asks, horrified by the bleeding boy chained to the wall in front of him.

"The dining room," Atia says.

Irritated, she wrenches her arm free from one of her vampire captors so she can wipe a smudge from her shirtsleeve.

"I don't exactly feel comforted by that reveal," Tristan says. "Couldn't they have taken us to the library instead?"

"You have a point." Atia looks to Sapphir. "Why not just kill us upstairs?"

"Oh please," Sapphir says. "I like those sofas."

She strikes without waiting another beat.

Her fingernails shoot out like arrows from the huntsmen who patrol the forests in search of foxes to feast on. They go for Atia's neck first—the sweet spot of veins—and then when Atia ducks, they try to claw for her stomach.

Atia jumps back, catlike as she maneuvers out of the way.

I'm shocked at the speed of her.

Atia is not ancient like Sapphir, a creature with nearly one hundred years under her belt masquerading as a teenager. Atia may have ancient blood, but she herself isn't ancient. She has grown up in the human world, surrounded by mortals.

Still, she is *fast*.

Gods, the sight of her is a thing to behold.

She ducks low, sweeping her leg across Sapphir's ankles, knocking her to the floor.

Quickly, she searches for some kind of a weapon, but when she sees there isn't one—apparently the vampires are smart enough not to keep silver daggers lying around—she jumps on top of Sapphir and punches her in the nose instead.

I think about throwing her the dagger I have tucked away in the back of my belt, but I think she's enjoying the fight too much to be interrupted just yet.

It's only when two of the other five vampires make to interfere that I glower.

One is the small girl from earlier, wearing the face of a child. The other, a tall and thin man who must've been turned well into his fifties. His beard is blood-soaked.

I step between them and Atia and wag my finger in a tut.

"I'd prefer it if you didn't do that," I say. "Actually, I'd prefer it if you just ran and left us to our business."

"You'd let us run?" the man asks. "I thought the Gods showed no mercy."

"I'm not a God," I say.

From the tie pin my wings burst free, wrapping around me and dissolving my body into shadow. Everything that I am becoming nothingness.

And then I'm behind him.

I pull out the dagger from my belt loop, letting the silver glint for a moment under the candlelight, before I wrap my arms around the vampire's neck, holding him in place.

"Do you yield?" I ask.

He merely cackles. "*Never.*"

"Tristan!" I call to the human, realizing there is no other choice.

I throw the dagger to him, and rather than catch it, he lets it clatter beside his feet.

I roll my eyes.

"His heart!" I say. "Stab it into the vampire's heart."

Tristan is wide-eyed. "You want me to—to—"

"*Now,*" I command as the small vampire girl screeches, trying to decide whether it's worth the risk to intervene.

Whether she should risk her life for her friend.

She stays still.

Tristan grabs the blade and charges toward me, his eyes half closed in a doubtful squint.

I am beyond shocked when his aim is true and the dagger plunges into the vampire's heart.

"Oh my Gods," Tristan says. "Oh my—"

He stumbles backward.

I drop the vampire's body to the floor.

It takes only a moment for his years to catch up with him, turning the fine and few wrinkles around his eyes deep-set, graying his speckled beard completely. Then his skin turns to ash, flaking from his bones. It decays over the weight of centuries until bones are all that's left.

Tristan dry heaves, dropping my dagger to the floor.

I pick it up and wipe the creature's blood off onto my suit jacket with a sigh.

Death is such a messy, unsightly business.

I'll be glad when I have nothing more to do with it.

The little vampire girl stares at her fallen friend. She looks at me, then at Tristan, just once, and flees.

The others follow suit, wasting no time in their escape.

They leave Sapphir to fight alone. Not a one of them wants to go against a Herald, even if it wasn't me who did the killing. They've heard too many horror stories, just like the humans.

I laugh, picturing their faces if they knew the limits to my powers, or why I was really here and what I really wanted.

Humanity.

My damn life back.

I count them as they run up the stairs, hearing the door pull open when they dart out into what's left of the night.

One. Two. Three. Four. F—

No, not five.

Where is the fifth?

I search the room for the last vampire and instead find Tristan, in the very corner of the room, pulling desperately at the chains of the captive.

"Don't worry," I hear him say. "I'm going to save you."

Behind him, the last of the vampires approaches.

I sigh, shaking my head at his gallantry. "When I'm human," I say, looking up at the ceiling like I'm speaking to the Gods, "I hope I'm not that stupid."

I rush to the other end of the cave, coming up behind the vampire just as he's about to attack. I grab the back of his long black hair and then push his head forward, slamming his face into the wall.

His body slumps to the floor and I grimace when I see a single white fang embedded into the stone.

Tristan turns, wide-eyed at the unconscious immortal by his feet. "Was he about to kill me?" he asks.

"Probably," I say.

"Thanks," Tristan says. "You're a real sport."

A sport.

That's one I've never heard before. People aren't usually grateful to see me, much less willing to give me fun nicknames.

I watch as Tristan continues to tug at the captive boy's chains. He heaves a sigh of frustration when they don't budge, and then a grin settles into his face as he turns and plucks the vampire tooth from the wall.

I'm shocked when he starts using it to pick the locks.

"You probably shouldn't do that."

I eye the mystery boy, who bites his lip keenly as he watches Tristan's attempts to free him.

"You don't know what he is."

"He's in trouble," Tristan says. "That's all I need to know."

Ever the valiant human.

"If you get eaten, I'm not responsible," I tell him.

"Just die!" I hear Sapphir scream.

I turn to see the vampire climbing on top of Atia, her face carved with the scratches of Atia's fingernails.

Atia, though sporting a bloodied lip herself, only laughs.

Sapphir pins her arms down and growls.

"Enough!" Sapphir roars.

She leans in as Atia struggles underneath her weight. I curse, realizing she's seconds from sinking her teeth into my new partner's neck.

I run over to pull her off, but I'm not even halfway before Atia smacks her head into Sapphir's nose and then takes advantage of the vampire's daze by kicking out, slamming the soles of her feet into Sapphir's chest.

The vampire skids roughly across the floor.

"Atia," I say, calling her attention.

She turns and I throw the silver dagger her way.

She snatches it swiftly out of the air and just as Sapphir readies to charge into her, Atia sticks the dagger out and pierces the vampire's heart.

"Good aim," I say, as Sapphir blanches.

Atia twists the dagger in, scratching it against the bone.

She doesn't blink as her once friend gasps out.

"You die first," Atia spits. "Traitor."

She pulls the dagger out and Sapphir crumples to the floor.

"The blood," I say, gesturing to the dagger. "You have to ingest some so you can absorb part of her life force."

Atia twirls the dagger in her hand. "That's really disgusting," she says.

Yet she brings it to her mouth. She casts a low glance down at Sapphir and then, slowly, runs her tongue along the flat edge of the blade.

She hides her flinch well. I imagine it tastes awful, but Atia doesn't let it show.

She tastes the blood and watches Sapphir decompose, her face blank.

It's not until the vampire is a pile of bones that Atia finally blinks, the color returning to her face.

"I can feel it," she says.

Her face lights up, any darkness brought upon it by killing swiftly replaced with the radiance of hope. Her smile grows wide as she stares down at her hands, squeezing them to fists and then stretching her fingers back out.

I can't help but frown when I look at her.

How can a person be so deadly and yet so beautiful?

"I can feel something in me returning," Atia says.

"One down, two to go," I tell her. "Now we just need to find a banshee."

"Haven't we already?"

Atia nods over my shoulder and I turn to see Tristan, walking toward us with the captive boy. His hand is slung over Tristan's shoulder, whose arms are secured around the boy's waist to keep him steady.

A banshee.

That's what he is. I knew he wasn't quite human, but I couldn't put my finger on it. A male is extremely rare.

The boy pauses at our stares and a worried look takes over his features. He pushes the red hair out of his face, which is streaked in dirt.

"What?" he asks.

His voice is croaky, but deep.

Atia takes in the frail look of the boy.

"He's only half," Atia finally says. She turns from the boy dismissively and pockets my dagger before I can argue otherwise. "It probably wouldn't work anyway. Leave him be."

She's trying to be dismissive, but I can see the truth in her eyes and that's exactly why she's avoiding looking at me.

She doesn't want me to see the mercy there.

"Come on," Atia says, more to herself than to me. "Let's get out of here before the coward vampires come back."

"Wait." The boy steps away from Tristan and toward Atia. "You must take me with you."

"I don't think so," Atia says. "We're going monster hunting and, no offense, but you can barely stand."

"Atia!" Tristan scolds. "He's wounded. We can't just leave him."

"You can't," Atia corrects. "I think I'd feel pretty good about it."

"I can help," the boy protests.

"Doubtful," Atia says. "Can you even transform?"

The boy presses his lips together, shaking his head.

"So you have no magic. Which means you're no help."

"I can still use a banshee's scream," he argues.

Atia scoffs and brushes past the three of us, ready to make her way up the stairs.

"And I can find others of my kind!" he calls out to her. "You said you want to hunt a banshee? I can lead you to one."

Atia pauses at the foot of the stairs, her curiosity piqued. Tristan may have knowledge from his books, but this boy's sense would be far more valuable.

"You can locate your kind?" I ask, when Atia stays silent.

The boy nods. "I can sense others like me if they are close enough. Not that I have ever wanted such a thing before."

At this, Atia lets out a disbelieving laugh. "Why would you

betray your own kind?" She swivels back to face the boy. "Better yet, why would we trust a traitor in the first place?"

The vampire's treachery has clearly irked her more than even she suspected it would.

For the first time, the banshee boy glares and I see a hint of defiance on his face. "Have you ever met a banshee?" he asks.

Atia stays silent by way of answer.

"They're vicious killers and the mothers have a habit of devouring half their young," the boy says. "Except for us *half breeds*, of course. We're not even worth the eating. I'm *not* one of them."

There is hate in his voice as he spits the words, born from what I can guess is a lifetime of pain because of what he is.

"They abandoned me," he says. "They could never accept anything about me. They're monsters."

"Aren't we all," Atia says.

There is a heartbeat of silence that follows, before Tristan clears his throat.

"I think we should take him with us. We all have our uses, Atia. Silas has his strength, I've studied monsters my whole life, and this boy knows how to find them."

I look over to Atia, who still seems to be mulling the decision over.

"He could be useful," I say.

"I know that," Atia declares tightly. "I have ears."

"And a really pleasant disposition to match."

She ignores me and focuses on the boy, studying him like one might study the clouds on a winter's day, trying to decide how they might turn.

"What's your name?" Atia eventually asks.

"Cillian," the boy answers. "Born from the Fire Kingdom."

At this, Atia smiles. "All monsters are born from the blessed realm of Oksenya," she says. "And if we do this right, we might just be able to get back in."

I thought Atia was more concerned with breaking the curse than she was about getting into Oksenya, but the grit of hope in her voice at the thought of going there suggests otherwise.

You've never even been there and yet thoughts of it consume you, Sapphir had said in an attempt to cut her.

How much truth was in those words?

I watch as Atia pulls the dagger she'd tucked away back out. I expect her to return it to me, but the way her knuckles whiten as she clutches it tells me that I'm not getting it back anytime soon.

Cillian swallows as he tries to anticipate what Atia will do next.

"In the future, never turn your back on a vampire," Atia says.

Then she hands him my dagger, Sapphir's blood still smudged across the blade.

"Welcome to the hunt, Cillian."

14

ATIA

B anshees are monsters of madness.

Their howls can only be heard by their intended victim, who they'll stalk for days, or even weeks on end, appearing as shrieking apparitions, driving them to madness long before they finally attack. And though *technically* banshees aren't known to kill their victims themselves—keeping them safe from the Gods' wrath—they often drive them to do it by their own hand.

A malevolent loophole.

They don't hunt for necessity. But because they truly despise mortals and all the things a human life gives that they can never have.

That's what makes Cillian such a conundrum. He's a banshee, but he's also a human. Usually banshees mate with gorgons in a sacred ritual, keeping their lines female. Cillian's mother must've taken a human mate.

It's rare and the consequence isn't just his sex, but that he can have all the mortal things his kind crave. It's probably part of why they abandoned him: They envied his mortality.

I don't have that problem.

"We have to leave Rosegarde," Silas says. "*Now.*"

He speaks as if he hadn't already been pressing the urgency of that very fact into me for the past half hour.

"I know," I tell him, as the rising sun snakes in through the window. "I'm packing, aren't I?"

"Yes," he says. "You're packing half the village."

Silas sweeps his black hair from his face in a sigh. The glasses he's fond of are now hooked in his front suit pocket, and when he pushes his hair back, they wobble uncertainly. Like they could fall and smash at any moment.

"You're an ancient monster cursed by the Gods and on the run from legions of monsters who'd have your head," he says. "How many cases do you need?"

I turn to him with my eyebrows raised. "Keep talking. That'll make me go faster."

Truthfully, I don't need any of the things I've gathered in this room over my weeks in Rosegarde. They're mostly knickknacks. Souvenirs. Small keepsakes of all the places that I've been, wrapped inside gowns from talented seamstresses that can't be bought outside Aura of the Sea's Water Kingdom.

I could leave all of it behind. I have done it so many times before, but now things are different. The Gods are trying to take enough from me, out of me, already.

I rifle through the last of my drawers as Silas taps his feet impatiently against the rickety floorboards, causing the whole room to creak.

"Can we pack your bed too?" Cillian asks.

He bounces onto the mattress and then flops down, spreading his arms across the sheets like he's making a snow angel.

"Make yourself at home," I say.

"I haven't had a bed in weeks," he tells me pointedly. "Let me have this."

"Sorry. No room left in my case."

I pull open the last of the drawers and find the final two objects I can't bear to leave behind.

A sheet of music my mother wrote, the notes scrawled hastily in her messy handwriting. She would sing it to me in the mornings, without fail, and wouldn't stop until I laughed and hummed along with her.

And a single flower petal from a purple iris, dried and pressed to almost look like a feather from our wings. My father used to slip it in between the pages of the books he read to me at night, so we'd always know where to pick up from the next time.

It is a key to unlock worlds, he used to say. *So we never stay trapped in our own.*

My throat feels dry.

Though I know my mother's song by heart and I haven't read a single book since my father died, I still can't leave them behind.

They were the only things I went back to the farm for, months after my parents had been killed and their blood had soaked into the carpet.

I'd taken them in a hurry, fearing the creaks of the floorboards would call the Gods back to finish the job.

I hold my breath now as I pluck the dried flower from the drawer, along with the music sheet.

I don't pack them into any of the two cases I throw at Silas's feet. Rather, I shove them into my coat pocket for safekeeping before anyone can see.

"You're taking *two* cases?" Silas asks.

"You have two hands, don't you?" I say.

Silas looks over at Tristan, who practically mocks me with his small briefcase, which I know contains only one shirt among the dozens of books he has squeezed in.

"I hope the next monster that attacks us devours your luggage before it devours any of us," Silas says.

In an odd response, my stomach roars in hunger, the grumble echoing across the small attic room.

All three of them turn to me.

"Speaking of devouring," I say, clutching at my stomach. "Is there a way for me to quell my hunger?"

Silas simply blinks, his face plain. "You eat."

"I've tried that," I tell him with a frown. "I can't sense enough fear to feed on it. So unless you have any better ideas, I might just start gnawing on your arm."

"I meant human food."

I jerk back. "No thank you."

"You clearly haven't tried chocolate," Tristan says, setting his case on the bed beside Cillian's mud-soaked toes.

I quickly open my old wardrobe to grab a pair of boots that have been here since I first rented the room, probably from a previous tenant. They're as red as his hair, with black laces bringing them up to the calf.

I barely have the time to toss them on the bed beside him—watching his face light up like a starry night—before Tristan unclips his case and says, "You also haven't tried cake. Or sweet pastries. Fried potatoes and—"

"Are you quite finished?" Silas asks.

"Not nearly."

Tristan flips open his case and I see I was right about the single shirt among the mountain of books. Beyond that, there is also a bundle of fabric, and when Tristan opens it, I see a small slice of what looks like a very squashed chocolate cake.

"Eat this and have your life changed," he says, as seriously as if we were discussing ways to kill more vampires.

I eye the brown smudge of cake in front of me, wrinkling my nose at the sticky frosting.

"I'd really rather not."

"Atia," Cillian says. He sits up suddenly, straight as an arrow in the bed, pausing the tying of his new boots. His eyes are as wide and urgent as Tristan's. "You *must* eat the cake."

I roll my eyes, but I take the fabric bundle from Tristan's hands nonetheless. Reluctantly, I dip my finger into the melted frosting. It's sticky and soft. I bring it to my lips and am hit with a smell that's good enough to make my stomach rumble all over again.

Once I finally taste it, I feel like I've been robbed my whole life. It's warm and sweet, melting in my mouth and slicking across my tongue. I can't remember anything ever tasting this good before. Even nightmares.

"Verdict?" Cillian asks keenly.

"It's nicer than any tears I've drunk," I say honestly.

He wrinkles his nose. "You're kind of foul."

"I'll assume it was a compliment on my father's baking though," Tristan says with a satisfied grin.

I nod and finish off the rest of the cake in only two more mouthfuls. The sponge is so light and moist that I find myself licking my fingers afterward, desperate to get every last morsel.

Who knew human food could be so delicious? A slice of this cake alongside a nightmare would be the perfect treat.

"If you're finished, we need to find the phial of eternity and a banshee," Silas says, shooting me an amused look as I pick at the crumbs left in the fabric. He casts a glance at Cillian. "Any ideas on where to start on the banshee?"

"Balthier of the Ash's Fire Kingdom," Cillian says, confirming Tristan's earlier suggestion. "They're obsessed with death and banshees love a little irony. It's where my mother's—"

He breaks off, looking pained at the memory.

"There are a few clans there," he says, recovering quickly. "They won't be hard to find. Especially if they're all trying to kill Atia."

"Good to know," I say.

If any of the Gods' monsters try their luck at hunting me, they're going to be in for a shock to find that I'm hunting them too.

"Then the Fire Kingdom is our first stop," Silas says. "And since Atia can't open gateways without draining her energy, it'll be easier for me to transport us there."

I frown at the reminder of what I've lost, feeling the holes inside myself more than ever. All the snags from pieces that are being ripped unceremoniously from me.

At least when I killed Sapphir, I felt something return, but it was small. So small that I'm not sure exactly what *it* even was. I know I'm not immortal again. Whatever it was wasn't big or life-changing, but I can still feel it all the same. A stolen piece of me returned, bringing me a step closer to being whole.

Perhaps with the next kill I'll be able to fully sense fear once more.

"Take my hand," Silas says.

He holds his palm upward in front of me. The life line, head line, heart line—all things I'd pretended to be intrigued with as I masqueraded as a seer. But with Silas, those things themselves are masquerades. His human form is as much of a lie as mine and those lines on his palm, those hints at destiny, are a greater illusion than any I could conjure.

We are both trapped in a lie and desperate to escape it.

A girl, who wishes to become a monster again.

And a monster, who wishes to become human again.

"I always thought you guys traveled by winged feet," I tell him. "Delivering your messages with feathers at your ankles."

"They were sandals," Silas corrects. "And they threw off everyone's balance. You wouldn't believe how many Heralds fell from the shadows because of those things."

"I heard it was helmets," Cillian says somewhat dreamily. "With cute little tufty feathers."

At this, Silas frowns. "Before my time and not conducive to being taken seriously."

"Plus it would ruin his hair," I tease.

I place my hand in his with a grin, surprised by the warmth of him.

I thought Silas would feel cold, hard and unrelenting, but his palm folds easily around mine, the heat of him blanketing me.

I'm hit once again by that scent. Spring on his skin. Fresh blossoms and new beginnings.

I press my lips tightly together.

"You too," Silas says, looking over to Tristan and Cillian. "Everyone link together. We need to be in contact for this to work."

Though he doesn't sound exactly sure it *will* work. I imagine Silas has never tried transporting anyone or anything but himself. Even the souls he ferries are taken to the After or the Never on little boats long before Silas turns to shadow.

"Are you sure about this?" I ask.

"No," he says. His smile is far too roguish for his own good.

His hand tightens around mine.

Then before I know it, wings burst from the small gold tie pin at his chest, as if bursting from his heart. They slip around him like a cloak and I barely have time to marvel at the magic before I am flung through the darkness.

It feels like flying, though rather than through the sky we are flying through the cracks of the world, slipping in and out of the hairline fractures that make up the universe.

I find myself getting caught on them, the fingers of shadows snagging inside me and pulling at my seams until I am nothingness, scattered in the wind.

Then I see Silas.

The parts of him that must also live in the wind, born of darkness and the secrets Gods hold. I reach out to him, fold into him, let his shadows run over me and his wings envelop me.

For a moment we are one and I touch the ancient power that runs in him.

I hear the calls of the dead, screaming out to me, the booming voices of Gods demanding orders. I run my fingers over the tightening of Silas's jaw as he ignores them all to stay here.

I sense the hope of the After and the fear of the Never.

I feel a part of it all. A part of *him*.

I fall to the hard floor, breathless but suddenly whole again.

I squeeze my hands into fists and see that they're no longer shadow but flesh. And we're no longer in the attic of the Covet but in a new, strange street with a roaring sun above us.

I look up to Silas, who stands above me, seemingly startled.

The wings fold neatly back into his chest, and his tie pin gleams in place.

His eyes lock on to mine and I wonder if he felt it too. The parts of me mingling inside the parts of him, making us whole for a split second.

"Wow!" Tristan says, laughing loudly into the night air. "What a rush! I felt like I was flying for a moment and then BOOM here we are!"

"I think I might be sick." Cillian bends over to gag on the pavement, his skin icy and pale.

"I guess it feels odd for anyone who isn't me," Silas says. His voice is hoarse. "Sorry."

His stare meets mine again. His eyes are fire, the black making way for something unrestrained, like he too had felt it. My fingers on his jaw as the darkness swirled around us.

I push myself to my feet.

"Silas—" I begin, curious to ask him what exactly *it* was.

Before I can, I'm interrupted by the rumble of my stomach once again.

"It seems three mouthfuls of chocolate cake is clearly not enough to satiate your appetite," Silas says.

The fire in his eyes quells and I find myself frowning at the absence of it.

"Come on." He shakes his head, shoulders relaxing. "Let's get you some more food before you kill us all."

15

SILAS

The Fire Kingdom is a far cry from Rosegarde and the Earth Kingdom that's been my territory for an eternity.

The glow of the cold flame rivers blankets, the streets of the capital, between oil lamps and ashy tree shadows with cinder leaves, sweeping in and out of the buildings that hunch over as if they're hiding from something. The flames burn a bright blue, dancing at the river edges and licking up the charcoal cobbles.

The streets are quiet as we weave in and out of them.

"I grew up in this kingdom," Cillian says.

He leads us to a nearby street vendor, with black umbrellas shielding his stall from the wind.

"I've wanted to forget most of it, but if there's one thing I'll never forget, then it's where all the best food is."

He points to the vendor in question.

Luckily, Tristan packed enough silver to buy Atia and Cillian six pastries between them, and himself a warm roll of smoked ham with honey mustard from the vendor.

They practically inhale the food.

"I'm sure you're supposed to chew," I say, at which point Atia flips me off.

Tristan practically chokes on his sandwich at the *unladylike* gesture.

I'll admit I'm mostly envious as I watch them fill their stomachs.

I don't remember what food tastes like, but it sure looks delicious.

Heralds don't eat. Nor do we sleep. We just exist.

And I'd much rather be eating pastries.

"Where do we go next?" I ask Cillian, growing a little impatient.

If we can find and kill this banshee, then it's just the God left before I can take back the memories that were stolen from me and discover who I once was.

Cillian wipes the pastry crumbs from his mouth and says, "Pythia will show us the way."

Atia rests against the largest of her cases. "Who's Pythia?" she asks.

"The one who helped me to leave the Fire Kingdom."

"She's a monster smuggler?" Tristan sounds genuinely delighted by the thought.

Cillian laughs at that.

At least he finds Tristan's excitement entertaining.

"She's an oracle," Cillian explains. "Able to see into people's futures. She also helps the monsters in this territory find their prey. Banshees especially. The clans like to hunt murderers and wrongdoers so Pythia passes their names along as a kind of justice."

"Can we trust her?" I ask.

Atia snorts. "I thought Heralds were eternal, not born yesterday. For all we know, this oracle is the one who sent Cillian into the arms of those vampires we found him with."

"She didn't," Cillian answers quickly. "I left the Fire Kingdom long before I arrived in Rosegarde. And the vampires ... well, it turns out that there are certain breeds of monster who hate each other on principle."

"Makes sense," Atia says with a shrug. "I hate everyone on principle."

"Except me," Tristan says, grinning as he does.

Atia merely rolls her eyes, though even I can tell it's true.

Tristan wouldn't be here if Atia didn't want him to be.

"Point is, Pythia isn't the traitorous type," Cillian continues, sounding certain. "She's big into justice and punishing the guilty."

"If she's an oracle, then perhaps she could also lead us to the phial of eternity you need. She could be a useful ally to have," Tristan says. He looks to Atia pointedly. "Oracles are almost as rare as you."

"Actually I'm one of a kind," Atia says with a proud smile.

At least, she tries to make it look proud, but there is a failure somewhere in the attempt where the left side of her lips does not rise quite as high.

The Last of the Nefas.

"How do we find her?" I ask.

Cillian shakes his head. "We don't. At least, not for two more days. The sun is up and Pythia only sees people between sunset and midnight, when the world is shifting. And only ever on the third day of the week."

I raise an eyebrow. "Why?"

"Something about it making her mind clearer when the pieces of the world overlap with each other. Night and day. Today and tomorrow. Plus she likes threes."

"That is entirely illogical," I say, crossing my arms over my chest to show our new ally how much I disapprove of this delay.

Cillian only shrugs and licks the last of the pastry crumbs from his fingers. "That's Pythia."

We decide instead to rest up for a while in the Fire Kingdom.

It isn't the safest place to stay put. Cillian said it himself; this is a hunting ground, but we've no other choice but to wait for the oracle's schedule to align.

After dropping Atia's and Tristan's cases off in a nearby lock-box that only required a single piece of Tristan's silver, we settle in the public gardens, cornered on three sides by graveyards that are bathed in the glow of the sun, turning the crisp grass almost yellow.

Cillian and Tristan lie out on the mossy steps overlooking the lake. The scholar is reading something out loud from one of his books, while Cillian stares up at the cloudless sky, listening to the facts he rattles off with a small smile.

Atia takes the bench across from them, her elbows settling onto her knees as she watches them relax. There isn't a hint of it on her own face.

"Are you worried about the banshees?" I ask.

I lean against the back of the bench and arch my neck over my shoulder to look at Atia.

I think about settling beside her but decide against it.

"No." She pushes her white hair from her eyes and turns to me. "Are you?"

"I'm the one that's still immortal. Why would I be worried?"

"My blood could stain your suit."

"I have spares."

Atia grins at me, delighted by the devilish comment. I smile back until I realize I've echoed the words of the Heralds in the sorting zone who joked about their ties being stained by a decapitation.

My laughter cuts short.

I am not like them, I remind myself. *I want things they have long since forgotten about.*

"You know, earlier I was a little jealous watching you eat," I admit to Atia.

Anything to distance myself from other Heralds.

"Jealous." Atia repeats the word as though it tastes strange. "You're the only one here who can flitter through worlds whenever you like. How does a Herald become jealous of pastries?"

"How can I not?" I ask. "I don't even remember what food tastes like."

Atia slings an arm over the back of the bench. "Is that why you want to become human then?" she asks, looking up at me. "You never answered before."

I don't answer now either.

Not only is it none of her business, but it's so much more complicated than that. I've had parts of myself taken away and stored for safekeeping by creatures I have never even met. I want to experience being human and all the finite joys it brings, but I also want to remember what it was like the first time.

I want to know my name.

"Humanity sucks," Atia tells me with finality. "Humans are weak-willed and petty. They find joy in awful things and anger in joyful things. They're impossible. You don't want to be human, Silas. Trust me."

"You cannot tell me there is nothing you envy about them."

Atia shrugs. "Sure I can."

I arch an eyebrow, bringing my foot to rest on the bench beside where she sits. "Not even pastries?"

"Okay, maybe there's *one* thing they do well," Atia says.

She bites the corner of her lips, pondering.

"And I suppose it's nice not being alone. Humans are surrounded by each other. Their lives are so entwined, coexisting on what those around them do."

Her jaw tenses.

"Monsters are always alone," she says, somewhat bitterly. "The Gods created us and abandoned us. Humans have it easy. The beloved ones. Not like us."

I'm jarred by her use of the word *us*.

"I'm not a monster," I protest.

Atia looks unconvinced. When she exhales, the wind grows stronger, the breeze turning her sigh far-reaching. It chills the back of my neck.

"We're all monsters," she tells me, as I pull the collar of my suit up to keep away the cold. "And we were all cursed long before this."

After two days of cramped inns and waiting in the Fire Kingdom's shadows for the next monster to attack, we finally follow Cillian to the temple, and from there to the gravestones that linger in its back field. The grass is withered brown and the names on each of the stones are smudged, as if they were burned on rather than engraved.

"This way," Cillian says, leading us through the field of dead.

We stop at a crypt, leaning against the iron fence haphazardly, as if it's only just being kept from crumbling.

"This is it," Cillian says.

He pulls out my dagger, still marked with vampire blood. I stare at it, frowning as he grips the winged handle fiercely.

I'd like it back, but it seems a little rude to ask.

"Can I have that?" Atia gestures to the dagger.

"I was just about to hand it to you," Cillian tells her with a smile. "I really wouldn't know how to use it anyway."

He holds it out to her.

"Let me guess, you're a lover and not a fighter?" Atia asks.

"I'd prefer to still be lounging on your bed, admiring my new boots," Cillian says.

Atia takes the dagger with a laugh, twisting her wrist to study the angles of the blade. I swallow as I watch her hand rotate, the specks of blood catching in the lamplight.

Atia notices me staring and stops. She inches it, imperceptibly, in my direction.

Take it back, if you want, she seems to say.

I shake my head.

I don't know why. I do want it back. Even if I've never been able to use it before, the blade has always felt like some kind of protection. *To keep the villains at bay,* just as Thentos said when he gifted it to me.

Atia smirks and slips the blade up her sleeve.

She needs it more than I do anyway.

"Fair warning about Thia," Cillian says. "She's not a big fan of humans."

He looks sympathetically to Tristan, but the scholar shakes it off. "Not to worry. I'm used to things trying to kill me by now."

Cillian barely suppresses his smile.

"And you probably shouldn't let her know that you're a Herald," he says, turning to me hesitantly. "Heralds can make people uneasy. What with you being so closely connected to the Gods."

"Not to worry," I say. "I can be charming."

"I've yet to see that," Atia says.

She turns away before I can shoot her a rebuttal.

I loosen my tie, letting it hang untidy at my neck. Cillian said not to look like a Herald and being unkempt is the only way I know to do that.

Heralds like order. We hate chaos.

Cillian knocks twice on the crypt door and it shudders in response. We take a step back, watching as the stone door cracks and splinters, the stone breaking down before it finally crumbles to nothing, leaving an archway where a door once was.

A young woman steps out.

She wears all black, the material gathering high at her neck and then slipping down to the curves of her ankles, where her black hair finally ends. Her lips are the same color, but her eyes reflect the blue of the flame rivers.

"You must be Pythia," Atia says, stepping forward. She angles her head to get a good look behind the woman and into the darkness of the new archway. "I don't suppose you have any banshees hiding in there, do you?"

SILAS

The oracle smiles down at Atia, her blue eyes unblinking.

"I prefer Thia, actually," she says in a dulcet rasp. "It rolls off the tongue a little better. Who might you be?"

"Just think of us as banshee hunters," Atia says.

Thia leans against the blackened archway, not looking like she's ready to believe a word Atia says.

"Why would you want to go looking for such horrors in the night?"

I suspect Thia already knows the answer, but Atia doesn't reveal the truth.

"Are they less horrible in the day?" she asks, a cool smile on her nightshade lips.

At this, Thia laughs. A rumble in the night air.

"People think the night hides things, but truthfully the day hides all the horrors. It coats them in light, making people feel safe in their lies. Give humans a little bit of sunshine and suddenly the world is a good place again."

"The world is never a good place," Atia says, with a chill in her voice.

She can't have seen much good in her life, but that's only because she's surrounded herself with evil. Seeing the good and not being able to be part of it is the true torture. Knowing it's out there and I can never touch it.

"Who do we have in your little brigade of banshee hunters then?" Thia asks.

Her eyes move past Atia and linger for a moment too long on Tristan before finally finding Cillian.

"Hello, Thia."

Cillian steps forward with a half wave.

"My sweet banshee boy," the oracle coos, delighted.

She grabs Cillian by the shoulders and places a soft kiss on each of his cheeks. The material of her clothes gathers like wings at her side.

"Didn't I help you escape this place not long ago?" she asks. "Must have been something awful to drive you back."

"You could say that."

"Tell me it's not your dreadful family that you're searching for."

At this, Cillian blanches, his face twisting into one of horror. "My mother—is she still—?" Cillian stumbles over the words.

"No longer in the city," Thia says, dismissing his fear.

Cillian lets out a relieved sigh.

"Some of the clan remains though. They split off from one another. I believe your sister spearheads a number."

"Half sister," Cillian corrects.

"Of course. Awful girl. Fantastic killer though." Thia steps back into her doorway.

I notice how she stays in the center of it, cutting us off from entering whatever place she just emerged from. Whatever lies beyond isn't something she wants us to see just yet.

"Can you tell us where there are banshees?" Atia asks, biting the words out. "Cillian said you could."

"Why, do you have a death wish?"

"Would it be bad if I did?" Atia asks.

"It would be interesting." Thia tilts her head to appraise how serious Atia might be.

She slips down a step, her bare feet on the grass. At her approach, the gravestones around us begin to sway as though bowing momentarily to her.

Atia notices it too and looks to me, raising her eyebrow as if to ask, *Do you see that?*

"Yes," I say, out loud. "I see it."

Thia smiles at the acknowledgment of her power. "Tell me," she says, looking to me now.

She's enjoying having a wonder at us all.

"Do Heralds usually travel with such a mix of creatures by their side? I thought you were all quite the loners."

I shouldn't be surprised that she recognizes me. It was stupid to think loosening my tie and staying quiet would make me unnoticeable in the kingdom that studies death so closely.

"This is not your territory," Thia says.

I shake my head slowly. "No, it isn't."

I can feel the call from the Earth Kingdom trying to beckon me back to Rosegarde and the other villages I'm responsible for. The messages that await my wings to carry them through the wind.

I try not to think too much about it, but a lifetime of duty isn't easy to brush aside.

"Are you looking for banshees because they've broken the rules a few too many times?" Thia places a hand to her chest and gasps. "Gods, am *I* in trouble for aiding in their murders?"

"We're not here for you," I say.

"Never mind that their kills are killers themselves," Thia continues, curling her lip. "It's all about the rules. You Heralds do like your rules, don't you?"

"Yes," I say, not rising to her tone. "We do."

"Your colleagues here in the Fire Kingdom must be overrun with work because of all the blood the banshees have been spilling."

Thia says it with a lick of her lips, as if imagining the bodies piling up with glee. She has vengeance in her heart. A vendetta she has been satisfying with the hands of other monsters.

"Yes," Atia answers, stepping in. "The Heralds are overrun and we're here to right the balance."

"Bullshit," Thia says, though she is grinning at Atia when she does, pleased with the lie. "Rather brazen to fib to an oracle, but lucky for you I enjoy that."

She winks at Atia.

"So you'll help us?" I ask.

Thia makes a small *hmm* sound.

"There is a place, not far from here," she says.

She watches me as she says it, but I'm watching Atia.

She has shifted, her body moving slightly to the left with every second that Thia speaks, a part of her in front of a part of me.

She does not trust the oracle either.

"It's not a place for the faint of heart, or those who wish to live long and healthy lives here in the human realm," Thia says. "I sense you are none of those things."

I tighten my tie back up, shifting it straight. Righting myself once again.

"Will you tell us where it is?"

"So long as you wipe your feet when you come in," Thia says with a shrug.

"You want us to come in?"

"Information is never free." Thia spreads her arm to the darkening archway. "And I always like a cup of tea before plotting a murder."

17

ATIA

Thia leads us into a theater of a room.

The walls are cloaked in purple velvet with candles cascading from them, the blue cold flame dancing across the fabric but not daring to char it. The carpet is the same grass as the graveyard, and in the center of it all is a small table with brightly cushioned chairs on either side and a mirror lying flat on its surface.

The door we entered disappears the moment we walk through.

Thia sweeps across the room and over to a small bar area.

She pours herself a drink.

I gesture to her glass. "I thought you wanted tea."

"Darling," Thia says, bringing the tumbler to her lips. "This is my tea. Now, what drives you to hunt banshees?"

"You're an oracle. You tell me."

Thia makes another *hmm* sound in place of a laugh and takes a seat on the brightest of the cushioned chairs.

"There's a difference between seeing the future and seeing the past," she tells me. "Besides, a little *physical connection* is always best when it comes to seeing destinies."

She winks.

I bite back a smile, not wanting to give her the satisfaction of slipping me into ease. If there's one thing I must do, it's keep my guard up.

The last person I trusted for help on this mission ended up

trying to sink their teeth into my throat and that was after knowing her for years.

Sapphir and I hunted together, we roamed villages together, and she didn't give murdering me a second thought. I knew we weren't ever really friends, but sometimes it felt like we were. Or at least I pretended that we could be.

I liked pretending.

My life had always been built on illusions, but I never realized just how many I've been creating for myself too.

I won't make the same mistake twice.

"Aren't oracles supposed to be aligned with the Gods?" Tristan asks.

He moves to take a seat, but Thia hooks her ankle around its legs and pulls it inward, away from him.

"Hardly," she says. "I'd rather steer clear of those pompous asses."

"So you've got no interest in appeasing them to get into Oksenya?" Silas raises his eyebrows, his arms folded neatly over his chest so that his tie bulges upward.

After what happened with Sapphir, he's as untrusting as I am.

"Oksenya." Thia slinks her head backward over the high arch of the chair. She lets it dangle there with a long groan. "Who cares about Oksenya anymore?"

I do, I think, as she pulls herself back upward to stare at us.

Everyone else might dismiss it, or prefer hunting in the human realm, but I'd like to know what sort of place birthed my kind and then threw them to the streets of humanity like rags.

If the Nefas had been allowed to stay, the ashen man and his band of killers wouldn't have been able to hunt down my parents.

One little slipup from me wouldn't have gotten them found.

"I saw it once," Thia says. She stares at me when she does, gauging my reaction. "The precious blessed realm. It came to me during a reading."

"What was it like?" Tristan asks in my place.

"Stuffy."

Thia finishes the rest of her drink in a large swallow and then uses her sleeve to wipe clean the mirror beside her.

"Time for the payment," she says briskly.

Cillian lets out a long groan and leans against the velvet walls beside Silas. "Don't blame me for this," he says.

"Destiny," Thia announces grandly. "Seeing pieces of your coming paths."

"Your price is seeing our destinies?" Tristan asks, so much curiosity in his voice. This world is still so exciting and fresh for him, all the things he once thought stories made true. "Why?"

"Because they taste nice."

Thia's unblinking eyes flicker, while Tristan's grow wide.

"Oracles feed on destiny," Cillian tells us.

"Oh, don't look so concerned." Thia waves a dismissive hand at Tristan's panic. "It's not a malevolent power." She turns to me and wiggles her eyebrows. "Though wouldn't that be fun? Stealing people's destinies for myself. I could have an entire library of them. Pick one from the shelf like a book and be absorbed into it."

She picks up the mirror and studies her reflection, cleaning the lines of her black lipstick.

"Ahh, what could have been," she says wistfully.

"Thia feeds off the energy from our destinies," Cillian explains. "She did it to me too. You see some images connected to your fate and that's all. It's harmless."

"*Hey*," Thia scolds. She practically throws the mirror down. "Watch who you go around calling harmless."

"So who goes first?" Tristan asks. "I'd quite like to know a thing or two—"

"Just one of them will do," Thia interrupts, nodding toward me and Silas. "Only the wickedest for me."

Tristan looks disappointed, while Silas seems offended at being called *wicked* in front of company. It's the same look he had when I called him a monster back in the gardens.

It's that easy to irk him—just compare him to the rest of us. Silas wants so badly to become something else that he forgets what he is now.

What we both are, beneath the guises we wear.

If Thia holds her mirror up to Silas, what will his reflection show?

Would he be disgusted by it?

I pull at the chair opposite Thia and her ankle unhooks, allowing me to slide into it. I flatten my palm down onto the table.

"Make this quick," I say.

Thia's lips slick into a smile. "What fun would that be?"

She places her hand on top of mine; the cold feel of her nails scratches over my knuckles and I swallow.

She feels like night.

"Everyone leave," Thia announces.

She waves a hand and one of the curtains shifts to reveal a small doorway that wasn't there before.

"That'll take you back into the graveyard," she says. "Wait there until I come for you." She tilts her head to appraise my hand. Her fingers run over mine in a tickle. "Destinies are private things. Not to be shared easily."

At this, Silas presses away from the wall and his crossed arms drop to his sides. "I'm not leaving her alone with you."

Thia turns from my palm and regards Silas as if he is a bug she'd gladly squash on any other day.

"Is that chivalry on your face?" she asks, unimpressed. "I don't like it."

"It's distrust," he says. "I need her."

I blink, letting his words resonate through the air. It's been a long time since anyone has ever needed me for anything.

"She's useful to me," Silas amends quickly. "I don't want to come back to find her dead by your hand."

Thia waves dismissively, bored by his outburst. "Go. I promise I won't kill anyone useful."

Silas hesitates, the stubbornness in his bones making his form go rigid. I'd bet he'd stand there all day, still as a statue, if only to prove a point.

Ever the protector.

Ever the stubborn fool.

"Just leave," I tell him. "I'm not frightened."

What is there to be frightened of? I've already lost my parents and now my powers. I can hardly succumb to fear over an oracle.

"Are you sure?" Silas asks me.

"If I die, you get to say I told you so," I promise him.

And you get to avenge me, I think to myself. *Don't let the oracle live long enough to tell everyone she killed me. That would be embarrassing.*

Silas turns slowly from me and walks toward the door. He glances back, just once, gray eyes sharp and narrowed, as if to confirm for a final time that I'm not in fear for my life.

When he finally leaves, and both Tristan and Cillian follow, a moment of cold creeps in.

"So, you're a Nefas," Thia announces. She all but claps her hands together. "How marvelous for you."

I arch a surprised eyebrow, somewhat impressed.

"Did my palm tell you that?"

"I could smell it on you actually."

I recoil a little. I hope that isn't a bad thing. "What does a Nefas smell like?"

"Trouble," she says, with a grin.

In that moment, I decide I like her.

I hope we don't end up trying to kill each other.

"I thought you'd be bragging about it," Thia says. "Such a rare creature to be. But then, I suppose the problem with a rare thing is that it's easily lost. Easily stolen."

Her hold on my hand tightens and her breath grows heavy. If she can sense what I am, that means she can sense what I am no longer.

"You saw me being stolen?" I ask.

"Don't you want to be stolen?" Thia asks back, as though it's a challenge.

I don't hide my confusion. "I would not wish the Gods' curse on anybody, let alone myself. I want to undo it."

"But the Herald has stolen you and you aren't complaining." Thia grips more firmly to my hand, her thumb rubbing over my life line like a burn as she digs deep into my mind. "He led you here, took you from your old life and thrust you into this one."

"I'm not one to be taken," I assure her. "Silas may have presented the deal, but I chose to accept. I'm here with him because I wish to be and I could leave any time I didn't wish it anymore."

"You're foolish to think of choices when you speak of that boy."

I lean back in my chair, as far as Thia's grip on me will allow. "You don't like Heralds very much, do you?"

"Perhaps you like them a little too much," she counters.

When I only smile in return, Thia lets out a long exhale.

"Traveling with a Herald is not something I'd advise under any circumstances," she says. "No matter how good their bone structure is."

I laugh at that.

If Silas were still here, I wonder if he'd blush knowing the oracle thought him pretty, despite the fact that she so clearly despised him.

"Did a Herald wrong you in some way?" I ask.

She may be an oracle, but she isn't the only one who can read people.

"I'm not the first person to have lost someone to the Gods," Thia says simply. "Or to blame them for it, even if it's illogical. Really, I'm quite the bitter old shrew."

Thia doesn't look more than a few years older than I am.

"You're not old," I say.

"But I am a shrew."

She holds up the small mirror to me.

"This will reflect parts of your destiny back to you as I search through it," she explains. "Don't be shocked."

The mirror ripples as if made of water and Thia's hands pinch over mine. I stare at my human reflection, nothing of who I am in the plain face that stares back.

For years, being a Nefas was the only comfort I've had. I may have been alone, but at least I had my power. It was a small comfort, but it was something. The feeling of magic in my fingertips and the knowledge that a part of my parents lived on inside me.

That is what the Gods took from me.

My family, twice over.

The mirror ripples once more and my face disappears to make way for a barren pit. A crack in the earth.

There is a necklace in its center, with a phial of crystal-blue water swimming inside.

"What is that?" I ask in a hush.

"Life," Thia says, breathless. Her eyes flicker backward as my energy rushes into her. "Aion's River of Eternity runs shallow, it has ever since the great war that destroyed him and split the Gods and their monsters in two. It cannot be refilled until what was taken is returned."

"But what is the necklace?"

"Water from his river that the Queen of Alchemy keeps for herself," she says. "Is it not what you wished to see?"

Vail.

My lips are dry with thirst for what the queen holds.

Aside from killing three beings, Silas said I'd also need to drink from the River of Eternity to break my curse. We knew there was a phial somewhere in the mortal realm, but I never thought it would be in the hands of the Alchemy Queen. I suppose it makes sense. Vail of the Arcane trades in magic and monsters, and that phial contains the essence of both.

I reach out to touch it and the phial recoils, blackening in the reflection.

"Be careful with your thoughts," Thia snaps, her eyes shooting open. "Monsters have gone missing for less."

I grow tense. Sapphir had said that same thing when she betrayed me.

"Who is hunting them?" I ask.

"I hear hushed whispers," Thia says. "Things uttered in dark places that only the queen is privy to. Why do you think she wears the necklace?"

I grit my teeth. "Vail."

The Queen of Alchemy is not just studying monsters and taking our corpses into museums, she is hunting us too. And she's protecting herself with water from the River of Eternity.

My knuckles whiten.

The Gods killed my parents for a single transgression, but how long have they been letting Vail of the Arcane get away with this?

How has she escaped them?

"Your kind is so shrouded in betrayal," Thia says, wincing.

I know that already, I think.

She looks so pained. I wonder if my grief is reflected in her.

"You can't run forever," Thia warns.

"I don't need forever," I tell her. "Just long enough to kill those on my bad side."

Thia sighs and the mirror dulls back to my reflection.

"That is all," she says, dropping my hand.

She licks her lips as though satiated.

I keep ahold of the mirror, hoping for more.

"That's it?"

Thia nods and I notice that her blue eyes have deepened, turning darker and darker. Her lips too, a far more midnight shade of black.

"You know what you need and where to find it," she says.

She walks over to the curtain and roughly pulls it back, arching her head through the doorway.

"In you get!" she calls out. "Before you let all the spirits in."

She looks quickly back to me, before the others begin to file inside.

"I'll warn you about the Herald one last time. If he is anything like the Gods he serves, then know this: They are treacherous creatures, through and through. He may be your undoing or your salvation."

"I'll be my own salvation, thanks," I tell her, as Silas walks back into the room.

He brushes past Thia and walks straight over to me, a strange note of what I could almost mistake for concern furrowing his brows.

"What happened?" he asks.

"She didn't try to kill me," I say, tucking the chair back into the table.

"And the banshees?"

I look over to Thia, who is already refilling her glass.

"The banshee cave is beyond the ash forest, where the largest of the cold flame rivers meets the sea. Only an hour's walk east," she says. "It'll lead you to the next step in your destiny. But I'm warning you, you won't like that step. The things you find will not be kind, but they will be useful."

"Just to clarify, our destiny isn't dying, is it?" Tristan asks nervously. "Because I agree that I would not like that."

Thia only smirks. "You can leave now. I have collected my payment."

"Wait," Silas says. He gestures back to the table. "I'd like for you to look into my destiny too."

Thia swirls her glass around. "You'd like me to look into your past," she corrects. "There's a difference and I've already quenched my hunger tonight."

"Please." Silas holds a hand out as if to stop her from turning her back on him. "I just need to know…"

He trails off, the word unfinished on his tongue. *Something.*

Silas just needs to know something about who he was.

The desperation in his voice makes me uneasy.

"Fine." Thia glides back over to the table and kicks out the chair opposite her roughly. "But don't blame me if you don't like it."

Silas takes the chair quickly, before she changes her mind.

I don't like how he moves, without the air of caution I've become used to. He should know better than to let his walls down right now.

"Aren't you going to make everyone leave the room?" Silas asks.

"No," Thia says.

He stares at her. "I thought destinies were private."

"Whoever said that?"

Silas looks to Tristan and Cillian, then to me, and his jaw grows tight.

He doesn't want me knowing the intimate details of his past and I don't blame him. It would be easy to use against him and he thinks me enough of a monster to do exactly that.

Thia holds out a hand and Silas folds his into hers.

She squeezes her eyes closed, then frowns and squeezes them tighter still. Her nose wrinkles and the moments pass in a long silence before she finally sighs and throws Silas's hand down.

"You're blank," Thia says, sounding disappointed. "The Gods did a good job erasing you. Well, except for…"

She trails off, toying with him as much as she can.

"Except for what?" Silas asks gruffly.

He can sense how much she likes having this kind of power over him.

"One word," Thia goads. "It's seared into you, like a scar. Or a brand, perhaps."

Silas clears his throat.

I can tell that a part of him almost doesn't want to ask. I think about questioning Thia in his place, if only so that fragile look is wiped from his face, when he finally says—

"What word?"

"Betrayer."

Thia thrusts the mirror out to him, barely giving Silas a chance to absorb the blow of her words.

"Hold this. It'll help me get a better reading."

"Wait," Silas stumbles. "What do you mean betr—"

"*Shh*," Thia hisses, closing her eyes once more in concentration. "Just hold it."

Silas grips the mirror so tightly that it shakes in his grasp, nearly losing the usual cool decorum he usually paints so well onto his face.

Betrayer.

Is that who Silas was in his past life?

The mirror quakes instead of ripples as it did with me, and no sooner than Silas sighs does the glass splinter. Cracks cut across it like cobwebs as an image comes into view.

In place of his reflection, four others emerge.

I don't recognize the first three, their reflections are all marred by the broken glass.

But the fourth face I know well enough.

It is unshattered.

And it is all I can focus on.

A face that has haunted me for the past three years. His suit is the same as it was then, the violet tie hanging loosely by his chest.

I can smell him, the ash on his skin like he was bathed in death.

"Who is that man?" I ask.

I keep my voice even, though it takes all the strength I have to do it.

Silas looks over his shoulder to me and I see his eyes flicker as he notes the anger in mine.

"It's Thentos," Silas tells me. "God of Death and creator of Heralds."

"Ugh," Thia says, turning to look away.

My hands shake at my sides.

"What is it?" Silas drops the mirror and rises from his chair. "Do you know him?"

Yes, I think. *I know him.*

He led the hunting party that killed my parents.

He let me live.

His voice chars into my mind.

Take this mercy and run as fast as you can from us all.

I grit my teeth.

This is no longer just about regaining my power. This is about the chance for vengeance I never thought I would get.

Found you, I hiss inside my mind.

I walk over to the mirror and look down at the cracked glass. The faces have disappeared without Silas's hold to project them, but it doesn't matter. I have it clear in my mind.

When the time comes, I know exactly which God I'm going to kill to regain my power.

And I hope he sees me coming.

SILAS

The banshee cave isn't hard to find.

Thankfully, Thia was true to her word, which isn't comforting. If she was telling the truth about this, it means she was telling the truth about everything else.

Like the fact that I was a traitor in my past life.

How? I wanted to scream the question at her.

I would've stayed there, glued bitterly to that mirror until the truth of it came out, if I thought it would do any good.

Who did I betray so badly it would lead me to this fate?

Or perhaps it isn't about who I betrayed then, but who I am betraying now.

I look to Atia, my monster of mischief, come to kill Gods by my side.

Do you have any loyalties at all, Silas? In this life, or the past?

I roll my shoulders back, shrugging the thoughts away.

One thing at a time, I remind myself. First I get my memories back and then I can worry about how bad they are.

We stand outside the banshee cave, staring into its depths.

It is jagged as a star edge and dripping with the embers, carved out from a stone hill that is broken only to allow a cold flame river to seep through and join with the sea. Thankfully, there's a bridge, because swimming in those rivers would surely kill everyone but me. Stories say they freeze you from the inside out.

"Banshees wail to predict death," Tristan says informatively. "Since I don't hear any wailing, I assume we're not going to die."

"Unless they scream once really quickly in your ear and then kill you," I suggest.

Atia snorts out a loud, brief laugh.

"We'll just have to kill them first then," she says.

She marches forward, my dagger outstretched in her hand like it's dragging her toward the cave.

"Wait!" Cillian calls after her. "Something's wrong."

Atia pauses, arching her neck back over her shoulder. "Wrong how?"

"I can't sense any banshees nearby." Cillian squints, as if trying to hone his abilities. "I should be able to feel them if they're so close."

"What do you feel?" Tristan asks. His fingers twitch as if he wants to pull out a notebook and jot down the answer.

"Nothing," the banshee boy answers. "Emptiness."

He shudders, as if the cold of that sense creeps through him.

Atia does not step farther from the banshees' cave. "You're sure?"

I step forward. "Cillian's abilities to sense others of his kind are why we allowed him on this quest. We should listen to him."

"I listened," Atia assures me. "But I'll need to see it for myself."

Of course she would not trust anyone after her last friend betrayed her.

Cillian shoves his hands into his pockets. "Fair enough. But I'm going to say *I told you so* when you walk into an empty cave."

"Deal."

Atia whirls back around to face the banshee cave, not hesitating before she bounds inside.

We're barely past the threshold of the entrance when we see the bodies. Twelve of them, stacked in neat little piles of three, one on top of the other like their killers had wanted to count to make sure.

The bodies are long and stretched, arms veined and their eyes red with fury. They are very much not human.

The banshees.

"They're dead," Tristan says, stating the obvious.

Cillian swallows, loud enough for us all to hear. He walks forward, looking across the piles of bodies until he seems to find the one he's looking for.

He kneels down beside it.

The banshee in question has willowy red hair a shade brighter than Cillian's that cloaks her body like it does the others, slipping over their torn white dresses. But the way Cillian studies this creature is different.

I remember Thia saying how he had family in these parts once but there's little resemblance. The banshee on the ground is pure monster, yet still Cillian's fingers shake over the ridges of her brow as he closes her eyes.

Tristan places a hand on his hunched shoulders.

"It was the Gods," Atia says, sounding betrayed by the slaughter. "If the banshees have been killing humans, even other killers, they broke the rules. The Gods probably decided a simple curse wasn't enough." She pockets my dagger with a sigh, upset it won't meet blood. "They do that sometimes."

"These bodies are old," I note.

I'm surprised we didn't smell them long before we stepped inside the cave. They are rotting, the flesh around the long claws of the banshees' fingernails receding.

It seems Cillian's feeling of nothingness was right.

"They've been dead for days, maybe even a week."

"What a cheerful observation," Atia says.

"If they've been dead that long, don't you think Thia should have known?"

Atia shakes her head, brow furrowing. "I know what you're thinking and you're wrong. If Thia wanted us dead for the bounty, she would've done it herself. Instead she showed us things that were helpful."

Helpful?

I'm not sure how calling me a betrayer was helpful to anyone, aside from Thia. She seemed to gain an odd satisfaction from unbalancing me.

Then again, I'm not the only one who gleaned something from her. I'd have been blind not to notice the look of pure hatred in Atia's eyes when she saw Thentos in the mirror.

I've seen a lot of monsters in my time, but never have I seen one look so full of murder.

I didn't ask again how Atia knew him.

I didn't need to.

Thentos is the God of Death and Atia is the last of her kind.

"Atia's right," Cillian says, pulling himself away from the bodies with a long sigh. "Thia isn't the kind to side with the Gods."

"And she did warn us we wouldn't like what would come from this cave," Tristan reminds us. "She only said it would lead us to the next step."

"I'm unsure the next step in our destiny is a pile of dead bodies," I argue.

Atia scoffs. "Don't you think that's an ironic thing to say? Since that's exactly what we planned to leave behind."

At that, a low growl rumbles through the cave entrance, shaking the rocks loose from the walls. They fall down like bread crumbs.

I curse and grab Atia's wrist, scrambling behind a nearby rock without wasting any time. Cillian and Tristan follow suit, shielding themselves behind us.

"I thought we were supposed to be hunting monsters, not hiding from them!" Atia hisses.

"Feel free to go out there and kill whatever just arrived," I say.

I see the creature's shadow first, beginning as one winged thing and then splitting into three. It quakes and molds itself human.

I dare a peek out from behind the stone wall and grit my teeth when I see the three women step into the cave and inhale the air, searching for our scent. Their hair is blacker than coal and slips across the floor behind them.

The Sisters of Erinyes.

Curse monsters, created from the bitterness of the most wronged spirits in the Never. I've only ever heard of them being summoned to the mortal world to inflict vengeance on the most awful of souls.

If they're here and hunting for us, that means the Gods sent them personally.

But why?

Did the vampires we left alive report a Herald by Atia's side? Did the Gods notice that I left my post in the Earth Kingdom to come here, when all their quills remained unwritten? Their messages undelivered?

Or maybe they're simply here for Atia, to finish the job her curse hasn't yet done.

"This is ridiculous," Atia says in a violent whisper. "What do we do if they attack?"

"If we still had your cases, we could throw all eighty at them as a distraction."

Atia glares. "Just because you only wear suits."

I straighten my tie. "I like suits."

"I know, you never take them off."

I raise an eyebrow. "Did you just ask me to take off my clothes?"

Shh.

I turn to see Cillian pressing a finger to his lips. The Sisters of Erinyes arch their heads in unison, then bend to sniff the bodies of the banshees.

They're trying to find our scent among them.

"I just wanted to keep ahold of some things," Atia says, her breath hot on my ear as she gets closer.

"What are you talking about?" I whisper in return.

"The cases," she clarifies, keeping her voice low as the Sisters search through the bodies. "I know it's ridiculous, but if I can just hold on to a few things that are mine, then it feels like I'm winning somehow. Like I'm stopping the Gods from taking everything from me."

That is ridiculous, I think. Yet it's not.

The Gods have taken enough from me that I understand the need to retain something. I might not have been able to keep my memories or anything from my past, but Atia has been able to cling to a few parts of hers and I can't hold it against her.

If I had something beyond the word *betrayer* to cherish, then I would too.

"Do you get it?" Atia asks.

I stare as a piece of her white hair slips into her face, catching in her eyelashes. She doesn't even notice, doesn't blink as her gaze catches mine and refuses to let go. She is so determined to be heard, to be *seen*, to not be erased like so many of us have been.

A monster of nightmares, trying to keep all the stars inside herself from burning out. And she is beautiful for it. Because of it. In spite of it.

"I get it," I say.

Atia smiles and a look of relief escapes her. Something in it catches me by surprise and I blink, quickly.

I can see how the Nefas were too dangerous—too illusionary—to keep in Oksenya. That smile could conquer worlds. Or destroy them.

"So you're not a huge stiff after all," Atia says.

It's the last thing she says before the shadow of a Sister slips behind her and wraps a hand around her neck.

19

ATIA

The Sisters of Erinyes are supposed to punish mortals for the truest of evils, but it seems anyone can be bought for the right price.

One of them grabs me by the neck, her grip a noose. I reach out and claw my fingernails down her cheeks.

She screeches and then throws me into the arms of another Sister, who is crouched down and waiting.

"A Nefas!" she yells in delight, dragging me to my feet. "Nefas!"

The other two scream with glee.

"Don't touch me," I seethe.

I hurl my fist out to punch her, but she grabs my arm midair and whirls me around to be presented to the rest of the room.

I wince as she twists my arms behind my back.

"A rare treat! A rare treat!" the second Sister says.

I struggle against her, but her hold remains tight.

"I have a rarer treat," the one who grabbed me from behind the rock says. Her voice is low and calm, reverberating around us like an echo in a storm.

The third licks a line of blood from a dead banshee's finger. "A Herald is here, or so it would seem."

Silas clears his throat as he comes into view, keeping his head held high and pompous. Like he so loves to do.

I think about swinging my head back to smash my captor's face in, but just one look at Silas, who moves his head slowly from side to side, gives me pause.

He doesn't think we can win a fight against them. Not without more of my power restored. These women are not simple monsters after all.

Damn it and damn him too.

Does he expect me to just stand here?

"Is that what he is?" says the first Sister, eyeing Silas as he side-steps her and comes closer to the one who has me in her grip. "A wandering Herald?"

The second Sister tilts her head, breath hot on my neck.

I recoil.

Silas's knife is still in my possession, I think, the cold of the blade hidden inside my pocket.

Perhaps we're not strong enough to kill the Sisters, but we could fight them off and then Silas could shadow us out of here.

If I could just reach it...

"There are humans here too." The first Sister inclines her head toward Tristan and Cillian, who step sheepishly out into the open. "Humans and part humans. Such a mix of cursed things."

The third Sister rips an arm from a banshee and rises with it gripped tightly in her fist.

Cillian lets out a tiny yelp, which the third Sister seems to enjoy.

No doubt she senses his heritage.

"Are you lost, eternal one?" the first Sister asks Silas.

I immediately hate the way she looks at him, like he is something rare and wonderful, to be studied and considered.

I wiggle my right shoulder as they all look to Silas, distracted.

My fingertips are just inches from my pocket and the blade that lies within.

"He isn't lost but looking," the third Sister says. "Looking for stolen things."

She shakes her head and discards the banshee's torn arm.

"I can read it on the tip of his thoughts. Boats that find ports in forbidden places."

"Was it not enough the first time?" says the first Sister, giving Silas a baffled look.

When he frowns, a dimple appears in the center of his forehead.

"I'm not sure I know what you're talking about."

He's trying to make sense of what they're saying, but I'm not sure why. They're creatures of nonsense. They've spent too long in the Never, cursing murderers and abusers, to know how to carry a normal conversation.

"His memories are as lost as he is," says the third Sister.

She turns her attention back to the pile of banshees, crouching low to search among them. For what, I'm not sure, but her hands delight in the blood.

A smile slips onto my face as my fingertips finally grasp the hilt of the blade in my pocket.

I wrap my hand around it firmly.

One. Two—

"This is your fault!" the second Sister screams suddenly in my ear.

She pushes me away from her, hard enough that I stumble a few steps forward and nearly trip over my own feet before I feel Silas's warm arms wrap around me.

The dagger clatters to the floor between us.

My chin hits his shoulder and on instinct I bring my hands up to steady myself, palms pressed against his chest.

Against the spot where his heart would be.

I hear Silas's breath hitch and I'm surprised when he doesn't immediately let go. He keeps ahold of me for a moment, a second longer than is truly necessary, but when I tilt my head to look up at him, his arms quickly drop to his sides.

A strange feeling rises up in my chest.

"Cursed creature!" the second Sister spits.

I pull back from Silas, ignoring the pounding in my heart.

"I shouldn't have been cursed to begin with," I say to her. To them all. "My quarrel isn't with you. All I want are my powers back."

"Never!" they scream in unison.

"It is sacrilege," the second Sister says. She spits the words like venom. "It must not be done! It cannot be done!"

She hurtles forward.

Silas's hand stretches out for mine, turning the air to shadow between us.

If I can just reach him, then he can transport us out of this place.

But the second Sister has already pulled me into her, away from him.

"I already told you, *don't touch me*," I yell.

I punch her straight in the nose.

Once. Twice.

I may not have all the powers I once did, but I'm not weak either.

The Sister cries out, her screams like the howl of a wolf.

"Monster! Monster!"

She swings out an arm and sends me flying across the cave.

My body cracks against the stone wall.

When I try to stand, a sharp, unyielding pain shoots from my spine down to my toes.

That is going to bruise in the morning.

I look up to see the first Sister cornering Silas.

I panic, wondering what she will do if she gets her hands on him.

She takes a step closer to him, and when Silas doesn't back away, I realize that she's *talking* to him. And what's worse is that he's actually listening.

He seems to have forgotten that we're about to be killed.

"Silas!"

My screams go unnoticed as the first Sister places a finger to his temple.

Silas freezes, caught in the web of whatever power she has thrust upon him.

"Cillian!" I choke out.

If the Herald can't help me, then I know someone else who can.

Cillian backs away as the third Sister creeps toward him, moving a finger from one of the dead banshees back and forth in a taunting gesture.

"Use your screams!" I call.

Cillian shakes his head, the fear in his eyes taking over.

He's more scared of his own scream, of what power he might hold, than he is of the Sister.

"I don't know if it'll work!" Cillian says. "I've never been trained to properly focus my screams on one person. I don't even—"

Surprising us all, Tristan throws himself suddenly into the Sister, trying to tackle her to the ground before she reaches Cillian. She grabs him easily and Tristan cries out as her touch burns into him.

"Cillian, do it now!" I demand.

Cillian casts a horrified look at Tristan and then squeezes his eyes shut. At first there is nothing, and Cillian sucks in a tight breath, cursing himself.

"Focus," I hear him hiss.

What follows is a moment of pure, immovable silence, as though the world can sense what is to come, before his lips finally part.

The sound is horrifying.

His wail carries through the air in a wave of grief and murder. I bring my hands to my ears in an attempt to drown it out, but the noise is like knives stabbing into me, twisting inside my mind.

I stand, my knees shaking beneath me, and wipe the stream of tears that seem to be running down my face.

There is grief in his scream and in it I see the faces of my mother and father. I feel the fear as they are cut from the world.

I swallow, pushing the memories low and deep.

It's nothing compared to the reaction of the Sisters.

Where I quiver, they writhe and scream. They are on the floor, their bodies rigid and twisted. Their hands shake as they try to bring them to their ears, but not a one of them has the strength.

It's then I realize that Cillian is focusing his screams on them. Or at least trying his best to.

What I'm feeling, what I'm hearing, is just the reverberations. The echoes of a banshee untrained in his power.

I run to grab Silas's fallen dagger from the floor.

"We have to go!" I yell, pocketing it for the next monster.

Cillian's scream tapers off and he grabs Tristan's hand, hurrying toward me.

"Silas!" I call, but he doesn't hear me.

He stays, staring at the first Sister with a horrified look. She reaches out to clutch at his ankle.

Whatever she did has bound him in place.

"We can't wait for him," I tell the others. "We have to go!"

Leaving Silas behind means leaving behind the only one of us with full use of their powers, but if we wait, then Cillian's scream will wear off and the Sisters will attack once more.

Besides, Silas is the only one of us who's immortal. The Sisters may be powerful, but surely they can't destroy a Herald.

We rush outside.

The moment my feet hit the grass that feathers along the cave entrance, I feel a fleeting sense of relief.

"The bridge!" Tristan gasps.

My relief disperses into horror.

The bridge that carried us across the river of cold flame has been broken. Snapped in two, its wooden slats charring as they linger in the water.

The Sisters wanted to make sure we had no chance of escape.

Suddenly, I very much miss my portals and my wings. If I had them still, I'd laugh at this attempt to keep me trapped.

I touch a hand to my back, willing my wings to break free from the cage the Gods have trapped them in.

They shudder beneath the arches of my shoulder but do not unfold.

"We have to swim across," I say.

"Atia," Tristan starts, "the flames will—"

"Not if we get out of the water quick enough," I tell him. "It's only a few meters."

"Are you sure?" Cillian asks. "The magic within the two of us could help to withstand it for long enough, but Tristan..." He looks uncertain. "He's pure mortal."

"Which is why he's going to swim fast."

I clasp a hand on Tristan's shoulder, in a gesture of comfort I've never given to anyone before. It's the first time that we've ever touched. So many conversations and stories shared, but never once have I felt the need to reach out for him.

Humans were things to be kept at a distance.

True friends gave you something to lose and I'd lost too much already. But Tristan is my friend in a way Sapphir was never capable of and I really don't want him to die.

I would fly him across if I could, but right now we don't have a choice. It's either try our chances with the river, or risk the Sisters tearing us apart.

"I mean it," I say to Tristan. "Swim fast."

Then I dive.

At first, the water isn't cold.

At first, I think it's boiling.

As I swim across, it feels as though my skin is charring, and I hear the hiss of my hair singeing behind me. It's only once I'm halfway across that I feel the ice. The pierce of something glacial.

There is winter in my heart and in my veins. It freezes me just inches from the bank. I reach an arm out for the threads of grass, but it's no use.

I can't move.

My teeth chatter against each other and when I gasp out, I see my breath is nothing more than a puff of smoke.

Atia, my father's voice whispers to me. *Don't be afraid. You never need to be afraid as long as we're here.*

But you're not here, I think. *You're gone. You're gone. You're gone.*

I choke out a cry as his face flashes before me, smiling, then crying.

Laughing, then bloody. My mother singing, then screaming.

All of it my fault as much as theirs. They broke the Gods' rules, but I broke their trust.

Atia, my father whispers as the monsters descend. As the God of Death himself comes for them. *Run. RUN!*

Only there's nowhere to run this time. No Gods that want to grant a scared child pity, when they can hunt them instead.

I am not a child anymore. I don't get mercy.

I think for a moment that I will be frozen, picturing my parents dying forever, stuck in this river as their deaths replay in my mind.

Then they shatter.

My heart cracks in the cold and all those precious thoughts and moments seep out, drowning in the water around me.

Then suddenly, I feel a pair of warm hands grabbing on to my numb, splintered fingers. They brush away the ice that has cascaded over my skin.

I'm pulled up and out of the river and onto the bank. The hands wrap around me, rubbing up and down my arms, my back.

Silas looks down at me, his dark eyes creasing.

"Your lips are blue," he says.

He runs a thumb over them, a strange line forming in the center of his brows. The shivers melt away.

"By the kingdoms, you got her!" I hear Cillian say. "You did it."

"Is she okay?"

Tristan's voice. I'm relieved to hear it, though I'm not sure how he and Cillian got through the river so quickly.

"Wh-what—?" I begin.

"Silas shadowed us across," Tristan explains. "We were about to chance the swim after you, when he came barreling out from the cave. If you had just waited one more second…"

My lips quiver.

I turn to the Herald.

How was I to know that he'd come?

How was I to trust that he would break free from the Sister's hold?

"Did you j-j-just s-s-save my life?" I ask.

Silas smirks, his hand moving from my chin to my lower back.

"Of course not, my little monster," he says.

Still, he keeps his arms around me. I'm pulled into him as he lifts me in his arms and carries me away from the cave. The cold is too intense for me to try and resist. It has embedded in me and Silas must sense it because he holds me tighter with every shiver, the warmth of him flowing into me and healing the cracks left inside.

SILAS

The Fire Kingdom doesn't have many taverns, so we gather at a graveyard instead.

"We don't know for sure if the Sisters were sent just for Atia, or if they knew of my involvement," I say. "But if the Gods didn't know we were working together before, they do now."

Atia sits on the ground beside one of the newer-looking headstones, the dewy grass creating droplets on the sides of her shoes. It has been mere days since the attack from the Sisters, and though she recovers fast—faster than any human would—her lips still look pale and tinged blue. At least she has finally stopped shaking.

I force myself to look away from her, not wanting to recall how she looked when I first pulled her from the river. Like a living corpse. She'd slept for nearly two full days, shivering in her sleep while I kept guard for any more of the Gods' assassins. Even when she woke this morning, demanding we waste no more time, her fingertips were still icy.

She should have waited for me, I think angrily.

She risked her life jumping into that river, and why? Because I let myself be distracted by the Sisters' magic.

If she died, it would have been on my hands.

She wouldn't even be in this mess if not for me.

"The Gods are onto us," Atia agrees. "Which means they know we're looking for a banshee and then coming for them."

"Speaking of that," Tristan says. "What's the plan for reaching the Gods if we live long enough? How do we kill them?"

He stands by Atia's feet, his briefcase of books held tightly in his hands.

I gesture to Atia's pocket, where my dagger still lies. "That is no mortal blade."

I don't tell her it was gifted to me by Thentos.

"And if it's not mortal, that means it's Godly," I tell the others now. "A blade meant to protect them, that I bet can hurt them. They're already hunting us, so once they realize all the monsters they're sending to kill Atia aren't succeeding, they'll come to finish the job themselves and we can strike. We're practically goading them as it is."

Tristan places his briefcase on top of the headstone beside Atia, clicking it open. "First things first, let's concentrate on the banshee," he says. "I've got a lot of notes in here on them."

"I don't think notes are going to help you." Cillian peers over Tristan's shoulder and into his briefcase. His red hair has been slicked back, finally giving view to the edges of his face. "Those who see a banshee rarely ever survive long enough to write about them."

"Then perhaps you can fill in the blanks in my research?" Tristan arches his neck, looking hopefully at him.

Cillian grins in return. "I can try."

It's all the scholar needs for his eyes to light up like he's just won some kind of prize.

"Though if the clan of the Fire Kingdom is already dead, I'm not sure where to start," Cillian continues. "Banshees are hard to track."

Tristan pulls a large notebook out from his briefcase, the

scrawls small and slanted enough that they could be mistaken for tiny pictures instead of words.

"I know all about their hunting patterns," he says. "And I'm sure you can help us nail down their weaknesses. We will have an armada of knowledge to help us vanquish them."

Atia leans back against the grass. Her white hair ripples over the greenery, like a blanket of snow. "Trust you to talk about books as if they're weapons."

"Knowledge is a weapon," Tristan tells her earnestly. "It's the truest power we can know. Through books, we're made wiser by those who came before us."

"Sure," Atia says. "And if all else fails, they're big enough to whack a few banshees over the head with."

"The question is, where now?" I shove my hands into my pockets and pace from one grave to the next. "If the banshee clans in the Fire Kingdom are gone, I can only think of one other place where we might find what we're looking for. It's dangerous, but at least the Sisters of Erinyes won't want to follow us there."

At this, Atia sits up, newly alert.

"That reminds me, what did she say to you?"

I stop my pacing. "Who?"

"The *Sister*," Atia says, throwing her hands into the air as though I'm being difficult. She pushes herself fiercely to standing. "She was talking to you in the cave, wasn't she? Keeping you in place somehow?"

"Yes," I say slowly. Carefully.

"And?" Atia asks, growing impatient. "What did she say that was so important you just stood there like a sack of potatoes? How did she manage to create such a hold on you?"

I clear my throat as I remember the Sister's words.

You cannot trust this path. You have walked it before. And you cannot trust her.

I'd seen Atia then, kicking out as the other Sister tried to lunge for her. I made to move forward, compelled to help her, but the first Sister stepped in my way.

Her finger whipped out to my temple, thin and callous as she slipped into my mind.

What have they done to you? she whispered. *How much have they stolen?*

I willed myself to move, but my feet stayed firmly on the stone floor and my arms remained strapped to my sides.

When I heard Atia call out, everything in me shook.

But still I stayed.

This was your ruin before eternity. Her voice spoke inside my mind. A tear slipped across the Sister's eyes. *She will be your ruin now.*

Everything after that was a blur under the echo of Cillian's screams.

It was a deceit, I quickly decided when I pulled Atia from the river and felt her shivering in my arms. Cursed words, designed to trick me. Something to turn me against Atia and splinter our alliance.

The Gods were desperate, trying to seed lies into my mind. That's all.

How could *Atia* ever ruin *me*?

"She said nothing of consequence," I tell Atia now, watching her frown as she decides whether or not to believe me. "Nothing that matters."

"It mattered enough for you to leave me to be strangled," she says.

"But not enough for me to leave you to drown," I remind her. "So let's not hold grudges."

Atia sighs, forcing the anger stubbornly from her face. "We need to go to the Alchemy Kingdom."

I blink, surprised.

"That's the kingdom you were talking about, wasn't it?" she says. "A place where no monsters will follow, unless they want to be put in Vail's museum of murderous things. Besides, Thia told me that Vail is the one who has been hunting the missing monsters."

"She's responsible for that?" I ask, hardly surprised.

Vail of the Arcane likes to collect things, so there's no reason for everything she collects to be dead. She'd likely keep living prizes too. A banshee would be a great one to add to her trophies.

Tristan slams his briefcase closed.

"Vail gives a bad name to her scholars," he says, seething. "We're supposed to study monsters, not—not"—he searches for the words—"not *entrap* them."

"How is she getting away with it?" Cillian asks. "Don't the Gods know?"

"Oh, I bet they know." Atia wipes the graveyard dirt roughly from her boots. "And they don't give a crap."

"Are you sure there's no other kingdom we could go to?" Tristan looks down to the grass and his voice grows quiet. "Alchemy is dangerous."

"Luckily we're just as dangerous," Atia says, clapping him on the back. "Besides, it has to be the Alchemy Kingdom. Vail has something else we need. The phial containing water from the River of Eternity."

"You found it?"

There is no hiding my surprise this time.

I feel the odd need to rush toward her and ask for any and all details, but I hold myself in place.

"How?"

"I saw it in Thia's mirror," Atia confesses.

I can't imagine how Vail of the Arcane would have gotten such a thing. Waters from any of the rivers are fiercely protected by each of the guards and if only one phial was bestowed on the human realm, why would it have been entrusted to someone as vicious as her?

"We need to regain my immortality before we take on the Gods, so we can have a fighting chance of killing one," Atia says. "And we need to hurry. Thia also mentioned the River of Eternity is starting to run dry."

"Dry," I repeat.

An odd pit rises in me, and I fold my arms across my chest to contain it.

Such a thing should not be possible.

Atia only shrugs. "Not our concern," she says. "What matters is the phial."

"The Queen of Alchemy really has it?" Tristan asks.

He chews on the corner of his lip when Atia nods.

"Then there's something I must admit."

Tristan runs a hand delicately across his briefcase.

"When I was a scholar for Alchemy, the queen had us track monsters for her, to study their habitats and find out more about their ways. It was standard practice."

Atia stands alert, her posture growing rigid with every word Tristan speaks.

"But then I found out that our academy wasn't helping her study the monsters we found, but capture them," Tristan admits.

"She wanted to harness their powers. Rumor in the academy was that Vail's museums doubled as secret dungeons to keep her most deadly captives."

Atia swallows and her voice is like knives. "You helped her do this?"

"No!" Tristan says, his voice rising in pitch. "I promise, Atia, the moment I found out what she was using our academy for, I dropped out. It's why my parents and I moved to the Earth Kingdom. To escape her. I had no idea she'd progressed to hunting monsters on such a scale."

Understanding dawns on Atia's face. "That's why she sent that man to look for you."

"The Queen of Alchemy was looking for Tristan?" Cillian turns to him with a hint of pride. "Should I be impressed?"

Atia sends Cillian a look of scolding. "Let him explain himself before you jump his bones, please."

Tristan clears his throat.

"I'd been doing my thesis on gorgons and one of my professors gave my research to Vail," he says. "We were told the queen was interested in learning from her scholars, but she took a particular interest in my paper. I was summoned to her palace and she asked me if I could find one for her, based on the hunting methods I'd stipulated. I promised that I could."

"And so when you left for the Earth Kingdom, she came to collect on that promise," Atia says. "That was the debt the man was after. Monsters, not gold."

The man who Atia killed.

I'd known he wanted Tristan, but not what for. I rub a hand to the back of my neck as the dread creeps in.

If Atia killed an agent of Vail, then it is going to make us far less welcome in the Alchemy Kingdom.

"Are you mad at me?" Tristan asks.

Atia's fierce gaze relents slightly at the worry in his words. "No, I'm not mad at you," she says, blowing out a resigned breath. "You didn't know and the fact that you left when you found out means something."

"I'm still sorry." Tristan hangs his head all the same.

"Not as sorry as Vail is going to be," Atia tells the scholar. "I may just take her head once we kill the banshee."

"Right, the killing," Cillian says. "Did I mention I'm really glad I'm on your team?"

"Because our team has pastries?" Atia asks.

Cillian nods enthusiastically. "Pastries and murder, what's not to love?"

Tristan looks shaken by the thought, which only seems to make Atia and Cillian laugh more.

Two monsters, cackling in the night at the thought of death.

She can't be my ruin, I think, as I stare at them. Forget what the Sister said. I'd never let Atia get close enough for that.

I'd never forget what she is.

Though as I think it, Atia's smile turns to me, just for a moment, and the memory of my thumb against her bottom lip awakens inside me.

The feel of her shaking chin cupped in my hand.

Her hair, wet and white, pooled across my knee as I held her up.

And that look in her eyes now, as she lets a moment of happiness into the dark?

Ruinous.

I shift, the world shifts, and I clear my throat to give it a chance to right itself again.

When it finally does, I hold out my hand.

"To the Alchemy Kingdom then," I say, ridding myself of the thoughts trying to weed into my mind.

Atia's palm slips into mine.

"To the Alchemy Kingdom," she repeats.

She reaches out to Tristan, who clasps his hand tightly around Cillian's. The four of us forming an odd kind of line. A barricade.

I close my hand tightly around Atia's and her fingers wrap around mine in response. It only takes a moment, a blink, before my wings burst free from my chest and I let myself dissolve into shadow, carrying us across kingdoms.

ATIA

The Museum of Monsters lives up to its name.

The building alone is a beast, with circular windows like a thousand eyes, stained in red glass. Each knob and crevice of stone is like a bump and a scar on the building's face. I look up at the large wooden doors, stretched open like jaws, inviting me to be swallowed in.

"Anyone else want to turn back home?" Cillian asks.

"What home?" I say.

I ascend the steps that tumble from it like teeth.

The others follow.

I hold my breath when we enter. I'm not sure what I expected to see, perhaps a few skeletons and some heads staged on well-polished spikes.

Instead, a row of polished glass cages line the walls, each depicting a monster—stuffed and propped—in some kind of scene. Some in forests. Others by the foot of young children's beds. Standing in the marble floor between them are cases, filled with body parts.

Clawed hands.

Vampire teeth.

Hoofed feet.

Humans crowd around the dismembered monsters, pointing and whispering at each of the creatures in turn. Some of the children laugh and run to hide behind their parents. A backdrop of music plays in the corner from a small band, consisting of a violin and piano. The music is delicate and soft, a contrast to the massacre this place holds.

"Do you think it's real?" one woman asks.

"Of course not," the man beside her says. "A vampire, I can believe—I saw one myself, you know. Fought it off with my bare hands," he says. "But who's ever heard of an aglaope before? Nonsense."

"Vail does love her theatrics," the woman agrees.

They move away from the cage and I step forward.

The aglaope's body has been submerged in water, her hair flowing wildly behind her. Her wings have been clipped and sheared beyond recognition. Her eyes are stapled open, to give the haunting illusion that her gaze is following you.

"Tell me again why we're here," I say, swallowing the bitter new taste brushing across my tongue. "All of the things inside this place are dead already."

"This is the front of the house," Silas reminds me. He doesn't look at the aglaope. "Who knows what creatures Vail might keep in the back? Living things, too precious to make into trophies."

"And how are we going to get in the back?" I ask, raising an eyebrow.

"We're not," Silas says. "Not unless Cillian senses there are other banshees nearby."

At this, Cillian clears his throat. He tears his gaze away from a lykai, who has been mounted in a forest scene in one of the largest cages.

"Banshees," he says nervously. "Of course."

"Are you okay?" Tristan asks, putting a comforting hand on his arm. "This must be rather unsettling for you. I'm not sure how I'd react to seeing someone I knew with their head mounted on a stick."

"Thankfully I don't actually know anyone here. No banshees behind the glass cages," Cillian jokes.

Still, I can tell he's unnerved.

Not that I'd ever admit it, but I am too.

The humans think we're the evil ones, but at least once we hunt our prey we leave them to the Gods. Let their bodies rest. No monster would dream of taking a human and *stuffing* it.

The last thing I'd want on my mantelpiece is the head of some guy I pulled from the streets of Rosegarde.

"Well?" I ask Cillian, desperate to get out of this place. The ceilings are perilously high, with the bones of harpies and other winged creatures I don't recognize hanging from them, giving the illusion that they're still flying. "Anything?"

Cillian shakes his head. "I'm sorry," he says. "I can't sense one anywhere."

I curse loudly enough that a nearby man covers his child's ears and gives me a hard glare.

"Oh boo-hoo," I say.

Silas quickly places both hands on my shoulders and steers me away from them, back toward the entrance.

"Try not to kill anyone," he hisses in my ear.

I turn to him, the picture of innocence.

If he hadn't saved my life so recently, I'd tease him about what a stiff he is, but my father always told me a favor owed should be a favor repaid, so I keep my mouth shut.

We head back out of the museum, and the pearl gates that enclose it squeak as Silas holds them open for me, one last cry from the beast.

"So what now?" I ask as we walk down the row of museums and royal buildings that line the street. "Where else in the Alchemy Kingdom do you go for living monsters?"

"There!" Cillian yells out, pointing.

He rushes forward, pushing through the crowds.

We follow after him.

"Right there!" he says again.

I ignore the crowds of people stopping to stare at us and look toward the eerie glow of the palace.

"Right, Vail's little house of riches," I say, sighing. I turn to Silas. "Should we shadow in and steal all of her gold?"

"Why, did you want to buy another pastry?" he asks me.

My mouth practically waters at the thought.

"Or perhaps a nice dress to kill someone in?" he asks with a sly smile.

·I wrinkle my nose at that.

"What? You don't like dresses?" he asks, raising an amused brow.

"I like dresses just fine, but I don't think they're very practical for killing."

Silas's laugh embeds itself into my pulse, quickening it so suddenly I almost jolt.

"I doubt you could steal anything from there," Tristan says with a sigh. "The Queen of Alchemy has protections against that sort of thing. Ancient wards to keep out magic. Or to drain magic, maybe." He frowns a little. "I kind of skim-read that book, if I'm honest."

"So that's a no to our heist?" I say. "Damn." I clap Cillian on the back. "Better luck next time. No ripping off the royals today."

"That isn't what I meant," Cillian says. He points again, shaking his finger at the grand palace. "In there. I can sense it. There's a banshee."

"In the *palace?*"

I groan inwardly when Cillian nods.

"You're sure?" Silas asks.

He nods again. "I can feel it."

I push my hair roughly from my face, dreading the thought. "How are we supposed to kill a banshee with the queen watching us from her throne room?"

"She won't be watching," Tristan says. "She likes to visit her Cousins routinely, like clockwork. If I remember right from my scholar days, she's not due back until the day after tomorrow. Besides, I'm more concerned with how we're supposed to get into the palace to in the first place," he adds. "I told you about the wards, Atia. Vail takes her magic seriously. We can't just walk in there."

"Of course we can," Silas says.

I turn to the Herald, surprised to see he isn't pinching his brow, or straightening his tie pin as he anxiously thinks of some kind of plan to resolve this whole thing.

Instead, a small smile slips onto his lips.

"You have an idea you want to share with the rest of us?" I ask, intrigued.

Silas rarely smiles. I wasn't even sure he *could.* His gray eyes glisten with the easiness of it.

"It's simple," he says. "If we can't break in, we get invited. Once the queen is back, we just need a little bait."

"Bait," I repeat, eyeing him curiously.

"Vail likes to collect monsters," Silas says. He unbuttons his cuff links, pocketing the small golden eyes. "So let's give her something to collect."

22

SILAS

Darkness descends while we wait to invade Vail's castle.

Daylight, Herald, Atia had said. *That's how we trick them into thinking it isn't an attack. Once the queen is back and the sun is shining, we descend.*

It's been so long since I've had to pay attention to the days and nights, and when they switched between, that I almost forgot there was a difference.

In daylight, monsters can easily masquerade as bait and a twisted queen might just be swayed into letting them inside her castle, so she can lock them in beautiful cages.

Daylight comforts people.

Nighttime is for nightmares and no queen of those is going to open her doors to monsters who master them. So our choice is to wait, to rest.

To refine our plans and hide away until the queen returns.

It's a much-needed break for the others, I'm sure. Having only stolen moments of rest between meeting oracles and running from ancient creatures must take its toll on them.

Not that Atia would ever show it.

She may have lost her immortality, but she refuses to be seen as fragile. She is a mighty wall and will not be toppled.

Even as she shook in my arms when I pulled her from the river, I could feel her struggling to let herself be saved. When she finally did curve into me, it was like I had experienced something rare that a finite few ever had.

"One room," the woman behind the counter says. "It's all we have."

The Inn of Illusion looks like the kind of place that rats might go to die, but my new allies are desperate for sleep.

They're like plants, requiring constant watering, care, and just the right amount of sunlight. I've gotten used to breaking every few hours for food, but I'd nearly forgotten the importance of a proper night's rest. The luxury of dreams they get to indulge in.

So this inn, the only one in the stretch of streets we've roamed that has any sort of vacancy, is what's required. Gray walls and a thatched roof with a hole large enough to be leaking rainwater onto the desk where Atia's finger taps.

Drip. Tap. Drip. Tap.

"I'm sorry," Tristan says, sensing the growing impatience of his Nefas friend. "But is there nothing else?"

"One room," the woman repeats again.

Drip. Tap. Drip. Drip. Tap.

"Two beds though. Are you taking it or not?"

"I assume you aren't open to negotiations," Atia says.

Drip. Tap. Tap. Drip. Tap. Tap.

"One room," the woman says again. "It's all—"

"Yes, yes," Tristan says quickly as Atia opens her jaw wide, either to laugh or devour the woman whole. "We'll take it."

Atia looks over to Tristan. "Do you even have any gold left in that briefcase or are we trading books for sleep?"

"You might've thought to bring some yourself," he says, popping open his case all the same. "It's not as though I'm the son of some wealthy merchant."

"Would you like me to rob the next person who attacks you before or after I kill them?" Atia asks.

"She's joking," Tristan says, snapping his head to the woman behind the counter.

"No she isn't," I say.

The woman stares, sighing loud enough to tell us that she really couldn't care less who any of us may or may not have killed.

This is Vail's kingdom, after all.

Drip. Drip. Tap.

I place my hand over Atia's, forcing her fingers to stop drumming.

"Let's go," I say, pulling her away from the counter.

When we reach the room, there are just two thin beds sitting directly above a floor littered by straw. The wind howls through a crack in the checkered window, lifting dust from the large red curtains.

Cillian wipes a finger across the small wooden table in the corner of the room. It comes away dusty.

"It's very homely," he says.

I move past him to light the overly charred wick of a candle stub that sits in the center of the table. The wax has bubbled over and melted to near nothing, but in place of a fire it might offer a little warmth for the humans.

I wave my hand across it and a flame flickers into being.

"Nice trick," Atia says.

Is it? I think.

It's barely even magic. Just an element, stolen for a small while. A little piece of Herald power not connected to ferrying messages or souls. It's not like I could summon a wave of fire to wipe out my enemies. But a small light to guide the way for the lost is something I can do.

"I don't mind sleeping on the floor if need be," Tristan says. "I'll probably be up until late reading anyway."

Atia flings herself onto the bed nearest the door, seeming delighted by that thought.

"I don't suppose you'd all agree to sleep on the floor and let me have both beds, would you?" she asks.

"Nice try," Cillian says.

Atia huffs out a breath.

"If your bookish friend will be up all night anyway, I'll bunk with him," Cillian suggests. "I'm a terrible sleeper, so at least I won't wake him."

Atia looks to me. "Is this the part where we fight over the lone pillow, Herald?"

"There are two pillows," I remind her. "And I don't sleep."

Atia looks surprised by this. "Ever?"

I shrug my hands into my pockets. "Ever."

A smile leaps onto her face. "Perfect!" Atia declares. "Tristan and Cillian can share one bed, and I won't have to worry about you stealing the covers in the other one."

She claps her hands together, a problem solved.

"I'll keep watch," I say simply, sliding beside the window. I draw the curtains closed, enough that only a slip of the outside world remains for me to see through. "In case anyone else tries to kill you."

Despite saying otherwise, Tristan and Cillian both fall asleep quickly. Within the hour, the banshee is wrapped up in bed and the scholar is next to him, a book resting on his chest as he snores louder than any foghorn I've ever heard.

Neither of them is disturbed or unsettled by their new surroundings. They seem used to travel, but this entire quest is my first time outside Rosegarde, and even if I did sleep, I think this night would be a restless one.

I stay by the window, moving the curtains every now and again to ensure the streets are free from monsters.

"You don't have to stand there all night."

Atia sits up in bed and stares over at me.

Her white hair cascades down her shoulders, the glow of night on her pale, freckled skin. She blinks, her eyes flickering against what remains of the candle fire.

"Really," she says. "Quit standing there."

"I told you, I—"

"Don't sleep," she finishes, rolling her eyes. "But you sit, don't you?"

I step away from the window for the first time in hours and perch on the far edge of the bed.

"Better?" I ask.

"You look like some kind of watchdog," she says, growing impatient. "This is the last place anyone would think to hunt us. It's one of the reasons we came here to begin with. Just relax, would you?"

"I am relaxed."

"So you're just naturally uptight?"

Pointedly, I shuffle backward and recline onto the bed beside her, my head sinking into the thin pillow.

It isn't exactly comfortable and the fabric makes the back of my neck itch, but my bones easily mold to the shape of the bed, softening against the fabric. A small sigh escapes me before I think to hold it in.

Atia opens her mouth in a gape.

"That is not what I meant for you to do," she says.

"Oh?" I ask, feigning ignorance. "So you weren't asking me to warm your bed for you?"

Atia takes a moment to stare at me, waiting for me to get back up and resume my post at the window. When I don't, she quickly crosses her arms over her chest and then throws herself back down on the bed too.

She stares up at the ceiling, her white hair splayed across the pillow.

"Are you like this at home?" she asks.

"Home?"

Why would she think I had anything like that?

"Well, don't Heralds go ... somewhere? When you're not delivering messages and bodies."

"Yes," I say, but I'd hardly call the sorting zone *home*. "But nowhere like that. What about you?"

"Home?" Her voice grows quieter, softer. "Not for a long time."

"Do you miss it?"

I don't expect her to answer. There's no reason for Atia to tell me anything about her past, just as there's no reason for me to expect anything from her future. This alliance is temporary, fragile, and not one of us owes the other anything past this quest.

Yet Atia's lips part. "I miss those that were in it," she says. "I miss my parents."

"What were they like?"

Another question. I can't help myself.

"Mine," Atia says.

She turns to me, her eyes like black holes, pulling me inward. They are deep and immovable. Everything about her is.

Unyielding.

"They belonged to me and I belonged to them," she says. "There was a comfort in that. A safety of knowing I was never alone."

She bites her lip to keep more of herself from slipping out, but I want so desperately for her to keep going. To tell me about her life before this. It's withering, this craving for her words and her stories.

Her life, in place of remembering my own.

There are so many things about her that I never thought to ask before, but now I find myself wanting to ask them all. Wanting to know who Atia and the Nefas truly are and why they turned against the Gods and caused the great war.

Looking at her now, she doesn't seem evil.

She doesn't seem capable of destroying worlds.

"Do you miss your parents?" Atia asks.

"I don't remember them."

My voice sounds distant, unrecognizable in its hoarseness.

"Right," Atia says, as if she'd forgotten for a moment who either of us were.

Creatures of myth and darkness. The creations of bored Gods.

"It must be hard," she says. "Not to remember anything of who you are."

"I was going to say the same to you," I tell her. "It must be hard to remember everything."

Whatever happened to her parents clearly still haunts her.

That's the price of being real and alive.

"The day they died I was so angry at them," Atia confesses. "My whole life was spent hiding in shadows, only ever seeing the human world at night. They always warned me how dangerous the outside could be, but that day I was just sick of it. I wanted to see the glory of the world in the sun for once."

She bites her lip, hesitant as to how much to tell me.

Everything, I think. *Tell me everything.*

"I snuck out," Atia finally admits. "Most human children sneak out when the sun is down, but the moment it was up I climbed from my window. There was some kind of fair going on in town. I could hear the jingles from our farm. Though I had no money, I begged the runners for just one go on this ceramic horse and they let me. I was probably a little too old for it, but I'd never seen anything like it. I rode round and round, sun on my face, listening to the laughter of the little kids and I thought, *See, the world isn't so dangerous.*"

She shakes her head like she should have known better.

"I must've only been there for half an hour before my father swept me up in his arms," she says. "I thought he'd be furious, but he was so scared. My mother was crying, and when they took me home, they hugged me for five minutes each. I wish I'd savored that," she says. "Instead I wanted to scream at them to stop treating me like I was so fragile, but they just kept hugging me and when night came my father read me a story like he always did and my mother sang her lullaby and I went to bed so mad."

The ache in her voice strips away anything else.

She is bare before me, plain and raw.

I swallow, my throat feeling dry.

"They died that night," she says. "The Gods smashed through our windows like stones and the first thing my parents did was tell me to run. They didn't bother to try it themselves. They just wanted me to be safe and that was all."

"Atia—" I begin, wanting suddenly to wipe away the grief like tears from her face.

"I know that sneaking out was what led to the Gods finding us," she says, not wanting to hear me suggest otherwise. She thinks she deserves to carry that blame. "Just as I know my parents must have done something awful to be hunted."

Atia glares at the ceiling.

"But whatever they did, they didn't deserve to die like that," she says.

She sweeps her hands over her face, erasing the suggestion of tears she refuses to let fall.

I want so badly to reach out for her, but my hands stay glued to my sides.

If I move, if I hitch a breath, what if it shatters her?

I think maybe I should use my abilities to ease her sadness. Dig deep into all the powers Heralds hold—the gifts to manipulate emotion so the dead can be placated. Calmed.

Could I bring her solace by reaching deep into her heart?

Can I take away the guilt she shouldn't be burdened with?

You have meddled enough in her life, Silas, I scold myself. *Let her be.*

"It was Thentos," Atia tells me. "That night, he led the hunting party that killed my family."

The pain on her face burns to anger at the mention of his name.

It is confirmation of something I already suspected, but it jars me to know that the God who comforted me in my first moments as a Herald and who gave me a blade of protection could be so brutal.

"He's the God you want to kill when the time comes?" I ask her softly. "Are you sure?"

The words rise up in my throat like bile. It feels wrong to probe her decision, but Thentos isn't just a guardian of the dead, he made me what I am. Even if I hate it, he did save my soul from suffering in the Never.

I've always felt a little indebted to him because of that.

When I started the quest to steal my humanity back, I never imagined Thentos would be the one I destroyed to do it.

"I'm sure," Atia says.

I want to tell her that Thentos is supposed to represent neutrality, not evil, but what he is supposed to be—what I thought he was—and what he truly is seem to be in conflict.

I thought what mattered most on this journey was strategy and that nothing was more important than regaining my humanity.

But that's not true.

Atia's grief and vengeance matter just as much.

"Aren't those the kind of memories you want to forget?" I ask her.

"I wouldn't trade my memories," Atia says in the darkness. "Even the angry ones. You have to remember the bad with the good. It's always the terrible memories that stick with us, but sometimes, if you're lucky, the good ones make up for it."

"Are you lucky?" I ask, wondering when my voice became so hoarse.

Atia nods. "I think I was," she says. Then: "Why do you want to be human, Silas? Really?"

The wind whistles against the curtains like a warning bell, but at the sound of my name from her lips, I choose to ignore it.

"There are two kinds of grief," I finally tell her. "There's the grief of having something and losing it, but then there's the grief of never having it at all."

It's a certain kind of loneliness to be void of anything, to have no memories or comforts to fall back on, no good times to cling to among the bad. To have your entire life just be erased.

Who you were, who you could've been, gone in an instant.

"Being human has to be better than what I am now," I say. I settle into the pillow, turning on my side to face her completely. "Why are you so desperate to be a monster?"

"Don't you ever worry that sometimes there's a darkness in you?" Atia asks.

She brushes a strand of moonlight hair behind her ears and sighs, like the first wave of wind before a storm.

How anyone could ever mistake her for human is beyond me. Even now, there is something otherworldly about her. A whirlwind in her eyes. She is a creature of Gods and it shows, a thousand tiny marvels tangled inside her every movement.

"If you're human and you have a darkness, then that darkness is all you are," Atia says carefully, as if she's trying to puzzle the words out in her mind. "At least as a monster you have forever to try and get it right. To be better."

"What darkness births around us can only be defeated by the lights we conjure inside of ourselves," I say.

"That's only because you don't remember how dark you might have been," Atia counters.

I gesture to my form. "Whoever I was and whatever I did, it can't be bad enough to deserve this."

"What if it is?" Atia asks softly. "What if it's worse?"

I contemplate that for a moment.

All I've ever wanted is to remember who I was, so much so that I've never really considered the possibility that I wasn't worth remembering.

"Then I guess I'm in good company," I tell Atia, not willing to let those doubts override me. "One monster to another."

At this, Atia laughs.

Her cheeks dimple.

My breath catches.

I don't know why. I've never needed to breathe—it's a habit if nothing else. A piece of the humanity I can't remember, left over and embedded into me. I don't need to breathe to live. And yet when she laughs, my breath sticks in my throat and I hold it there, not wanting to make a sound to break the moment. The spell of her smile.

Is this what it means to be in the company of a Nefas?

Is this all part of the illusion?

How could I ever be sure which parts of her are real and which are conjured to draw me in as she has drawn in so many prey before?

She will be your ruin.

"One monster to another?" Atia says, her voice wavering with sleep. "I hope we bring every single God to their knees, not just Thentos. As long as they're alive, they get to decide our destinies. The only way we choose our own is by burning their house down."

She closes her eyes, not waiting for my response. She pulls the sheets up high, tucking them under her chin, and lets dream take her.

Just like that, comforted in the promise of destruction.

I can't help but watch, unmoving from where I lie beside her. Long after her eyes close and her breath slips to sleep, I stay. I watch.

I wonder which of us will ruin the other first.

23

SILAS

If someone had never seen Vail's palace before, they could almost mistake it for the moon, pulled down from the night's sky and tethered to the realm.

The rounded building glows a strange white blue, seeping black waterfalls from either edge. Each carefully carved window looks like a crater.

It's truly a building of magic, fit for a ruler of such terrible things.

"I'll bet she has more jewels in that place than all of the Cousins combined," Cillian says. "How does someone get that rich?"

Atia only shrugs. "You just have to kill a few people. It really isn't so hard."

"Now why didn't I think of that?"

"You were too busy being chained to a wall by a bunch of blood-suckers."

"Oh, right," Cillian says, snapping his fingers. "*That.*"

The day is bright, and beaming up ahead of us, the streets are filled with people visiting the museum or stopping to admire Vail's palace. When they get too close, the guards put a hand on their swords and the people scurry quickly away.

"So when you said you were going to be bait," Tristan says, "what did that mean? Assuming Vail is indeed back, we will need some sort of display to show how rare and powerful you are, so that she'll *want* to collect you. The guards must get dozens of scholars presenting monsters to them, but Vail's picky. She loves drama and intrigue."

"Drama and intrigue." I study each of the dozen guards that line the gates. "I think we can give her that."

I hold out my arm, skin catching the light before it eventually becomes shadow.

"Your hand!" Cillian exclaims, his eyes growing wider than I thought possible. "Everyone will see!"

"That's the point," Atia says. "Drama, remember? Silas's abilities will make Vail think we're powerful monsters that Tristan has captured, who are now trying to escape. The best way to find a hunter is to make them think you're prey."

I let my wings free from the pin. They spread across my body, covering me in unyielding black.

Atia's smile dawns.

I return it, just for a snatch of time, then I disappear.

I reappear feet from where I stood, my wings carrying me in flickers through the folds of the world. Crowds of people stop to stare. A few of them gasp, unsure if it was a trick of the light or not.

So I do it again.

I become shadow before their eyes, and then re-form a blink later.

That's when the screams start.

"Cillian," I say to the banshee. "You're next."

If the groan is anything to go by, Atia understands what I'm asking of our new friend.

Quickly, she places Tristan's hands over his ears, and then secures her own around her head, ready to block out the shrill screams.

Tristan looks momentarily confused, but when Cillian's lips part, he ducks down, crouching on the ground with his head between his knees.

Cillian's wail punctures through the street like a surgeon's needle. Those in the crowd who can, disperse quickly, but some are caught on the hook of his calls. They writhe on the ground. Cillian's voice wavers a little, but he doesn't stop. He controls himself just enough, causing them pain instead of death.

I let myself fall to the shadows again. Cillian's cries have no effect on me, but the crowds scream in terror at the combination of our powers.

They run.

Atia keeps her hands firmly to her ears as the panicked crowd rushes to safety.

Then a man knocks into her and nearly sends Atia tumbling to the ground. She regains her balance, scowling after him as if her glare were a weapon.

Without thinking, I take her hand in mine, snatching her from the chaos.

Atia falls into my shadows, letting them engulf her without question. She stares at our interlaced fingers as the darkness whips around us.

We become half smoke, half people, entwined in the air and into each other, so that her sharpest points find solace against my own.

I feel the thrum of her, the melody that lives inside her catching my ear. There is so much pain and grief contained in that mourning song, beyond anything I've known in all my years as a Herald. She holds an infinity of heartbreak. It's in the eyes of her father that flash before me and the delicate smile of her mother, whose blue lips proclaim lullabies.

"Herald," Atia says. A tear slips down her star-freckled cheeks. "*Silas.*"

She can feel it too. A part of her is twisted inside a part of me, memories and melancholy seeping out of her and into the shadows that birth around me.

Yet neither of us lets go.

Letting go would mean being alone and we've both had too many years of loneliness between us to want more.

I'm sorry, I think to her, wondering if she can hear. *I'm sorry for cursing you and bringing you into all of this.*

"You there! Enough!"

Atia drops my hand, and the shadows wither, breaking the connection between us with jarring urgency.

Cillian's screams have stopped. I'm not sure when they ended, but now two guards have him secured between them. A third grabs Tristan by the arm; a fourth, fifth, sixth come for me and Atia.

We let them take us.

The gates of Vail's castle clink open like gold falling into a chalice. When we enter the dome, I'm hit by how quiet it is. Even our footsteps are silent on the marble. Whatever magic Vail has blanketed over this place keeps everything uninvited outside, even sound.

The guard holding Atia pushes her gruffly forward. "Wait here," he says.

"You might want to be less heavy-handed," I say, noting the way Atia licks her lips when she looks at him. "A show of respect for creatures who could kill you."

"You're not killing anybody," the guard says with a laugh. "Not in this place."

He looks up at the ceiling, gesturing around us to the vast

emptiness. I can feel the wards that Tristan warned us about, eradicating all power that isn't hers. It battles against me, trying to fight its way inside and steal what its creator demands stolen.

Vail doesn't fear monsters, because the ones she takes into this place can't fight back.

"You feel that, monster boy?" the guard says. "Your power doesn't work."

He grabs Atia's arm, as if to prove the point that she can't fight back.

"Very well," I say. "But just so you're aware, I wasn't threatening to kill you. I was just letting you know that she would."

I gesture to Atia, who smiles up at the guard sweetly, and then slips my dagger from her shirtsleeve. She swoops it upward, catching the guard's cheek.

It's a shallow cut, but the line of blood across his face makes her grin.

"Oops," she says.

"Oops?" he snarls, wiping the blood away.

She shrugs. "I meant to go for your neck."

The guard growls, more beastly than any of us, and raises his arm to strike her.

"That is no way to treat our guests."

The voice cuts through the room.

Vail of the Arcane, queen of the Alchemy Kingdom and middle of the five Cousins, descends the stone spiraled staircase. She looks as though she has been carved from one of the statues that sits in her museum, a woman of cold marble. She is dressed in the night sky, a purple-black cape flowing down her legs, littered with diamonds masquerading as stars.

The phial of eternity hangs from her neck.

I would know it anywhere.

The water sparks inside and I am overcome with the urge to reach out and rip it from her throat.

That doesn't belong to her.

She should not have access to such a thing.

Take it back, a voice inside me demands.

"You seem to be causing quite a commotion both in and out of my palace," Vail says. There is a smile on her face that does not leave, as though it has been etched there. "One might wonder why you'd do such a thing. I was planning to rest after my travels."

"It was my fault, High Queen." Tristan steps bravely forward. "I am—"

"Oh, I remember who you are, Scholar of the Arcane."

Vail would not forget the scholar who wronged her. I'd bet Tristan was the first. A few may have wanted to run, but they'd never had the gall to actually do it.

"Have you come back here with apologies?" Vail asks. Her eyebrow arches high, permanent smile growing expectant.

"With more than that," Tristan says, swallowing the lump I can hear in his throat. "I ran because I could not find the monster I had promised you. I panicked. But for my misgivings, I have brought you three more creatures. I could not wrangle them alone, but thankfully your guards were able to intervene."

Vail's hand lingers on the staircase, perched like a bird. "Such a tale you tell. How much truth lies within it?"

"You may assess them yourself, High Queen," Tristan says quickly. "You, of all, cannot be tricked."

Vail's smile stretches at the flattery, but I can tell she is no fool.

"Which monsters did you decide to bring me?"

"A banshee," he says, pointing to Cillian.

"Oh, my favorite. And a *male* too. What a rarity indeed. What else?"

Her words grow gasping with hunger.

Tristan turns to Atia and a panic rises up in me. If he tells Vail what she truly is, it could be catastrophic. The Last of the Nefas. The only one of her kind left in existence. Atia is special and Vail likes special things far too much.

We can't risk her separating us in her cells.

"She's a lykai," I say, before Tristan has the chance. "Half, like the banshee. Filthy little things."

Tristan clears his throat. "Y-yes," he says. "A lykai."

Vail's eyes swarm to me.

She glides down the last step, her hand finally slipping from the banister.

"And what might you be?" she asks. "I would dare to call you *young man*, but those eyes don't look so young. There are lifetimes in them."

Her words catch me off guard. Vail has surrounded herself with enough magic to see through me, into me.

Does she see something hidden in my past?

Is it the same thing the Sisters saw?

I scowl, begging my mind to reclaim just one memory from my old life, but there's only a blank in my mind, as there always is when I try to look back inside myself.

"What do you know of me?" I ask.

"I don't need to know in order to sense," she says. "And there is a sense about you. A feeling of magic where it doesn't belong. Of forbidden things, wedged inside of you. Secrets, tucked away. Who put them there?"

"He's just a vampire," Atia proclaims loudly. "Hardly special."

Vail lets out a small, triumphant laugh. "You forget what a collector I am. There is no vampire in this boy. Nor monster, if you look closely. Still, he has a beautiful face for immortality. I wonder how it got there."

She turns to her guards.

"Take them to the cells," she orders. "I'd like them to be confined until we're able to test their blood for origin."

She looks at me when she says it. Not at the rarest creature of all, Atia, who curses right in front of her face.

"I shall see you soon, dear boy," Vail says.

We're led down to the cells, which lie beneath Vail's grand staircase, the guards not letting up their hold.

The cells are rows of large gold bars that weave in and out of each other, like rope knots. They play host to dozens of creatures, but when any of the things inside get too close, peering out of their cells to get a good look at us, the bars sizzle and the creatures jump back, as if shocked.

We walk down rows of growls and bared teeth, until suddenly Cillian stops dead in the midst of it.

"Move," the guard says, shoving him.

Cillian turns to me and nods.

A banshee, I think. He senses one of them here.

I nod back, and when the guard goes to shove Cillian again, I shadow behind him, grip my hands around his head and smack it into the stone wall.

That'll keep him knocked out for a few hours.

"What the——?"

Another guard yells out, bringing his sword up to my neck.

But in a blink I'm on his other side, shadow whipping around the room as I knock out each guard in turn.

The magical protections here might diminish a monster's power, but I can feel mine still surging through me. Vail's wards and tricks might work on the creatures in these cells, but they don't work on me. Perhaps it's because Heralds are formed by Gods. We began as humans and were made something else by their infinity.

"How is he—?"

Atia punches the last guard straight in the mouth, sending him tumbling backward against the gold bars. They fizzle against him and his body writhes with the current of magic.

The vampire inside the cell laughs.

"Where is it?" I ask Cillian. "Where's the banshee?"

Cillian shakes his head and his eyes widen at something just behind me.

"Which cell is it in?" Atia urges.

"She's not in a cell," Cillian finally says, pulling Tristan behind him.

I turn to see what made him pale so quickly.

A banshee stands before us, unchained.

Not a prisoner, I realize.

That's why we didn't see any banshees in the museum. Vail doesn't collect them to imprison and display.

She uses them as her guard.

The creature's hair is a fire-bitten red and her nails are inches longer than Cillian's. She sucks in a breath of delight.

Beside her, three familiar figures stand.

Women with bodies like cloaks and hair slick as oil.

The Sisters of Erinyes.

"Son of a—" Atia curses in disbelief.

They move aside to let Vail of the Arcane past.

"You're working for her?" Atia spits at the Sisters.

"No," I answer in their place.

The Sister of Erinyes, twisted as they are, are creatures of integrity. Not like the treacherous souls they inflict vengeance upon. Disloyalty and mistrust are traits they revile.

If they are here, it's because the Gods wish it.

Because they're the ones who are truly orchestrating the downfall of monsters.

"They're working for the Gods," I say to Atia. "And so is the queen."

Vail reaches to her neck and thumbs the phial of eternity that lies there.

"Which of them gave you that?" I ask bitterly.

Vail's laugh echoes through the cave like a song. "Why, the High Gods, of course," she says. "A gift, along with my wards, for purging monsters from this world."

The High Gods.

The very beings who shaped the world and set the rules for monsters not to murder or harm humans beyond repair. They cursed Atia and countless others like her. They cursed *me* for whatever transgressions I had committed in my human life, and yet they murder monsters.

Uncursed monsters.

Innocent monsters.

I should have known it wouldn't simply be the River Gods' doing.

And they haven't just given Vail the phial of eternity, but weapons in the form of the Sisters. How have they passed judgment on us, when all the while they have become killers themselves?

I should have never told them about Atia.

"Of course those hypocrites are in league with scum like you," Atia growls. "So they're just waging war on everyone now?"

"You know nothing of war!" the second Sister cries out. "Except how to cause it. That is all your kind do. You are erasers of Eternity."

"We told you this path would lead you to ruin." The first Sister is saddened as she stares at me. "It is not too late to come back to our side. Join us, once more."

I set my jaw. "I was never on your side. Not really."

The third Sister strokes a finger along a piece of gold thread that dangles from her hand. "So many chances, but the choices remain the same," she laments.

"Send word to the High Gods that I have their enemies in my dungeons," Vail drawls to the Sisters.

"We should stay," they intone. "We should subdue them. We should kill the girl. She should not exist. She should not be."

"I don't need your help," Vail snaps. "My banshee and I can deal with them. Now go. And tell the High Gods that I expect to be rewarded."

The Sisters dip their heads in unison. "We will tell. And they will reward."

The thread the third Sister held begins to fray, fibers spiraling out until they create a storm within their wake. A gray cloud in the shape of a door.

It creaks slowly open and the Sisters step through it, gliding across the floor like spirits, before it slams violently shut behind them, swallowing them like the jaws of a beast.

Only the banshee remains beside Vail now.

She stares at Cillian, who does all that he can to avoid looking back. He is quieter than I've ever known him to be.

Does the banshee sense him as he sensed her?

"Now, what shall we do while we wait?" Vail asks.

The phial around her neck grows brighter, blue, blue, blue.

Not hers to harness.

Not hers to hold.

Take it back.

Vail turns to her banshee.

"Subdue them," she orders. She runs her fingers tenderly through the banshee's long hair. "And make it painful, won't you?"

The banshee steps forward and Cillian gasps.

The sound is like a wail in itself.

It is not until I see the horrified tears in his eyes that I realize something.

"I'm begging you," Cillian says. "Don't do this."

No sooner does he utter the words than the banshee's mouth pulls open in a bloodcurdling scream.

Before I have time to process the recognition in Cillian's eyes, I see Atia collapse to her knees as the banshee's scream scrapes inside her mind. Blood pours from her nose.

Vail reaches into her cloak.

I move forward, throwing myself in front of Atia just in time.

The blade slips from Vail's fingers and through the air fast as an arrow, shooting straight into my neck.

24

ATIA

The blade sinks into Silas's neck, deep enough that only the hilt is visible.

"Separate them from the Herald. Do not let them escape," Vail snarls.

I stagger backward as her banshee advances.

Silas chokes out something, a warning perhaps.

All that comes out is a waterfall of blood.

My hand twitches with the urge to pull the dagger out and try desperately to nurse his wounds, forcing the blood back inside.

He can't die on me now.

He is immortal, I remind myself. *He will live.*

Unlike me.

I wipe the blood from my nose.

I didn't realize how much more powerful a full banshee would be compared to Cillian, especially when able to target her screams so accurately.

Vail's banshee prowls forward.

The queen herself stays back, away from danger.

Now that she has disabled Silas, our only means of escape, she'll try to stick us into one of her cages. Maybe mount our heads in trophy cases ready for the Gods.

I'll be damned if I'm going to let that happen.

I lunge with Silas's dagger, but the banshee's arm swings out, the beastly claws of her hand slashing across my shoulder as she knocks me into the bars of one of the nearby cages.

My skin chars against them.

I cry out and Silas's dagger drops from my hand.

The vampire inside howls and then darts for me.

I leap quickly out of the way, its teeth just nipping the edge of my neck.

"Opportunistic bastard!" I yell.

The vampire runs its tongue along its tooth, relishing my blood. "Nightmare eater," it says in a growl.

I snarl, just as the banshee yanks me backward.

"Nightmare eater?" she echoes.

Her voice is like shards of glass in my ear.

She opens her mouth wide and her tongue licks across my neck.

I swing my head back to smash into her face, but she catches me by the hair and pulls, holding me in place.

"Mmm," she moans, turning back to her queen. "This one contains the most rarities. She is a fear bringer. A child of nightmares. A *Nefas*."

"Is that so?" Vail asks.

Her voice trickles into the air like the first drop of rain.

The banshee keeps ahold of me, gripping my hair so fiercely that my jugular is exposed.

She runs a pointed nail across it.

If I move now, she could slice my throat.

I grit my teeth, biding my time.

"And to think," the queen continues. "I was going to put you in a tidy little case with the others. Perhaps you'd be better suited beside your companion instead?"

She rolls Silas onto his back with the tip of her foot.

I flinch at the sight of his closed eyes.

Heralds don't sleep, he'd told me.

So wake up, Silas, I want to scream. *Wake up. WAKE. UP.*

"A God's messenger alongside a nightmare," Vail says, mulling over his corpse-like form. "Such an intriguing display it would make."

I angle my elbow, readying to ram it into the banshee's ribs when—

"Please, just stop it!" Cillian yells.

Not to the queen.

The banshee's attention clips onto him.

"You of the sullied blood," she says, disgusted. "Why have you come?"

Cillian flinches at the insult, as though the banshee had struck him dead in the face. His lip quivers in anger, or perhaps sadness.

I lower my elbow, holding off on the counterattack for a moment.

"You two know each other?" I ask.

"She's my half sister," Cillian says.

"*You* are the half thing," the banshee screeches. "And you were the Mother's downfall."

I can hardly believe what I'm hearing, nor can I stomach the distraught look in Cillian's eyes, finally being faced with part of the family who abandoned him.

The banshee's grip on me does not waver as she snarls.

Even if I throw my elbow into her ribs and am able to reach Silas's blade once more, what then? How am I to kill this thing if she is kin to Cillian?

I hesitate, letting the banshee keep her grasp on me for the moment, as I puzzle out how best to end this.

"What happened to our mother?" Cillian asks. "In the Fire Kingdom, I saw some of the clan—"

"Dead," the banshee hisses, her fangs catching on her lips. "Dead by me, for the power that should have always been mine. The Mother was not worthy. She let you live. *Disgusting*, sullied thing. I tore her apart first. Burned her body in the rivers until only ash remained. The others were left as a warning to any who oppose the new Mother that is I."

"How delightful," Vail drawls from the corner of the room, her face smug.

The banshee is elated by her queen's approval.

She wants to taunt Cillian further. I feel her thirst for it.

Cillian's eyes well.

Tears for a mother he never truly knew, or who never bothered to know him. Tristan's hand slides into Cillian's and he squeezes, offering the smallest comfort.

"You really killed her?" Cillian asks.

His voice is a ghost.

"You would not understand our ways," the banshee chides. "You are not banshee. You are *nothing*."

My lips curl.

"And you talk too much," I say.

I don't hold off any longer.

Having heard enough, I finally jerk my elbow back and into her ribs, bone connecting with bone.

When the banshee drops her hold on me, I once again swing my head back. Only this time it connects, cracking against the banshee's ghostly face.

The creature wails and the high-pitched screech of it nearly stops me in my tracks, but I fight through the pain, running for the edge of the cage where I dropped Silas's dagger.

Quickly, Cillian leaps onto the banshee's back, his arms strangling around her neck to give me time.

"I won't let you kill my friends!" he shouts, just as I find Silas's blade.

"Stop!" Vail screams at Cillian, lurching forward. "Release her!"

But before she gets close enough, Tristan pounces and punches the queen right in the mouth.

"That's enough from you," he says.

Vail tumbles to the ground in a heap, just as the banshee throws Cillian off.

He slams into the wall and I hear the pop of his shoulder as Tristan runs to his side.

I hold out the blade.

The banshee seethes, her attention returning to me.

"Nightmare eater," she says. "How will your blood taste?"

"Like acid in your mouth," I spit back, ready to end her just as I did the monsters that came before.

The banshee's laugh only lasts a moment.

Before she can see for herself, a familiar set of shadows slithers around her waist, choking up her neck until they obscure even her face.

The banshee pulls back, tearing wildly at the smoke, but it slips easily between her fingers. It slides up her nose and into her eyes, turning them black as night.

With a terrified gasp—a desperate attempt at a scream that is foiled by the shadows—she falls to the floor.

Silas stands over her unconscious body. His clothes are

blood-soaked, and though there is no sign of the gaping hole in his neck, the look on his face is grave.

Deathly.

"You're supposed to be killing the banshee, not letting her kill you," he says.

I shoot him a rueful look. "What took you so long?"

Silas's jaw tightens as his eyes flick to the claw marks on my shoulder and neck.

"Are you okay?"

His voice is changed, heavy and somber.

He reaches out a hand to run down the edge of my neck. I swallow, my skin pricking at the feel of him.

Without thinking, I place my hand on top of his, tightening my fingers around his. For a moment, it almost feels like it did when I was wrapped inside his shadows, the two of us becoming one, his powers mine and my memories his.

"Are you healed?" I ask.

"I'm immortal," he responds.

He offers me a smile, but it is weakened by the baleful look in his eyes.

"I've never been stabbed before." His hand drops to his side, leaving me cold. "I've never had to test this whole invulnerability thing."

I rub at the spot where the banshee's nails pierced into my flesh. "Welcome to my world."

"Vail's guards will be coming any minute," Cillian says. "Perhaps the Sisters too, with the High Gods. We need to leave."

"No," Silas says. "The Gods would have come by now if they were planning on it. They know what we're up to and they're not going to risk giving it to us, by coming here so we can kill them. We have time. Especially now the queen is out."

Thinking of the Arcane Queen, I turn to see her still slumped on the floor.

Tristan must pack one heck of a punch.

"Atia," Silas says. "You have to kill the banshee."

I glance down to the creature at my feet. She is still alive, the curve of her chest heaving with shallow gasps.

"It's the next step in undoing your curse," Silas reminds me. "We might not get another chance like this."

"But Cillian—" I whirl around to face him.

"Do it," Cillian tells me, as he stares down at the banshee.

"Cillian, I—"

"Do it," he repeats, jaw set firm. When his eyes lift to meet mine, I know he means it. "You heard what she said, Atia. She killed my mother and any of the clan who wouldn't follow her. She tried to kill all of us just now."

The blade feels unusually heavy in my hand. "Are you certain?"

I know what it is to lose family and I don't want to inflict that grief on anyone else, especially someone I care about.

"There is no going back."

"I'm sure," Cillian says, letting out a long, resigned breath. "She isn't my family. There is nothing but evil inside of her."

I accept his words, gripping on tight to Silas's blade. "Are you ever going to give me that back?" Silas asks, gesturing to it with a teasing half smile. "It was only supposed to be a loan."

"Come and get it then," I say.

I crouch over the banshee's body.

She stirs, her eyes widening as she sees me hovering over her. She opens her mouth, a scream on the edge of her lips.

I slit her throat before it comes.

The blood splatters across the ground like acid, bubbling over the rough tiles. As with Sapphir's blood, I bring the dagger to my lips and taste the kill.

It is acrid and bitter, burning as I swallow it down, but what comes after is like the sweetest nectar.

In a heartbeat, I feel the power returning to me. *My* power. Eons of my family's magic drawing back into my blood and calling out in celebration.

It shoots through me like lightning, striking at the tips of my fingers and threatening to set me alight in magic.

The fear of each of the caged creatures around us salts the air.

I could grab on to it, knowing I could twist it into reality if I so wished.

"Did it work?" Tristan asks.

"It worked," Silas says.

His smile tells me that he can see exactly what lies beyond my eyes.

My body feels harder, like a shield, my skin glistening under the low light. The blue veins in my arms deepen, a tease of my true form. I may not be able to transform just yet, but with one more kill that power will once again be mine.

"Grab the phial," I say to Silas.

"Fools," Vail gasps out.

I look down as the queen stirs.

She clutches at her neck. I blink, horrified as I see the chain has only a shard of glass hanging from it. Vail's shirt is damp with the spilled water.

My hands shake at my sides.

There is glass littering the floor beside the Arcane Queen.

The phial has been destroyed.

No.

"It's gone," I say in a gasp. "The water from the River of Eternity is gone."

Silas presses a warm hand to my shoulder. "We'll find another way," he promises.

"What other way?" I ask, the panic rising. "Without that phial, we'll need to drink straight from the river, which will be more closely guarded than ever. That also means confronting the Gods before I have my immortality, so how—"

"Atia," Silas says, his voice firm enough to snap me back to reality. "We will find another way." He repeats it like a mantra. Like an oath. "We're going to break your curse and get your immortality back. That I swear to you."

I want so badly to relax into him at that moment, to fold my body into his and find a second of calm and comfort in the chaos. Then Vail's laughter echoes through the tomb of the dungeons.

I turn to her with a snarl. "Is something funny?"

"You'll die trying to get that water," she says. "I hope I'm around to see it."

I grit my teeth together.

"Your Highness!" A legion of voices tumble down the stairs toward us.

Vail's guards.

"Okay, *now* do we leave?" Tristan asks. "I'd rather not be killed here."

"You won't be," I assure him.

I wave my arm and my heart flickers when a gateway pulls easily open.

The world bends to it.

To me and my power.

"Gods," Tristan says. "It really did work."

I kneel down and reach into the pocket of one of the guards we'd knocked unconscious earlier, curling my hands around his keys. Across from us the trapped monsters slam their hands against the bars of their prisons, sensing the chaos to come.

Their fear is replaced quickly with sly hope.

I throw the keys into a cell, where the vampire who grazed me sits.

"Open the cages," I say to him. "Free yourselves and escape this place before it's too late. Silas, you grab the queen."

I gesture to Vail.

"If she's in league with the Gods, then she could have information we need," I say.

Silas drags her from the floor.

"What are you doing?" Tristan asks, horrified at the thought. "Atia, she's a *queen*. We can't kidnap her."

"It's not kidnapping," I say. "You heard her. She wants to be around when we find eternity." I smirk at the Arcane Queen. "Allow me to grant your wish."

Without hesitation, I walk toward my gateway.

"You're all doomed to fail," Vail hisses.

Maybe, I think. But I've been doomed my whole life, from the moment I was born and forced into hiding, to when the Gods killed my parents, to when they cursed me. It always felt as though doom followed me and I was destined for nothing else.

But not anymore.

Cillian, Tristan, and Silas are at my side, and together the four of us feel like a great barrier. Like we are unstoppable in the face of anything, even doom.

"What now?" Silas asks.

"Two down," I say, smiling at the Herald by my side.

He grips Vail's arm tightly.

We step forward, letting the gateway pull us inward.

25

ATIA

We step from the ravages of Vail's cells onto the wide balcony of a high manor that overlooks the hillside.

I reach under the plant pot that sits by the doors, housing a tiny winter tree that I planted myself during last year's festival, when the snowfall blanketed the grass with soft tufts.

The key is still hidden beneath.

I grab and then throw open the large double doors, stepping back into a room I haven't visited in months.

It's just as I left it, albeit a little dustier. The groundskeepers may keep the topiaries sharp, but they never enter the manor itself. Still, it seems to have done well on its own to keep the cobwebs away, which I'm glad for. The last thing I need right now is to jump into a bed of spiders and mothballs.

We practically throw Vail down onto a nearby chair.

"Sit," I command. "And be quiet."

She glares at me, folding her arms neatly across her chest.

"Suddenly I'm a little ashamed of the quarters we had you staying in back at the Covet," Tristan says.

It's true that the bedroom is opulent, carpeted in red and gold, with high ornate ceilings and a bed large enough to sleep four, which I once rolled over six whole times in before I fell off the edge.

A large stone fireplace sits in the corner waiting to be lit, a plush pink armchair nestled invitingly beside it.

Of all the places I've visited, human kingdoms unrestricted to my power, this is one of my favorites.

Tristan runs his fingers across the spines of the books that sit on the nearby desk. A small collection of fairy tales and ghost stories my father used to read to me.

I don't usually leave pieces of home or myself for others to find, but this is one of the few places I've ever been able to return to: a manor on the edge of the Water Kingdom. The third home to a wealthy landowner who now resides in Elphina of the Sky's Air Kingdom and only visits once a year, on the anniversary of her wife's death. It's haunted, the locals say, by her ghost. And so nobody ever steps foot inside.

I've never met her, but if I did find her ghost stumbling across the halls one night, I'd compliment her on the tapestries.

"Where are we?" Cillian asks.

"Water Kingdom," I say.

A peaceful place where its scholars study healing.

I watch Silas, who remains by the large doors, not yet stepping inside.

His eyes stay focused on the queen.

"In or out?" I say. "You'll bring in the draft."

He steps forward and closes the doors softly behind him. He draws the curtains, blocking out the sunlight.

"Why here?" he asks.

I shrug. I'm not sure why, but it's the first place I thought of as an opposition to Vail's spite and the cells that run rampant beneath her palace.

Aura of the Sea has created a land wild and free, focused on peace and healing, with wide fields that cascade over dewy hilltops and waterfalls that slip from the sky like lines of silk.

"Vail's guards won't think to look for us here," I say. "Aura enjoys harmony. Her kingdom is a sanctuary. Who wants to wage war beside glittering waterfalls and sapphire cloud pools?"

I turn to Vail.

"It's the last place they'd expect someone as bloodthirsty as you to be."

Vail smiles in place of a retort. "Think as you like, but if the guards don't come for me, the Gods will."

Not if I come for them first, a part of me thinks.

"Are you sure about this place?" Silas asks.

He moves to my side, his footsteps gliding across the carpeted floor, like the kiss of the wind in autumn, twirling leaves through the air in a dance.

My heart pounds, thinking of his hand pressed to my neck, tender against the wound.

"You feel safe here?" he asks.

I nod. "I do."

"Okay then," he says.

Just like that.

I touch a finger to my neck at the memory of him.

The wound hasn't healed. I may be able to create gateways again, but there is more of me to be restored yet. The question is, with the phial of eternity smashed, where do we start?

Silas ties the Queen of Alchemy to my favorite pink chair.

Vail of the Arcane sits pleasantly, watching us all with judging eyes as we gather in a circle around her. I'd have thought a full day locked up in this place with no food and little water would do wonders to show her she needed to loosen her tongue if she hoped to survive.

It seems I was wrong.

"When did the High Gods give you the phial?" I ask. "And why?"

Vail's lips turn to taunting, but she stays silent.

Silas leans against the fireplace, his hand fading in and out of shadow as he readies for Vail's attempts to escape or attack.

I wish he were closer and not so focused on her in this moment. If she tries to escape, we'll deal with it, but for now I want the comfort of his presence by my side.

The feel of his hands on my skin again.

I wish I was brave enough to tell him that.

"There must be other phials in the human realm," I try again, pressing the queen. "If you were given one by the Gods, who else did they give one to?"

"Perhaps all the Cousins are in league with them," Cillian suggests.

His arm is in a makeshift sling Tristan fashioned from old pillow-cases, giving his injured shoulder a much-needed rest.

"They could have given a phial to each of them, so they'd be safe to do their bidding for as long as they needed."

At this, Vail finally scoffs. "Trust you to think everyone is as insignificant as you are," she says in a low murmur.

Cillian's eyes narrow. "Excuse me?"

"You, who is not special or worthy of anything." Vail shakes her hair from her face. "Putrid little boy. You could have been glorious and instead you are this."

My mouth drops open in shock.

"You don't know him at all and you should be ashamed for thinking such things," Tristan says, stepping to Cillian's side.

"Ashamed for calling a spade a spade?" Vail is unimpressed. "For calling a nothing a nothing?"

My hand twitches by my side.

"Watch who you talk to like that."

I would slap the smile off her face if I thought it would do any good.

"I'll speak as I see fit to creatures so far beneath me," Vail says.

"Hey!" Tristan shouts, at the same time as I reach forward to punch her right in the face.

Forget whether it'll do any good. At this point I just want to see her bleed.

Silas catches my fist in the air. I'm not sure when his hands turned solid, or when he moved so swiftly from the fireplace and to my side, but his hands wrap around mine now.

"What are you doing?" I protest. "She—"

"She is not the focus right now," Silas says calmly.

He nods over to Cillian, whose jaw is clenched tightly.

"Don't rise to it," Cillian says, though I hear the shake of anger in his voice. "It's fine."

I rip my hand away from Silas, incensed. "It really isn't."

"That's not for you to decide." Cillian's voice is firmer than I've ever heard.

I swallow and unclench my fingers from their fists.

Vail cackles from her bindings, and though it makes my blood boil, I keep my focus on Cillian.

He lost the last of his family just yesterday to my hand.

He steadies himself and walks calmly from the room without another word.

"I'll go after him," Tristan announces.

"No," I say, stopping him moments from the door. "You stay. Find something in your damn books to crack through that thick skull of hers. Or smack her over the head with one, I don't care. Just do it."

Silas double-checks Vail's restraints, as though her comments were sharp enough to cut through them.

"And *you*," I say, pointing to him. "Put some of that Godly magic to use, won't you?"

Silas straightens. "What is it you'd like me to do exactly?"

"Use your imagination," I say, turning on my heel to follow Cillian out the door.

It doesn't take long to find him in the kitchen with a glass of water in hand and a look of utter irritation on his face.

I'm not sure if my presence makes it worse.

"I couldn't find any tea," Cillian tells me. He jumps up to sit on one of the countertops, feet swinging beside the sink. "Well, unless you count pure alcohol."

"Thia would."

Cillian snorts and puts his glass down with a sigh.

"I apologize," I say to him, crossing the length of the kitchen toward him. "For everything."

I've rarely spent time in this room, having never had to eat until recently, but it's grand enough to be three times the size of my bedroom back at the Covet, with marble furnishings and gold handles. I bet the widow and her wife had some fantastic parties here. It's a shame it's fallen to cobwebs.

"I didn't mean to overstep," I say to Cillian. "I suppose I'm just a little protective of you. Especially after all that's happened."

"You mean our latest banshee attack?" Cillian asks. "I don't blame you for killing her, just to clarify. She was evil and the world is better off for it."

I lean against the countertop he is perched on. "I'm still sorry."

"When we first met, you considered killing *me*," Cillian reminisces with a small smile. "How times change."

I laugh, thinking how long ago that feels now. We have come so far together, I struggle to think about a future when the four of us will go our separate ways.

Isn't that what I wanted? To get my powers back and return to how I was?

No friends.

No commitments to make me weak.

Alone again.

"Did you want to speak about it?" I ask Cillian. "What happened or what Vail just said—"

"Vail?" he says, with a roll of his eyes. "I've dealt with jerks like that my whole life. It's hardly new."

I picture her smug face.

"That doesn't make it okay."

"I never said it was. I just don't consider it a success to give someone who clearly wants a reaction exactly what they crave. Vail isn't going to suddenly see me differently because you beat her to a pulp."

I shrug. "We won't know unless we try."

Cillian snorts. "You're so sinister. I do love it," he says, nudging me with his knee. "Do you remember when we first met, I told you that banshees were vicious killers who could never accept anything about me?"

I nod. It was right after I'd sunk Silas's blade into Sapphir, killing one of the few people who knew I existed.

"My mother and sister hated me from the moment I was born," Cillian explains. "I know all monsters are different and some aren't capable of love the way you or I are, but they're capable of hate. They hated what I was." He bites the corner of his lip. "I was too different for them. I don't care about what some stranger thinks, but Vail's words were the same as those of my own family. That's what hurts."

The gnaw of anger rises in my stomach.

In a world of such wonder, who would choose to reject love, of all things?

"I don't care that my half sister is dead," he says. "Maybe I don't even care that my mother is. But somehow I still care what they thought of me. Isn't that ridiculous?"

"No," I say quickly. "It isn't."

Families have a strange hold on us, and even in death that never truly disappears.

My parents lied to me about so much, setting rules they themselves then broke. I should hate them for it, but I don't. I can't. Before this quest, I still sang the lullaby my mother sang to me and clutched my father's petal at night wishing there were others like me out there.

Wishing the Gods and the world they created wasn't so cruel.

"I have nobody," Cillian says ruefully.

"That is not true," I protest. "You have us, don't you?"

And I have you, I think.

We might not be with others exactly like us, but it doesn't mean we're alone.

Not anymore.

Family isn't only about blood, but something far more rare and sacred. A bond forged in choice.

"When this is all over, I just want to live my life," Cillian says. "Have fun and not worry so much about every little action I take and whether my mere existence is going to offend someone. Do you think killing the Gods will solve that?"

"If not, I can kill everyone else too," I suggest helpfully.

Cillian all but cackles. "What are you going to do if we can't find any more water from the River of Eternity?"

I don't want to think too much about that.

I've finally regained the parts of myself I thought were lost and the idea of not getting the rest would make every victory hollow.

"Tristan will find a way," I say with certainty.

Cillian smiles. "He always does."

I don't miss the blush that creeps onto his cheeks. "You know," I say slyly. "I saw how fiercely he tried to protect you back in Vail's dungeons. And just now, when she was shooting her mouth off."

Cillian shrugs sheepishly. "I think he's a little bit in love with you."

"Funny, since I don't recall him yelling *my* name when the banshee attacked," I say. "People contain multitudes. Tristan hasn't looked at me in a while."

Cillian swallows, trying to hide his grin. "We talk," he says. "I like his stories. Or the way he reads facts as though they could be stories. He's ..."

Cillian trails off.

"He's Tristan," I finish for him.

Cillian beams. "Exactly that."

I'm glad to see the joy on his face and to know that Tristan has met someone who will want to stroll along the lake and watch the stars with him. It wasn't something I could ever give to him, or that I imagined finding for myself.

I frown inwardly as Silas's face brightens into my mind, his suit so neatly pressed, but his hair disheveled as his gray eyes stare straight into me.

His voice in my ear.

His fingers on my neck like they could heal me with just one touch.

Silas would not cower from the monster in me and I would not be afraid to show it to him.

My true face.

As though Cillian has now become an oracle, he hops down from the counter and says: "He always tries to protect you."

"What?" I nearly stumble over the word as it falls out of my mouth so quick.

"Silas," he clarifies. "When Thia wanted to read your future alone, or when he saved you from the cold flame river. Oh and, uh, just about every single time you're in danger."

I blink, a little offended. "I'm perfectly capable of saving myself."

"Yes, but the point is that Silas always tries," Cillian says with a wink. "The way he looks at you ..."

"Like I'm getting on his last nerve?"

"Like he doesn't want to look anywhere else."

I grow silent.

The thought of Silas's eyes on me makes my heart twitch indescribably.

I have never wanted to let someone in, thinking it made me vulnerable and that caring for people was how you got hurt, but everything Silas has done is in contrast to that. Cillian is right: He has protected me and done all he can to help me regain my power when others have tried to strip it away.

I feel something for him that I have never felt before: trust. I think I could trust Silas not just with my life, but with myself. Who I truly am.

I imagine opening up to him and letting him see every part of me. Feeling his hands thread through mine as he comforts me, warm and caressing.

His fingers brushing my lips.

Suddenly the room feels hot.

"I have an idea!"

Tristan bursts into the kitchen like a stampede.

I clear my throat, brushing my hair from my face.

"Oh?" I ask, the only word I can think to utter that won't betray the shaking in my chest.

"I know how we can get information from Vail!" he practically yelps. "Thia!"

"Thia," I repeat, raising a brow.

"She's an oracle, isn't she?" he says, as though I'd forgotten. "If we want to get inside Vail's mind, then who better to do it?"

"Tristan, that's brilliant," I say, because it's true.

If Vail has secrets hidden, then he's right in thinking Thia can uncover them for us. Whether it be about the River of Eternity and any other phials in the human realm, or about the Gods themselves.

It's one step closer to getting everything I've wanted.

Soon, I will have my powers back.

Soon, Silas will have his humanity.

And together, we will fix all the wrongs done to us both.

SILAS

There is little light left in the day when Atia and Tristan announce the plan to bring the oracle to us. I didn't know what the *ah-hah!* meant when Tristan first screamed and ran from the room, but when he came back with Atia and Cillian in tow, I didn't think it was anything good.

"I want it on record that I do not agree with this," I say, as Atia pulls her boots back on and readies to open up her gateway.

"Noted," she says, hopping from the bed.

"We still can't be sure whether Thia betrayed us back in the banshee cave," I remind her. "She could betray us now."

"I told you, she's not the traitorous type!" Cillian calls over his shoulder.

He has lit the fireplace beside where Vail is still tied up and plops himself down on the rug, warming his hands over the flames. It may be winter in the Earth Kingdom, but here in the reaches of the Water Kingdom it is already spring and so the air hits with a more subtle chill.

"That's too hot," Vail says indignantly, glaring at the fire.

"Good," Tristan says. He takes a seat beside Cillian. "Let it burn away your foolishness."

Atia snorts at the scholar's gibe and turns back to me. "Be a little more trusting, won't you?" she says, sensing my growing reluctance.

She pulls her white hair from her face and into a low ponytail. Her cheeks are red with cool air and she looks—

She looks what? I think to myself.

Like someone I should not be staring at so intensely, comes my own reply.

I shake the thoughts of her cheeks and lips from my mind. Now is not the time for such things.

But when is?

Will there ever be a moment when I can give in to this craving for her?

"You could be in danger," I say.

"If Thia betrays us, I promise to kill her." Atia holds up a pinkie in a promise. "Feel better?"

"No," I say plainly. "I'm coming with you."

Atia shakes her head. "Did you forget we have a murderous queen tied up in the bedroom? You need to be here in case she tries anything. We can't just leave Tristan and Cillian alone with her."

Atia sweeps an arm over the room and her gateway tears into reality as quick as a lightning strike. As it engulfs the room in wisps, I see Thia's graveyard on the other side. I know I have nothing left to counter with but even so, when she moves toward it, my arm jerks out on instinct.

"*Atia*," I say, clutching firmly on to her wrist, stopping her in place.

I think about letting go. I know that I *should* let go and she should go to Thia and ask for her help, but I can't shake the idea that she's going to get hurt if I let her out of my sight. She may have some of her abilities back, but some is not all, and the wounds that banshee left on her neck, on her shoulder and arms, are still so visible.

I was not fast enough to protect her then.

I won't make that mistake twice.

"Just—" I pause, trying to think of exactly what I wish to say to her among the many things. "Just be careful," I say.

Atia softens. "I'll be back in seconds," she promises, untangling my hand slowly from her. "Just close your eyes and count to ten."

Atia slips into the gateway and it swallows her whole in response, folding in behind her like the pages of a book closing.

More than ten seconds pass. Minutes. Enough so that I begin pacing the length of the room, back and forth, wondering how long I need to wait before I can go after her.

"Do you think she got herself killed?" Vail asks in a silky drawl.

When I turn to her, she smirks and straightens in her chair, ever the royal posture.

"I promise that if someone brings me her head to stuff into one of my museums, I won't charge you admission for the viewing."

"Keep talking," I say. "The next binding will go over your mouth and I'll make you listen to Tristan read out loud from the dustiest book he can find."

Vail's lips purse together in a glare.

"That's the worst form of torture you could think of?" Cillian asks in disbelief.

"It would work on me."

From the rug, Tristan casts me a glare. "You're just as pleasant as Atia. You two are bad influences on each other."

And Atia should have been back by now so we could be bad influences together.

I glance at the grandfather clock in the corner of the room.

Six minutes.

That is more than enough time to kidnap an oracle, I decide.

My body is already half engulfed in shadow as I prepare to head to the Fire Kingdom myself, when the room cleaves in two.

Atia emerges from her gateway with her arms linked through Thia's like they've just come back from a tavern. I eye the oracle, dressed in a black nightgown with fuzzy purple slippers and a look of utter devilishness as she clasps onto her mirror.

"Could she not get dressed first?" I ask, as Atia unlinks her arm from Thia's and points over to Vail.

"As though anyone would look away from me regardless," Thia says, giving me a wry smile. "Is that her?"

Atia nods.

"*Oh*," Thia says. "You weren't joking."

Atia shakes her head. "Told you."

"Wow," Thia says, sucking her teeth in a wince.

"I know."

"Her aura is all—" Thia swoops her hands around in a jumble.

"That'll be the murders," Atia says.

Thia kicks off her slippers and jumps onto the nearby bed. "You should've let me bring the tea," she scolds. "I'm going to need it for this one."

Vail eyes the pair of them in a mixture of disdain and curiosity. Two monstrous women ready to inflict unknowns upon her mind.

I hadn't noticed it before, having been too focused on finding the answers to my own past and future, but I see now how the oracle and Atia seem at home with each other.

Did it happen when Thia showed her glimpses of her destiny? Or was it before that, when the oracle first opened the door and invited us in to plot murder with unblinking eyes?

Thia is not yet a friend, but I can see in Atia her desire for the oracle to be just that, somewhere down the line.

The two of them together would cause chaos in the world.

I'd kind of like to see it.

"So how will you pay for my services?" Thia asks.

"The service is the payment," Atia informs her. She gestures back over to Vail and wiggles her eyebrows. "Ever wanted to dine like royalty?"

Thia hums a laugh.

"What is the meaning of this?" Vail hisses.

It's then that Cillian pulls himself up from the rug and stokes the fire casually. "Pythia is an oracle," he says. "And she's going to show us all the dirty little secrets in your mind."

Vail blanches, the fury a tangible musk that rolls from her. "You would dare to summon an oracle into my mind?" the queen seethes. "Me, of holy birth and divine origin?"

"You, of utter crap," Cillian clarifies.

"Your mind will be a dark and awful place for us to ask the oracle to go," Tristan says, crossing his arms over his chest. "But I'm sure she'll manage."

Thia shrugs. "I've had worse."

She pulls herself from the bed in a long stretch, her arms high in the air. I hear the crack of her back.

"Besides," she says. "I've always wanted to taste a queen. Good thing I skipped lunch."

Vail swallows and for the first time her look of menace is replaced with one of dread I'm glad to see.

She must have felt so invincible, untouchable under her bargain with the Gods, with water from the River of Eternity hanging around her neck.

Now she knows better.

Vail struggles against the ropes that bind her for the first time, wrenching and tugging as if they will snap with her will.

"Enough of this madness!" she says. "Unhand me."

"Our hands are nowhere near you," Atia points out. "Now be a good little queen and sit still."

As Thia approaches Vail, I move to Atia's side. There is a warmth still radiating from her, left over from the jump between kingdoms. The residue of her gateway is like static. I can feel it jumping from her skin to mine.

Thia holds up her mirror high enough for us to be able to see what will be reflected in it.

Her other hand, she places on top of Vail's.

"Do not dare!"

The queen spits in her face.

Still, Thia doesn't blink.

"Unpleasant," she says, wiping the queen's saliva from her cheek and onto the rug. "If you're quite finished with that behavior, let's begin."

She places her hand back over Vail's, though this time her nails dig in deep to the queen's flesh. Vail cries out, but Thia keeps her hold strong.

The mirror shakes.

"That's it," Thia says, closing her eyes as Vail's teeth grit together. "Let me see what's hiding in there."

Vail gasps out in horror and on Thia's mirror three figures materialize. At least, I think they are figures. They appear more as smudges.

The first is made of utter darkness, the second of pure light, and the third a perfect mix of the two in blinding gray.

Three *Gods*, I realize then. The High Gods—Skotadi, Imera, and Isorropía—who created all things and cursed me to my fate.

"This we give you to undo a grave mistake," they say in unison.

Their voices are the sound of music and melancholy.

"You must kill as many monsters as you can. Destroy them before they destroy us."

"Is it the only one?" Vail asks now, as though she is reliving the memory.

She thumbs her neck keenly, where the phial would have been.

"There is no more," the smudged images of the Gods say. "There can be no more. For the river is vengeful. For eternity is lost to us."

"It is the last then," Vail confirms, her voice high in glee. "I am your chosen one."

"Yes, the last," the High Gods repeat. "It is the last."

Atia's face is crestfallen and I feel the disappointment in my own bones. My shoulders slacken.

If there really is no more water from the River of Eternity in the human realm, the only place we can find any is in Oksenya and what little remains there.

We will have to invade the world of Gods to get the last part of Atia's cure, putting her in danger. She'll have no immortality to guard against the Gods when we face them.

Not to mention that I don't even know how to get into Oksenya. I thought the Gods would chase us themselves when they figured out what we were up to, and we wouldn't have to invade Oksenya to get what we needed.

But now I would tear the blessed realm apart to help Atia break her curse.

If only I knew how.

"Stop," the queen begs, shaking under Thia's grip.

The mirror cracks, just as it did with me, the images of Gods too much for it to bear.

Thia releases her hold on Vail, and as soon as she does, the mirror crumbles to ash.

"Damn," Thia swears. "I'm going to need a new one of those." She looks down to the remnants of the mirror. "Remind me to send you a bill for that."

"I'll work on it after we destroy the Gods," Atia says.

"You cannot destroy the Gods," Vail warns. Her eyes flutter as she struggles to hold on to consciousness.

Thia must have delved awfully deep to extract that memory from an unwilling host and it seems to have taken a lot out of the Queen of Alchemy.

"You will bring chaos to us all," Vail warns.

"Good," Atia says. "I fully planned on chaos."

Vail gasps out one last time before her head drops to unconsciousness.

"I consider that a success," Thia says. Her eyes are darker, filled black from feeding on Vail's memories.

"You look extra creepy now," Cillian informs her. "Just so you know."

Thia grins, glad for it.

"A Nefas, a Herald, and a queen in such a short space of time," she says. She pats her stomach. "I'm so full from all your treats."

"Come with us next," Atia offers. "To Oksenya."

"Join you in waging a deadly war against the Gods and possibly getting yourselves killed?" Thia slips her fuzzy purple slippers back on. "No thank you."

"We could use your help," Atia says.

"I'll send you good thoughts."

"We'll need them," Tristan pipes up with a sigh.

When did he become the pessimist among us?

"Are you sure?" Atia asks the oracle again.

"I'm more about intrigue and evil plotting than all-out war," Thia says simply. "But I'll do this for a favor: I'll keep the queen with me in the Fire Kingdom for a few days. Stop her from running to her guards or the Gods."

"Just a few days?" I ask.

"I'm an oracle, not a hotel," she says. "I'll harbor your kidnapped queen for as long as I can, but she is still a *queen*. I can't keep one of the five Cousins my prisoner forever."

"Can't you just kill her then?" Atia offers.

"No," Thia says, though the look on her face tells me she's tempted after the spitting. "But if I don't hear from you, I'll hand her over to her Cousin. Balthier of the Ash would love to hear about how she made a pact with the Gods that excluded the rest of them. And how she was keeping waters of eternity all for herself. It never quite sat right with Balthier how Vail murdered her way to the throne. The old king was his favorite uncle, after all."

Thia's wagging eyebrows are nothing short of menacing.

I'm glad for the favor, but that still leaves us having to find a way to get into Oksenya, since the Gods clearly aren't going to come to us.

Atia helps Thia lift the still unconscious Vail from the chair, swaying a little under her weight. She laughs at something the oracle says and then waves her arm to open a gateway to the Fire Kingdom.

She is so at home in this world. She belongs to it in a way I've never felt I have. Atia is too much of a wonder to ever stay normal.

When this is all over, where does that leave us?

Will we still work in each other's worlds?

Would she even want us to?

I roll my shoulders back, but the thoughts stay with me.

Everything I ever thought I wanted, but no Atia.

"Do me a favor," Thia says as she steps toward Atia's gateway, lugging Vail like a case. "Cause as much chaos as you can when you find the Gods."

Atia smirks. "That I can promise."

"And you," Thia says, looking back to give me a reluctant smile. "Look after her, won't you?"

I swallow the lump in my throat as I nod.

That I can promise, I echo in my mind.

Until the end.

27

ATIA

Night falls like a blanket over the manor once Thia leaves with the Arcane Queen.

Cillian and Tristan are tucked away into the bed like little treasures for safekeeping, but I sit awake on the small chair by the fireplace listening to the crackles of the flames while Silas stays by the window like a guard.

Every now and again, when the wind shifts and the stars blink, he twitches, as though expecting an attack.

"Vail is gone," I remind him. "You can relax now."

My voice is heavy with night.

"Not with the Gods still out there," Silas says. The shadows dance around his fingers in anticipation. "I won't be caught off guard again."

"You said so yourself, they won't risk exposing themselves to us now," I remind him. "You really don't ever relax, do you?"

I pull myself up from the armchair. The power inside me buzzes with restlessness after so long away.

"Come on."

I hold out a hand and Silas eyes it suspiciously.

"Do you want money for food?" he asks.

"No, Herald, I want you to come with me."

When Silas doesn't move, I sigh.

"I'm getting itchy feet just sitting here," I say. "I'm not used to not being on the move. Especially at night."

For years, I've wandered the streets when the moon descends and the time spent without my power left me feeling chained. Too long spent at the mercy of humanity, without my own means for escape. Now that I have that escape back, that notion of exploration returning to my veins, I can hardly ignore it to wait until sunrise.

"Just come with me, won't you?" I ask. "Let *me* take *you* somewhere for once."

Silas slips his hand into mine and I blink, surprised at how little convincing he needed.

"Okay," he says.

That word again, so simple and trusting.

I wave a hand over the balcony doors and they split open in a seam down the middle, the ripples of a world beyond echoing through them.

Silas's hand grips tighter on to mine and he nods back over to Tristan and Cillian, sound asleep in bed. "What if something happens to them while we're gone?"

"We're not going far," I promise. "Wonders are never far."

My gateway takes Silas to the edge of the manor grounds, a small clifftop that overlooks the ocean below. It's cold out, air fogging from my lips the moment our feet meet the grass.

"Quite the view," Silas says, looking down at the chasm of water below.

"Not there," I say. I lift a finger to his chin. "Look up."

When he does, his eyes shift, mirroring the crystal waters that cascade above us. The sky waterfalls of Aura's kingdom decorate much of the land, weaving through the clouds, but I've always found the view of the one by the manor to be the best. The water is a seaweed green, like a glimpse of the forest falling from the sky.

It's a thing Silas can't ever have seen, confined to the Earth Kingdom before our quest. So much power in his hands and yet he has never been able to properly use it. To hold the chance of new worlds at his fingers and be forced to walk in just one must be something grave.

Freedom. It's what I ached for when my parents hid me away out of fear for our lives, and it must have been all he's ached for since becoming what he is.

The chance for adventure.

"It's beautiful," he says.

I smile. "Thought you might like it."

Silas pauses and it's then I realize that our hands are still entwined, his fingers laced so carefully through mine.

He is a magnet pulling me in, and I don't try to fight it any longer.

Never once did I think I could meet someone who would understand me so well, taking the good with the bad and not acting like either of them was a burden.

"Why did you bring me here?" Silas asks, suddenly serious.

"Because we're about to kill a God," I answer honestly. "And if that goes wrong, if anything happens to us, then you may never get another chance to see something like this again."

I remember what he said back in the Alchemy Kingdom about there being two kinds of grief: the grief of losing and the grief of never having had something to begin with. I could see his own mourning, feel it urgently against my own. I have lost so much, but Silas has never been given anything to lose. Or if he has, he can't remember it.

"I don't want you to grieve for those things you never had," I tell him now.

Silas breaks his hand from mine to bring it softly to my cheek.

My name is a mere breath on his lips, a quiet wish on a clifftop in the middle of nowhere.

My father's petal hums inside my pocket. I've been carrying it with me since I left the Earth Kingdom, tucked safely away by my breast. Only now can I feel it pulsing alongside my heart.

It jars me with my every breath. A reminder of what I am and what I've lost. Of years spent alone, thinking that was the only way to be safe. This entire journey started with me wanting that safety back: the comfort of knowing I can't just be cut down by anyone. Of attacking before I'm attacked.

I thought I'd turned hollow after my parents' deaths, but here I am on a cliff's edge all but shaking with the notion of Silas's touch. Of comfort and longing for someone else to see me outside of these shadows.

I think back to Tristan and Cillian, tucked away in their bed. Friends, who are risking their lives for me. They have put such a deep trust in me that I worry I won't be worthy of it. I broke my parents' trust the day they died by sneaking out and endangering all our lives.

It's something I've never been able to make up for.

I can't lose Tristan and Cillian.

I can't lose Silas.

I don't want to be alone anymore.

When this is all over, I want us to be together, no matter what.

"Your grief rolls off you in waves," Silas says to me, as though he can truly sense it. *See it.*

Perhaps he can.

"I think that's why the river of cold flame affected you so much," he says. "You're so haunted by your past, Atia. You let it drown you."

I know he's right, but it's hard to move on when I've never felt like I have something to move toward until now.

"You're not to blame for what happened to your parents," he says. "You must realize by now that it was inevitable. The Gods wanted them dead, as they seem to want all monsters dead. There was nothing you could have done."

Deep down, I know he is right, but I don't know how to separate my grief from my guilt. They have been intertwined for so long.

"You must have faith in who you are today and not think so much of who you were or who you think you need to be," Silas says.

He doesn't understand that it's who I am that scares me.

"There's a darkness in me, Silas," I warn him. "If you want to be human at the end of this, you should know that. It's been inside me since my parents died and I'm not sure I'll ever be able to escape it. I don't know what I've become without them. You saw what I did to that man who attacked Tristan. The Gods cursed me for it."

Silas doesn't break my stare, brushing the hair from my eyes so tenderly I find it suddenly impossible to imagine he has ever been so much as touched by death.

"You're not to blame for that either," he says firmly. "Believe me, you're not. The curse isn't your fault."

"There is a darkness in me," I repeat.

"Look around, Atia," Silas says, gesturing to the waterfall, to the sky. "Where there is darkness, there are also stars."

The moment he kisses me feels exactly like stepping into a gateway.

A new world, a new horizon, a new sensation inside my heart.

His lips press gently against mine, a taste of each other so delicate that I swallow when he pulls away, my craving running too deep for such softness.

Thankfully the break only lasts seconds, and then he is against me again, this time hungrier. His hands slip to my lower back, making me shiver.

He presses me closer to him and yet it is not close enough still.

Beside us, the waterfall cascades down, washing the sins from the sky as we try desperately to ignore the sins inside each other. The petal in my pocket thrums, thundering against my quaking heart.

I ignore it.

I push my hand under his shirt and let the world fall away until there is only him, only us, and the solace we find in each other.

28

SILAS

When the new day dawns, I'm joined by the sound of seabirds, leaping in and out of the waterfalls to bathe themselves.

Beside me, Atia stirs but does not wake. She has been asleep for only a handful of hours, gently stirred to dreams just as night began to grow husky with the promise of day.

I don't want to wake her to coax her back inside the manor. She seems at peace for the first time since we met, as though last night lifted a weight from her that she'd been struggling to bear for years.

It would be one of the worst things I could do, to disturb that rare peace.

One of.

Though by far not the worst I have done to her.

This is all your fault, I think to myself. *You threw her into this chaos.*

"Atia!" Cillian's voice tumbles up and over the grassy hills toward us.

I see a flash of his red hair as he pants, waving his hands erratically.

Beside me, Atia's eyes snap open.

"I've been looking for you everywhere," Cillian says, finally reaching us. His hands fly to his knees as he draws in a series of sharp gasps. "You have to come quick!"

"What happened?" Atia stands to attention, like a soldier in battle, all sign of sleep erased brutally from her face. "Was there an attack? Is Tristan okay?"

"He's better than okay," Cillian says. "He found something!"

"Found what?" I ask.

Cillian smiles. "He found the Gods."

Atia regards the pile of books across her once bed with a frown. In the middle of them, the scholar sits cross-legged. He grins when we enter and holds up a volume, pointing to a line in the center of the page.

"I found it!" he exclaims. "Utter genius, if I do say so myself. I told you, didn't I? I said that knowledge is our greatest weapon and this is the proof."

Atia frowns at him. "That's what you two were doing all night?" she asks with a raised brow, staring between him and Cillian. "*Reading?*"

"Why?" Tristan says. A pair of glasses is perched on the edge of his nose as he looks between us. "What were you two doing?"

Atia blinks and then quickly picks up one of the books Tristan had long since discarded.

"Anything about me in here?" she asks brazenly.

"No," Tristan says. "You elude the written word. Now *focus*."

Atia salutes. "What did you find in your research?"

"The entrance to Oksenya," he says proudly.

At this, Atia's attention is piqued, as is mine. We both walk forward, crowding around Tristan's book to see his discovery.

"It doesn't mention it by name," he says. "But you all kept

calling it the blessed realm and right here it talks about a land of holiness where all things find rest. Now, that vampire Sapphir—awful person, truly—said how she didn't care about *traveling* there. Then the Sisters of Erinyes—again, just awful women—"

"Tristan!" Atia exclaims, trying to make sense of the text in front of us. It all looks like gibberish to me. "Focus, remember?"

"Oh, right," he says sheepishly. "Sorry. Well, they mentioned boats finding port in forbidden places and it all got me thinking: Oksenya is guarded by rivers. Now if there's ports, surely there's boats."

"What kind of boats?" I ask, unsure.

"One of *your* boats," Tristan says. "The ones you use to ferry souls to the other side."

"The After and the Never," I correct.

"Right!" Tristan says, clicking his fingers.

He holds up his book again, a volume I can see titled *Beyond Our World and into Theirs: An Exploration of the Realms' Gods and Monsters.*

"It talks about Firia's river being the gateway into Oksenya that only the worthy can cross, but then it says right here how the Gods' messengers—that's you, Silas—transport lost souls to the After or the Never via the River of Death. If all the rivers surround Oksenya, it means they're all connected. So if we hop a boat to the River of Death, it'll take us right to the unguarded River of Eternity, so you can drink without needing to try and go inside Oksenya. Then, once you're immortal, you can pick a River God to kill."

"River *Gods*," Atia says quickly. "One for me and one for Silas too."

I'd almost forgotten that was the deal Atia and I struck when we first agreed to help each other. I help her break her curse if she helps me kill the God of Forgetting and regain my human memories.

The life I had before her.

"So now Silas just needs to call his death boat—"

"It's not called a death boat," I interrupt.

Tristan ignores me. "—and we can be off. Personally, I think it'd probably be best to kill the God that guards the River of Death. If he created Heralds, Silas could use their connection to throw him off balance. What's his name again?"

Atia's jaw clenches, but she stays silent.

"Thentos," I say, feeling her anger within me.

I want her to have that chance more than anything. She deserves the peace it will give her to finally avenge her family.

"I could actually kill him," Atia says.

She frowns down at her hands, as if his blood is already there and she can't decide how to wash it off.

"Isn't that a good thing?" Tristan asks. "You kill Thentos and this is all over."

He does not realize what this God means to her.

She has only ever told me about that night.

Atia ignores Tristan and looks up at me.

"Do you really believe that?" Atia's voice is tight. There is torment there, but she swallows it down. "Is that what's best for the realms, to kill a couple of River Gods, break both our curses, and flee?"

"No," I say honestly. "I don't think it is."

My voice is hoarse.

The realm Tristan and even Cillian have called home—that I

want to explore and that Atia has shown me the wonders of—will be chipped away by deceit and evil if we allow the High Gods to continue stealing and punishing monsters, changing the rules whenever they please. Their alliance with Vail has proven that.

The High Gods are the ones who must be destroyed for the good of the world.

"You told me once that the Gods would never rest, and that as long as they were alive, we would never have control over our own destinies," I say.

I understand now that Atia was right.

She steels her face. "I also told you that the only way to change things was to burn their house down."

"So let's burn it down," I tell her. "Together."

Atia eyes me, like she can't be sure whether I'm being serious or not.

Killing all three of the High Gods is a far bigger task than simply breaking a curse or two.

"That's if you believe we can really do it," I add.

"I believe in us," Atia says, not missing a beat. "And I trust you."

I do not have the words to respond to that. I want to pull her in close to me as I did last night and let her find all the comfort she needs in me.

Atia has come so far. In the face of getting everything she wants, she is willing to go the extra mile and risk death at the hands of the High Gods to protect the realms.

She trusts in me, I think, the thought hitting me like a fist, strong enough to knock me off-kilter. *Will she come to regret it?*

"To be clear," Cillian says, looking between us. "We're no longer talking about sneaking in to break a curse or two, but about stealing the powers of River Gods to then go on to kill the three divine beings who created us? All to save the world's monsters?"

Atia and I both nod.

"You gave me the impression neither of you were noble," Cillian says with a glare. "I feel very lied to."

"Does that mean you're in?" Atia asks, surprised.

"What, like I'm going to let you have all the glory?" Cillian scoffs.

"You know I'm not going to miss out on adventure either," Tristan says, before Atia can ask.

He does not bother to look up from his books.

"It's actually a war," I correct. "Just so we're clear."

"Right," Tristan says. "But now we have a plan. So is it possible to divert your boat?"

"Theoretically yes," I say. "But in order to call a boat I need a lost soul, which we don't have. If we go to find one, there will be a Herald there. The Gods know I'm working with Atia and I wouldn't be surprised if they assign multiple Heralds to each soul. Any power I have, they do too. We can't risk them getting the upper hand.

"Besides, I only take souls to the *entrance* of the River of Death, which we call the sorting zone," I continue. "I pay the guide a coin for safe passage, and from there he takes them across. Heralds aren't allowed to go farther."

"So what you're saying is that the best way to intercept one of these boats is to go to this sorting zone and commandeer one from the guide?" Atia asks.

"That's not exactly what I said—"

"A trip to Herald headquarters to steal a death boat and invade the blessed realm of the Gods?" Cillian muses. "Oh, I am *so* in."

I touch a finger to my temple, wondering just what in the Never I have started.

"Okay," Atia says. She claps her hands together, a deadly smile painted onto her lips. "So how do we get into the sorting zone?"

29

ATIA

Apparently, a Herald cannot simply use their shadow wings to get into the sorting zone, instead there is a secret entrance to what Silas likes to call the Library of Souls.

"The Library of Souls," he says, voice as if we were sitting around a campfire with a torchlight on his face. "Is a very sacred place. It's where we store every memory, every thought of the dead for safekeeping in case the Gods need it. Heralds go here after we hand souls over to the guide."

We ascend the steps of a very human library.

It is a small and unassuming place, like most of the Earth Kingdom it resides in. Where Alchemy has buildings that look like starlight and Water has waterfalls dripping from the sky, the Earth Kingdom has simplicity. Buildings encased in ivy and flower petals, like this one.

"The Library of Souls also serves as an entrance for Heralds who do not have lost souls but need to access the sorting zone for whatever reason," Silas continues.

He pushes open the single stone door leading into the building, which can't be any bigger than the average house, or the downstairs of the Covet tavern.

"Reasons like the weekly staff meeting?" I offer.

I can't help but find Silas's seriousness endearing. The way his jaw sets hard and his brow pinches together.

I press my lips together in the memory of his kiss.

I wish I'd had the time to ask him what it meant for us going forward. Or to speak to Tristan and Cillian about it and see what they thought it could mean.

I wish that I could kiss him again, right here and now.

"Reasons like receiving divine messages," Silas continues. "Or having to combine the files of deceased families, or speak to other Heralds about related deaths in the area to establish a pattern and whether or not it is related to the supernatural or the natural."

"That sounds like a staff meeting to me," I say with a shrug.

Cillian snorts and it echoes in the vast emptiness of the small room we have stepped into.

There is a single counter, with a largely mustached man asleep on a wooden chair behind it, his glasses having slipped to perch on the very tip of his nose.

Books line the countertop and every wall, going up and over the single window and curving to the rounds of the door we stepped through. There is not a space for bricks or lantern lights on any wall, where instead there could be chapters. Two rocking chairs sit in the center of the room, piles of ink-wet paper and quills at their feet.

New stories, ready to be born.

"So this is the Library of Souls?" Tristan asks.

"No," Silas says. "This is a library that contains the entrance to the Library of Souls."

"That's convoluted," I say.

"That's the Gods for you."

"There must be more books cramped into this room than into the entirety of any of Vail's libraries combined," Tristan says in wonder. "How do they all fit?"

He takes a step closer, inspecting a shelf of books by the door handle.

"It's almost as if they merge together. You can only really differentiate one from the other when you squint up close."

"It's called magic," Silas says. "Don't act like a traveler."

"Are these all books on monsters then?" Tristan asks.

"No." Silas points to a volume just above Tristan's head. "That one's on potatoes."

I stroke my stomach. "Don't tease me," I say. "It's been an age since we've eaten."

"It's been an hour," Silas corrects.

"Exactly."

The warm raisin buns we'd had before coming here did not suffice.

"Not that I'm not enamored by the wonder in Tristan's eyes," Cillian says, lowering his voice to a whisper. "But are you sure we're in the right library?"

At this, the man behind the counter awakens. "Do you have your library card?" he mutters drowsily.

Silas points to his tie pin. "I do."

"Good," the man says gruffly.

He closes his eyes once more and the sound of snoring quickly fills the room again.

"Wow," I say. "Heightened security measures."

Silas laughs. "Nobody but a Herald can sense the entrance anyway."

"So where is the entrance?"

"In a book," Silas says, as though it's obvious. He looks to Tristan. "Like the scholar once said, their stories transport us."

"I didn't mean it quite so literally," Tristan says. "But I'm marveled by the reality. Do all of the Heralds in the world come through here?"

Silas runs his fingers along the spines of the books nearest to the door, searching for the right volume.

"There are different libraries for Heralds of different territories," he explains. "Each one a closely guarded secret. But this is how most of the Earth Kingdom's Heralds get in without a lost soul."

He pauses, his hand lingering on one volume before he sighs and then moves on. Not the right one after all.

"Can we help look?" I ask. "What's the book called?"

"Something new each time," Silas says, sounding frustrated with the odd rules of our world. "I'll know it when I feel it. It won't take long."

"What if another Herald comes in here in the meantime?" I ask.

"Don't let them know we're planning treason."

I elbow him in the ribs and Silas jolts, a teasing smile on his lips. My heart flutters at the sight of it. I can't help myself. I can still taste him, feel his hands against my back and pulling me into him. *It wasn't enough.* I ache to have him touch me again.

I clear my throat before my cheeks start to blush and begin scouring the bookcases.

Despite Silas's insistence that only a Herald can find the entrance, I study each line of books carefully, searching for something ghostly among their colored spines.

I'm halfway across the room when I feel my father's petal begin to hum inside my chest pocket. At first I mistake it for my pounding heart, but the vibrations become clear, pushing against my chest just as they did when Silas kissed me.

I move back a step, away from the bookcase and the humming stops. I step closer again and it resumes. Quickly, I run my hands along the books, palm flat across them all until I hit one volume and the humming intensifies so much it feels like my chest is being punched.

I pull the volume from its shelf, my hands shaking.

It is plain black, a single word inscribed in gold along its spine, mirrored in equally small font on the cover.

Baíno.

To enter.

"It's this one," I say.

Silas frowns from across the room. "You can't know that."

But I do.

My father's petal practically screams out to me.

Here here HERE.

Silas steps to my side, taking the book from my hands. The petal quiets the moment it's removed from my grasp.

Silas blinks and the frown deepens on his boyish face.

"You're right," he says. "How could you possibly know that?"

"With this."

I take the petal from my pocket, holding it out for the three of them to see.

"This belonged to my father," I explain. "It guided me to it."

"A petal guided you to the entrance?" Tristan asks. "Is that... a normal thing for petals to do in this world?"

"No it isn't," Silas says, eyeing the petal. "That looks familiar."

"Familiar how?" I ask.

"It seems to be the same kind of flower petal that decorates our quills," he says. "It was your father's?"

I nod and close the petal in my palm. "Is it possible my father has been to the Library of Souls before? Could the petal be carrying the memory of that?"

"It's possible," Silas says, albeit skeptically. "I don't know why he'd have a reason to, or how he'd have gotten that petal, but there's a lot we don't know and there's only one way for us to get answers."

He lays the book gently onto the floor at our feet.

"The High Gods and their lower children guide me here," Silas intones.

Immediately the pages begin to flicker, the book searching itself for what we need. Eventually it comes to a stop on a completely black page with the outline of a simple white door in its center. The book pauses for a moment and then shudders, a blinding white light exploding from it.

A door bursts from its fragile pages.

"Follow me," Silas says.

He pushes the door open and we step inside.

The Library of Souls is not a library at all, but a filing room. It is rows of cabinets and drawers, higher than I can even see, pulling across the room in an endless line. It is immeasurable and my vision blurs long before I can even begin to see where it might end.

We move forward and as we do the blue cabinets seem to move along with us. They ripple like the waves of the sea against a backdrop of unending black.

"What is this place?" I ask.

"Eternity," a voice whispers.

My eyes widen as from somewhere beside us, I hear a quiet laugh. A giggle that sets my toes on edge. From one of the drawers, a creature slinks. Gray-limbed with eight spindly fingers across each hand, gripping over the drawer's edge to peek out at us.

It licks its thin lips.

"Young boy of old worlds," the creature says. "You have brought some very special lost things."

30

ATIA

I leap forward to slice the creature in two before it can sound the alarm and warn the others of our presence, but a pair of firm hands grabs me by the waist, pulling me backward.

"Let go!" I say against Silas's grip. "We have to deal with it."

"He's harmless," Silas says.

His breath is hot against my ear. I ignore the way his heart drums against my back, pounding through me.

"He'll be more harmless when he's dead," I say.

I grit my teeth hard and the creature in front of me slinks farther from the drawers. It straightens up its bow tie and then, rather indignantly, says, "I have been dead for quite a while already, thank you."

I soften against Silas's grip and he lets go, sensing the fight leaving me.

"Dead?" I ask.

"All things here are dead," the creature says. "Maybe even you."

I point my dagger at it. "Don't threaten me."

"Atia." Silas blows out a breath, pushing his tousled hair from his face. "This is the Keeper of Files. And as I said, he's harmless."

"Keeper of *all* these files?" Tristan asks, his eyes roaming the great expanse of the room.

The creature nods.

"You must really like reading," Cillian says. He nudges Tristan. "Birds of a feather, aye?"

The Keeper of Files hesitates, his jaw pulsing in a frown. "I don't like birds. They shit on everything."

"Truer words never spoken," I say. "Now don't mind us, we're just going to go about our business."

The Keeper of Files sidesteps, his tiny frame barely reaching my hips but blocking my path all the same.

"What are you?" he asks me curiously.

"A Nefas," I say, my eyebrows raised in a challenge.

"Odd." He sniffs the air. "You smell funny for a Nefas."

I stiffen at the insult.

"Though not as bad as that human." The Keeper of Files points to Tristan and then whispers, "A very bland scent to that one."

Beside me, Silas does not even try to contain his snort.

"Why are you pretending to be human? That skin isn't your true one," the Keeper of Files says, regarding me like a curious thing.

An experiment, or a trophy akin to the ones in Vail's museum.

"It's a long story," Silas says. "Are you going to tell anyone we're here?"

"Oh," the Keeper says. He looks from Silas to me, then back to Silas again. "She's *that* Nefas." He sniffs the air around me again. "Yes, yes, you do smell rather cursed."

I cross my arms over my chest indignantly. "I smell just fine."

I showered before we left the manor and even used some lavender oils I'd found left under the sink, either from the widow or her late wife.

"I say," the Keeper yelps out. "There's a banshee here too!" He seems far more delighted by Cillian than by me. "What eclectic company you've been keeping! What else are you collecting?"

He peers behind us, to see if any other monsters have followed.

"And what exactly are you?" I ask, eyeing him with the same look of morbid curiosity.

"Very old," the Keeper says. "And always very tired."

Welcome to the club, I almost say. *Having people try to kill you every day is equally as exhausting.*

"Can you help us?" I ask instead.

"Probably not," the Keeper says. "But ask me anyway."

"We're looking for a boat to ferry us to the River of Death so we can kill a River God, gain entrance into Oksenya, and wage a battle against the High Gods. Can you help with that?"

"Atia!" Silas's eyes grow wide.

The Keeper of Files only blinks, unoffended by the idea of murder or treason against the High Gods.

"They don't keep the boats here," he says. "But I know where you can find one."

The Keeper slips open the door from the Library of Souls and scurries out. We wait only moments before his head slicks back through and he waves for us to follow, signaling the path is clear.

The first step I take from the so-called library and into the halls of death is like stepping from a cliff's edge and falling, spinning down to the rocky doom below.

My heart leaps into my chest as my feet tap against the solid floor. Marble white, the walls a forest of moss and molding red berries.

"It's that way," the Keeper says, pointing a spindly finger toward a throng of doors all jammed together like a bundle of overripe fruit. "The purple one."

"Gods," Tristan says in awe. "This is what death looks like?"

"This is what a corridor looks like," Silas says. "And it changes. No doubt someone just collected the soul of a gardener or something. Blink and it'll go another way."

He isn't exaggerating. In a moment the walls shift and ripple, the halls re-forming themselves. Beneath my feet the floor jolts and suddenly I am standing on polished wood, the maze of walls around us as black as the night sky, with tiny stars embedded into each door.

The Keeper sighs, searching the hallway. He points again.

"There," he says, spotting the purple door from earlier. He walks quicker, hurrying toward it before the hall reshapes itself to the whim of the next lost soul.

It is then that the hallway fills with Heralds.

Black suits, black ties, and gold winged tie pins that mirror the world back to them. They are tall and short, thin and curvaceous, dark-skinned, light-skinned, freckled, and scarred. Yet they all look the same.

Their hair, whatever the shade or texture, is clipped above their ears. Their faces are an unchanging blanket of seriousness, drawing their mouths to straight lines. And their skin, no matter the color, is muted and tinged gray. The suit falls the same on each of them, moving in the same way over their shoulders and in fitted lines to their sleeves.

They are perfect echoes of each other.

They are nothing like Silas.

The suit he wears looks so different from the identical nature of each of theirs. His hair, unkempt, threatens to descend past his ears. His bright skin and gray eyes and the way his lips quirk in a sigh as he passes them.

There is nothing of them in him.

"Remember to act natural," Silas says. He leans to whisper into my ear, his voice tight. "Do not engage or make eye contact. Eyes are the windows to the soul, Atia. You can't let them see into yours or they'll know what you are."

I look down to the floor as the Heralds glide past us.

"Eyes down," I say, glancing back to Tristan and Cillian.

But the two are already staring at the floor.

I can feel the Heralds' stares as we pass through the halls, their sharp eyes lingering on me for a beat too long before they pass. There's no doubt they can sense something isn't right.

"Why aren't they attacking?" I ask Silas, lowering my voice as far as I can to not be heard in the silence.

Even their footsteps make no sound.

"Heralds don't ask questions," Silas says. He draws me closer to him, moving me out of one's path. "They do not think or act without cause and provocation. And especially without orders."

His fingers tighten around my shoulder with every word.

"And they like rules," the Keeper says. He is walking faster now, waving his hand so we keep up. "If I ordered them to attack you, then they probably would. Or if they discovered who you are somehow. But they cannot just assume. That is the way Thentos built them. Heralds cannot act on instinct or think for themselves. It isn't in their nature. They are servants and messengers, yes, yes, nothing more."

His words make me irate, and it's not just at the mention of Thentos, reshaping people's lives and even their personalities to how he sees fit. The Keeper is talking about Heralds as if they are just puppets, paying no mind to the fact that Silas is standing right beside us.

"He can think for himself just fine," I say, pointing to Silas.

The Keeper looks back at us, baffled. He wraps his fingers around the handle of the purple door and pauses.

"When did I say that he couldn't?"

He cracks open the door and a rush of wind hits us, blowing dirt and damp into my eyes. I recoil, but Silas brings his hand to my back.

"We have to go through," he says, ushering me in.

"It *stinks*," I protest, gagging as the door shuts behind us.

Long gone is the changing hallway and the finely dressed Heralds. We are transported to a cavern, with water spitting from the ceiling and dripping onto jagged rocks below. The staircase is a long slope of barely chiseled stone that descends toward a mottled green lake.

"This is worse than half of the taverns in the Earth Kingdom," Tristan says, holding his nose.

"Remind me not to visit your tavern in the future," Cillian says. He brings his arm over his face. "Really, it smells like someone died in here."

We turn to face him.

"Oh," he says with an embarrassed smile. "*Right.*"

We descend the staircase, the wet stone slippery beneath the soles of my shoes. I walk as quickly as I can, but it seems to go on forever.

"Is it much farther?" I ask.

The air of death that lingers in the wind is beginning to make me dizzy the farther we descend into the cavern.

"Such impatience," the Keeper says. He takes the steps two at a time, hopping down each one as if it were a game. The claws of his feet dig into the stone. "So much like the others."

"Do you happen to sneak a lot of people through this place and to the ferry boats?" Cillian asks. "Do many wish to find Oksenya?"

"Many wish, none do," the Keeper says. "And I have nothing to do with wishes. They may want, but they never try. You are the first to attempt re-entry. I was talking about those who left."

"Those who left Oksenya?" Tristan asks, ever curious. "Who would ever do that?"

"Those who didn't have a choice," the Keeper says. "Those who were blooded with her."

He pauses momentarily to point to me.

I stop dead in my tracks, his words like a piercing blade.

The Keeper merely shrugs and carries on regardless, shuffling down the steps.

"They were here once too," he calls over his shoulder. "In the time before the time before. When the world was new and so were they, still burning from banishment."

"Wait—you knew my parents?" I ask, hurrying down the stairs to catch up with him.

I nearly slip and Silas grabs my arm to stop me from tumbling.

I shrug my elbow from him and continue down the steps, not stopping for a moment.

"You met them?" I press the Keeper.

"They passed by in a boat, thrown from Oksenya after the war. They were not meant to last, but Gods and guards have funny phases and eternity felt kind that day. They passed right by, ferried all the way."

The Keeper looks to Silas.

"You're too young to remember."

"I wasn't a Herald then," Silas reminds him.

"Exactly," the Keeper says.

I sigh, growing frustrated at this creature's riddles and the flippancy with which he regards us. "My parents came through here after they were banished from Oksenya?" I ask. "I thought they were thrown straight to the human realm from the blessed realm."

"Thrown, ferried." The Keeper waves his hand. "Meant to be thrown, instead ferried. Such a mix-up. But you look like them," he says. "Not so much your mother. She was very pretty. You don't have much of her in you. Except maybe the scowl."

"Excuse me." I glower, folding my arms over my chest.

"But your father, yes," the Keeper says. "His eyes are in you and his ears too. Thankfully not his mustache. A terrible mustache he had. Ghastly. I gave him the idea to shave it. Said he didn't want me to keep that in his file forever, did he?"

"Why did the Gods throw them out?" I ask, desperate for answers. "You must know the reason the war began. My parents rarely spoke of it."

After all I've seen, I can't believe it was simply because the Nefas were too mischievous, or that one day they just decided to turn against the Gods with no provocation. Something must have *happened*.

"It wasn't just the Nefas," the Keeper says. "So many files for so many things. What happened then was awful and bloody. I read the files over and over, trying to make sense of it."

"And what did you discover?"

"That the Gods like to betray," the Keeper says.

He snaps his fingers and the lantern at the edge of the dock lights up. In the distance, another light flickers in response.

Together, they illuminate the river between them and all its horrors.

Beside me, Tristan gasps and stumbles backward, but I remain frozen at Silas's side, both of us staring into the murky depths of the water. Among the dull green ripples, there are bodies.

Souls drowning in its depths, their mouths wide open in fear.

"The beginning to the River of Death," Silas says, voice quiet. "Where those sentenced to the Never must first be banished. Their first torment is to watch other souls be ferried to the After instead of them."

I grimace as I watch them, left to float endlessly in the waters.

"A boat is on its way," the Keeper says. "Make sure to pay for your ferry and don't fall in."

He turns to leave and I move to grab on to him.

"Wait," I say, but the Keeper slinks easily from my grasp.

He frowns at me.

"Do not grab," he scolds.

"You can't just go," I plead. "You have to tell me more about my family and the war that got them kicked out of the blessed realm."

"I keep the files, I do not reveal their contents," the Keeper says, growing impatient. "Files, not stories. That is my meaning. You will find what you're looking for when you find what you're looking for."

He nods toward the river, where a small black boat makes its way across the shores.

"Your father was not the forgiving type," he says. "I wish you luck where he had none. You're far more amenable at least."

"I don't think anyone has ever used that term to describe Atia before," Tristan says.

"She forgave him." The Keeper points to Silas. He checks his watch. "I really must be going. There are files to be sorted."

"Forgave him for what?" I ask, as he begins to make his way back up the stairs.

"For your curse," the Keeper yells back. "Your strange smell."

I look back to Silas, confusion taking over.

Silas pushes away from the dock stake where he had been leaning in wait. I find myself noticing how his suit has wrinkled at the edges, fine creases forming in the usually well-pressed fabric.

For some reason, this makes me frown even more.

"Atia, I have to tell you something," he says.

"Tell me what."

My voice is set on edge, my entire body bracing.

"I thought by the time you found out that you wouldn't care, because you'd have gotten what you wanted," Silas says. "Or that I wouldn't care because I'd have gotten what I wanted. I didn't expect us to become..."

He trails off. I shake my head, unable to speak as the suggestion of betrayal becomes all too heavy. It leaves me breathless.

"Being cursed wasn't your fault," Silas says.

"What are you talking about?" I swallow, my throat dry and cracked. "Of course it was my fault."

"No, Atia."

Silas's voice wavers, as unsteady as I feel.

I curl my hands into fists to stop myself from shaking. At the edge of the dock, the lost souls begin to claw their way up from the river. Sensing the approaching boat, a chance at salvation, they lift their ghostly hands from the water to clamber for the dock. For our ankles.

Neither of us move. Silas holds my stare.

"I planned this," he confesses. "It's my fault that you're cursed."

31

SILAS

*T*ake *her power.*

That was the Gods' command, when I let their quill scrawl a tidy message back in the sorting zone before Atia and I had struck our deal.

Take her power now.

Encourage her wickedness.

Curse the monster, before she curses us.

After the Keeper had alerted the Gods to Atia's whereabouts as I'd instructed him to, they ordered me to destroy her.

Force her to break the rules.

So that's what I did.

It was darker than usual that night and I'd been hunting for Atia, following her scent so I could follow the Gods' orders.

I found the man first.

His anger burst from him, turning the air around him stale. I could smell Atia on him—the impression of a confrontation long passed. Monsters always leave traces and Atia's were like bright lights across his aura.

"Hello," I said, corporealizing into the world. "Are you looking for someone?"

The man had stumbled for a moment, stepping back as if he'd imagined me blinking into existence. He arched his neck to look behind me, checking for shadows in the well-lit street.

"What's it to you?" he asked, gruff and smoke-soaked.

"Perhaps I could help. I'm good at finding things," I said. "Is it the seer you're looking for?"

"*Seer?*" The man spat at the mere mention of her. "I don't want anything to do with that damn meddler. It's her little friend I was after and now I've failed I'm going back to the Alchemy Kingdom to face my punishment."

"Friend." I repeated the word.

It stuck out to me most. I wasn't aware that Nefas had friends they didn't like to torture. But if the Gods wanted Atia cursed, then this presented the perfect opportunity.

Besides, the man had killed so many times. It radiated from him in delight. He was an evildoer and so I felt no guilt when I said:

"You're giving up on whatever mission you came here for? Just like that?"

I felt the bite of his frustration as I baited him, the strings of his anger palpable.

Heralds have always been able to manipulate emotions to placate the dead and ease their transition.

This time, I did not placate.

I pulled harder, pushed harder, letting the man fray in the grasp of my power. All the anger and frustration he held inside, I forced to rise to the surface.

It was a volcano and I pushed it to erupt.

"Why not see it through?" I urged, as his face warped to a snarl. "What is his name? The seer's friend you're after."

"Tristan Berrow," the man said, voice unsteady as he tried to sort through the new anger.

Tristan Berrow.

I focused, locking on to the name the same way I'd locked on to so many souls before.

"I know where you can find him," I finally said. "Follow me."

It didn't take long for Atia to appear after that.

A hunter, looking for her prey.

A protector, following her friend.

From there, things moved quickly.

"Stay out of this," the man had spat. "It's between me and the boy."

"It's between you and his parents," Atia said back. "Tristan shouldn't suffer for their misdoings."

There was a sadness to her voice I hadn't expected or prepared myself for. I watched from the shadows, telling myself to ignore it because the Nefas were masters of illusion. Though I wasn't sure why she would have chosen sadness as her illusion in the heat of such a confrontation.

"People like you are why monsters like me exist," she told the man.

And monsters like you are why I exist, I thought in return.

I blamed her a little for my curse.

There wouldn't be a need for so many Heralds, if there weren't so many monsters in the dark.

"Atia," the scholar begged, as the man convulsed under her grip. "Stop."

Only she didn't stop.

And I didn't move to interfere, though I knew I could put a stop to it all. I led this man here so that she would do this, hoping that endangering her friend's life would force her to act.

I swallowed as I watched her, unable to look away.

This was my doing.

Betrayer.

When it was finished, Atia's eyes grew empty.

"He's dead," Tristan had said.

"I didn't mean to," Atia whispered, at the same time I thought it too.

Only one of us was lying.

I'm no killer, I'd told the Keeper of Files.

But it wasn't true.

"You did what?" Atia says to me now, outrage dawning across her face like an eclipse.

I would do anything to make it right, smoothing out the wrinkles of betrayal in her brow to bring her smile back to me, though I know I don't deserve it.

"I told the Gods about you," I explain. "And they were planning to curse you, no matter what. They wanted you to break the rules. They wanted me to force your hand so they could steal your powers."

Atia's hands shake at her sides.

"Why would you follow that kind of an order?"

"Because I am a Herald and it was my duty," I say. "Because back then, I assumed it was inevitable."

But more than that, because the conversation with the Keeper had been whirling around in my head. Thoughts of destroying a God to reclaim my humanity and the frustration of not being able to do it myself.

"And because I needed your help," I finally confess. "A monster, desperate enough to help me. Someone capable of killing to do my killing for me, wielding my dagger in a way I could never."

Atia all but gasps at the realization.

"You wanted this to happen to me," she says. "You wanted me to be cursed so I would be desperate enough to help you."

The betrayal on her face shatters me like a mirror. A thousand pieces of bad luck, stabbing inside my heart.

"You just said Heralds can manipulate emotions," Atia says. "You used it to make that man continue to hunt Tristan. What about me? Have you used it to manipulate me into—"

She breaks. Her jaw is set firm, eyebrows raised in a challenge, daring me to reveal more before that volcano inside her erupts again.

"What is it that you think I've manipulated you into feeling?" I ask.

"You know exactly what!" she bites back. "Was that kiss even real? The night we had together?"

I flinch at the accusation.

"What kiss?" Tristan asks, looking between us. "Which night?"

"Gods, Atia," I say. "I would *never*."

"You'd never betray me?"

She spits out a laugh.

"That's what Thia meant when she said you were the one who took me from the life I had. You made sure I'd end up here," she says. "She warned me not to trust you and like a fool I ignored her."

If I thought she'd believe me, I'd explain to her that Heralds cannot create emotion from nowhere. We cannot construct false-hoods. We can only heighten or calm what is already there.

What is there? I wish to ask her.

What is it she feels so severely that she could suspect I would have placed it there myself?

"I care about you," I tell her honestly. "More than I have ever cared for anyone or anything in my—"

Atia has a dagger to my neck before I can finish.

"You don't have a life to remember," she says. "Would this blade even hurt you?" She presses the dagger—my dagger—deep enough that I feel it slit the skin.

"Do you feel anything at all?" she hisses.

"It hurts," I say softly. "It could kill me."

The blade was a gift from Thentos himself, after all.

To keep the villains at bay.

Was I the villain here?

Was I the thing that needed to be kept at bay?

"Perhaps I should kill you now," Atia seethes. "You were carved by a God, weren't you? Perhaps that'll be enough to cure me."

"It won't."

Atia steps closer, nicking the blade against my skin. Her voice is low, a growl beside the sea of souls swarming at our feet.

"There's only one way for me to find out," she says.

But before she can, something descends from the clifftops above.

It lands with a thud beside us and grabs Atia by the throat.

A hand.

A claw.

Nails, long enough to wrap around her entire neck.

It yanks her backward, ripping Atia from me and throwing her to the dock.

She skids across the rough wood and only just manages to stop herself from tumbling over into the river of souls.

The creature lets out a malevolent roar, flies weaving in and out of the gaps in its teeth where rotting flesh is still caught.

Its emaciated body is coated in a thin layer of black skin marred by blood, and the thin bones of its fingers host nails long enough to curve in on themselves.

"What is that?" Tristan asks.

The creature turns its glowing eyes to the scholar.

"Eurynomos," I say, as it approaches him.

A monster created to torture the souls of the Never, peeling the flesh from the skin of their mortal bodies and devouring it in front of them.

I sprint forward, grabbing the creature's shoulder and swirling it back around to face me. I throw a punch, but it's barely a distraction. The creature howls and digs its nails into my shoulder, lifting me above its head.

I see the concavity of its ribs, so sharp that the blood gets caught between them. Then I'm thrown against the stone steps we descended.

"Wait, it's Euryn—*what*?" Cillian asks.

"A creature from the Never," Atia says.

She stabs my dagger into its back, the blade catching between its shoulder blades.

"It feeds on the flesh of rotting corpses, leaving only their bones."

The blood runs black.

Eurynomos licks its lips, a prince of death and pain. It rolls its shoulders back in a loop and the dagger slides from its skin and clatters to the deck.

"The blow will need to be a killing one to do any good, straight in the heart!" I tell Atia.

"In the meantime, will someone kindly tell it that we're not rotting corpses?" Tristan yells. He stumbles backward, holding an arm over Cillian's waist like a barrier between him and the monsters. "And also that we'd very much like to keep our flesh!"

I pull myself up from the steps, touching a hand to the blood that cakes my hair. I'm dizzy with it.

"I don't think it'll listen," I say. "It was sent by the High Gods to kill us before we could infiltrate Oksenya or the rivers."

"If it kills you first, that'll save me a job," Atia says.

She kicks out, her foot cracking against the bones of Eurynomos's protruding ribs. The creatures stumbles backward and roars, lines of spit and flesh flinging into the air.

"Cover your ears!" Cillian yells, bracing us for his screams.

Quickly, Atia and Tristan throw their hands over their ears as Cillian's wails rip through the cavern. The souls in the river shake and scream, their reaching hands quaking and disappearing back under the water in retreat.

Eurynomos does not move. Does not flinch.

It flings its great arm out, whipping Cillian across the cheek. He flies to the ground, his scream silenced as great claw marks carve across half his face.

"You son of a bitch!" Atia screams.

She lunges for Eurynomos, forgetting perhaps that this is a monster worse than her, even when she had her powers.

It catches Atia in the air, using its claws to choke the life from her. Its jaws widen, tongue running a line across its chipped fangs.

The growl that escapes is low and hungry.

It will rip the flesh from Atia's bones while she is still alive, feasting on her.

And it will be my fault.

I, who brought her here and set her on this path for my own selfish reasons.

Without my interference she would've left Rosegarde and never seen that man again.

My hands ball to fists, a low growl of my own escaping.

I sprint toward Atia and the creature, charging with all my might. There is not a chance that I will let that thing hurt her.

Eurynomos turns and makes to swipe out at me, but I shadow to its other side, ripping its hands from Atia and twisting its arm backward until I hear the snap of bones.

Atia falls to the deck and I turn toward her, taking just seconds for my eyes to roam her and check for injuries.

There's no blood. I sigh in relief, but those two seconds cost me.

Before I realize it, Eurynomos has lurched its unbroken arm back, claws pointed like knives toward me.

In a blink, those knives go through my stomach.

It slices me open like a grapefruit, twisting its hand to twist all that is inside me.

I can barely gasp out from the pain.

I only hear Atia scream my name, just once, before Eurynomos throws me into the river of lost souls.

SILAS

I am swept under by the current of the dead.

Their hands grab at my ankles, dragging me into the depths of the river that binds them.

The water fills my mouth, salty and ashen. I try to spit it out but choke on it instead.

Blood pools around me, staining the water red as my wounds take hold. The dead feed from it. It attracts them like sharks.

Above the surface, I see Eurynomos straddling Atia, its claws rising and falling in slashes she barely avoids before they threaten to cleave into her chest.

It is going to kill her while I watch.

I twist beneath the water, wincing as my wounds seep more fiercely with every jolt.

I don't stop trying even as my foot is caught in the web of the dead. I look down and see them, great white shadows stretched into the current. Their mouths are pulled open in eternal cries of longing.

They drag me closer, closer still.

I lose sight of Atia.

Please no.

If she dies, then a part of me—a part of this immortal form I have been given—will die along with her.

It is my fault she is vulnerable.

It is my fault she is in danger.

I kick out, but the hold of the dead is firm.

Can they sense who I am and all I have done? Am I so coated in death that they think I am one of them?

I swim upward, fighting against them the best I can to get to Atia. Somehow, I manage to reach out a hand for the surface, my fingers clipping the edge of the water.

Atia, I think. *Atia Atia Atia.*

The souls scream louder each time I struggle, and each time the blood spills from me with as much strength as the waterfalls Atia showed me when we kissed.

I wish to be back in that moment with her more than anything.

I wish I had kissed her before and since, again and again.

My chin rises above the water just briefly, a flash of the world, before the cries of the lost souls and the forgotten overtake me and I am pulled back under.

These souls will never let me escape their clutches.

They will keep me here, drowning beside them forever.

Then suddenly I am being pulled from the water by a swift pair of hands. By three pairs.

I look up to see Atia reaching toward me, Tristan and Cillian at her side. The three of them grab at me, batting away the lost souls that try to pull them down too.

"Get off!" Atia yells out to them. "I've done enough drowning in rivers!"

Somehow, they manage to yank me upward. I'm dragged gasping from the river and back onto the dock.

"Oh Gods," Cillian says.

The slashes across his cheek are a bright red, reopening old wounds the vampires once gave him. His eyes shoot to my stomach and the holes that puncture through me.

I try to speak, but I only spit up ashen water instead. It dribbles down my chin as Atia lays me down flat, lifting up my shirt to inspect the wounds.

"Eurynomos," I manage to choke out.

"Not a great swimmer," she says. "Well, not after being stabbed in the heart by a Godly blade."

I glance behind me to see the creature's body floating atop the river, before the weight of the dead drags it downward in my place.

Dead people Eurynomos may have devoured itself. Souls it may have delighted in torturing as it fished them from the edges of the river where it dwelled.

"Will he survive?" I hear Cillian ask.

I think he is talking about Eurynomos, until Atia's eyes catch mine and a wrinkle centers in her brow.

"He can't die." She picks up the dagger on the dock by her feet. Eurynomos's black blood coats the blade so thickly I can no longer see the silver. She pockets it without bothering to wipe the blood away. "Not unless I kill him myself."

"The boat!" Tristan yells.

The world winks in and out of existence. In the distance, a light grows larger. A lantern. I see the long arm that holds it.

The guide. *The Charon.*

His black boat glides easily past the descending corpse of Eurynomos, rippling through the waters as though they were at peace.

The souls flee from it, scattering like fish threatening to be caught in a net.

Everything is hazy and blurred.

I blink, trying to focus back in on the world, and bring a hand to my stomach. The bleeding won't stop.

"Why isn't he healing?" Tristan asks. "Shouldn't he be back up and running by now?"

"It's fine," Atia says sharply. "*He's fine.*"

But Tristan is right.

I should have healed by now, or at least felt the wounds begin to close and stitch themselves back together. I have never been injured to this extent before, or felt this much *pain*.

Atia glances down at me, and when she bites her lip, I can tell she knows.

Something is wrong.

If the Gods sent Eurynomos to kill us, the creature may well have succeeded.

Its claws are no doubt imbued with the same ancient power as my blade.

A power to kill any creature.

The small boat docks, and beneath his black hood, the Charon speaks. "What happened here?" he asks.

His voice is a soft winter song. In one wrinkled hand he holds the lantern and in the other a skiff pole that doubles as some kind of hammer. He looks frail and elderly, like the kind of soul that welcomes me when I approach, ready to discover the delights of the After.

Only the Charon is no soul. Nor a frail man, ready to depart.

If Atia and the others were to try and force their way onto that boat, he would kill them in an instant.

"Eurynomos happened," Atia answers the guide. "It attacked us."

"Because you do not belong," the Charon says. "Because you walk in worlds that are not yours. Worlds they do not want to be yours."

"Thanks for the riddle," Atia says.

She moves to step onto the boat, but the Charon whips his skiff pole across his body in a barrier.

"Let us pass," Atia says, her voice growing impatient. "We need to get to the rivers."

"You cannot pass," the Charon says.

I make to stand and talk to him in her place, but trying to do so causes the pain to splinter through me.

I gasp out and Atia's face contorts.

"He is one of you!" she yells at the Charon. "Will you just let him suffer?"

"He is used to suffering," the Charon says. "He is made for it. It is his punishment."

"He needs payment," I call out, gritting my teeth. "The coin."

I reach into my pocket for the obol.

It is a small coin, embossed with the face of a High God. I can't even remember which. The face imprinted onto the silver looks so plain and void of anything resembling humanity.

My hand shakes as I hold it out to Atia.

She kneels beside me, her hand sliding into mine as she takes the obol.

"This is most unusual," the Charon says. "You are not dead."

"Not yet," Atia tells him. She squeezes the obol in her hand. "But everyone is trying really hard to kill me."

Atia nods over to Tristan and Cillian, signaling for their help as she slings my arm over her neck. It is agonizing and I can't help but cry out. Atia merely grits her teeth, pressing her lips tightly together as the three of them pull me to my feet.

My blood soaks into Atia's shirt.

"Here," she says.

She holds out her free hand to the Charon and presents him with the obol.

The Charon plucks the coin from her, examining it with a wry smile. "Isorropía," he says, in musing. *Balance.* "She is my favorite of the High Gods. Such a wicked beast."

Swiftly, he moves his skiff pole out of the way, allowing us on board.

"Take us to the rivers," Atia says, lowering me down to the floor of the boat.

With every movement, I can feel myself slipping.

Too much blood. Too much pain. Too much bright, bright world, even down here.

"He requires his eternity back," the Charon says simply.

He lowers the skiff pole into the waters, wading his way through the souls that float around us.

"That's where we're going," Atia says firmly. "The River of Eternity can heal him, can't it?"

I shiver, feeling the cold creep into my bones where before I have only ever felt nothingness. Not even warmth, until I met Atia.

Is this what it's like to be human?

Feeling everything all at once, a muddle of pain and brightness all blurring together until the world becomes too much to bear?

I close my eyes, allowing it to all fade away.

"There may be no healing him," I hear the Charon say, as the world grows hazy and out of focus. "Perhaps that is his punishment too."

ATIA

We drift through the dead.

The farther we travel the more I am thrown by the smell that drifts up from the souls as the Charon guides us forward. They smell of rot and curses, their evil growing as a fungus would.

Silas said this was a place for those sentenced to the Never to be banished as their first torment and I see why. Forced to swim in their own decay, watching others be ferried to some place beyond, with only the low howls of their tortured friends for company.

"What happens when we get there?" Tristan asks. "Do you think the Gods will be waiting?"

"Yes," I say. "They'll be waiting."

"And they're going to try to kill us again, aren't they?" Cillian asks.

He touches a hand to his bloodied cheek and the claw marks that now ripple through one half of his face.

I flinch when he does.

"I shouldn't have dragged you both into this," I say. "Perhaps I should have sent you home. Created a gateway to take you back, or at least left you to wait in the sorting zone until our return."

"I don't think that would have been safer," Tristan says. "The

Gods know we've helped you. Surely they'd find us wherever we went."

I lower my head, feeling the shame of it. "It's my fault that you're in danger."

Cillian sighs, brushing his red hair out of his face with a huff. "It's really not. Do you not remember me pleading with you to come? You saved me from dying, Atia. You and Tristan and—"

He looks to the bleeding Silas, unconscious beside me. I shift when I realize how close our hands are. Silas doesn't stir.

My hand twitches as I feel the urge to touch it to his cold cheek and try everything to coax him awake.

I ball my hands into fists instead.

"I would have been tortured and killed by those vampires, but you got me out," Cillian continues. "And you made me a part of something. My whole life I've been pushed to the side and told I don't belong. But with the three of you I have never once felt that way."

Neither have I.

It's strange, but hearing Cillian speak makes my heart release a little, as though it has been tightly constricted all this time. I never thought I'd know what family was after my parents died, and truthfully, I'd consigned myself to being alone for the rest of my long life. I didn't think it possible to open my heart and risk caring for anyone, especially for people who didn't share my immortality and would inevitably leave me again.

Yet here, now, with these people, I've allowed myself to do just that.

Tristan and his books, his stories and need for adventure breaking through my walls. Cillian's jokes and his love of pastries, and how fierce he has been in the face of his family's hate. I cannot believe anyone would ever think he was unworthy. He is miraculous and kind, and I'm proud to have him by my side.

"You're saying you belong in a world of reckless, death-defying quests?" I say teasingly.

"This reckless, death-defying quest is strangely the safest I have ever felt," Cillian counters with a smile. "Because for once, I'm not alone. For once, I have a family."

"Hear, hear," Tristan says.

I snort at him. "You've hardly spent your life being shunned, Tristan. You have parents who care and will mourn you if you die."

"But look at the world you've shown me," he says, gesturing around us. A moment passes, then he grimaces. "Okay, this part isn't exactly a great example, but still. Monsters and magic and Gods. Atia, I've been studying these things my whole life, never knowing what is fact from fiction, but hoping that one day I could find out and explore the hidden world around us."

"That's awfully sentimental."

Tristan scoffs. "Then I'll just remind you that me and my books have saved your life," he says proudly. "You'd be lost without me."

Cillian nudges him. "She'd be lost without me and my banshee screams saving the day."

"I'd be lost without all of you," I say, shaking my head in a smile.

"All of us?" Cillian asks.

His eyes flicker to Silas.

"Both of you," I correct myself.

Cillian and Tristan exchange a look that I choose to ignore.

Silas has been unconscious for the better part of our journey. If

I didn't know better, if I was able to ignore the blood that stains his suit, marring the crisp white of his shirt, I could almost be fooled into thinking he was sleeping.

He looks peaceful, beautiful.

I want to scold myself for thinking it, but I can't help it.

Gods, he is so *beautiful*. When his lips part in a sleepy gasp, my heart jump-starts, flashing back to that moment beside the waterfalls. His hands in my hair and my name escaping his lips like a sigh before he pulled me into him. Not close enough, not nearly, ever, close enough.

There is a hunger in me for him. A longing for this immortal boy, this creature of Gods, who somehow understands me better than anyone has ever dared to before.

The anger inside me begs to forget it, to take the dagger I've slid into my waistband and plunge it into his chest as a price for the betrayal.

Instead, I reach out a hand and brush a tuft of hair from his damp forehead.

I care about you more than I have ever cared for anyone or anything.

That's what Silas told me before I held the blade to his throat and had to use every ounce of strength within me not to sink it through his jugular.

How much of it was true?

How much of anything between us actually mattered to him?

I know that I bear the responsibility for taking that man's life, no matter how much Silas may have manipulated the situation, but it still hurts all the same.

He put Tristan in danger, hoping it would force my hand, so that I could help him escape his fate.

He allowed the Gods to manipulate us both.

But more than that, he *lied*.

"Is it much longer?" Cillian asks the Charon.

"Time is fickle," he says, not turning to face us. "Possibly one night and one bright."

I curse.

What if Silas can't make it that long?

"How exactly do you ferry all the souls of the world when it takes so long each time?" I ask bitterly.

"I am many," the Charon says. "I am all."

Tristan raises an excited eyebrow. "So there are multiple guides?"

"There is just me," the Charon says. "I am multiple."

I cast him an awful look, resisting the urge to take his skiff pole and smack him over the head with it. He and the Keeper of Souls must make great friends.

"Atia?"

Silas stirs, his head lolling as his eyes flicker back open.

A great worry rises up in me. He looks weak for the first time since I've known him, and that isn't the ideal position when we're about to attack a land of Gods.

"You haven't bled to death yet," I say. "So your immortality must be holding up against Eurynomos's murderous abilities."

Silas manages a chuckle, though he's wincing by the end of it. "Atia," he says again.

"Will you stop saying my name like that?" I say gruffly, unable to bear the vulnerability in it. I swallow down the dryness that tacks my throat. "What is it?"

Silas smiles. "You're always so unpleasant," he says. "Did I ever tell you that I want to kiss you the most when you scowl?"

I open my mouth in shock. "You—"

"We are here," the Charon announces.

I turn swiftly to face the old man. "I thought you said it would be a day?"

He shrugs. "I said time was fickle. Perhaps it has been."

I take in the barren pit where the water ends and we have come to a stop. It stretches into a wasteland, but around it I see the rivers of the Gods. They branch off from this pit like the arms of a tree, like the veins of life, each of them pulsing and thrumming.

The River of Death that belongs to Thentos, black as night with the glitter of stars inked in its waters. It flows slower than the others, trickling along the waterbed. I see Lahi's River of Oblivion, cloudy and marred by a great fog. And Kyna's River of Sorrow beside it, filled with tears, the rushing water sounding like sobs as it tries to escape.

I cannot yet see the River of Eternity, but I can see the River of Fire, the farthest away from us. It spits and bubbles, smoke cascading from the surface.

The final gateway to Oksenya, where only the worthy can cross without being burned.

I will be plenty worthy once I kill Thentos and take his power for my own.

I frown.

Suddenly, I realize something.

Among the flames and the tears, the river boundaries are empty. I see no Gods or guards. No Firia, guarding her fire river, or Kyna beside the River of Sorrow. No Lahi or Thentos. The rivers are abandoned.

"Fled," the Charon says to me. "To the safety of Oksenya. Perhaps they knew you were coming."

Cowards.

"Where is the River of Eternity?" I ask, surveying the wasteland in front of us. "I cannot see it among the others."

The Charon regards me with what seems to be a rare flicker of sympathy. "This is it," he says, pointing to the pit. "This is what remains of the eternal river."

I blanch.

Thia mentioned the river had begun to dry ever since Aion's demise in the war . . . But this.

The pit in front of us crumbles in its drought, not a single drop of water to be seen. It is a long trench that stretches for eons, the old riverbed nothing but sand and dirt, blown easily by the wind.

My father used to tell me stories of the River of Eternity and how it sparkled in ripples of such a clear crystal blue you could see your reflection in it. He spoke of lily pads and frogs leaping between them. Of fish that matched each color in the rainbow and of the wildflowers that sprang up as if from nowhere, allowing them to dart between.

It was a river of life. The first river.

A place where the High Gods made their vows to protect the world and received their gifts of immortality. Where they created the River Gods from their children, blessing them with great power and tasking them with monitoring all the beauties of these gateways. With helping mortals and monsters in their journeys.

Now it is nothing.

The River of Eternity is gone.

It cannot be true.

Only this is the vision I saw in Thia's mirror, isn't it? Vail's necklace, the last drop of eternity, in an empty, desolate pit. And the High Gods had told her there could be no more.

They gave the last drops to Vail, and when we destroyed it, we destroyed all hope at regaining my powers and breaking my curse before facing the Gods.

All hope of saving Silas.

"How is this possible?" I ask the Charon. "What happened?"

"You should know the answer to that already," a voice intones.

When I turn, I see the man of ash and shadows.

His hair is long and black, ending in a straight edge at his collarbone, where his shirt is open a button to reveal the heaving of his dark chest. His eyes are the same color, unyielding, without reprieve. The suit he wears is much the same, fitting him so perfectly it looks like a second skin, like he would not be able to remove it even if he wanted to. It slinks to the edges of his wrists.

He looks the same as he has done every night in my memories.

Thentos, God of Death, murderer of my parents.

He looks to Silas and sighs deeply, stealing the breath from the air.

The wind grows still with his frown.

"So you have returned," he says, shaking his head as Silas manages to push himself to standing. "I wonder, is it to save us or to destroy us?"

34

ATIA

Silas pales in the shadow of the God's voice.

"Thentos," he says, so much reverence in the word, the name.

I am almost surprised he doesn't take a bow.

Thentos narrows his eyes somewhat. "If it is a war you want, you'll be disappointed to see we have no soldiers waiting."

What I want is to wipe that smug grin off his face.

"Isn't that what you wish for?" I ask, imagining how it would feel to rip his damn throat out, after so many years of waiting. "A war?"

"It's what your parents wished for," Thentos says. "Look where it got them."

I lurch from the boat.

"Do not," I say in a low growl, the tip of my blade so tantalizingly close to the tip of his throat, "*ever* speak of my parents."

Thentos doesn't move, doesn't bother to look afraid as I stand mere inches from him, ready to slice his throat open.

"You would allow her to threaten me?" He looks to Silas with a wave of betrayal. "After all I have done to help you both."

"How brazen you are!" I hiss. "I'm going to kill you and I'm going to enjoy every mo—"

"Atia, wait."

Silas steps meekly from the boat.

He winces with every movement and it makes me want to wince too.

"What do you mean 'help'?" he asks the God of Death.

"Ever the questioning one." Thentos shakes his head.

"Answer him," I say, the dagger trembling in my hand as I try to hold in my fury for a moment longer. "Tell us what you meant so I can slice out your heart like you did mine, and this can finally be over."

"Atia of the Nefas, last of your kind." Thentos heaves a great sigh. "What a burden you bear."

He straightens out his suit, an echo of Silas.

I shift seeing it. The similarities in how they move.

"To clarify," Thentos says calmly, "that was not my idea."

"What wasn't your idea?" I ask. "Killing my entire family?"

"Killing everyone," he says with a shrug. "Destroying worlds."

The casualness with which he says it only makes me want to hurt him more. This man has lived forever watching others die and it has hollowed him. Shelled him out to the point where only emptiness remains, no notion of pain or sympathy for the lives he stole from me.

"Imera, Skotadi, and Isorropía have always ruled Oksenya with fists and fury," Thentos explains. "Long ago, creatures were ranked and imprisoned, created and destroyed on their whims."

"I don't need your bedtime stories," I snap.

"Of course you do," he chides. "Don't all children require such things to understand the world?"

He moves to take a seat on the edge of the Charon's boat, his weight not jolting the vessel even a fraction, as though he is made from air and little else.

I tense.

If he makes a move to run, I am going to gut him.

"One such creature did not wish to bow to the High Gods," Thentos says. "They did not wish for the blessed realm to be so rife with corruption and un-peace. Can you guess which creatures they were?"

"The Nefas," I say, without hesitating. "My parents."

"Indeed," Thentos says. "The Nefas, mischievous little things, so full of illusion and laughter. Weaving fear and taking it away too. Creating melancholy and solace. And your parents were the most wondrous of all. Enthralling creatures. They created quite the movement. They wanted to leave Oksenya and go beyond its gates to live in the mortal realm. They wanted to be free."

At this, I frown.

"My parents hid from the humans."

The God laughs a bitter laugh. "They weren't hiding from humans," he says. "They were hiding from us."

Never get involved in the business of humans, Atia, my father always said. *That is how they trap you.*

By *they*, did he mean the Gods?

Beings who would use the humans to trace and curse us.

"The High Gods were furious that a thing they created to entertain them had outgrown them," Thentos says. "That fury tore the skies in half. It led to a great war, the Nefas and their allies against the High Gods and theirs. After the Gods won, they imprisoned as many betrayers as they could and sentenced the rest to be stripped of their powers and die among the humans."

I shake my head, not understanding. "But my parents didn't lose their powers."

"Yes, well," Thentos says, looking disgruntled. "My brother,

Aion, took pity on the monsters, as he was prone to do. He helped them escape to the mortal realm intact. "

"But the Nefas killed the God of Eternity during the war," I say, confused.

"Aion was alive after the war," Thentos corrects sharply. "Despite the stories. And he roped me into helping them escape too."

"*You* helped my family?"

"Don't be grateful," Thentos says, looking insulted. "I've come to regret it."

I am tempted to try and stab him again.

"The High Gods found out, but oh-so-noble Aion took the fall for us both. So the High Gods destroyed him, and his River of Eternity has run dry ever since."

"So the Gods killed one of their own and then blamed my kind for it?"

Thentos merely nods. "After all was said and done, the Gods invented a curse, waiting for the monsters he helped escape to slip up so they could be found and punished. They didn't think you could live peacefully among humans, but so many creatures did that the Gods resorted to trickery. It was only a few years ago they managed to locate the remaining Nefas by chance at some fair."

The day I rode the ceramic horse.

I narrow my eyes. "Do not try and blame me for this," I warn.

"I'm simply telling you that finding them was all it took for the Gods to kill them," Thentos says, the first hint of regret finally entering his voice.

I swallow, my throat tacky as the realization sets in.

"Are you telling me that my parents didn't break any rules or kill anybody?" I ask. "They were innocent?"

Just like I was when they told Silas to curse me.

Thentos bows his head slightly in a nod.

The tears come quick then, threatening to spill over and buckle me at the knees. All this time I believed they must have done something awful to be hunted by the Gods, but it was a lie.

"How could you kill them if they were innocent?" I want to scream, but the words are a hoarse whisper, barely audible. I swipe away my tears, hot and angry as they pour down my face. "Especially when you claim to have helped them escape the war?"

"I didn't kill them." Thentos looks angry at the mere thought of having to explain himself. "I was there to help you."

Help me?

"I knew it was what Aion would've wanted, but I was too late," Thentos continues. "I couldn't save your parents, so I saved you instead. I killed the monsters to protect you. One last vestige of the Nefas."

My brows knit together as I try to line up all the awful fragments of that night I have tried so hard to erase from my heart.

My mother's screams. My father telling me to run, and oh how I ran, for my wings could not yet lift me to fly.

And then the ashen man—Thentos—came, lifting me up from the mud and the grass when I had tripped.

This is what happens when you displease the Gods, he said. His hand was so tight and my wrist was so small, but he squeezed hard. *Take this mercy and run. Run far and as fast as you can.*

"You weren't part of the hunting party," I say in a whisper.

Thentos crosses his arms over his chest. "No, I was not. The High Gods assumed your parents and the monsters they sent had all just killed each other. They never knew of my involvement, especially in your escape. If they ever discovered such a thing, I would not be here talking to you. They would've done to me what they did to Aion."

The revelation makes my head spin.

Thentos saved my parents from the High Gods after the war.

Then he risked his own life to save me from the hunting party I thought he had led.

I can't kill him knowing this, but that means going up against the High Gods without being restored to my full power.

Would we even stand a chance?

"I have a proposal for you," Thentos says, though he seems reluctant to offer it. "The High Gods have sent me here to tell you that they do not wish for more war with you or your kin."

"Is that because Atia has nearly succeeded in reversing the curse and evaded every attempt by your so-called High Gods to kill her?" Tristan asks defiantly. "Or is it because they're afraid which of them she might kill next?"

"Or maybe," Cillian says, raising his brows in a challenge, "they're just sore losers."

Thentos's smile grows tight. He rises from the edge of the boat. "They sent me here with a gift."

He holds out a phial. At first I think it's empty, but then I see a single droplet gathered at the bottom, a clear crystal blue so bright it could crack the glass that contains it.

It is just like the one Vail had.

"This is all that remains of my brother's river," Thentos says. "Just a single droplet containing his eternity."

"I thought Vail had the last one," Silas says weakly, his eyes never leaving the phial as Thentos carries it toward me.

"Don't be a fool for once," Thentos barks. "Vail had one of the last, but of course the High Gods would have another. One for the mortals and one for us. They are willing to let the Nefas have it to make peace."

Thentos focuses in on me, his eyes like black pits that destroy any hope of light.

"Regain your immortality and return to the human realm, Atia of the Nefas. Let there be no more bloodshed between us."

I open my mouth to ask what the catch is and if the Gods really think I'm going to trust them, especially when it will mean not regaining the full might of my power, when Cillian gasps.

I turn just in time to see Silas collapse to the ground.

Eyes wide, I rush to his side. He looks so pale, the blood from his stomach a thick, dark red.

"Silas." I press a hand to his cheek and it feels cold. "Get up. Don't do this now. Not when we're so close."

His eyes flicker.

When he coughs, a line of blood draws from his lips.

"He won't get up," Thentos says darkly. "That dagger you tried to kill me with is imbued with the same magic that lives inside of Eurynomos. Godly weapons, both."

I clench my jaw. "He can't die."

"All things can die," Thentos says. His hands grip fiercely around the phial. Almost shaking. "Though of course, there's always a choice."

He holds up the phial he presented to me, with the droplet of eternity.

"You could always give him this."

I narrow my eyes.

If I give that to Silas, it'll heal his injuries and restore him to what he was, but in doing so I give up the chance to regain my own immortality and break my curse.

I would never be a true Nefas again.

Saving him would mean losing myself.

I look down to the Herald.

To the beautiful boy who chained me in curses and then freed me over and over.

"Don't," Silas manages to say. He shivers under my touch. "Don't you dare save me."

I steady my breath.

Silas is part of the reason I'm cursed in the first place. He led that man to me and Tristan, then lied about it. He manipulated me so he could regain his humanity.

And yet.

When I bite my lip, I feel the ghost of his mouth to mine and what it meant to no longer be alone in this world. Feel his hands on my skin, trailing down my body until I shivered in delight.

I hear his words telling me that there are always stars in the darkness.

"Choose," Thentos demands, his voice echoing across the rivers.

Silas shakes his head and his body shakes along with it, convulsing as the killing blows from Eurynomos take hold.

He is going to die in my arms.

"You can have your immortality," Thentos says. "Or you can save his life."

35

SILAS

Atia's eyes glow against the darkness, her silver hair dripping down her shoulders as she looks between me and the God of Death.

"Do not," I tell her.

If the Gods are scared enough to offer Atia her immortality back without having her risk her life for it, then she must take it and forget any ideas of war. This is her chance to undo most of what has been done to her without the need for more blood to be spilled, including her own.

It isn't the same as having her full powers back, but it is something.

It is *safety*.

Atia bites her lip, and if I wasn't already on the ground bleeding to death, I suspect it would have knocked me sideways.

"Give me the phial," she says, holding out her hand to Thentos.

The God of Death hands it over wordlessly.

No tricks or debates.

"Silas," Atia says.

"It's okay," I tell her. "Just drink it."

Atia glares, her hand scooping around my neck. "Don't try to be a hero," she snaps. "Just shut up and take this."

She pops the cork off the phial and places it to my lips.

I try to bat her away, but Atia's glare only deepens.

"I swear to the Gods I will shove it down your throat, phial and all, if you don't stop being so awkward," she scolds.

"If he doesn't want it, I'll happily be immortal," Cillian says, raising a hand.

Atia scoffs and then looks back to me with soft eyes. "Part of me wants to kill you myself," she says. "But the other part wants to save you even more. Please don't make me rethink the decision."

Gods, she is a wonder.

I was so desperate to leave behind this life in favor of one I don't remember, but I didn't think about how that would mean leaving behind Atia.

She is a miracle where there were only ever horrors before.

The water slicks down my throat like honey.

I can't even feel the moment my skin begins to re-form, ousting old wounds and pulling skin back together again. The second I swallow, blink just once, the pain is gone.

I look down to my shirt, where the blood has dried a deep red. When I lift the hem, my skin is smooth and flat, not a scar to show.

Atia's smile widens and I wish with all my might that I could kiss her.

I wish the God of Death wasn't smirking at us, as though this had been his plan all along. "I wonder if she will regret that choice," he says, as Atia pulls me to my feet.

I ignore him and focus my attention on her. "You have to keep going," I tell Atia. "Screw any deals. You have to continue on to Oksenya and find where the rest of the Gods are hiding and kill them. I can't trust they won't have kept more water for themselves. You must find it."

"You would betray the deal we just made?" Thentos asks, though he is not angry. "How unsurprising."

I glare at him and the use of that word *betray*, which has followed me for some time.

Atia shakes her head. "I can't pass the River of Fire without the power of a God. It won't deem me worthy." She casts Thentos a dirty look. "And since we can't kill him after everything he has said, there's no other way."

"You don't need power to be worthy," I tell her. "In fact, it's the opposite. Look at what you just did."

"He is right," Thentos says. "Sacrificing power is far worthier than having it handed to you."

"Why do I get the feeling you just want me to burn up in that river?" Atia asks him.

"If I wanted to kill you, you would be dead," Thentos says. "Lest you forget who I am."

"So you want me to kill a High God?" she asks. "Why? I thought you wanted me to take that phial and leave?"

"I want nothing," Thentos says. "Except peace for Oksenya."

"If you're lying," I tell him, "remember we still have that dagger. If she dies, so do you."

Thentos's smirk tightens. "Same old, same old."

Whatever he means by that, I don't care, because I'm not speaking in riddles or hidden code. I mean what I say. If Atia suffers so much as a single burn, I will drive that dagger into whatever heart Thentos has left.

"What about us?" Tristan asks, looking uncertain. "Can humans cross the river, or should I build a bridge from my books?"

"What about half humans?" Cillian pipes up, looking equally nervous. "I really don't want to blister."

Thentos sighs, as though just speaking to them is a trial. "Jump in and find out."

Atia rolls her eyes.

"Let's just go."

Her hand slips so easily into mine, pulling me back toward the Charon's boat, that I don't think she even notices she's done it until she feels the tug of my resistance pulling her back.

"I'm not coming," I tell her. "Not yet."

A flash of something crosses her face. Anger. Hurt.

"What do you mean you're *not coming?*"

I gesture back to Thentos. "He knows who I was," I say. "He isn't the God of Forgetting, but maybe he can tell me about my past and what I did to become like this. I have to know, Atia."

She shakes her head, adamant. "I'm not leaving the two of you alone."

I squeeze her hand in mine, angry at myself when I finally let go. "This is my quest, Atia. I came here for this. And you came here for them."

I gesture toward the River of Fire and the High Gods, who lie in the gateway of Oksenya beyond it.

"This was never just about your immortality. It was about your parents and what they did to them and the rest of your kind," I say. "Breaking your curse, but also breaking their cycle of tyranny so nobody else would have to suffer like you have."

Atia flinches.

"I understand that now," I assure her. "I understand *you.* You have to go to Oksenya and find the High Gods, for both yourself and your family. So go. Find out where they're hiding and wait for me there. If we delay any longer, who knows where they'll flee to, or if they'll come here to attack us first and cause us to lose the upper hand."

"We could both die," Atia tells me. "If we split up now, what's to say we'll ever see each other again? We're stronger together, Silas."

"I'm not allowed to die without your permission, remember?" I say in a laugh, thinking back to her words before she dragged me on the Charon's boat. "And you have so much of your magic back already. You can do this, I know you can. Find them and *wait for me*."

Atia doesn't smile.

"Even if I can find the Gods, how will you find me?" she asks.

I reach up to my tie and unclip the pin that has been a part of me for all the years I can remember. I have never taken it off. Not in a single moment since becoming a Herald.

I place it inside Atia's hand, my blood coating the wings.

"I don't think they work here," I say. "But I'm connected to them. I'll be able to find you, wherever you are."

Atia's hand closes around the pin. "You're giving me your wings?"

I fold my hand over her closed fist. "I'm giving you all that I am," I say. "I'm truly sorry, Atia. I'm sorry for everything I've done to hurt you."

She shakes her head. "Don't say goodbye like that," she tells me fiercely. "Don't you dare."

Her hand hooks around the back of my neck and she pulls me forward, pressing her forehead to mine.

"You say goodbye like this."

Atia's lips crash against mine, the taste of her satiating a deep, unwavering hunger in me.

My hands move against her back, the silk of her skin against my fingertips enough to set me alight. I do not wish to ever let her go, ever stop holding her and adventuring with her through this world.

I was empty as a Herald and perhaps I was also empty as a human. Two lives lived and neither of them could compare to the time I've spent by her side.

Her hands tangle in my hair and she gasps out as I slip my hands lower, pressing her closer still. She feels like fireworks across my skin, exploding and charring all that came before until there is just her.

Just the burning I feel for her.

Thentos clears his throat and the reminder of death breaks the brief spell.

I pull away from Atia, feeling the hum of her lips on mine like a memory, embedded in my skin.

"Surely a kiss that dramatic means someone is now going to die," Tristan says with a dreaded sigh.

Cillian nudges him. "Why do you think I haven't kissed you yet?"

When he winks, Tristan blushes and looks down to his feet, like his shoes are suddenly very interesting. I see the small smile in the corner of his lips and the wish in it.

"Silas," Atia says. She brushes her hair from her face, her eyes filled with worry. I snap my attention back to her as she pushes my dagger into my hands. "Kill him if you need to."

She gestures over to Thentos.

"You're finally returning this to me?" I ask.

"It's a trade," she corrects firmly. "And you better live to give it back."

I squeeze the blade back into her hand.

There is no way I'm letting her search for the High Gods without the one weapon that could protect her.

"It's yours, Atia," I say. "As am I. Now take it and go."

Atia nods and then steps back onto the Charon's boat.

Tristan and Cillian follow.

"Good luck," Tristan says to me as the Charon pushes his skiff pole back into the water. "Don't take too long."

"And please don't nearly die again!" Cillian calls out.

"I'll be fine," I assure him, but I'm looking at Atia as I say it.

She swallows, loud enough for me to hear even over the spitting of the River of Fire in the distance. As the Charon carries her away, I think maybe I can even hear her breathing. The deep sighs that would mirror my own if I could do such a thing.

"I have to give Lahi credit," Thentos says. "She did her job well."

I turn to face Death. "What does that mean?"

His laughter is acrid and filled with disappointment. "Erasing your past. How glad and furious I am."

A snarl makes its way onto his cool face, twisting his pointed nose to a wrinkle.

"Though really, falling for a Nefas? What were you thinking?"

"I'm thinking my love life isn't your concern."

"Then again," he continues, as if I'd never spoken. "You always did have a soft spot for them."

The cold creeps into my bones with every disgusted shake of his head.

"This started with you and them. All those years ago."

"What started with me?"

Thentos tightens his tie, squeezing the knot close to his jugular.

I suddenly wish that I'd gotten onto that boat with Atia and the others.

"The war," he says. "Surely you must remember by now."

I blink, the cold shaking into my heart.

"You can't have forgotten everything," he says. "Can you, Aion?"

36

ATIA

The Charon's boat stops at the cusp of the River of Fire, the waters singeing the edges of his skiff pole as they bubble over the small rocks we perch beside.

Firia's domain is even more deadly up close. The bright orange rivers boil in their stream, cracking the shards of black rock that reach out from beneath like great limbs. Steam curls up from the glow, following the flow of the river until it eventually cascades down into a waterfall that breaks to ash at the bottom.

The High Gods knew what they were doing when they made this the river to protect the entry to their home.

I resist the urge to look back to Silas.

Not having him beside me feels wrong. It itches, a small whisper in the wind telling me to turn back and look at him one last time, for strength.

But I don't.

I know that if I do, then I won't be able to resist actually going back. And I must go forward. He was right when he said we each had our own battles.

His past is his, and my past is mine.

Beyond this river lies Oksenya and the High Gods, who ordered my parents' deaths. Who cursed me and ordered mine.

I cannot turn back, even for him.

I must find out where they are hiding so we can have the upper hand in our attack.

I jump from the boat and onto a small rock that seems the most untouched by the fire, too high for the river to bubble over onto it.

"Wait here," I say to Tristan and Cillian. "You can't risk crossing with me."

"Are you serious?" Tristan shakes his head, adamant. "We aren't leaving you, Atia."

I place a hand on his shoulder.

Tristan was the first friend I ever made, even if I lied to myself for so long that he was nothing more than another temporary human in a sea of such things.

He never abandoned me even when he saw the most monstrous parts of me, and then he risked his life to help me try to steal my own back. I have never known a friendship like that. I didn't think it was possible to have a person care so much about me, without motive or greed behind it.

I would take him with me if I could.

I *want* to take him with me.

"You must stay behind," I say.

"No way," Cillian objects. "We didn't come all this way to stand at the sidelines. Didn't you hear anything I said before? We're in this together, Atia."

My heart quickens at their loyalty.

"I heard," I say. "But this is different. It's a literal river of flames, and looking at it now, I don't know if I can even cross, let alone two humans."

"I'm half banshee," Cillian says pointedly.

"So maybe only your human half will have the skin melted off," I retort.

Tristan folds his arms across his chest. "I think the Charon should attempt to ferry us all safely across and see what happens."

The Charon blinks at him. "Humans are funny."

"You can't do it?" he asks.

"I ferry souls to the After and the Never," the Charon says. "Oksenya is neither of those. My boat would burn and char. You are fortunate I have taken you to the rivers and stopped there. I could have kept going, beyond, beyond to the Never and its delights."

"And you think we're safer here with this man than with you?" Tristan says to me, disbelieving.

"I have to do this," I tell him. "And I have to do it alone."

"You're not alone, Atia," he says urgently. "You don't ever have to be."

I know in my heart that is true and I understand that Tristan and Cillian want to protect me, but what they don't understand is that I want to protect them too. If it's a choice between them saving my life, and me saving theirs, then I know what I'll choose every time.

Too many people have died for me, *because* of me. Death has followed me my whole life and I will not let it follow my friends any longer.

"Wait for me here," I say to them. "I'll return, and when I do, I swear it'll be with the head of a God under my arm."

"You're really scary sometimes," Tristan says.

I smile. "That's precisely why you don't need to worry."

I turn to face the River of Fire. It is scalding, rippling the air as I threaten to move forward.

"Would you like me to push you?" the Charon asks.

I glance over my shoulder. "You better not."

"Know that if you die, I shall be here waiting to guide you to where you belong," he says. "It should be quick. If you are not worthy, I am sure you will liquefy in moments."

"You're really a very comforting person to have in death," I say. "How lucky the humans have been."

The river spits at my feet, sensing my plan to invade its waters.

"Are you sure about this?" Cillian asks from the safety of the boat.

"No," I call back. "But I'll do it anyway."

For my parents and every other creature the High Gods have cursed or imprisoned or betrayed.

I jump into the River of Fire.

When we swam across the river of cold flame to escape the Sisters, I felt the scorching of its waves, and then the freezing of my own heart as I tried to reach toward the bank. I'd thought I would die in those waters, gasping in my memories, drowning in the images of my parents.

I think that's why the river of cold flame affected you so much, Silas had said. *You're so haunted by your past. You let it drown you.*

When I jump this time, I don't think of my parents' deaths. I think of their lives and mine, forever entwined. About the words Thentos spoke of their rebellion, their desire to be free, and how they plucked immortality from the Gods and spent lifetimes, eons, eluding the most powerful creatures in the world.

I think of their strength, running through my blood.

Of their legend, carved into my bone.

I do not jump into this river to escape. I do it to move forward. To run headfirst into the hunt.

You must have faith in who you are today and not think so much of who you were or who you think you need to be.

Silas's words back at the manor wash over my thoughts.

I am predator, not prey.

The Last of the Nefas, created by Gods to be Godlike. Even without my abilities I have killed powerful, immortal creatures. I have conquered vampires and banshees, defeated queens and vengeance deities. I have captured love in my wake, tasting his lips as the sky fell around us.

I know who I am.

The water slips over my body. As I swim, I feel the tingle of its malice, threatening to swallow me whole. But it is just that: a tingle. A sense in the back of my mind. The rest of the water feels warm, comforting. The final hug before a long goodbye, the tender moments between sleep and waking.

It does not burn.

It does not ache.

The river froths and sears around me, charring rocks and melting anything that dares slip into its path.

But not me.

It cannot devour me, because I refuse to be devoured.

If this river is for the worthy, then it is mine to cross.

I claw my way onto the bank.

My clothes are singed, the ankles of my trousers crisp and a few holes in the lining of my shirt. Some of my skin is smudged and blackened, but when I panic and wipe at it, I'm relieved to see it is mostly ash beneath. Though my skin is reddened, I am unblistered.

Nice try, I think to the High Gods. *But I'm still here.*

I turn to see my friends across the way and wave my safety to them, but there's no sight of them beyond the thick smoke that bursts up from the River of Fire like lightning trying to pierce back into the sky. They are hidden beyond the fog.

I look back to the edge of the River of Fire I stand upon.

My parents never described the gateway to Oksenya, but I always pictured a large set of iron doors, stretching the lengths of the sky and back, manned by all manner of creatures and magic.

Instead, I'm presented with a window.

It is arched and wide, the inside a bleary film of white light that obscures all that is beyond.

"You are worthy," I remind myself. "You were born from this place. And you will be the one to put an end to the wretched Gods."

I step into the window.

Rather than being greeted by enchanted forests, I stumble and trip into a small stone room. The ceilings are low and gray, the only light crawling through from the small window I entered, which is now somehow barred, great iron rods trapping whatever was meant for this room inside.

I think quickly that this must be a trick from the High Gods. That Thentos and even the Charon conspired to have me sent here, lying about what the River of Fire truly led to.

I touch the tie pin.

Silas will find me wherever I am, even if that place is a prison.

Then I see the thing in the center of the room, on a low stone pillar; a blue orb that swirls before my very eyes. As I look around, I realize there are dozens of them, lining the various indents in the stone walls. They brighten as I approach.

My father's petal pounds against my chest.

It feels like being punched. Stronger than the hum when I kissed Silas, or the thump in the library when I found the entrance to the sorting zone. This is a hammering in my heart, so strong it begins to hurt.

I rip the petal from my pocket and hold it in the center of my palm. It quivers the closer I move toward the orb on the pillar.

I bend down to peer inside the strange object, and the white swirls that knock against the glass that secures them. They howl when I'm within reach.

I jump back.

Souls.

There are souls inside the orb, trapped in an eternal glass.

Who are they?

What could they have done to deserve such a fate?

The God of Death's words ignite inside my mind, as I remember what he said about the rebellion my parents waged and how all those who dared question them were imprisoned.

"This is their prison," I gasp.

A place where none could escape because they had no physical form. The High Gods trapped their essences here.

My father's flower petal jumps in my hand, as if it is being pulled toward the orb. He told me once that it was a key to unlock worlds, so we never had to stay trapped in our own.

Is this what he meant? Was he trying to tell me all this time?

I hold the petal out to the orb, feeling the pull of it.

My father did not die in vain. He left me something, a memento, a *key*. A way to free the creatures the High Gods trapped. He'd always meant for us to come to this place together and right a wrong.

"Here," I say, touching the petal to the orb.

The souls rush to it, pressing against the surface of the glass.

"Take it," I say. "Be free."

Only they just keep pounding against the glass.

I curse.

There must be a way to unlock the petal's powers. Surely if my father left me this, he would've also left a way to make it work. I search in my mind for anything my parents may have said, for any gifts they had left behind.

This petal is the only thing remaining of my father, the very thing he made certain I'd treasure as he tucked it between the lines of our bedtime stories. There is nothing else.

I pause, realizing that may not be exactly true.

My mother did leave me something too, didn't she? The song she'd sing to me every morning, not stopping until I hummed along with her so I'd never be able to forget.

I hum just a single note and the souls inside swirl, wild with the music. A splinter cracks across the glass of the orb. I part my lips, remembering the lullaby that my mother taught me so well, ingrained in every part of my heart, body, and soul.

Before I can let it explode from me, I feel a crushing in my chest. A hand, reaching inside me and squeezing. The melody is choked from me.

I fall to my knees and three apparitions burn into view.

One as bright as a star, blinding in her radiance. The other a dark smudge of a man, his top hat bleeding into his face. And the third, deep skin and a glowing smile, one eye of light and one of darkness.

"Atia of the Nefas."

The High Gods speak in unison.

"We had hoped you would choose not to die tonight."

37

SILAS

A *ion.*

The name slams into me. The name of a God and a guardian to the River of Eternity that is now barren before us.

It can't be.

"Aion is dead," I say, refusing to believe it. "And I was a human before I was a Herald."

"You were a God before you were anything!" Thentos snaps. "To be unmade. Not to die, but to live as though you were dead. That was your punishment for what you did."

"What I did?"

"Your *sympathies*, brother." He spits the words as if they are dirt in his mouth. "You helped the Nefas stage their rebellion, and when it all went wrong and the High Gods resolved to have them banished with no power, it was you who let them drink from your river and carry immortality to the mortal realm. You who convinced me to help you, but then refused to let me shoulder any blame by your side."

I frown as the story weaves into my mind. A God and a league of monsters allying, only for it to end in bloodshed.

Is that who I am: Bringer of war? Causer of chaos?

Betrayer of the Gods.

"It isn't true."

Thentos's glare darkens. "Why do you think your river runs

dry now?" he asks. "You absorbed our parents' wrath for your-self. After you were banished, it disappeared along with you. The High Gods were barely able to capture a few droplets. Not that they minded. They were thrilled nobody could ever use it to rebel against them again, leaving immortality only theirs to grasp. We have suffered for centuries over you, Aion. *Eternity.*"

I flinch at the use of the name and the word that has followed me since the start of this journey.

Eternities are ever changing, the Keeper of Files once said to me. Did he know? Is that why he spoke to me of breaking curses? And the Charon, so willing to help intruders cross the river. Had he known too?

Was I the last, surrounded by creatures who kept the secret of my past from me?

"You started all of this," Thentos says.

He advances toward me, his patience eclipsed.

Suddenly I realize the stature of him. The wideness of his shoulders and the sharpness of his jaw. How tall he is compared to me, like a shadow ever growing.

"Your brothers and sisters were forced to condemn you," he says. "I, to turn you into one of the Heralds, and Lahi, made to steal all that came before. Do you know how she cried when she stole every piece of her face from your mind? Our sister's river, erasing all that you were so she would not enrage our parents more."

Sister?

For so long I have been alone, the thought of family hadn't crossed my mind. I imagined any I had as a mortal would be dead, but instead I am faced with a family of immortals. Of furi-ous Gods, stung by my betrayal.

Have I been betraying them again by helping Atia?

This was your ruin before eternity, the Sisters had said.

Or no.

This was your ruin before, Eternity.

I move a hand to my belt loop, but it comes away empty. My palm tingles with the memory of the dagger. Of Atia.

"That blade was your favorite," Thentos says. "You called it the Caduceus. If applied to the dead, it brings them to life. If applied to the living, it removes their eternity. You were especially proud of it, so it was the first thing our parents took from you. And the very thing I sought to give back in case they decided to try to take your life," Thentos explains, "rather than have us erase you and unmake you every one hundred years."

"Every one hundred years?" I repeat.

How long have I been a Herald for?

Thentos's arm snaps out, hands curling around my neck in a vise.

"Though perhaps you should die after all, brother," he says. "Is that what you want? Coming here with a Nefas and no real plan?"

I don't struggle. I let my arms fall to my sides as he squeezes my throat.

Atia Atia Atia.

"For someone who knows me so well, you forget one thing," I say to the God of Death.

"Oh?" He raises a brow, hands further tightening around my neck. "What's that?"

"I don't need to breathe."

I bring my palm swiftly up, aiming for his nose.

He catches my hand and twists my arm, turning my whole body with it. I bend to the point of breaking before I crash my other elbow against his lip.

Thentos stumbles backward.

I don't give him the chance to regain his footing.

I raise my boot high in the air and kick out at his chest, sending Thentos straight to the ground.

He laughs as I hover over him.

"Not bad," he says, leaning back onto his elbows. "I thought you'd be out of practice, but perhaps you're ready after all. What do you think?"

He arches his head over my shoulder, and when I turn, I see that he isn't speaking to me.

The three remaining River Gods eye me with indecision.

Firia is the tallest of the women and looks the most distrustful of me, her fire-red eyes flickering like embers as she takes in my form. Her orange hair slinks down to her shoulders, jagged and black-tinged. Flaming arrows are secured to her back, alongside her trusty bow.

Beside her, I see Kyna, God of the River of Sorrow. There is such mourning on her face, it is hard to escape. Her hair is blue as tears and the look of betrayal in her eyes when she sees me nearly knocks me to the ground.

And then there is Lahi. With bright blond hair and cherub cheeks, she looks ever youthful and bright.

There is a familiarity to them that makes my heart nearly leap straight from my chest.

I know these people. These Gods. And I know them well.

"You've truly returned," Firia says, her voice deep as a cavern. "I must say, I expected your entrance to be more bloody, Aion."

"There's always *my* blood," Thentos says, touching a hand to his lip. "Or does that not count?"

"It most certainly doesn't count," Kyna says.

Thentos pulls himself up from the ground. "That hurts," he says. "Why am I the one who gets tasked with testing his strength?"

"Because it serves you right," Firia says simply. "For being his accomplice to begin with."

I look between them and at the way they are all now avoiding looking at me, as though something about my face hurts them to remember.

It is only Lahi who keeps her gaze on mine, unblinking.

She smiles. "Hello, brother. I've missed you so."

Would I miss her too if I could remember?

"Would you like me to help with that?" she asks, as though my thoughts have been whispered to her on the wind. "I'd very much like to undo all this, so we can be reunited."

Her voice is as delicate as a promise, begging to be kept.

I nod as she approaches, her arm out to touch a finger to my temple.

"It won't hurt at all," she says. "Not like the last time."

"Perhaps make it hurt a bit," Firia says. "I'd feel better for it."

Kyna elbows her sister, but I don't get a chance to see what Firia does in return. The moment Lahi touches me, a life flashes before my eyes.

My life.

In the days before the days, when the world was chaos and nothing else.

All that existed were my parents: the Day, the Dark, and the Balance. They molded the world into realms and from the chaos they created children to guard and patrol.

I hated patrolling.

The centuries bled into each other because there were no days.

It was a never-ending guard of a never-ending river and I was so very *bored*.

All the power of a God and all I got to do was watch a river?

To see souls be ferried to an afterlife of bliss, or see Godly creatures cross the boundaries into the blessed realm.

My siblings and I made games of it, guessing what a soul did to deserve the After or the Never, debating which monsters could cause the most chaos if they ever went against the High Gods.

We hoped for it. An end to our monotony and the rampage of our parents.

Then one day it happened.

One day, the monsters came.

I was floating in my river, arms spread wide as I looked up at the utter lack of sky, my clothes wet but never dragging me under.

Then, out of the corner of my eye, there were monsters.

"You shouldn't be here," I said, not bothering to look.

"And that is precisely why we've come to you," one said. "Because we want to belong elsewhere."

I sighed and turned my head to see the most strangely beautiful creatures.

A man and a woman, blue skin and great golden horns weaving in and out of each other like glorious cobwebs. Their eyes glowed white and their hair too, and from their red lips their voices entwined into song.

The Nefas.

Illusion makers.

Mischief bringers.

I smiled as I swam back to shore. I smiled further when they told me how they longed to be free and how they sensed I wanted the same.

They asked for an alliance.

"To betray my parents?" I asked. "To betray the High Gods and all that has ever been, so we may escape Oksenya together?"

"Yes," the man said. "Exactly that."

This time, I grinned.

The thing about being immortal is that you don't grow or change, especially when you aren't allowed the chance. You are stuck as you are, living each day endlessly the same.

No new experiences to give you wisdom, no new people to tug at your heart. Everything means nothing.

I hoped that joining with them would change that and that the freedom they longed for could be mine too. So I assembled armies in their name. I told them of other monsters, monsters my siblings and I had predicted in our games would cause the most damage if they rebelled, and helped them amass their following.

The result, I thought, would be freedom.

The result, it turned out, was slaughter.

Thentos was right about one thing: The fury of the High Gods did tear the skies apart, and when they won, they stripped the powers of all they didn't kill and locked them in an orb of endless torment.

Until I freed them.

Until I convinced my brother to help me betray our parents further.

Not many—there wasn't time for that—but enough.

I took a petal from the sacred tree of life and I sang the ancient melody that created us, and their prison shattered. When it was done, we took them to my river and let them drink, restoring all that they were. Then Thentos ordered the Charon to ferry them to the mortal world and I made them promise to hide for all the eternity I had given them.

"Betrayer," Skotadi had hissed.

"Night Bringer," Imera had howled.

"Unworthy," Isorropía had spat.

My parents descended on me like wolves. They held me under Firia's river, letting the ripples scorch my skin until I screamed and blistered.

They pushed me into Lahi's waters until I was swept away and choking on the memories being pulled from me. Drowning in the emptiness.

Then my brother came, and with tears in his deathly eyes, he ripped my form from me and gave me a new one. One of a loyal Herald, never questioning and never able to escape.

The High Gods erased all that I was in hopes it would never surface again.

But I remember now.

"Now what?" my sister asks, the wisps of her light hair still against the furious wind.

Lahi. How could I have ever forgotten her?

My beautiful sister, fierce and kind until the end.

She looks to me to lead, as they all do. As they have done ever since we swore our oaths and promised to put duty to the High Gods above all else.

Always, they have looked to me.

If I had kept the allegiance we swore to our parents, none of this would be happening. If I had stayed loyal to my family, Oksenya would not be under attack.

"Who do we kill, brother?" Thentos asks.

Killing.

I had forgotten I could do such a thing.

Heralds are incapable, but not Gods. Not me.

"Speak the names," Thentos says.

His hand clasps around my shoulder.

It has always been us, the five of us against the world. The only loyalty none of us would dare to break.

"Is it our parents, who threw their rage onto you and stole you from us?" Thentos asks. "Or do we kill the monsters who caused your downfall to begin with?"

The answer is clear.

There is only one way to end this.

"We slay the beasts," I tell him. "Every last one of them."

ATIA

My limbs are not my own. They are pulled in all directions, ripping and tearing at my skin until I feel as though I'm burning from the inside.

I slam into the walls of the prison cell.

The High Gods stand tall and resolute as statues, while my body cracks against the stone. Their power carries me up into the air and then throws me back down, pushing against my heart until I hit the floor next.

My chin scrapes against the rough ground.

"Atia of the Nefas," they say. "You do not belong in this place."

I spit blood onto the floor.

"Then why am I here?"

I certainly didn't ask the gateway to pull me into this place of all in Oksenya. I'd simply been thinking of the Gods and how much I wanted to take them down.

"Oksenya is what you want and always what you need." Their heads tilt to the side, musing. "You think you need to be a hero. A flaw, we admit. It will be fixed. It will be changed."

Their monotone voices are so void of emotion. They are not human, not monster, not anything I have seen or felt before.

I point to the orb in the center of the pillar. "What is that?" I ask, trying to catch my breath before their next attack. "Are your prisoners in there?"

"Traitors, alive and dead," they say. "Mingled together, the corpses and the living."

I blanch.

This is what the High Gods do: They abolish anything in their way. They are not creators. They are destroyers.

"Why did you kill my parents?" I ask bitterly. "They didn't murder any humans! They didn't break your rules!"

"They broke many rules," Skotadi, God of the Dark, says, breaking from the others. "Perhaps not in the mortal realm, but in this one. Those sins are never forgiven."

If it is a matter of sin, then these beings have done more than most.

My jaw hardens as my parents' screams echo in my mind.

Run, Atia! RUN!

"You will pay for what you have done," I promise. "You will pay in blood."

Even if it takes my own to do it, I will not let the High Gods live long enough to cause anyone else the pain they have caused me.

"What do you imagine will happen here?" Skotadi asks.

"I imagine I will kill you as I have killed vampires and banshees," I say. "I will break my curse, regain the full might of my powers, and snap your so-called blessed realm in two."

The High Gods laugh, their unison returned.

Their arms shoot out, a perfect dance, and I am lifted in the air once more.

Their powers choke me.

I linger beside the prison orb, kicking my legs out to try and throw myself from their grasp. It is useless. A grip nobody can escape.

"You are alone, Atia of the Nefas. You have lived alone; you will die alone."

I clench my fists together.

"Burn in the Never," I spit.

I kick my leg out, as hard and fast as I can, colliding with the orb beside me. It bounces to the stone floor and the High Gods gasp.

They drop me with a thud as they watch the orb roll across the ground.

It doesn't smash. It doesn't shatter or chip.

All that remains is the tiny splinter from when I sang my mother's song.

Still, the Gods are furious.

"Silly child," Skotadi yells. "A prison cannot be broken so easily."

He approaches me with eyes like great spheres.

"But you can," he says.

I lift my chin, refusing to cower before this creature.

The High God grabs my arm, twisting until I hear the bones click.

He will break me in two if I let him.

I will not let him.

I wrench Silas's dagger from my pocket, and with my free hand I swipe wildly out behind my back.

Skotadi merely laughs, flinging the dagger from my hand.

It skitters across the prison floor, coming to a stop by a familiar set of polished black shoes.

"I'm glad we have not missed the massacre."

My heart leaps at the smooth intonation of Silas's voice. It's all the strength I need to writhe from the God's grip.

He found me.

I wrench my arm from Skotadi's hand, pushing outward to escape.

The High God stumbles back, but his scowl is no longer directed at me.

It is to Silas and the four River Gods who stand at his side.

Death, Sorrow, Forgetting, Fire.

Where the High Gods are mighty statues, the River Gods look more like warriors, fierce and ready for battle, with arrows and swords hooked every which way on their bodies.

"Aion," Imera says. The God of the Day speaks in a whisper, her voice alive in light. "You have returned. You have become whole."

My lips part as she looks to Silas.

"*Aion?*" I repeat.

Briefly, Silas's eyes move to mine and a flicker of uncertainty passes over his chiseled face.

He swallows when he sees the blood dripping down my chin, but he doesn't speak or move to wipe it away.

"Why have you returned?" Isorropía asks. "What hangs in your balance, our dearest one?"

"The world," Silas says.

His voice matches their monotone so perfectly that I flinch.

There is something new and awful in his eyes that I don't recognize. His gait is no longer rigid and proper, the stiff Herald I'd grown to care for. I'd grown to cherish his moments of unrest and the unruliness that set into him after a battle, mussing his hair and loosening his jaw.

Now those cherished moments seem cursed.

His posture is too relaxed, slack and arrogant. His hands no longer slink into his pockets and the reluctant smile I'd come to crave in the mornings is replaced by an easy smirk that doesn't sit right on his face.

"As you have wished," the stranger Silas says. "I have come to make amends for my past mistakes."

The moment it clicks, I stumble backward.

Everything we have been through, every oddity about him that never made sense before, suddenly fits perfectly into place.

Silas is the God of Eternity.

His powers weren't affected by Vail's magical blocks, because his powers were Godly.

He didn't look like the other Heralds—dress like them, feel like them—because he was never truly one of them at all.

The Sisters did not want to kill him, but to save him from monsters.

Aion.

He is not dead. The once ally of my kind is here and he looks nothing like the boy I thought I knew.

His shoulders seem broader, everything about him sharper and foreboding, even alongside the casual shrug of his shoulders.

He is like a storm on the cusp of exploding the skies.

"You remember who you were," I say in a gasp.

He stares at me, silent.

"What does that mean for us?" I ask.

Silas is a God and I am a monster. Two sides of a coin, of a *war*.

"Speak!" I demand.

Silas's eyes are like arrows, shooting into me.

He says nothing. He does nothing.

Skotadi laughs. "I knew you would come to your senses after living lifetimes outside of our blessed realm, seeing the horrors the monsters wrought. Well done, boy," he says. "You are returned to us, worthier than you left."

The High God points to me, the darkness descending into his eyes.

"Now help us kill the monster before it taints this place further."

Silas—*Aion*—nods.

His divinity is newly piercing as he reaches downward to pick up the blade that we once shared. The first gift he gave to me, that I tried to give back so he would return to me unharmed.

He lifts it from the floor.

"This isn't you," I say, shuffling backward as he approaches. "I *know* you, and I know that you don't want to kill me."

"You have no idea what he wants," Skotadi spits.

Aion, God of Eternity, spins the dagger in his hand.

"Silas—"

"My name is Aion," he interrupts, jaw strung tight with every word.

The High Gods look pleased, their smiles a perfect mirror of each other.

Behind him, the remaining River Gods are unblinking, awaiting their commands.

"I am son to the High Gods," Aion announces in a boom. "Brother to the River Gods and guardian of eternity."

He pauses, his smile a caress.

"And most important," he says. "I am always an ally to monsters of mischief."

Quickly, he throws me back the dagger and I swipe it from the air with a surprised yelp.

The arrogant ease to Silas's movements is suddenly replaced

with a familiar straight back. He tightens his tie and gives me a wink.

"What are you doing?" Skotadi demands.

"Finishing what I started," Silas says, whipping his head to face them.

He steps to my side, his hand lingering close.

I reach out to him, threading his fingers through mine, the rough skin of his knuckles a familiar relief.

Skotadi's eyes widen in betrayal, just as a new door appears and swings open behind the River Gods.

To my surprise, Tristan and Cillian rush in, each of their hands filled with iris petals identical to the one my father had given me.

"Got them!" Tristan says, holding the flowers out toward Silas. "Did we miss it?"

"Humans? *Here?*" Skotadi yells. "What is the meaning of this?"

"I told you," Silas says.

His hand tightens around mine.

He came for me.

"I need to undo a grave mistake," he says. "Letting you win the first time."

It is then that Thentos steps forward, his ashen scythe like a spear in his hands.

With one nod from Silas, the God of Death brings the scythe into a swooping arc in the air, and then clear across his father's neck.

39

SILAS

Skotadi catches the blade before it can cleave all the way through. My brother's scythe is embedded in his neck, caught between bone and the High God's hand.

Isorropía's screams are loud enough to shake the orbs from their walls.

Skotadi pulls the scythe from his neck and flings an arm out. His hand whips across my brother's brow.

Thentos flies through the room.

"Now!" Firia screams in rage.

She heaves her bow into her hand and grabs a flaming arrow from the quiver across her back.

God weapons.

Blades and armor just like my dagger, forged here in Oksenya from the very essence of the Gods to protect them from any being, now brought to kill them.

As Kyna swoops forward, her tearstained axe aimed at Imera's throat, I turn to Atia.

"Get to the orbs," I say, grabbing on to each of her shoulders. "You must set the prisoners free. Use the petals. Tristan and Cillian will explain."

I turn to the battle, but Atia shakes her head, confused.

"*You* explain," she says, pulling me back to her. "How is any of this possible, Silas? You—you're a *God*."

I shake my head. There isn't time. Across the room, Imera grabs Kyna's axe from the air, ready to slice open my sister's stomach.

"Silas," Atia presses, as my siblings wage a war in my name. As my family tries to kill each other for their versions of peace. "Who are you?"

I sigh and press my forehead to hers. A brief moment of tenderness that I wish I could stay in forever.

"Yours," I tell her in a breath. "Only ever yours. Now go!"

I push Atia from me and sweep into battle, throwing my mother Imera to the ground.

She hisses.

When she reaches for Kyna's axe again, I step down on her wrist, hard.

Her bones crinkle like paper.

"Finish it," I tell Kyna. "And make it quick."

My sister nods, the tears clear in her eyes as she descends upon our second mother.

It is necessary, I tell myself. *They will not stop terrorizing both the human realm and the blessed realm if we do not stop them first.*

They are unforgiving. Unmerciful.

I have seen and felt their horrors firsthand.

Out of the corner of my eye, I see Tristan and Cillian gathering by Atia's side. Between them, they amass the petals from the sacred iris tree, readying to crack the orbs that line the walls.

Once Atia speaks the blessed words, assuming Tristan and Cillian remember them, they can free every soul trapped inside this place, as I failed to do the first time.

I whirl as the sound of clashing scythes and arrows piercing stone fills my ears. Firia and Thentos are keeping Isorropía at bay, but Lahi stands alone with our father.

He grabs her hair and pushes her into the stone wall.

Her blood coats the unbroken orbs.

I run toward my sister, fury alight in my bones. I will not let my father destroy her as he tried to destroy me.

He throws her to the floor like a rag doll, staring down at her tiny body with malice. The morning star Lahi was gifted as a child lies on the floor by her feet, and I barely get to her before my father grabs it and brings it high in the air.

I block his blow, grabbing the hilt before the iron spiked ball can split my sister's head in two.

I wrench it from my father's hand and swing it back around at him, but Skotadi jumps out of the way just in time.

The spikes rip through his shirt but miss his marbled skin.

Lahi rushes to stand, her blond hair matted by blood.

"I can make you forget, Father," she begs. "I can release your hate and give you peace. It can be like it was in the before times."

"Foolish thing," Skotadi scoffs. He rips the morning star from my hand in a flash. "I will not be manipulated by the very children I created!"

He swings the weapon into the air, releasing it so quickly I only just dive out of the way.

It embeds into the wall behind us.

It's then I hear Thentos's booming voice.

"No!" he cries out.

I look over to see him leaping forward, just as our mother Imera plunges the axe into Kyna's back.

She rips it out, then strikes a second time.

A third.

Kyna falls, eyes wide. The tears cascade down her cheeks like rainfall.

The blood is everywhere.

Thentos freezes, just steps from our sister's body. Too late to save her from our cackling mother.

"All of our children are such disappointments," our father says, staring over at Kyna's lifeless body. "And all of you will die here."

He whips out of the way just as one of Firia's arrows shoots toward him.

"You missed," he says with a tut. "Idiot girl."

I charge forward, but his hand lashes out, quick as a whip, and suddenly Atia is dragged from the other side of the room and into his hands.

I freeze as he holds her close to his chest, the crook of his large elbow against her throat.

"Do you really believe that you can best us?" he asks.

"Let her go," I say, my voice as dark as my father's has ever been.

"Or you will try to kill me?"

I rip Lahi's morning star from the stone wall. "Or I will succeed."

"Just do it, Silas!" Atia screams, trying in vain to wriggle from my father's grip. "Kill him!"

Only I can't. Not with her in the way.

I won't risk hurting Atia further than I already have. She is the one thing in this world that has given my life meaning.

Skotadi's hold on her tightens.

"You will live forever with this on your conscience," he says. "The death of an entire race, down to you. I wonder what will—"

In a snap, a flaming arrow shoots straight through my father's skull.

I whirl to see Firia with her bow raised.

"I didn't miss that time," she says.

Our father drops to his knees, the arrow piercing one side of his head and protruding straight from the other. The flames catch across his face.

Thentos rushes toward him, raising his scythe high in the air once more.

"For Kyna," he says.

Skotadi barely has the time to blink, his mouth opening in a wretched gasp, before Thentos's scythe cuts clean through his throat, finishing the job.

The God of the Dark's head thumps to the floor.

I bite down on the small ounce of grief for him that remains. My once father, who fell victim to greed and power. It takes a moment, our weapons hanging in the air, silence ripping across the prison, before his body shudders.

A shadow explodes from him—*becomes him*—transforming his body into pure smoke. It shatters through the barred window, bending the iron bars as it heads for the night and soaks into the darkened sky.

Only his severed head remains, open in that final gasp for mere moments, before it dissolves into the shadows that coat the stone. The God of the Dark is dead. Returned to the formless essence he once was in the time before corruption and malfeasance.

"Murderers!"

Our mothers' screams rattle the world.

"Atia!" I call out. I don't give my father's body a second glance. "Get the prison orbs! You must shatter them all!"

She races toward them.

When Imera and Isorropía whirl around to stop her, my siblings and I all charge. Scythes and knives, arrows and morning stars. We lunge at our two mothers in a melee of blood and slaughter, allowing Atia the time she needs to unleash a legion of warriors.

40

ATIA

My mother's song was made for dancing.

It was a thing she whispered to me whenever the sun rose dewy and pink through my window, and then again whenever it set in a haze of orange that rippled across her cheeks. It was stolen moments of laughter, spoken in clucked tongues and sweet humming.

My mother smiled whenever the longing melody parted her lips and drifted through the air like a summer breeze.

She was happy when she sang it.

She was free.

Tristan and Cillian said it was simple: touch the petals to the orbs and speak the words. That was what Silas told them to do.

Only they weren't words, not really. The harmony was far more complicated than that. It was a language, I think, but not one I ever knew to exist in the human realm.

It was a symphony of sound, echoing the noise of the world in all its wonder, and every inch of that noise, of that chaotic beauty, danced through my memory.

I throw the petals into the air, a dozen irises leaping from me.

For a moment, they are butterflies, fluttering across the stone prison. Some land on the orbs, others cascade to the floor below them, but when I begin to sing, all of them shake.

I let my mother's music tumble out of me, filling the cavern.

The Gods grow still as the petals lift up from the ground in a whirlwind.

Tristan and Cillian throw theirs into the air too, and like magnets, they find their way to the orbs, kissing against the glass.

First, the orbs splinter. And then they shatter.

The glass explodes from the walls, pieces so tiny they turn to dust at our feet. In moments, the souls flee. It is a frenzy. Flurries of white-blue light whip against the walls, the might of their anger and shared joy a palpable force that winds me as they rush by.

Silas's eyes catch mine in the chaos.

The warm glow of him is like a beacon. His cheeks are flushed, suit marred with blood and dirt, an urgency to him I have never seen before.

He looks like Silas, but he looks like someone else too. Someone new.

"Foolish child!" the God of the Day screams. "You have no idea what you have unleashed."

I gasp a smile.

Surrounding us now, there are no orbs.

There are warriors. There are monsters. And they are angry.

The monsters, dead and alive, bare their teeth. Souls, flickering in and out of being. Those the Gods trapped while still alive are finally able to clench their fists, after years of being stripped of their forms.

"You cannot win this," Silas tells his mothers. "You are outnumbered."

"We are Gods," Imera says.

Silas gestures to his brothers and sisters. "As are we."

"Not for long."

From Imera's hands, light births. It radiates from her palms, a warm glow at first, but when her hands shoot out, the light grows into a scalding white.

It is brighter than any sun or star could be.

The freed monsters charge.

Imera laughs.

The beams scatter from her hands, blinding the warriors. Silas and the River Gods wince back, shielding their eyes, but those not quick enough to hide from the light are absorbed by it.

Their eyes turn red and then explode inside their skulls.

My vision blurs, but as Tristan, Cillian, and I stand behind Imera, we are sheltered from most of her power.

She has eradicated more than a third of the free warriors with a single blast.

Silas! I scream his name in my mind.

I have to reach him before the God of the Day sends another wave of power.

I barrel toward him, but Isorropía sweeps into my path, snarling before me.

"Now we can finally be alone," she says.

I frown, until I realize what she means. Imera is keeping Silas and the others at bay for just long enough so the other God can kill me herself.

"Get away from her!" Tristan yells.

He throws himself into Isorropía's path, but she is quicker than he will ever be. She merely flicks a finger, as if swatting a fly, and both Tristan and Cillian collapse to their knees.

They clutch at their throats, unable to breathe.

"What are you doing?" I yell. "Stop!"

Isorropía dismisses me with a wave of her hand. "The spares mean nothing to me."

"What does mean something to you? It certainly isn't your children or the world."

The God of the Balance does not respond.

She looks between the dead Skotadi and the still-living Imera, holding back the warriors as best she can.

The Dark and Day she has lived beside for eons.

Isorropía simply sighs.

Then she lunges.

I expect to be thrown to the floor as the God collides with me, but instead she jumps through me.

Inside me.

There is a flash of blinding red, like blood being poured into my eyes.

I scream and stumble backward.

When I open my eyes again, I'm no longer standing where I once was. The prison walls are gone, and Silas and his siblings have disappeared.

There is simply a black void with me in the center.

"What is this?" I ask.

Isorropía's cackles echo around me, bouncing off the black. "Perhaps you are dying."

"It's a trick," I yell out to her. "An illusion!"

Isorropía steps forward, appearing like fog from the nothingness. "You would know all about illusions," she says. "Let's see which is your favorite."

The nothingness shifts and Silas appears from the darkness.

"Silas!" I call out, rushing to him.

Relief fills my heart as I wrap my arms around him.

"Isorropía has trapped us in some kind of illusion and—"

I pause as I notice a flicker in his eyes that I have never seen before. That deep-set gray, the color of winter nights, is darker than usual.

I pull back, pull away.

This is not Silas. This is *Aion*. And the difference is clear.

"I know what my mother has done," the young God says.

His voice is cold and distant.

He pulls his tie loose, rugged.

"I know because I asked her to. Because I am loyal to my family, above all else."

I narrow my eyes. "You're not him," I say, skittering backward.

He arches a brow. Too precise, too cruel. "Aren't I?"

I grit my teeth together as the conjured Aion stalks toward me. "I trust Silas," I say.

After everything that has happened, I know in my heart he would never hurt me, just as I would never hurt him. We are kindred and whoever we were when this journey started is no longer who we are today.

He is mine and I am his, that I know more certainly than anything else.

"You won't scare me like this," I tell the God. "Unlike you, I know where Silas's heart truly lies. Imera can only hold him off for so long. He will come for me and—"

"*Aion* will be dealt with." Isorropía's voice bursts from his lips, as though his name is a curse. "Just as he was before. He cannot find me here anyway. I am inside of you, little Nefas. Tucked deep. The only way to kill me now would be to kill you too."

"Then stop hiding behind your son and get it over with!"

The conjured Aion shrieks, the God's voice a banshee-like howl escaping his lips.

"Then deeper we go," she says. "All the way down."

Aion disappears into smoke and is replaced by screams.

The cries of my mother the day she died. Back then, she begged me to run, but now she pleads with me to save her.

Please, Atia, she begs. *Do not run and let us die!*

Atia! my father bellows. *For the love of Gods, save us!*

I am paralyzed as their bodies appear before me, bloodied and mutilated.

Please, the ghost of my mother screams. *Don't leave!*

From her mouth, tiny insects crawl. I gasp as they creep past my mother's lips and then scurry onto my feet.

I try to jump backward, but the insects skitter up my arms and into the creases of my neck. The holes of my ears.

"H-how are you doing this?" I manage to stutter out.

"I am the Balance." Isorropía's voice echoes around me, ever calm. "I exist in all things, even insignificant creatures like you."

Insignificant.

The word burns through me with its untruth.

I am not insignificant.

If I was, then a God wouldn't currently be trying to kill me.

"Enough!" I yell out. "I already know that my parents are dead!"

It aches to say the words, but once I do the voices silence.

My parents' bodies vanish in a shimmer.

"But do you know whose fault it is?"

The voice belongs to my father.

He steps from the dark, with my mother at his side.

"Atia," he says.

I cannot breathe as I take in the image of them both, close enough for me to reach out and touch.

"Father." I nearly choke on the word. I have craved to say it aloud since I was fourteen. "Mother."

"We are here," he says.

And then his hand lashes out across my cheek.

I hit the floor, hard. The pain makes my vision haze at the edges, black spots dancing across my eyes.

"Did you think we would not return to seek justice for what you did?" he asks. "You left us to die, Atia. After you caused us to be caught, you fled."

I stammer out a breath, my lips trembling at the accusation.

You're not to blame, I tell myself.

But a little voice in my mind, a voice too hard and jagged to be my own, whispers, *Are you sure?*

"Guilt is a strange thing," my mother says, looking down on me as I clench my fists against the ground.

Her voice is just as I remember.

A perfect copy of hidden lullabies.

I ache to hear her sing to me just one last time.

"Guilt only comes to those who deserve it," my father finishes, as my mother steps slowly backward, almost becoming shadow.

"You deserve it for what you did to us, Atia. How could we ever love a child as selfish as you?"

My lips press together.

The words do not hit as they intend to.

I may fear the memories of the night my parents died, but I know the difference between a truth and a lie.

Between a scared child and a conniving God.

Fear is not real unless you give it the power to be.

I throw my body into the illusion, wrapping my arms around

his waist to push him to the floor. We collide in a mess of limbs, hitting the ground with a crack.

My false father throws me off and growls; a line of blood runs down to his lips, mingling in his teeth.

My heart throbs.

It isn't him, I remind myself. *This could never be him.*

My father would not be so stiff and brutal in a fight. He would be lithe and graceful, gliding in and out of motions. He would focus on bringing forth nightmares, instead of trying to battle hand-to-hand.

This conjured image is a bad lie.

As is the one of my mother, whose mouth curls to a smile. Not her smile, not even close.

I watch as the image of her fades into the nothingness.

"You little bitch," my false father spits.

He backhands me and I only have a second for my body to graze the floor before I am being lifted back up.

He picks me up by my hair, pulling me from the ground like he is plucking a weed from a meadow.

"Your screams will satiate me until the mortal realm crumbles to ash."

I wince under his grasp.

Isorropía.

This image of my father isn't just an illusion. *It is a mask.*

The rage ignites in me. This God thinks she can use the memory of my parents to make me weak when they have only ever made me strong.

"My parents loved me," I say. The tears sting at my eyes. "They loved me so much that they would've done anything to keep me safe, even if it meant spending their lives in hiding. They are not my fear. They are my *strength*."

"I'm going to watch your soul leave your body as I watched the souls of your family leave theirs," the God promises.

I swallow.

Grind my teeth together.

"Fuck you."

I spit my blood into her eyes, and my father—the God wearing his face—flails backward, knocking me to the ground.

Quickly, I grab Silas's dagger and stab it right in the center of her foot.

Isorropía only laughs, her face transforming back into her own.

"That was not a killing blow," she says.

"It doesn't need to be."

Blood is all I've ever needed to absorb the power of monsters. The blood of the treacherous vampire Sapphir and the blood of Vail's banshee. All of it, painted on this dagger and then brought to my lips to restore my magic.

I rip the dagger from Isorropía's foot, and before she can stop me, I taste her blood.

Isorropía pales as she realizes what I have done.

"You little—!"

But it's too late.

I rise to my feet as I feel the last of my powers restored. My veins are lightning, surging through me. I could explode with it.

There is no immortality, but the rest...the rest that was once gone is there again.

The Last of the Nefas, restored.

All the power of my family, coursing through me.

Awakened, again.

"You want fear?" I say to the God in a challenge. "I'll show you fear."

It doesn't take long. Hers are written all over her mind, barely disguised in the haze of anger and hate.

She fears being ousted.

She fears being overrun.

She fears being forgotten.

I sear the images into her like brands, letting them grow and multiply around her. The fear of her fading away, of her dying after living so long as an immortal, and of nobody caring to remember her afterward.

"Stop!" the God screams out.

I don't.

I let my eyes turn white and my skin return to blue, as the fears overrun her.

I do not feel hate and desperation, as I did with the man who tried to hurt Tristan. This isn't about that. It's about doing what is right to keep my friends and the world safe.

It's about making sure nobody else must suffer, as my family did.

I do not feed on the God like a grand meal. I let her fears slip away as they come true.

I promise to forget her the moment she is gone.

Her hair streaks white and she holds out a shaking hand to me. One last attempt before she fades.

"I will not go alone," she says.

The black seeps from her fingertips like ink and shoots into my heart.

I only just see her collapse to nothing, before I am thrown to the darkness.

The world blinks away.

When it returns, I am home.

In the farm by the daisy fields I used to live in with my parents, with the smell of fresh apples we'd feed to the horses.

My parents stand in the kitchen, smiling at me. They are bathed in a glow of endless light. It beams from their smiles. It is soft and warm, their bodies slowly blinking before me as their souls try to hold on for a little longer.

"You're really here," I say. "It's not a trick?"

My mother shakes her head.

"Nothing ever really dies," she says. "Especially not people. We live inside of you, always, a tiny fragment of our souls embedded into yours."

My father steps around the kitchen island to lay a hand on my shoulder. The feel of his touch releases a breath in me I have been holding on to for years. The relief of knowing he is not gone.

Not truly. Perhaps not ever.

"We have watched you grow and we are so proud, Atia," my father says. "Proud of the woman you have chosen to become."

I bite my lip as the tears roll into the creases of my mouth. "I've missed you both so much."

"Oh, Atia," my mother says. "Our beautiful Atia."

Her eyes flicker to my heart, and when I look down, I see there is blood. Thick and dark.

It crawls from me, just like the insects.

"You can fight this," my mother says. "Evil slithers inside of you, but you have the power to cast it out. To absorb it and make it anew."

The melody of her voice brightens the room that much more.

How is it possible to miss the sound of a person so much?

"The choice has always been yours," my father tells me. "What happens next is for you to decide."

"I just want to be with you," I say, afraid of this moment ever ending. "Forever, the three of us here. Just like this."

"A part of you will always be with us." My mother touches a hand to my cheek. I close my eyes to savor it. "But a greater part of you knows there is more to do, Atia. More to see. More to love."

I bite my lip as I feel the tingle of my hand being pulled back.

Atia! a familiar voice calls out. *Stay with me, please!*

My heart pounds.

"All these years I've missed you too much to bear," I tell my parents. "I can't lose you again."

My parents each take one of my hands and squeeze tightly.

"You never lost us," my father says. "And you never will. If you want to stay and rest, you can. If you want to fight for more, you can do that too."

I want both, I think to myself.

But deep down I know which one I want more.

"I love you so much," I tell them.

Then I make the choice and let everything else fade away.

41

SILAS

Atia is on the floor and she does not move.

Cillian and Tristan crouch by her side, but no matter how much they shake her, she refuses to wake.

"Get out of my way," I say.

The God of the Day licks her lips as she stands between me and Atia.

With my mother of the Balance disappeared, she is the only obstacle I face.

Years of tyranny and anger, of curses and cruel punishments to satisfy my parents' power, and now there is only one thing that remains.

A single clear and crystallizing thought.

Kill her. End this.

"Move," I say.

I clutch on to Kyna's axe, her sorrow coursing through me. I miss the feel of my blade—the Caduceus—clutched in Atia's seemingly lifeless hands.

I want it back.

I want her back.

And I will not let anything stand in my way.

"What use do you have for vengeance now?" Imera asks.

She glances at the unleashed monsters who surround her, unburned from her first light blast.

"You have freed your captives, your curse is lifted, and you have taken your father's life as vengeance. Is it not over, Aion? Is it not enough?"

"Vengeance?"

That is what she thinks I want, more than justice or righteousness. So corrupted by the notion of creation she carries in her veins that she could not imagine wanting anything not rooted in greed or selfishness.

"You cannot comprehend a quest spurred by need, rather than vengeance, and carried through by love rather than hate," I say. "I started this because I thirsted to know who I was. I will finish it because I know who I want to be."

I step forward, axe in hand.

"It ends now," I promise.

I turn to the warriors, the monsters who growl at the thought of tearing my mother apart, limb from limb.

"The kill is mine," I tell them.

I hurtle toward my mother.

We crash in a mess of blows, her fist pounding into my stomach and sending me flying backward with the force of it. My siblings descend next, Thentos's scythe jutting out like a spear.

Our mother need only fling her arms out, sending rays of pure sunlight into their eyes.

They stumble backward, dazed.

"Idiot children!" she roars. "Betrayers of creation!"

The monsters do not hold any longer.

They run for her and I see the brief flicker of panic in the God's eyes at the idea of their fury. She waves an erratic arm and a ring of fire surrounds her in a protective circle.

The monsters flinch back, hissing at the flames.

"Hold!" I order, trying to keep them at bay. "I told you that she is mine!"

If they attack, my mother will surely kill them. Perhaps not all, but even one more monster's death at her hands would be too many.

She has spilled so much blood already.

I pull myself back up and surge forward, leaping across the fire. It burns at my ankles.

The pain means nothing.

I whip Kyna's axe through the air and it smashes against my mother's cheek, sending sparks of light shattering like glass across the floor.

The God falls to the ground, seething.

A desperate thing, trying to cling to power in a losing battle.

She may be mighty, but she is outnumbered. Four Godly children and a legion of monsters at her feet. She cannot win and she knows it.

But this isn't about winning.

The God rises to her feet.

It's about destroying whatever she can, while she can.

"Firia!" I call out to my sister.

"I know!" she yells in return.

The arrows burst from her bow, a trio flying at our mother. They split in the air, one puncturing each of her outstretched palms and the other shooting straight into her chest.

Her heart.

Their flames spread, crawling up her arms and threatening to engulf her whole.

Thentos springs into action. He sends his shadows ripping around our mother, the clouds of deathly smoke puncturing her like knives, leaving slits and cuts across her skin.

Imera cries out and the walls of the prison begin to splinter. Cracks appear through the stone, giving a glimpse of the true Oksenya beyond this prison.

The blessed realm.

"Lahi!" I command. "Now you!"

My sister is already primed to strike.

"Enough, Mother," she says in a caress, placing a hand on her shoulder. "Let me take it away."

Imera gasps as my sister pulls the memories and anger from her mind like weeds.

Lahi trembles. "I can't get it all. It's so wedged in there."

She falls to her knees alongside our mother.

Thentos rushes to her side, catching our sister before she collapses completely.

"Only a little," Lahi says in gasps. "I could only take a little."

"Shh, sister," Thentos soothes, caressing her hair from her face.

"A little is enough," I say, towering over our mother.

Her head lolls as she sits on her knees, dazed from whatever few memories Lahi stole from her.

We end the war by ensuring all of the High Gods can never return.

So end it, Aion. Silas. God of Eternity and wars, both new and old.

The air around us shimmers as my mother tries to right herself.

"You cannot win," Imera pants. The white of her blood drips down her chest where Firia's arrow still burns, and then onto the floor. She is coated in it. "You cannot save her from the Balance."

She casts a glance to Atia and my jaw ticks.

"She doesn't need me to save her," I say.

I lift Kyna's axe high in the air.

"She'll save herself."

Without another moment of hesitation, I bring the axe down clean through my mother's skull.

She doesn't make a sound as it cleaves into her.

It feels wrong, even though I know it is the right thing. I have never liked killing, never had a taste for it even in war. Eternity whirls in my veins and that means more than just living forever. It means worshipping the infinite and hating all that is finite.

I step back as the monsters descend on my mother's corpse in a melee. Each of the once-trapped warriors take their turn to tear pieces from the old God and ensure she can never rise again.

As I watch my mother die, the light fading from her ever-bright eyes, I know it is for the good of the realms. To save humans and monsters alike.

To help Atia.

Before the monsters know to cease, a light erupts from the body of the once God and creator of the day. It is a brightness like no other, not searing and angry as the blasts she had sent to kill us, but ethereal. *Divine.*

The monsters stagger backward.

Only once they are clear does the light explode upward, blowing through the roof of the prison and shooting for the sun behind the night. For the stars and all the brightness of the world that exists beyond this one.

For the thing the light used to be before it knew malice.

The prison walls crumble to dust around us.

It's over.

I throw the axe to the floor and rush to Atia's side.

Her hands are cold and slack, her skin far too pale and sticky beneath my touch.

"Atia! Stay with me, please!" I kneel, cradling her within my arms.

I clutch on to her as a lifeline.

If she dies, then nothing matters.

In all of eternity, I have never known this feeling before we met, of being so consumed by somebody else that I'm not sure where each of us begins and ends. I am tied to her, all the pieces of me most worthy wrapped up in her smile and her touch.

She is a monster and a miracle. A thing of light and of shadows. Without her, the world does not make sense.

"You can't die," I say.

Atia's hand tightens around mine, as if a reflex, but then slackens again in moments.

"Tell me how to fix it," I demand. I push her silver hair from her face. "Tell me what I need to do."

When she doesn't stir, I touch a thumb to her lips to wipe away the blood that dribbles to her chin.

I know she may think it is easier to give up, to rest after a life spent in grief and hiding, in fear and battle with the Gods. But the world needs her.

I need her.

She has so much more left to do, left to experience, left to live.

Atia has the power to change the world and I want to be there when she does.

"Choose me, Atia," I whisper. I press my lips to hers, my own tears falling down her cold cheeks. "Choose us."

42

ATIA

I open my eyes to see the world I've chosen to stay in and the person I want more than anything to stay beside.

Silas, battle-bloodied and achingly beautiful, searching me for any signs of pain.

Only I don't feel pain.

I feel *strong*.

The power explodes through me and into my lungs, so that with every breath I take a new wave of it settles into my heart. I look down at my hands, veins like lightning coursing up my arms.

They glow.

My body comes to life in light.

"Atia—?" Silas begins.

"The Balance," I say in return.

I can feel it now—not just my powers but hers too, tangled up inside of me so there is no clear divide between us.

For a moment I'm scared, but then I realize that they don't feel hard or empty like Isorropía was. This power is light and warm. It is the true essence of Balance that the God herself lost over the eons.

I close my eyes to savor it.

When I open them again, the glow fades to a mere shimmer, settling inside me like it has always belonged there.

I look around me.

The walls of the prison are gone, and beyond the crumbled rocks I finally see the world that created my parents and birthed all the wondrous monsters of the realms: Oksenya.

The skies are alight in purples and blues, the sun and the moon now sitting alongside each other in an endless twilight that wasn't there before. Clouds drip down like waterfalls, into star-speckled lakes that disappear past an endless field of wildflowers. Great trees stand alight with birds of fire and forests, some with wings of moss and others wings of ember.

The skyline ripples with mirrors much like my gateways, promising new horizons beyond.

I swallow, my breath catching at the vastness of it. The beauty that could never be done justice by stories.

Around me now are dozens upon dozens of warriors gathered in a circle, bloody but alive. My parents aren't among them, and I feel a small needle in my heart at the thought that it will be a while before I see them again.

"Atia," Silas says.

The pain lessens when his eyes collide with mine, his face riddled with anxiety.

"Hi," I say.

It only takes a moment before his arms are wrapped tightly around me.

I breathe him in, savoring his touch. I hold on to him hard as his hands thread into my hair, making sure this moment isn't another kind of trick or illusion.

No, I think, when I feel him tighten around me. *This is Silas.*

I would recognize his touch anywhere.

"Is it over?" I ask.

Silas nods against me. "It is," he promises.

I clutch on to him like life support, my bloodied cheeks pressed against his and the sweat slicking between us, but I don't care because it is *real*. He's here and I want to hold on to this moment as tightly as possible.

Silas pulls back just briefly to run a finger across my cheek, brushing the hair from my face. Running a trail across my lips.

He kisses me and all the throbbing in my limbs fades to nothing under his touch. I would stay wrapped in him forever if I could, our lips together and nothing else in the world existing beyond that.

I break apart from him with a deep sigh.

"Atia," he says. "You're a *God*."

I bite my lip, not even knowing what that means, or how Isorropía's powers are now inside me.

"Is everyone else okay?" I ask, a far simpler question.

"Good of you to inquire," Tristan says, with a shake of his head.

"Really, I thought she'd never ask," Cillian adds with a grin.

I look up, feeling such relief when I see them safe and alive, no longer grasping at their necks. Aside from a few scrapes and bruises, they are fine.

I survey the rest of the damage. There are over a dozen ashen piles where I know more warriors once stood, burned away by Imera's light.

"What happened?" I ask. "Imera?"

"She's gone," Silas says. "Her powers returned to what they once were, before she took form. The world has long surpassed the need for selfish Gods. They forgot to guide and unite the creatures they created. Instead they became meddling parents who couldn't respect free will. The realms will be better now, without their menace."

Firia secures her bow onto her back, unfazed by the new power she can surely sense in me. "It was justice," she says.

Then she walks over to her fallen sister's body, where Lahi is already standing guard. The God of Sorrow is still on the ground and Lahi reaches over to close her eyes in one final act of peace.

Firia kneels beside her, red-hot tears rolling down her flushed cheeks.

Thentos clears his throat, the shimmer of grief in his own eyes, but he doesn't let it overcome him. He keeps his focus on me. "What happened with you and Isorropía?" he asks, scythe gripped untrusting in his hands.

"Isorropía," I repeat quietly. "She jumped into my mind and forced me to see my worst fears."

My eyes shoot to Silas as I remember the conjured version of him, so rough in its edges, without the worried dimple in his brow that he has now.

"I overcame them," I assure him. "And I regained my powers. I was able to show her own fears to her in return. It destroyed her."

"You didn't destroy her," Thentos says. "It seems that you absorbed her. You *became* her."

"I am nothing like Isorropía," I bite back sharply.

How dare he even imply that after everything?

"He means that Isorropía was inside of you when she died," Silas explains softly. "So rather than her powers returning to the realms, as those of the other High Gods did, they remained in you. You have her magic now, Atia. You are born of monsters and of Gods."

I swallow as the weight of it sinks in.

Does that mean I must stay in Oksenya and try to rule? The thought leaves a sour taste in my mouth. As beautiful as this realm surely is, I don't want to be trapped in it, and I don't think what Oksenya needs is another ruler.

"We weren't sure what to think when you passed out," Tristan says, interrupting my inner panic. A grave worry line is imprinted in his forehead. "We thought maybe she possessed you, but then you started bleeding."

He nods to my chest and I press a hand there, surprised to feel that the blood has dried.

"Technically, Silas healed you," Cillian explains. "Not that you need it now you're all Godlike, but his tears flow with the same water as the River of Eternity, so it restored your immortality."

Silas frowns at him. "Don't say it like that, please."

I let out a long, deep laugh.

Whatever my new powers mean, I know something for sure: No more curses and running from monsters to try and regain my powers. No more Gods telling me what I can and cannot be, deciding my fate for me.

I link my hand into Silas's.

There are a great many things I want to say to him, but in that moment all I can think to say is: "You cried for me?"

"You didn't wake," he says softly. "Even after you healed. I thought that maybe—"

He breaks off, unable to bear finishing the sentence.

"We were so worried," he says.

"Speak for yourself," Thentos announces. He finally lets the scythe drop to his side. "I was perfectly straight-faced."

Silas rolls his eyes. "Are you okay?" he asks. "Do you feel different now you have all your powers back? Now that the Balance is . . . inside of you?"

I pause.

Being restored in Isorropía's dream world was one thing, but now that I'm back in the real world with my immortality running through me and all of her strength too, I feel *awake*. Like my whole life I have been sleepwalking and now finally I can see everything, feel everything.

There is a spark inside my blood, gateways pulling inside me, daring me to leap into any world I wish. And beyond it all, a familiar scent. Fear.

I am still a Nefas, after all.

I focus in on Thentos, my eyes boring into the God of Death as I dig in deep to explore the terrors that live inside him.

"Hey now," Thentos says, holding his hands up in a barrier as he backs away. "None of that after we just became such a good team."

I look up to Silas with a grin. "My powers really are back."

He tucks a strand of hair behind my ears. "And then some."

I swallow, asking him the question I dread. "And yours?"

When he nods, I'm not sure if I'm relieved or distraught. He knows who he is, finally, and he has the power to do as he wishes rather than be caught in the curse of his parents. He is free from them.

But what does that mean for us?

I take in the new stature of him, how polished and smooth his skin looks against the echoes of his mother's conjured daylight. The way the trees around us seem to bend in toward him and his siblings, as if nature itself is feeding from their presence.

He is a *God*.

But then, so am I.

What do we do with that?

The warrior monsters around us wait, as if for orders or

guidance. A notion of what will become of us all now that the High Gods are dead and their prisoners are freed. Among them are the Nefas, great and beautiful things with horns of green and red and an array of colors curling from their wild hair. Their eyes are alight in reverence and familiarity.

Whatever happens next, I am not alone.

I am no longer the last of my kind.

More than that, I am connected to the entire world, Oksenya and the human realms. Realms of Gods and realms of the monsters. I can feel the call of them in the back of my mind, their song as familiar as my mother's lullaby, wishing for change. For guidance. For balance.

Unite us, they say. *Set us free.*

43

ATIA

We discuss the fate of the world on a long bridge.

It arcs over a pool of rose-petal water, the wooden slats scattered with leaves that look more like stars, sprinkling from the ever-burning tree above. The first bridge between the worlds, created by the Gods when the realms were new and they had not known corruption.

The four remaining River Gods stretch across it, their wounds healed and their armor newly shining. It has been mere days since the battle, but you would think it had been weeks considering how fresh they all look.

Silas, God of Eternity, lingers by my side.

We are surrounded by the gateways of mirrors that make up Oksenya. They appear on pathways and treetops, on the lip of the vast oceans and the kiss of the skies, sweeping beneath the clouds. They allow all creatures here to travel to any part of the infinite blessed realm, catered to their wants and needs.

But all I have needed these past few days is Silas.

All I have wanted is him.

It has been bliss, days wrapped up in each other while we healed and rested, limbs tangled and kisses never far.

Though it has been tainted by this approaching meeting and the futures we will discuss. That first night after the dust settled, Silas led me to a small clearing he used to visit often as a young

God when he needed time to think. We spoke of what we wanted to happen next, for us and the realms, but words are easier than action, and the more we discussed it over the days, the more I have been afraid of what his siblings and the realms' monsters might think.

The mere thought makes my heart fit to burst with anxiety and so this past night we spoke of it no more, and I chose instead to savor the feel of Silas's arms around me and his body warm on top of mine. No talk of Gods or the worlds outside the room we had made our own.

Now I can't delay it any longer.

"There is much to consider," Thentos says. "First off, what will you do with your new powers now that Oksenya is without a true ruler?"

"Are you worried she's going to tread on your toes?" Silas asks.

"I'm worried that she's going to let it go to her head," he rebuts. "We are the ones with experience here, Aion."

I try not to let his caution irk me, but it does.

"I forgot about your years of experience doing whatever the High Gods told you, until I came along and saved the day," I say with a sweet smile.

The God of Death smirks.

His scythe is hooked onto his back like a quiver, the edges of his black hair draping over the tip of the blade.

Trust Thentos to bring a weapon to a meeting.

"High God powers or not," he says. "You're still just a Nefas."

The idea of being *just a Nefas* is as insulting as it gets. My people have been the most formidable creatures of the Gods since our creation and now, through me, we'll be the key to their downfall.

There is no *just*. The Nefas are mighty monsters.

As I dwell on his words, my hands begin to glow, bright and hot.

These new powers are still taking some getting used to.

Still, once I feel the song of them across my skin, I lean in, embracing the day and the dark that now live inside me. A swirl of shadows dances over one side of me and rays of light sprint across the other.

"Keep talking," I say, as my body burns more fiercely.

Thentos's hand twitches as if to reach for his scythe. "You're not going to pick a fight with me."

I raise an eyebrow, enjoying the glimpse of fear I see on his face.

Perhaps he has saved my life more than once, but he's still an arrogant ass and he deserves to squirm a little.

"One more God's powers to absorb?" I tease. "It could be fun."

Thentos presses his lips firmly together.

"Wow," Lahi says, impressed. She pats her brother on the shoulder. "That's the first time anyone has gotten him to shut up in centuries."

Thentos casts her a look that could quite possibly kill. "None of you are worried about a child being granted so much power?"

Firia, who has paid little mind to any of us since we arrived, aims one of her flaming arrows high in the sky.

"Pipe down, brother." She focuses on a red cloud up ahead that has shaped itself into a target for her. "Or you're going to get thrown into your own river."

Firia shoots the arrow and it curves upward, shooting through the center of the cloud. She smirks, satisfied.

"Look." I take in a calming breath. Balance's powers recede inside me. "The last thing Oksenya needs now is rulers. It needs leaders whose example they can follow. Gods to guide them, not dictate their lives."

"Which, by the way, is evidenced by the fact that a bunch of Gods are meeting here, without all the warriors and monsters, to discuss their fates," Silas says. "We're not exactly doing things differently from our parents."

My worries melt away and any uncertainty I have quiets with his voice.

"Enough with dictators and Gods with big egos," I say firmly. "Being here, so disconnected from the world, does a God no good. If I am to truly become the Balance and act as a bridge between worlds, then I need to live in those worlds."

"Meaning what?" Firia asks, lowering her bow to face me. "You don't want to stay in Oksenya?"

It is a decision that I've thought long and hard about, but I know it's the right one. As much as I have longed for the blessed realm, thinking it was the place I was supposed to be, now that I am here, I know that isn't true.

I'm a Nefas.

I'm supposed to be exploring the world. That's what my parents fought for the right to do.

I don't want to become like the High Gods before me, distanced from the creatures they created. I am the center to a web of connections now, with the possibility to be connected to all things if only I search deep enough.

Humans, monsters, Gods.

"I'll keep the Balance, ensuring good and evil remain in check, offering guidance to monsters and humans," I explain. "But I can't do that here, watching from afar."

The River Gods stay silent, taking in what I'm truly saying. They're actually listening, even Thentos, which is more than Silas and I expected so quickly.

"There will also be no more curses," I say. "And no secret plans to kill monsters."

"What of those who take human life?" Thentos asks. "They must be punished."

"Monsters who can't live in peace with the human realm will be brought into Oksenya, where they will be free to indulge their needs and where we will teach them the new way."

"Sounds like a party," a familiar voice says.

I turn and try to hold in my grin when I see Pythia, accompanied by Tristan and Cillian.

She tugs the Queen of Alchemy along the bridge, holding on to her rope-tied hands.

I gesture to Tristan and Cillian. "I was afraid you guys had gotten lost."

I'd tasked them with bringing Pythia to Oksenya hours ago, and though that might not seem like long when traveling from a realm of Gods to the human realms, it should have been a quick task considering the mirror I had given them. A small, pocket-sized shard of glass, taken from the castle of the High Gods, which housed the only mirror here that could travel not just through Oksenya, but out of it.

"If you're going to send us to the Fire Kingdom in search of an oracle, you can't expect us not to stop for cake and a quick drink first," Cillian says matter-of-factly. "I've missed indulgence."

"By quick drink, he means five. Indulgence indeed," Tristan admits. "We actually visited the Covet first, so I could let my parents know I was still alive."

"Wild place!" Cillian says, sounding thrilled by it. "Tristan's parents were a hoot."

"You'd think anyone who tells you they *never knew banshees could be so handsome* was a hoot," Tristan maintains.

Cillian doesn't deny it. "Anyway, our new Nefas-God-High Person," he says to me, with a small bow that makes me roll my eyes. "You ask and you shall receive."

He waves his hands over Thia like she is a prize. And she does look like one, covered in a shining gold dress that slinks by her ankles, with her inky hair braided to one side in a makeshift bow.

"I heard you got a power boost," Thia says to me, a glint of mischief in her eyes. "Please tell me you're going to use it to whip everyone here into shape."

"I'm already perfectly in shape, thank you," Thentos says indignantly, adjusting his tie the same way I've seen Silas do so many times in his Herald form.

A piece of his brother, inherited onto him.

"Ugh." Thia looks over to Thentos in a groan. "Who invited Death to the party? Literal killjoy."

I muffle my laughter with a small cough, which seems to delight Thia.

"By the way," she says, leaning forward in a stage whisper. "You look really badass."

I arch a brow. "And that's new?"

I suppose the midnight-blue trousers and coat I'm wearing, lined with threads of silver armor, is a little more warrior than peacemaker, but I wanted to make a statement.

"Excuse me," the Queen of Alchemy says.

I blink.

I'd nearly forgotten our captive was still there.

Vail lifts her chin, trying her best to look high-and-mighty, despite the restraints.

"What are you planning to do with me?" she asks.

"Cillian and your scholar friend filled her in on the new hierarchy," Thia says. "War, bloodshed, yada, yada. End line: She's not thrilled you're in power considering she tried to kill you."

I only shrug. "I don't hold grudges."

Silas practically snorts.

I shoot him a glare and he clears his throat to try and cover it.

"You needn't panic," I say, turning back to the queen. "I'm not going to kill you."

Vail looks suspicious.

I don't blame her. We don't exactly have the best track record.

"I'm going to have you returned to the human realm and to your throne," I promise.

Tristan gapes. "Tell me you're joking."

"Can't we at least return her to the human realm as a slug?" Cillian proposes.

"The human realms have their leaders."

It is not up to us to dictate that.

"But things are going to change," I vow, looking straight at the queen. "You have a new duty, to help keep the monsters you'd once have in your museums safe. You will continue to instruct your scholars to study and learn about them, but with the mission to educate humans and bring to light both the dangers and the good of monsters, so that a peace may be reached."

Vail does not hide her scoff. "Why would I do that?"

"Because she won't kill you?" Silas offers, jaw tensing. "Believe me, I tried to talk her out of that mercy."

And he had, repeatedly. Not so much advocating for her death, but definitely not behind the idea of an alliance after she had tried to kill us.

You were covered in blood, he'd said. *If I hadn't woken up when I did, then Vail and her banshee would've—*

He broke off then, unable to finish the words, and I'd placed a delicate kiss on his lips, reassuring him that I felt the same. That if anything ever happened to him, then I wouldn't know what to do with myself. But we cannot throw the human realms into turmoil because of a little murder plot.

"In return for your help, I'll give you a new phial," I offer now.

This piques the queen's interest, her stance straightening.

"One for each of the Cousins," I announce. "Five rulers and five rivers."

Vail was the only one of them who had struck a deal with the High Gods, but it seems right that each of them have a connection to Oksenya now, as they did before.

After all, the stories say that when the Gods created the world, their miracles split into five elements that became the rulers. They were once connected to this place and its Gods.

The queen cannot hide the hunger in her eyes.

She practically licks her lips at the thought.

"Of course, I shall be meeting with your family to discuss this too," I clarify. "Provided they agree to the missions I will also task them with, then the Gods will trust you all as guardians of the phials. It will seal our new treaty and show that we wish to work alongside the human realm for peace."

"Though be careful, Vail of the Arcane," Silas adds, his voice low. "The phials are a representation of trust. If that trust is ever broken, you will have made an enemy of Gods and monsters alike. And we won't all be so merciful."

He steps toward the queen, who staggers backward at his new stature.

"The Gods see all," he warns. "So behave yourself, won't you?"

The queen nods. "I accept this bargain," she says, somehow still managing to sound haughty.

What a talent.

"I don't suppose I get a phial of some sort for all of my troubles?" Thia asks, searching the bridge as though there is one lying about.

"You get this instead."

I present her with a small shard of glass, identical to the one I'd given Tristan and Cillian. A portal between worlds.

"You can use it to travel wherever you like, be it in the human realm or this one," I explain. "Just think of how many destinies you could devour if you weren't stuck in the Fire Kingdom."

"Oh, delightful!" Thia plucks it from my hand. "This means you'll be wanting me to visit then?"

"I'll keep a jug of tea around, just in case."

Thia's smile is wicked as she waves a hand over the glass. It ripples, before stretching to the size of a full door before our eyes.

"Come on then," she says to Vail. She unfastens the rope that bound the queen's wrists and then gestures to the new doorway. "Let's escort you back to your throne."

The queen steps swiftly through, barely giving Thia time to shoot me a quick wink before she follows.

The doorway vanishes.

I turn back to the River Gods, who watch me with a slight look of bemusement.

"I'm assuming you had no objections to any of that?" I ask.

When I'm met only with silence, I clap my hands together.

"So it's settled," I say. "I'll stay in Oksenya for a short while, to help ease the transition, but I won't be stagnant. I'll move through the worlds, as the Nefas were always meant to, and do the job this bridge failed to: be the uniting force between them. And I ask you to help me keep an eye on the human rulers. *Especially* Vail."

"You could stay, you know," Thentos says, albeit reluctantly. "And to be clear I'm not disagreeing so you can threaten to flay me or drown me in my own river."

I smirk at that.

"But Oksenya can be your home," he says. If I didn't know better, I'd say he was being earnest. "It could be your base to return to. You've earned the right to paradise."

I shake my head, not needing to think on it for another moment.

"If I've learned anything over the course of this journey, it's that I don't want to be trapped in one place," I explain.

I want to experience the wonders of not trying to stay hidden all the time for fear of the Gods, or of being too afraid to make connections and find friends, *family*, like Tristan, Cillian, and Silas.

I want to be a part of the world that I used to try so hard to close myself off to all these years.

"What about you?" the God of Death asks his brother.

My pulse quickens at the question.

I know what Silas and I have discussed, but he has been reunited with his family and that may sway him. I chose not to follow mine into the afterlife, but that doesn't mean he won't stay with his.

"I've lived many eternities," Silas says. "All of them were the same."

He gathers my hand in his.

"I'd really like for this one to be different." His eyes connect with mine. "I'd like it to be with you."

His words are a promise I cling to.

"I think I'd be okay with you sticking around," I tease.

Thentos mimes a gagging sound, but I ignore the petty God and focus only on the God right in front of me.

Silas sweeps me into his arms. "Is that so?"

His lips touch mine all too briefly, his fingers against my lower back so that I feel like a flame ignited to a roaring fire.

When we break apart, I know Silas's words are mine too: This new life we both have will be different. After losing my immortality, I know to hold on to the fleeting moments and the time that could so easily be lost. I want to keep changing and find out who I could be at the end, rather than live lifetimes the same.

The humans have it right: Their lives are gifts. Over in a blink, cherished for an eternity.

"Then we leave and we explore," I tell Silas, squeezing his hand in mine. "Together."

"What of the rivers?" Firia asks, hooking her bow over her shoulder. "I think this new plan is all well and good, but we still need guards, Aion. We need to protect their power from all who might abuse it and ensure Oksenya stays safe. With Kyna gone, the River of Sorrow will soon dry up, and if you leave, then the River of Eternity will have no guard once again."

"It's true," Thentos says. "We didn't free this land from our parents in order for it to become barren. How will we protect it?"

"There are a legion of warriors around you." Silas opens his arms to gesture to the land that surrounds us and all the creatures living within it. "Monsters of magic who are beyond worthy to become guardians."

"He is right," Lahi says, her usually small voice growing bolder. "We should honor the warriors that were imprisoned and appoint them, imbuing them with our powers. Listen to them as we rebuild this blessed realm in their image too."

I smile at her support.

Silas's siblings will thrive here, without the High Gods trying to influence their morality. Oksenya was made to be a paradise and that can only be done by letting all creatures choose how it is shaped. And by opening the gates to Oksenya once more, to those in the mortal realm who wish to return.

Monsters, who are not all that monstrous after all.

"Does this mean we're finally going home?" Tristan asks. "Because I never thought I'd say this, but I'd like to go back to reading about monsters instead of battling them. At least for a little while. And possibly have a very long nap."

I cackle a laugh, but Cillian is quiet beside us.

He hugs his arms to his chest.

"Where's home?" he asks. "For each of us it's something different, isn't it? Somewhere apart?"

I reach out for his hand, joining him to Silas and me. Tristan slips his fingers through Cillian's too, and together we form our line.

Our wall, our indescribable boundary.

"Home is anywhere that the four of us are together," I say in a promise. "It always will be."

I slip into the room as the human sleeps.

The lock flicks open with a wave of my finger, window sliding upward without a sound.

The human boy is young, his arms are sprawled across the pillow, mouth tugged open.

I inhale and dive straight into his sleeping mind to find the
fears that dwell.

Small spaces.

Great heights.

Vampires.

That one nearly earns a laugh.

The nightmares fall from my fingers, creeping under his covers. Dreams of death and blood, with nobody to hear his calls.

The boy stirs.

He mumbles, cries out, thrashing between the sheets.

I taste the sweetness of his fear, letting it wet my lips before I
feast.

When he wakes, this will be gone and I will be fed. The nightmares will fade, as they always do.

But I will remain, somewhere, in the back of his mind.

A monster.

A Nefas, if only he knew what that was.

Once I've had my fill, I retract the boy's terror and conjure up
images of smiling faces and first kisses to settle him. His breath
becomes steady once more, and when I am sure he's back to a
peaceful sleep, I jump out of the window and onto the ground
below, satiated.

I'm about to open a gateway and hurry back into the warmth of
my bed with Silas, when I spot something in the distance.

A vampire woman, green dress the same shade as the woods
she is slinking off into, with a human prey in her arms, unaware
of what he is so freely walking into.

I can sense the fresh kill on the monster. The intent to kill again.

Naughty, naughty, I scold, resisting the urge to wag a finger.

I push my hands into fists, my illusions teetering on the edge of my fingertips, ready to conjure all manner of things.

Ready to save the human and escort the vampire into Oksenya.

I have already created illusions like wards, in towns and villages ridden with lykai and monsters too bloodthirsty to use caution. It stops them from ever entering, their own worst fears coming to life as soon as they try to cross the town lines.

A fun trick, but my work is not done.

Luckily, it's never boring.

With a smile, I follow the monster into the woods.

EPILOGUE

SILAS

The waterfalls dance around us, as the sun warms the back of my neck.

"It never gets old, does it?" Atia asks.

I shake my head in response.

We have visited a lot of the mortal kingdoms over these past months, dozens of towns and palaces, weaving through the tree mountains of the Earth Kingdom and the floating temples of the Air Kingdom. But the Water Kingdom remains our favorite. And this spot by the manor where Atia first showed me the wonders she knew is where we always return.

Home, I think, as I tighten my hand in hers.

A home we've stolen for ourselves.

We get to choose who we are and where we go from here. The voices that once swarmed us with doubt have been erased, and all that exists is the clarity of who we can be when we listen to our hearts, instead of those who wish to break them.

I still don't sleep, but for once I don't mind. I dream while I'm awake, in every moment Atia and I hop through kingdoms, through worlds, and explore them with thirsty hearts.

"What do you think?" Atia asks, peering over the edge of the cliff face, to the daring waters below.

Her gateway dances just atop, a portal to a new world.

It reflects in her eyes, as though she herself is a doorway to new worlds. I know the truth of that. It's because of her that I was able to find myself and then lose myself all over again to the beauty of the kingdoms.

When Atia and I left Oksenya, we left as more than we were before.

I refilled the River of Eternity I'd spent my life guarding, ready for the new watchman my siblings would choose. And Atia refilled the Nefas. They used to be able to open gateways to any dimension they wished, to move between the After and the Never, from Oksenya to whatever world the Gods gave them permission to.

It changed after the war.

And so after our war, we changed it back.

Atia gave the Nefas the true essence of their powers. The legend that should have lived in their blood all along.

And I'd refilled the River of Eternity easily. The power came to me quicker than a memory, and when I held out my hands, the water flowed from me like sunshine pouring through forest leaves to light up a once-forgotten pathway.

"If we're planning to explore a world of eternal midnight, do you think we should get Tristan and Cillian to come along?" I ask. "You know how they get when we go on adventures without them."

Atia leans forward, her words a warm whisper in my ear.

Her feet tap against the grassy verge in excitement.

"Not this time," she says. "This one's just for us."

I grin as I take in her mischievous smile. A world where the stars reign and the night sky is blanketed by four brightly colored moons, each to mark a compass point.

"I suppose Tristan and Cillian can do well without us for a few days," I say.

Atia's eyes brighten. "Tristan is probably having too much fun questioning the Keeper of Files on which myths are true or not anyway," she says. "You know how he likes to pop in and out of Oksenya and the sorting zone for his research. And I'll bet Cillian is busy trying to find the best pastries paradise has to offer while making sure the new River Gods stay in check."

It's true, the two of them have taken to Oksenya and the monstrous world more than we thought. For Tristan, to research to his heart's content, and for Cillian to live and laugh among creatures who see him as unique and brave. Monsters who find his humanity a blessing, rather than the curse the banshees made him believe it was.

We travel alone, we travel together, but we always end up in the same place: We always end up home.

And even Atia enjoys going back to the blessed realm, to ensure the future we are trying to create is flourishing. I used to feel guilty that I could be reunited with my family so often, when hers was far out of reach. The statue tributes in the iris forests of Oksenya, for all who died and were punished at the hands of the High Gods, stand tall in the image of her parents. But when we last visited, Atia told me that she never feels sad to look at them. She knows she will see them again, sometime. Somehow.

There is an infinity of power between us and nothing will ever be impossible again.

"Come on," Atia says, guiding me toward the new world.

She gives me a quick kiss and heads forward, but I tug her backward, brushing my finger against her lips before I pull her all the way into me.

Nights spent in her arms, sweat slicked with her cheek pressed against my unsteady chest, it never gets old. Each day with her feels new.

She sighs against my lips and I swallow to keep from becoming undone.

"Let's steal another adventure before lunch," Atia says, grinning.

I would steal a thousand of them at her side.

I let her guide me to the edge.

She gives me one final wink, and then with a gasp of laughter, together we leap.

The new world shines below, pulling, drawing us inward. Promising magic, monsters, and adventure we will have an eternity to relish.

ACKNOWLEDGMENTS

Wow. Book 5. When did that happen? If you've followed me all the way from my debut to here, or if this is the very first book of mine you've read, I want to say *thank you*. Thank you, my readers, for making this wild dream of mine come true. For allowing me to continue putting pen to paper (or, actually, fingers to laptop keys). Each book I write, I do so with my whole heart. Atia's and Silas's story was no different. I loved writing their tale, weaving Greek mythology between kisses under waterfalls, battles with banshees beside quests for self-discovery, and new worlds appearing at the wave of a hand. I hope reading this gave you as much joy as it did for me while writing it.

There are a lot of people who helped make this book a possibility. As always, my agent, Emmanuelle Morgen, for being the best champion of all the weird ideas I pitch her. And to Whitney Lee, for spreading my stories across countries!

To my publishing team at Feiwel & Friends, for whom I'm so grateful. My wonderful editor, Holly West, who can fix any worries I have in a single Zoom session. My awesome marketing and publicity duo Teresa Ferraiolo and Morgan Rath. As well as Sage Kiernan-Sherrow, Lelia Mander, Kim Waymer, Kelley Frodel, and the rest of the fab team.

To Julie Dillon, who created the masterpiece US cover, along with Meg Sayre. What a dream!

To my UK publishers at Bonnier Books/Hot Key, for being epic in all ways: Ruth Bennett, Tia Albert, Talya Baker, Emma Quick, Rob Power, and Isobel Taylor. And of course Steve Stone and Dominica Clements, for bringing a magical UK cover to life. It gleams!

Of course, I have to thank my family, who still get so excited whenever they see any of my books in stores and then send me endless pictures. Who listen to every story pitch and try not to look horrified when I start talking about fear-eating monsters going on murderous rampages. And to Nick, for still reading my books, even if only to check this page for your name (we both know it won't be anywhere else in the book!).

My friends, both old and new, in the publishing world and out of it. You are all such a bright light in my life, helping me escape deadlines with wine and great food whenever I need it, and encouraging me to throw myself back into these stories whenever I need that too.

And finally to you, Daniel, to whom I dedicate this book. Thank you for giving me strength and for taking on the world with me.

Also from bestselling author and TikTok sensation
ALEXANDRA CHRISTO

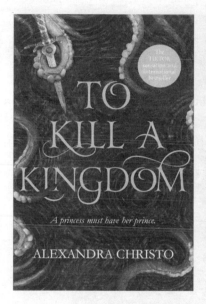

Discover a world of dark fantasy in the
HUNDRED KINGDOMS novels.

Also by Alexandra Christo

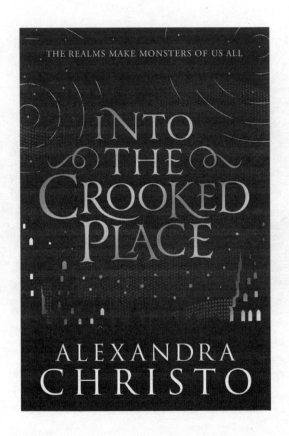

The first book in a spectacular fantasy duology.

Also by Alexandra Christo

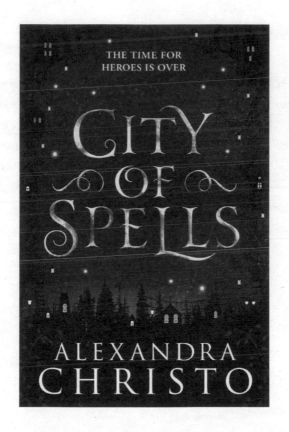

The thrilling sequel to INTO THE CROOKED PLACE.

ALEXANDRA CHRISTO is a British author whose characters are always funnier and far more deadly than she is. She studied Creative Writing at university and graduated with the desire to never stop letting her imagination run wild. She currently lives in Bedfordshire with a rapidly growing garden and a never-ending stack of books. Her debut novel *To Kill a Kingdom* is an international bestseller and her Young Adult fantasy books have been translated into over a dozen languages worldwide.

Follow her on Twitter: @alliechristo
and Instagram: alexandrachristowrites